The Tenth
Volume Two

by
R.W. Peake
and
L.R. Kelly

Also by R.W Peake

Marching With Caesar® – Birth of the 10th
Marching With Caesar – Conquest of Gaul
Marching With Caesar – Civil War
Marching With Caesar – Antony and Cleopatra, Parts I & II
Marching With Caesar – Rise of Augustus
Marching With Caesar – Last Campaign
Marching With Caesar – Rebellion
Marching With Caesar – A New Era
Marching With Caesar – Pax Romana
Marching With Caesar – Fraternitas
Marching With Caesar – Vengeance
Marching With Caesar – Rise of Germanicus
Marching With Caesar – Revolt of the Legions
Marching With Caesar – Avenging Varus, Part I
Marching With Caesar – Avenging Varus Part II
Marching With Caesar – Hostage to Fortuna
Marching With Caesar – Praetorian
Marching With Caesar – Usurper

Caesar Triumphant Parts One and Two
Caesar Ascending – Invasion of Parthia
Caesar Ascending – Conquest of Parthia
Caesar Ascending – Pandya
Caesar Ascending – The Ganges
Caesar Ascending – The Han

With L.R. Kelly
The Tenth

Foreword

With *Volume II* of *The Tenth*, as readers of the *Marching With Caesar* series know, the training is over, and the men of the new 10th Legion are going to be marching to war for the first time. For young men throughout the ages, and frankly, until very recently when viewed on a historical scale, there was nothing more glorious than the idea of marching to war. It was, and to some extent still is, a siren call that has seduced countless young men. And, as modern-day combat veterans will tell you, that no matter how harsh the training, how dangerous and realistic it is, it's never the same thing. And, in an era where combat was as "up close and personal," as it was for Titus and his comrades, I don't think any kind of training can prepare you for that.

Otherwise, I think readers will notice a change in the portrayal of Spurius Didius; at least, that's the intention of Larry and myself, and our hope. As "pro-Titus" as I am as his creator, I also want to make him, and all of my characters, as authentic as possible, and that extends to Titus, and his descendants. We all have our blind spots, and Titus is no different; in his view, Spurius Didius is the first, and in some ways most important antagonist in Titus' life, and I think that each one of us has a "Spurius" in our lives, the person that tormented us, or thwarted our ambitions, and I'm willing to bet that many of you (and yes, I include myself), will have the name of that person jump into their minds.

If we're lucky, as the years pass and we hopefully gain wisdom, we might begin to view our Spurius with a more sympathetic eye, as we begin to appreciate that, just like us, they might have faced challenges and obstacles that made them the person they were. But, if we're being honest, it's just as likely that many of us view our Spurius in exactly the same way as Titus views his, as someone who did whatever he could to make our lives miserable, and there's no excuse for their actions.

In other words, even Titus Pullus has a blind spot, and as the story of all of the men of the Tenth Section, First Century, Second Cohort of the 10th Legion unfolds, maybe Didius will redeem himself at least partially, at least in the eyes of the readers. That is, after all, one of the purposes of this "Band of Brothers" tale is about, and why I thought my friend Larry was on to something when he said, "I have an idea..."

Every character has a story, and it's all of their stories that make up *The Tenth*.

Semper Fidelis
R.W. Peake
May 26, 2022

Historical Notes

In the Historical Notes to *Marching With Caesar-Birth of the 10ᵗʰ Legion*, I explained that there is precious little in the way of primary sources about Caesar's campaign in Hispania, and unfortunately, there has been no earth-shattering discovery of a set of scrolls from that campaign since I released the First Edition of *Marching With Caesar-Conquest of Gaul*. What little there is out there can be found in Napoleon III's biography of Caesar from 1865...all four pages of it.

However, while I'm not including the maps from the Barrington Atlas that are available in *Birth of the 10ᵗʰ*, I do want to provide the location of the islands that feature in the end of the rebellion. The first island attacked by the 10ᵗʰ is actually a pair of islands, but they're separated by a channel that's barely forty yards across on the western side, away from the coast, so that to the naked eye, it looks like one island. They're called the Islas Cíes, and are one of the most visited tourist sites in Portugal as the Galicia Atlantic Islands National Park.

The second island, the larger one where there was a settlement, is Isla Ons, and is also part of the National Park. There's a town, Ons, with a population of 83 people.

Ancient Gades, modern-day Cadiz, was well known, and is in fact the site of one of the most famous anecdotal scenes about Gaius Julius Caesar, as related by Plutarch, when a thirty-two year old Caesar is standing at the base of the statue of the Macedonian King Alexander, whereupon Caesar supposedly bursts into tears, distraught at the fact that, by the time Alexander was his age, he had already conquered most of the known world, whereas Caesar's career had been, shall we say, less than distinguished. It is one of my favorite stories about Caesar, and I don't know if it's true, but given what transpired, I like to think it is.

The Temple of Hercules Gaditanus, or Melqart as the Carthaginians called him, was a real site in Antiquity, and was one of the "must-see" spots in Gades, even for a couple of men of the Legions like Didius and Atilius.

Table of Contents

Chapter One

Departing Scallabis, three days after crossing the Anas, Caesar and his army experienced their first contact with the rebelling Lusitani, although this first time was something of an anticlimax. It so happened that it was the 10th leading the way on this day when, from midway down the column, one of the *Corniceni* sounded the series of notes that alerted the men that enemy troops had been spotted. Naturally, this caused a ripple of excitement among the new men, but when the Lusitani were sighted, it was nothing more than a party of three mounted men, sitting atop the ridge that overlooked the track the army was following. The next few miles were passed with the veterans teasing their new comrades unmercifully for their overreaction, which the new men took with varying degrees of good humor, having become accustomed to being the butt of the jibes and practical jokes all new men endured when they were under the standard. The next day, however, was a different story.

A force of several hundred men, all mounted, were spotted as the army was breaking camp, and while there was no overt action taken, either by the Lusitani or by the Romans, this enemy force shadowed the army as it continued its northward march. As a precaution, Caesar ordered what was the safest but most difficult formation used by the Legions, the *agmentum quadratum*, a box formation with an entire Legion on each side of the box, with the baggage train protected in the middle. It took up a great deal of space, and being on either side and the bottom of the box could be very difficult if the enemy decided to put pressure on the formation, requiring the men on the sides to face outward and sidestep, while the men at the rear had to walk backward if the enemy actually tried their chances at an assault. Fortunately, the Lusitani were content to keep their distance, and once this became apparent, Caesar ordered the army back into their normal marching column, allowing for the pace, which was never fast enough for Caesar, to increase.

The first attack came at the end of the day, when, from behind the 10th, who was in the middle of the column now, the *cornu* sounded the same alert at the rear of the column; within a matter of heartbeats, a new series of notes was played that indicated that not only had the enemy been sighted, but contact had been made. Caesar immediately had his personal *Cornicen* play the command to halt, leaving the men farther up the column to stand in place while craning their necks to see what might be happening behind them. While none of the new men were aware of it, this would be the first of thousands of moments like this; men who were removed from the action were understandably interested in what was taking place elsewhere, and it was a universally shared obsession by men of all ranks and experience to know as much as they could about their situation at any given moment.

That, however, meant they weren't paying attention to the front and flanks, which was what prompted Pilus Prior Crastinus to bellow, "Eyes front, you *cunni*!" He began striding towards the rear of the column as he said, "Let me find out what that racket's all about!"

The instant Crastinus left the First behind, the speculation in the ranks began immediately, and in the Tenth Section, it was Scribonius who asked Pullus, "What do you think it is?"

All Pullus could offer was, "The gods only know."

Calienus, knowing how quickly this could get out of hand, spoke up.

"My guess is that those bastards who've been following us picked off some stragglers."

Calienus wasn't the only veteran to offer this assessment, and there was a buzz of conversation as the speculation continued, prompting Vinicius to move up from his spot at the left rear of the Century.

"Keep alert," he warned the men as he walked up towards the standard to take Crastinus' place. "Don't keep your attention on the back of the column. This may be a trick to draw our attention from some other point."

While he wasn't the only one who realized his attention had wandered and hadn't noticed the mounted force's absence, only Pullus was bold enough to ask, "Where did those horsemen go?"

"They peeled off a mile or so back, a little while before the alarm sounded," Vinicius told him.

A few moments later, Crastinus returned, shouting to the men to prepare for the march to resume, and a few heartbeats later, the column was marching again, leaving the men to wonder what had happened.

They learned after they stopped to make camp, and the men of the 10th were in the process of doing their part to construct it, packing the spoil and laying the turf on the top of it to form the rampart, when the cavalry escorted a Century and a wagon through the gap where the *Porta Praetoria* would be. The work stopped, but whereas Crastinus would have normally been wading in among the men with his *vitus*, he understood the importance of this moment, so he watched silently with his men as the wagon passed by. Its driver's seat was soaked in blood, while the sides of the wagon still had javelins protruding from it, although it was the extra cargo that had been thrown in the back of the wagon atop a number of crates that rendered not just his Century, but all of those within eyesight, silent.

"Pilus Prior, do you know what happened?"

Without taking his eyes off the men escorting the wagon, he said to the new Gregarius from his First Section who had asked, "One of the mules pulling that wagon went lame, and the Sixth of the Third of the 8th was detailed to bring a spare from the pool and protect the wagon." He hesitated, debating whether to impart another piece of information, then realized that it would be all over the camp by the time the fires were lit anyway. "Those Lusitani that were following alongside us weren't alone. There was another bunch of them following behind us, and they must have sent one of their own to the group we were watching to come join them. They surrounded the Century, but they held the bastards off until the cavalry arrived." Turning away from the wagon that was now past them and reaching the forum area of the camp, he shouted, "That's enough gawking! Back to work!"

The mood that night was somber, and not just in the 8th Legion, who had suffered the casualties, the conversations quieter and not as boisterous as normal, which Calienus had expected. While it wasn't the 10th, yet, the army had just suffered its first casualties, making things very real in a way that nothing before had been able to accomplish with the new men. Vinicius had called the Sergeants together for a quiet word, relaying to them the information he had received from Crastinus, that there were two Roman dead, but they had also inflicted a number of casualties, and as they sat around the fire, Calienus waited for his moment.

It was Remus who broke the silence, saying, "Well, at least they took a few of the bastards with them."

"I was talking to a friend in the 8th," Calienus spoke up, offering a silent prayer to the gods for forgiveness in telling this small lie, since it had been Vinicius who had been the source of information, but he thought it was in a good cause. "They said there were more than twenty bodies around that wagon. Now that," his voice was still quiet, but carried an intensity with it that wasn't lost on any of the listeners, "is how a Roman dies. Taking as many of the *cunni* with them as they can."

The others offered some sort of assent, although they were each acutely aware that they didn't really *know* this as a truth, at least not yet. They lapsed back into silence, which was how Crastinus found them; the Tenth was the last section of his Century he was visiting, but he had five other Centuries to go after this.

Dropping into a squat next to the fire, he spoke in a conversational tone that was another unusual moment in an unusual day, saying, "Evening, boys." The men, glancing at each other, either nodded or murmured something, then Crastinus asked quietly, "How's everyone holding up?" Just as had already happened nine times with the other sections, the reaction of the Tenth Section was uniformly one of surprise, and Crastinus explained, "It's always a shock when you see men killed for the first time, I don't care who you are. And," he continued, "that's the one thing that we can't train you for, that moment when you see your first dead comrade." This elicited universal agreement, although it was in the form of nodding heads. "But," he went on, "if you're being honest, you're also a little bit relieved that it's not you, or one of your friends. Am I right?" Once more, there was agreement, but while he hid it, he was amused to see that it was only after glances were exchanged between the section members, and while the heads moved, it was not with as much enthusiasm. "That," he assured them, "is normal. Don't think there's something wrong with you for feeling this way. It doesn't mean that you're not sorry to see good men die when you're happy that it's not someone you know. If they were alive and you were the dead ones, they'd be feeling the exact same way." Standing up, he said, "That's why we train so hard, so we have as few of these moments as we can. If I do my job right, none of you will have to feel how the men in that Century are feeling tonight."

He left then, heading down the street to the Second Century, leaving in his wake a group of young men who were almost as confused as they were reassured; this was a side of their Pilus Prior they had never seen before, and Calienus remained silent, listening with amusement as they debated among themselves whether their Centurion had taken a blow to the head, or if he had been inhabited by some *numen*.

The army stayed in the same camp the next day, which was a regular practice after a few days of consecutive marching. While the Legions rested, Caesar's scouts were extremely active, and returned to inform the Legate of the location of the first town of any size a day's march away so that, when the march resumed, the Romans made a straight line for it. There was an air of anticipation for the entire day, while there was speculation about whether or not they would go immediately from the march to the attack. Reaching a large plain, the town was clearly visible from a distance because it perched atop a lone hill that jutted up from the otherwise flat ground. For the men, especially the new Gregarii, the approach march seemed to take forever, and there was even speculation that there was some sort of magic spell involved, cast by the barbarians' sorcerers, that kept the town tantalizingly out of reach.

However, two-thirds of a watch before sundown, the horn finally sounded the halt, bringing the march to a stop about a mile from the town. As soon as the entire column had arrived, Caesar immediately sent the orders for the army to array for battle, beginning with the 8th Legion, which had the vanguard that day in honor of their fallen. Just as they had trained, three of the four Legions moved into position, in the three-line *acies triplex*, with the 8th anchoring the right, the 10th in the middle, and the 7th on the left, with the 9th in reserve. Packs were grounded, the leather covers stripped from shields, and the men were fully armed and armored, yet by the time the army was arrayed, it was close to sundown, and the speculation was rampant. Were they really going to go into battle this late in the day?

They got their answer shortly, when the Pili Priores returned to their Cohorts from their meeting with Caesar, informing their men that they would be making camp, yet instead of the one large one, they would create two camps, with two Legions apiece.

"The way it's going to work," Crastinus explained, "is that we're going to stay here in formation, while the 9th makes the camp. Same for the other two Legions: one works, the other watches. The one thing that we're going to change is that we're moving into a single line to extend our coverage of the ground here." As he expected, the news that they were escaping the work of making a camp aroused a small cheer and smiles. "Go ahead and laugh now," he growled at them, "because sooner or later, Fortuna is going to piss all over us."

The sight of the smiles instantly replaced by scowls at this reminder that all things equaled out in the long run made Crastinus happy, though he didn't show it, and he left to inform the other Centuries. It was past dark when the camp was completed, and the 10th marched into it to join the men of the 9th, forced to move in the darkness because Caesar had forbidden fires that night. Nevertheless, as was their habit, the Tenth Section, like their comrades, was sitting in a circle around where their fire would have been, chewing on cold bacon and the morsels of bread they had learned to squirrel away when

Crastinus and Vinicius walked up. Squatting down, Crastinus was only barely visible between the half-moon and the handful of torches on the walls.

"We attack at first light. The engineers are going to be busy tonight making scaling ladders, and we're going to assault the town from two sides. The artillery will begin a barrage a third of a watch before sunup and soften up the defenses." He paused, but as he expected, he could tell they were listening intently, no longer even chewing their food. "I doubt that what we have is big enough to knock down any of that wall because it looks pretty strong, so it will probably be the ladders that will get us over the quickest. The 8th is going to use the ram to assault the main gate, which is the most heavily defended. The other two Legions will be support, which is why we're in the camp together." Pausing again, he wanted this to sink in before he continued, knowing that he was imparting a lot of information in a short period of time. "You'll receive more detailed orders in the morning, but I just wanted all of you to know what's going to be happening. In the morning, we'll assign the sectors of the wall and who will be the first over it. So," he stood up, "get some sleep, because tomorrow is a big day."

As he left the section behind, they were all silent, until Domitius broke it, saying, "I bet we're one of the first over the walls."

Perhaps if it had been someone other than Domitius, Pullus' closest friend, Didius would have kept his mouth shut, but before he could stop himself, he boasted, "That just means my first *Corona Murales*!"

It was Pullus who answered coldly, "Or you'll be the first man dead."

The fury came boiling up from his gut, and Didius snapped angrily, "As you could be, Pullus. Don't forget that."

Rather than let Pullus get another word in, Didius leapt to his feet and stalked away, leaving his comrades in an embarrassed silence, until Calienus turned and said quietly to Pullus, "Remember what I said."

"I will," Pullus assured him, then stood himself and stretched. "I have to go piss."

Sleep was in short supply that night, at least among the new men; in the Tenth's tent, only Calienus was sleeping soundly, although some of the others had managed to fall into a doze. Around midnight, Domitius was unable to stand it any longer, and despite knowing he was risking the wrath of not only his best friend but the rest of his section, he still couldn't help himself.

Rolling over towards Pullus, he whispered, "Do you have it in a safe place?"

Pullus wasn't sleeping, as Vibius had known, and Pullus managed to bite back a curse that would undoubtedly rouse the others, whispering back with a patience he didn't feel, "Yes, Vibius. I have it in a safe place. It's wrapped in the greased leather bag in the bottom of my pack...the same place it's been the last four times you've asked me about it."

"I know, I know," Vibius apologized. "It's just that..."

"I understand," Pullus sighed.

They fell silent, and this time, Pullus had just begun to doze off when Domitius pressed, "And you remember what to do?"

"By the gods!" Pullus groaned, this time the volume above a whisper. "Yes, Vibius, I remember!"

"Tell me," Domitius insisted. "What are you supposed to do?"

This roused Pullus, who sat up, and he was now angry, glaring at the shadowy figure next to him, but when he opened his mouth to snap at his best friend, his ire dissolved; after all, they were talking about Domitius' death. Instead, he sighed again, "I'm to take your ashes not to your family, but to Juno and give them to her. Then I'm to tell her that she's no longer bound to you and has your blessings and prayers for her happiness."

Pullus' hope this was enough lasted only long enough for Domitius to demand, "And what else?"

Pullus didn't answer immediately, mainly because he didn't even want to think about it, but just as Domitius was about to repeat himself, he whispered, "I'm to tell her that you died well, facing the enemy. Even if..."

He refused to finish this, and Domitius did for him. "...Even if it's a lie. I want her to always remember me in a good light,

Titus. Surely you can understand that."

"Yes, Vibius, I do understand that," Pullus replied. "It's just that neither of those things are going to happen. I won't have to lie because you're not going to die, and even if you do, you're not going to die with your back to the enemy. It's just not in you."

"I hope you're right," was all Domitius would say, rolling back onto his back to stare up at the ceiling of the tent.

Spurius Didius had been awake, listening to the exchange, yet despite his feelings for Pullus, and to a lesser extent, Domitius, he actually took comfort in hearing that he wasn't the only one who was worried, not just about dying, but being a coward. Nothing was ever, or would ever be said, but the truth was that everyone else—Scribonius, the Mallius brothers, Vellusius and Atilius—had all listened to their two comrades, and to one degree or another, taken the same comfort. In fact, the only one who was far from comforted was Pullus, not because of the prospect that faced them all the next day, but his friend's mention of Juno had been like a stab to his heart. While he thought that he had accepted that the girl who had been the reason for a ten-year-old Titus Pullus rescuing a boy whose head was being shoved into a chamber pot loved that boy instead of him, despite Vibius' failure at stopping the bullies Marcus and Aulus from tormenting her, and had agreed to marry Vibius before their departure from Astigi, it didn't hurt any less, the most potent sign that he hadn't actually come to terms with it. Pullus had been smitten by her when she was a flat-chested girl who still didn't have all her adult teeth, although she was anything but flat-chested now, and Juno had been the cause of their most serious falling out. While Didius wouldn't have appreciated it, Juno was actually the cause for Domitius viewing him with sympathy after he had endured the humiliating beating at the *rudis* of Pullus a couple months earlier, because Pullus had used the exact same tactic to smash Domitius' nose in a fit of teenage jealousy over the fact that Juno had chosen his best friend. Now, like Domitius, Pullus was staring up at the ceiling of the tent, but he wasn't thinking of the next day.

Inevitably, the sun came up in the morning, Caesar ordering that fires be made so that a full breakfast could be cooked before it rose. Even men with prodigious appetites like Pullus had to force themselves to eat, but since it seemed important to their officers that they have a hearty meal, for the most part, they complied. The sun wasn't up yet, so the assembly was done by torchlight, and like the other Pili Priores, Crastinus assembled his entire Cohort in a semicircle around him so that he only had to relay orders once.

"As I told you all last night, we've been selected by Caesar to be the assault element on the walls of the town, while the 8th Legion will be conducting a simultaneous assault on their front gate. Our assault is going to work like this. First, Second, Third, and Fourth Cohorts will be the first over the walls. The First and Second Maniples of our Cohort, commanded by me, will scale the walls, while the Third Maniple will provide javelin cover at the base of the hill. Once we're over, the Third Maniple will follow suit. An artillery barrage will precede the assault, and all the scorpions from the 9th and 10th are being assigned for our use. They'll station themselves on that small rise a couple hundred paces away, and they'll be providing close support, only lifting their barrage when we begin climbing the ladders. That should make those bastards keep their heads down while we take care of business." Pausing to let the men absorb this, Crastinus continued, "There's also a slight change from what I described to you last night. Instead of acting as our reserve, the 9th is going to march to the far side of the hill, in order to ensure that there's not a sortie by the enemy from the rear gate, or any escape when we take the town." As he knew it would, it took a moment for his words to sink in and register, which he saw when the men began looking at each other, muttering about the fact that Crastinus had essentially informed them that no quarter would be given to the people in this town. "So tonight when we're victorious," he resumed, his voice hardening, "and we *will* be victorious, we'll be spending the night under a roof, in a nice bed, and maybe there'll be a woman beside you." He smiled then, but it was a cruel one as he finished, "Willing or not."

As he expected, and hoped, the Cohort burst into a rousing

cheer, but they were far from alone, although it wasn't coordinated, and the sound rolled across the camp, mingling with the bellowed cries of the other Cohorts of both Legions, and Pullus wondered if the Lusitani could hear them, and if they knew what it meant.

What the men under Caesar's command, both veterans and new Gregarii, learned that day was that there was always a reason for Caesar's seemingly random decisions. Because the town was oriented in the traditional manner for those times, where the front and rear gates were oriented on a north/south axis, Caesar's decision to align his new 10th Legion on the eastern side, along with having them assemble in the forum then march out of their camp before first light, meant that the defenders in the town were greeted by a sight that, had they known, they were only the first of many of Rome's enemies to see in the coming years. Not only were they greeted by the sight of a full Legion of Rome, perfectly aligned and waiting silently, they quickly learned that their task was made harder by the early morning sun shining directly in their eyes. The 10th wasn't alone either; Caesar had galloped over from where he had been with the 8th Legion, who were readying the ram, with the Centuries of the First Cohort aligned behind their First Century, so that when the sun peeked over the horizon, the Lusitani saw him, his black-plumed helmet and polished cuirass gleaming, and his scarlet *paludamentum* draped across the hindquarters of his mount, which was next to the Legion eagle. While they were out of the range of archers, and the Lusitani disdained the use of artillery, the leading Roman line was still close enough that the men could see individual warriors lining the wall, which was crenellated. Once Caesar was satisfied, he turned to look back in the direction of the 8th Legion, then raised a hand in an obvious signal. The meaning of it became clear when, from behind the Legionaries, a Tribune, identifiable by the same kind of black plume as that worn by Caesar, just smaller, nudged his horse through the lines, holding a javelin to which was attached a large square of white cloth.

"Maybe they'll surrender without us having to do anything," Didius muttered, temporarily ignorant of how that would sound to his comrades, given his boasting of the night before.

"Maybe," Calienus, who had the misfortune of being to Didius' left in the middle of the rank, said, his tone neutral.

What he didn't say was that, even if this town surrendered, there would be one who wouldn't, and this would repeat itself all over again, which was why Calienus, the other Sergeants and veteran rankers across the 10th, along with their Centurions and Optios, hoped that today would be the day their Legion would spill, and shed, its first blood. Because they were near the end of the right end of the first line, the men of the First Cohort and the first two Centuries of the Second Cohort had enough of a view to watch the proceedings as the Tribune neared the town wall. He came to a stop, and suddenly, another figure appeared, but this one was on the wall, having stepped up onto one of the crenellations, presumably so he could see and be seen clearly by the Tribune. Too far away to hear what was being said, the observers were consigned to trying to guess just by the gestures each man was making, which started out calmly enough, the Tribune lifting his free hand in the universal gesture of wanting to talk. Then the Tribune pointed, and they could see the Lusitani, presumably the chief or headman of the town, turn and look in their direction. They could tell he was bearded, but what caught their attention was the color of his armor, which was a dull golden in color, and unlike their mail shirts, this armor was scaled, resembling a fish. A high conical helmet was on his head, and his response to the Tribune's gesture was to make one of his own, thrusting an accusing finger down, first at the Tribune, then in Caesar's direction. From that point forward, the gestures became more emphatic, while later, some of the men claimed that they could hear their shouted exchange drifting across the space between them.

Things changed dramatically when the armored man suddenly twisted at the torso and looked down behind him, extending a hand. What happened next occurred so quickly that nobody could react with anything other than open-mouthed shock, because an unseen man handed the Lusitani a heavy spear which, in one fluid motion from the moment he took it until he released it, his hand pointing down to the spot he was aiming, he hurled it downward to strike the Tribune in the chest, transfixing him. This was instantly followed by a shower of smaller missiles, throwing javelins that hit his body and that of the horse, which reared and threw the Tribune from his saddle, who hit the ground with a limpness that signaled that he was already dead. His landing broke the spell of silent shock, and every man of the Legions who was in a position to see what happened began roaring their anger and hatred for their enemy. Suddenly, it was no longer an abstract thing; the Lusitani had been the enemy, but there hadn't been much passion in the invective against them from the ranks. This all changed, but the Lusitani didn't appear daunted at all, the warriors lining the wall opposite the 10th leaning out and screaming their own challenges, accompanied by gestures inviting the Romans to come test their will. Caesar's face appeared as if it were set in stone, but he was repeatedly hitting his thigh with his fist, the only sign of his anger, and he kicked his horse and trotted it out in front of his waiting men, placing himself where he could be heard by as many men as possible.

When the men saw their Legate, the noise subsided so that they could hear Caesar shout, "Soldiers! You have just witnessed one of the most abominable acts any supposedly civilized nation can perform, the slaughter of a defenseless emissary under a flag of truce!" They hadn't noticed that, as he was speaking, he had drawn his *gladius*, which he now used to point directly at them as he challenged, "What do you propose to do about it?" He got his answer, but not just with their voices; from somewhere around the middle of the formation, men began banging their *pila* against their shields, not haphazardly but in a rhythmic manner that created a distinctive noise that bounced back off the town wall. Caesar was content to allow this to continue for a moment, then lifted his free hand to silence them. Once it subsided again, he said, "Very well, I have your answer. Now," he pointed to the wall, "show me your answer in deeds." He dropped his left arm and reached to his waist, extracting a purse that he held aloft. "I will give one hundred *sesterces* to the first man over the wall, along with the reward of a *Corona Murales*!"

Without waiting for an answer, he wheeled his horse,

leaving the 10th once more roaring their promise to his back as he galloped to the 8th to repeat his offer.

"A *hundred sesterces?*" Pullus gasped, standing in his spot on the outer file and the rear rank of the First. "That's a fortune!"

Scribonius, standing next to him, had been calmer than his comrades, with the exception of Calienus, something that the Sergeant had noticed, and it fueled his growing suspicion that Scribonius' past was more extensive and interesting than he let on. Now, he glanced over and smiled at Pullus. "I wouldn't call it a fortune, but it is a fair amount."

"*Gerrae*," Pullus retorted indignantly. "I've never seen that much money in my life!" He hesitated, then asked, almost shyly, "Have you?"

"Not often," Scribonius assured him, "but a few times." He hoped this would suffice, but while he was looking at the wall, he could tell he was being studied, so on the fly, he lied, "The man I worked for driving cattle, once he sold his herd, he'd have more than a hundred *sesterces*, almost twice that, usually." Shrugging, he finished, "He let me look in his purse a time or two."

Whatever Pullus might have said was cut off, by Calienus, who was the first man to spot the impending trouble, groaning, "Gods, why us?"

Doughboy had been in an agonizing state that was somewhere between anticipation and abject terror, yet he was proud of himself that, when the Legion marched out of their camp, he was with them and attired in his armor with his *gladius* strapped to his *baltea*. He wasn't particularly happy about the fact that, being an officer, he wasn't carrying a shield, but he consoled himself with the thought that he hadn't suddenly come down with some sort of malady like he had intended. Mingling with the other Tribunes, all of whom had been informed that their place as the Legions went about their business was anywhere out of the way, he had watched Caesar nervously, wanting to be seen by the Legate, but not to the point that Caesar wanted him to serve as a messenger or something of that nature, and he thanked his household gods that he hadn't been as foolish as that Tribune who had volunteered to be Caesar's emissary. In fact, he felt a stab of envy; now that Marcus Creticus Appulianus, the Tribune in question, was dead, that meant that his fellow Tribune, Tiberius Mucianus Kaeso, suddenly had a tent all to himself. Once Caesar galloped off to the 8th, he had only hesitated for a moment, then, proud of himself for making an independent decision, he dismounted and walked directly towards the 10th Legion eagle. The fact that Primus Pilus Favonius hadn't been near the standard was what led Calienus to sight the fat Tribune as he waddled down the line of the first three Centuries of the First Cohort. As far as Doughboy was concerned, it was good that Favonius was standing with the other two Centurions of the front line, along with that oaf Crastinus, who happened to be facing in his direction, although he was the man who warned Favonius of his arrival.

The Primus Pilus turned but didn't salute, which Doughboy graciously decided to overlook, putting it down to the nerves of the moment, and he raised his voice so the rabble in the ranks could hear him say, "Well, men! Are we ready to go over the wall and spill some Lusitani guts and get our hands wet?"

"Of course, sir." Favonius actually gave him a smile, the first time he had done so, and it made Doughboy feel warm at this sign of regard. That feeling evaporated in an instant, when Favonius continued, "As long as we know that you'll be the one leading us over the wall."

To this moment in time, Doughboy had never been punched in the stomach, but he was certain that it felt just like he was feeling now, and it *was* as if his breath had gone because it took him two tries to stammer, "P-pardon me, Centurion?"

The smile vanished from Favonius' face.

"That's Primus Pilus, if you please, sir." Favonius' tone was coldly polite. "It's just that I worked hard to get here, sir, and well, it's my proper title."

As dull as Doughboy was, he knew he was being mocked, yet there was nothing in this oaf's words that he could latch on to as some sort of an insult. More than anything, it was Favonius' level gaze that convinced him to drop the matter.

"Forgive me, Primus Pilus." He emphasized the rank.

"You're correct, of course. Anyway," he returned to what was clearly the most important thing, "back to what you were saying earlier."

"Yes, sir." The smile came back to Favonius' lips, and his tone was suddenly almost cheerful. "As I was saying, we'll follow you anywhere you choose to lead us. Isn't that right, sir?"

How, Doughboy thought miserably, had things gone so wrong so quickly? And, by the gods, what was he supposed to say to that? Was Favonius *mad*? Did he really expect him to lead these men and be first up one of the ladders? In order to stall for time as his mind worked feverishly to come up with the best way to extricate himself without it making him look like the utter coward that he secretly knew that he was, he began stroking one of his chins, frowning thoughtfully at the ground as he nodded his head.

"It's just that you're a young man on the rise, sir. Nothing makes a young patrician's career like being the first over the wall," Favonius offered helpfully. Then, he turned his head and indicated the other Centurions who, to this moment, had maintained a solemn demeanor. "Besides, that sort of thing is a young man's game, isn't it, boys?"

Naturally, the other three Centurions, Crastinus included, despite being the youngest of this group, all nodded their heads vigorously, murmuring their unanimous agreement that, yes, the act of scrambling up a ladder to face a screaming savage who wanted to gut you was a pursuit best left to the young.

With a rising sense of desperation and knowing he had to say something, Doughboy cleared his throat, a nervous habit.

"It's just that if I'm first over the wall, I won't be able to assess the overall situation, you see? I thought it would be better for me to remain in a place, *close* to the wall, of course," he emphasized, "not completely out of danger, but far enough back so I can have an idea of what's going on."

Now it was Favonius' turn to remain silent for a moment, rubbing his one and only chin, and while he looked sincere enough, Doughboy couldn't escape the nagging feeling that the Primus Pilus was toying with and mocking him.

"I do see your point, sir. Indeed," he nodded, "I'm not sure of these things, so you're no doubt correct. I'm sure that you've read many more manuals than I have on the subject...sir."

By the time Favonius was finished, Doughboy no longer held any doubt that he was being mocked and ridiculed by this low-born brute whose only real talent was killing, and his face burned from the humiliation now that the full realization hit him, while at the same time he reminded himself that Favonius *was* a killer, and like every Tribune before him, Doughboy had heard the stories about angry Centurions using the chaos of a battle to exact revenge for some slight.

Somehow, he managed to get out, "Right. Well, then, carry on."

He spun about and stalked away, at least remembering to march, despite it rubbing his thighs raw. Just as he reached the edge of the formation to take a right turn to head to the rear of the battle line, two things occurred: the barrage started, but while the cracking sound of the torsion bars of the *ballistae* slamming forward was loud, it didn't drown out the roaring laughter of the men who had witnessed their Primus Pilus humiliating a Tribune who was too stupid to know just how stupid he was. Not, it must be said, that Doughboy saw it that way.

The barrage unleashed on this Lusitani town was unlike anything the inhabitants had experienced before, and for the duration of this time, the men were allowed to stand at ease, or as it was called, *otiose,* where they were allowed to lean on their shields and turn around as long as their left foot remained in the same position as they watched the stones launched by their artillery sailing through the sky.

Vinicius was standing in his spot at the left rear of his Century, when Domitius, taking advantage of the *otiose*, pivoted to face down the rank and call to Pullus, "Do you have it in a safe place?"

By this time, Vinicius had heard about Domitius' obsession with his will, so he wasn't surprised when Pullus, pivoting to face his friend, picked up a dirt clod, threw it at Domitius, then grabbed his crotch as he called back, "Oh yes, it's in a safe place, all right. It's right here. I used it to wipe my ass this morning."

"You mean you're smart enough to wipe your own ass now?" Domitius scoffed. "I guess it's true that the Legions can teach *anyone* if they can finally teach you!"

"It's going to be hard for you to talk with my foot up your ass," Pullus shot back, which made absolutely no sense to Vinicius, and he decided to put an end to this.

It wasn't that he was opposed to this kind of lighthearted moment right before battle, but he had awoken in a strange mood this morning, one that he had never experienced before, and while nobody, not even Calienus, would have noticed from his demeanor, he just wasn't in the mood at the moment.

"All right, you bunch of women," he spoke up. "Shut your mouths." He feigned a yawn. "I've heard you two going back and forth about that damn will for too long. Can't you talk about something else?"

"Don't yell at me," Pullus said indignantly, pointing at his friend, "yell at him. He's the one who keeps asking!"

Oh, Pullus, why do you make it so easy? Vinicius thought, while he said blandly, "Yes, and you keep answering him, so who's the bigger fool? The fool who asks or the fool who answers?"

The sight of Pullus standing there, mouth open as he tried to determine if this was a question for which Vinicius was expecting an answer caused one corner of the Optio's mouth to lift, which Pullus had learned was a sign of Vinicius' amusement, and with a roll of his eyes, he faced back to the front.

By this time, the 8th had reached the gate with the ram, and was slamming it in a rhythmic manner against the double wooden gates, each impact creating a small tornado of dust and fragments of wood, while the artillery barrage had scored gouges out of the western wall in several places, which as the veterans knew, were actually misses. As Crastinus had said earlier, the walls were too strong to be breached with the artillery, so Caesar's goal was to inflict casualties among the defenders on the wall, as well as damaging the buildings in the town itself. He had considered using fire but decided against it, not wanting to complicate the assault for his unblooded Legion, knowing how the presence of fire and smoke could make things even more confusing.

The Lusitani, however, had no such compunctions when it came to the lengths to which they would go, and it was the thin trails of smoke rising into the air from inside the town that prompted Pullus to lean over and ask Vinicius, "What's the meaning of the smoke, Optio?"

Vinicius had been thinking of something else, so his reaction was delayed, but after a glance at the town, he turned to face Pullus, and without emotion said, "I imagine they're heating up some pitch to pour down on us, or maybe some sort of oil." Vinicius wasn't surprised at Pullus' reaction, one that was more or less shared by the others, which was a shudder. "Would you rather have me lie to you?" he asked quietly.

"No, Optio." Pullus shook his head. "But still..."

"I know, boy," Vinicius assured him, then turned away and repeated to himself, "I know."

Before anything else could be said, the order to come to *intente* sounded, cutting off all of the conversations like this taking place with the assaulting Cohorts, yet while Vinicius moved at a trot to take up his spot at the rear and opposite end of the formation, his mind was still on the conversation with Pullus. He couldn't have explained why, but there was something about the subject of it that wouldn't leave his thoughts. The use of boiling pitch or oil was a common defensive tactic, and he had faced it before, so why was it lingering in his mind?

He couldn't spend any more time worrying about it because Crastinus began speaking, forced to come close to a shout as he ordered, "Before we start out, I want everyone in the assault elements to pass their *pila* back to our supporting Maniple. You won't be able to throw them from a range where they'll do any good, and they're going to be useless once you get on the ladders. Give them to the boys who'll be supporting you, and they can deliver them to the bastards for you."

The chuckles at this grim joke was more because it was expected, and the men of the Fifth and Sixth Centuries, designated as the supporting Maniple, came forward to take delivery of the javelins, which the men passed back to the rear of their formation, freeing the men about to make the assault from holding on to both their shields and their *pila*.

Once this was done, Crastinus continued, "Right, I want my veterans up front to pick up the ladders." Each Sergeant left his spot, including Calienus, moving through the formation to pick up the pair of ladders the Century would be carrying. "They're going to be the ones carrying the ladders and will be between files so the rest of you boys can hold your shields up to cover them since they'll have their hands full."

Five men carried each ladder, which were heavy because they had been made sturdy enough to bear the weight of four or five men at one time, and Crastinus positioned them between the second and third file, and the eighth and ninth file, which required some shuffling to create the proper spacing so that the men carrying the ladders would have overhead protection should it be needed.

Once he was satisfied, Crastinus said, "Now, listen and listen carefully. I'm going first up the ladder. Normally," he explained, "I wouldn't, but since this is you boys' first engagement, you just follow me and everything will be fine." Gesturing to Vinicius, Crastinus went on, "The Optio will be the first up the other ladder. We'll need one man, one very strong man to brace each ladder against the wall while the others ascend." As he could have predicted, almost every eye in the entire Century turned to the rear of the formation where Pullus was standing, clearly visible, but this was when Crastinus sprang his surprise, the one that he and Vinicius had decided on days earlier. "No," he shook his head, "not Pullus. He's been the best in training, so he's going to be after me." He grinned then, and joked, "Besides, the very size of him is going to scare half of those bastards to death before he lifts a finger."

Then, Crastinus scanned the ranks, and the first man he pointed to was Didius, who looked anything but honored, and in fact, while he acknowledged the Pilus Prior's order, it was with an edge that earned him a glare from Crastinus. The other ranker, another new man named Gnaeus Macro of the Second Section and was considered to be the third strongest man in the Century, accepted his selection with a shaking voice. All along the twelve Centuries of the first line of the first three Centuries of the first four Cohorts, identical or very similar orders were being issued, whereupon each Pilus Prior stepped a few paces forward so they could be seen by their Primus Pilus, raising their *viti* in the signal that they were prepared. In turn, Favonius ordered his *Cornicen* to sound the signal to alert Caesar that the 10th was ready. Meanwhile, the cracking sound of the *ballistae* continued, punctuated by the lower-pitched but similar cracking sound when a stone slammed into one of the logs of the wall. Then it was Caesar's turn, ordering first his *Bucinator* to sound the alert that orders were coming, which was acknowledged by each Cohort of the 10th dipping their standards, then ordering his *Cornicen* to play a series of notes that actually put the Legion into motion. The 10th's part in the assault was now beginning.

The First Century of the Second Cohort stepped off along with the other Centuries, which also was the signal for the smallest artillery pieces called the scorpions to begin loosing. Launching what was in essence a large bolt with a wooden shaft, iron tip, and leather fletching that served the same purpose as feathers on arrows, while its range wasn't that of a *ballista*, it fired in a flat trajectory at incredible speeds, and a skilled crew, consisting of three men from the ranks who would join their comrades once their job was done, could launch three missiles within a span of fifty heartbeats. A good crew chief, who was responsible for aiming the weapon before pulling the cord that released the pin holding the torsion arms, could put a bolt exactly where he aimed with remarkable precision, which the men of the Tenth Section were about to learn firsthand. Once the scorpions began their own barrage, the Lusitani defenders were forced to duck behind one of the crenellations after the first couple of their fellow tribesmen learned the hard way that the missiles moved too fast to dodge. Consequently, they were forced to try and peek around a crenellation to keep track of the progress of their attackers, and it just so happened that one of those unfortunates was on the wall directly in front of the First of the Second, a Lusitani warrior who chose the precise instant that the bolt was arriving to stick his head out. The bolt barely slowed down as the top half of the warrior's head exploded, the remnant flying off to the right, while the bolt continued onward, leaving a bloody spume behind it that tracked its progress as it vanished in the distance above the town. Every man who saw it happen had some sort of reaction, either a gasp of shock or some expression of awed surprise, but it was Scribonius who best summed up the sentiment of his comrades.

"Remind me not to ever to get in front of one of those things."

This was met with unanimous agreement, but as they got closer to the wall, Pullus realized something, and while he didn't want to break the discipline of the moment, he couldn't see any choice in the matter.

"Optio," he called out, but Vinicius didn't look in his direction, and he had to raise his voice, hoping that Crastinus didn't hear him, or if he did, he didn't recognize his voice. *"Optio!"*

The manner in which Vinicius' head jerked made it seem as if his mind had been elsewhere, but he did turn and look down the rank at the large Gregarius.

"What is it, Pullus?"

"How am I supposed to get from here," Pullus pointed to his spot on the outer edge of the formation in the last rank, "to up there?"

He pointed to the last man who was carrying the ladder two files over and a couple of ranks ahead.

Vinicius sighed, shaking his head as he answered, "You follow the file of men with the ladder, idiot. The Pilus Prior will be there at the base of the ladder while the ladder is being lifted. Then you follow him."

"Oh."

It was all Pullus could think to say, although he thought that somehow this might not be as simple as Vinicius made it sound. Before he could dwell on the matter any longer, the front rank of the assaulting Centuries reached an invisible line that served as the signal for their enemy that it was time to begin inflicting their own punishment. It was Crastinus who bellowed it first, but it was instantly echoed by every other officer down the line.

"Testudo!"

Like his comrades, Didius responded immediately and automatically, his left arm lifting up and slightly forward so that his counterpart in the Ninth Section ahead of him was covered by the lower half of Didius' shield as he took what was only a half-step to his right because of his proximity to Pullus on the outer edge, and even with all that was happening, he experienced a flash of pride in how quickly the First responded, a sign that the grueling training was paying dividends. While the men of the First were all in time, it wasn't a moment too soon, and within a heartbeat, all the noise that had gone before was like a whisper compared to the stone shot from Lusitani slings that slammed into Roman shields. Although he had never experienced it personally, Didius imagined that this was what a hailstorm sounded like, with the exception being that this hail could kill a man. The only damage the first volley inflicted was gouging a few shields, but with the second, along with the cracking noises that signaled most of the shots had been blocked, Didius heard a slightly different sound, a deeper, meatier sound from directly ahead of him, perhaps two or three ranks up, followed immediately by a grunt. Even with the slower pace required by the *testudo*, Didius was unprepared for the moment when he had to step over a member of his file, recognizing him as another new man from the Sixth Section, Percennius his name, and one of Didius' dice victims, which did cause a pang of what might almost have been shame. Although he did notice how Percennius had rolled up into a ball, at this point, he was too inexperienced to recognize this as an actual good sign, because it meant that his comrade at least had his wits about him. In the moment, he was just an obstacle, and while he tried to be careful as he stepped over Percennius' body, his left arm moved and created a bobble in his shield that opened up a gap between the shield of the man of the Ninth Section ahead of him. More quickly than he could have believed, some sharp-eyed slinger on the wall spotted it, and sent his missile directly for that gap. Thankfully, either his aim was slightly off or Didius recovered in time, but the shock of the impact against his shield was such that it almost yanked the shield from his hand.

"Didius! You can't let your shield dip like that! Don't do it again!"

Didius recognized Vinicius' voice, which had a conversational quality to it, despite the fact that the Optio had to yell to be heard over the cacophony of noise. With Percennius gone, it also meant that Didius had to move up a rank in order to keep the integrity of the *testudo* intact, which was an integral part of the *testudo* training, and he took an extra stride, leaving nine men in the Tenth Section as part of the last rank, the first of his section to do so. By the time they had gone another hundred paces, the First Century lost three more men, including a man from the Eighth Section in Pullus' file, placing him at Didius' right front quarter two ranks up. This time, the sound of the stone shot striking the man reminded Didius of someone striking a piece of iron with a hammer, making a ringing noise, but it was the manner in which this man collapsed that drew his attention, and to his horror, he saw that this man, Dentatus, had clearly taken a glancing blow that struck the rim of his helmet, but in one of those things men ascribed to the gods, instead of caroming off, it had deflected the stone downward and destroyed the bridge of his nose and burrowed into his brain. That Didius could see this was because Dentatus was lying face up, eyes open, but it was the spray of blood that was shooting up several inches, pulsing with every beat of the man's heart, that was burned into Didius' mind, haunting his dreams for the next several days. Before he looked away, for an instant, it appeared that there would be more catastrophe because Papiria of the Ninth Section and the man who marched immediately in front of Pullus actually tripped over Dentatus' body, his shield moving so much that a ray of light the width of a man's hand and about two feet long briefly illuminated the dark interior of the *testudo*. The men around Papiria, Pullus included, shouted in alarm, but while there was a rattling of three or four stones slamming into shields, including Pullus', nobody else was hurt. It was at this moment that, from somewhere up ahead in the formation, a man shouted out the traditional prayer of the Roman Legions marching into battle.

"Jupiter Optimus Maximus, protect this Legion, soldiers all!"

It was a sentiment with which Didius fervently agreed, and for the first time in his life, he began offering his own prayer to the gods, all thoughts of winning glory and a *Corona Murales* gone from his mind.

For Publius Vellusius, his first taste of battle was decidedly not to his liking at all. As he marched next to Domitius, the one lasting memory from this first time was the darkness and stench that, as he would learn, was normal when marching in *testudo* in combat. The darkness he had become accustomed to from the training, but he realized that before this moment, he hadn't noticed how bad it smelled, and he was certain that at least one man had *cac'*ed on himself, although that wasn't the only odor. Although he was long accustomed to the smell of sweat, while it was a similar smell, there was a rankness to it, and like his other comrades, he would learn to identify the difference between sweat from labor and the sweat excreted by men who are afraid.

Once the Lusitani slingers began loosing their stone missiles, it was so loud that Vellusius couldn't even think, but like his comrades, his body moved in concert with them, and while his left arm began to ache, he was determined to keep his shield in position, not wanting to be the cause of the death or wounding of his comrade in the Ninth Section just ahead of him. Nobody was saying anything, but he did hear a few men crying out, their voices alarmed, which he assumed was because of a near miss from a missile, then he heard someone shout something about Jupiter Optimus Maximus, but this was also the moment when the First hit the base of the hill. Of course, like everyone else, Vellusius had looked at the slope while they were waiting, but neither he nor most of his comrades had the experience to be able to gauge just how steep it would be when they were forced to hold their shields above them, under fire from enemy slingers, after already covering two hundred meters. And, as it would turn out, it wasn't Vellusius' error, it was the man in the Ninth Section in front of him, another new man named Titus Sido who, becoming fatigued from the unexpected steepness of the slope, dropped his shield. Not much, just a crack, but the ray of light that shone through fell across Vellusius' face, temporarily blinding him, but almost before his mind could register this, he was struck a terrific blow to his right collarbone, followed instantly by pain of an intensity he had never felt before. He felt himself falling backward, then he hit the ground with terrific force, the back of his helmet slamming into the rocky ground, and he thought he heard what sounded like Domitius shouting his name, although he wasn't certain. Somehow, just before he lost consciousness, he retained enough awareness to pull his shield up over his body; then, all went black.

Pullus had been almost as badly shaken as Didius by the sight of Dentatus and, like Papiria, Pullus had been forced to step over the corpse, trying not to retch at the feeling of the spray of warm blood that drenched his lower leg. Despite Papiria's bobble, the stone loosed by one of those Lusitani *cunni* had only struck his shield, and while it was with a great deal of force, Pullus' arm didn't move like those of his comrades. By the time they were halfway up the slope, Pullus' rank had four men missing from it, and he missed what happened to Vellusius, but what he didn't know was whether Domitius' absence from the rear rank was because he had moved up, which he could see that Didius had, or he was lying somewhere behind him. This worried him to the point he became distracted, and the fact that it wasn't from fatigue that caused him to move his shield didn't matter, and this time when the stone slammed into his shield, aimed at him by a Lusitani to the right of their formation, the range was short enough that it did jerk his left arm down. Thankfully, this was the last of the barrage, because the Century finally reached a spot close enough to the wall where any Lusitani who wanted to use their sling would have to lean out over the wall, and just behind the First and the other three assaulting Centuries, were the Fifth and Sixth, all of them with extra *pila*, ready to launch them at any enemy warrior who exposed themselves. To Pullus, and his comrades, the sensation was as if the hailstorm had suddenly stopped, and Crastinus bellowed the order to break out of *testudo*. Even with all that was going on, there was a collective and audible gasp of relief as the men finally dropped their left arms, including Pullus, although he had only to move his left arm back across his body so that it was in its original position. Things began moving quickly from this point, while the veterans carrying the ladders immediately left their spot in the formation and moved to where Crastinus was standing, just a matter of four or five paces from the base of the wall, looking up at it, watching for any threat. Pullus, momentarily forgetting that he was supposed to have followed the ladder bearers, took a ferocious satisfaction at the sight of hurtling *pila* coming from behind him, seeing at least one Lusitani warrior, with a heavy brown beard and battered helmet and whose own arm was drawn back with a javelin in his hand, take one in the chest, falling backward and out of sight.

"Didius!" Crastinus bellowed. "Get your sorry ass up here!"

Pullus hadn't noticed that Didius hadn't moved either, and he glanced over and saw his nemesis, with an expression on his face Pullus had never seen before, moving up between the files, turning sideways, ignoring the other men jeering him for his tardiness. Crastinus grabbed Didius by the arm, turned him, then shoved him roughly down to the ground with his back to the wall, while the ladder bearers immediately began raising the ladder, with Didius grasping the vertical legs of the ladder on either side at Crastinus' specific instruction so that he didn't have to worry about his hands being stepped on when his comrades ascended. This was something they had never practiced, meaning that it was a new sight, which was one reason why Pullus was still in his spot at the rear, essentially gawking like a spectator at a gladiatorial game.

"Pullus, you big oaf. Go get behind the Pilus Prior!"

Vinicius was already heading for his ladder as he shouted this, but it got Pullus moving, and to his relief, he managed to make it just behind Crastinus in time for the Pilus Prior to see him when he glanced over his shoulder. Then, Crastinus began his ascent, but Pullus was once more distracted when a second volley of *pila* came slashing overhead, but this time, he could only hear one strangled cry of pain.

"Get up there, you stupid bastard. We're right behind you," Calienus said from behind him, and this got Pullus scrambling up the ladder after Crastinus, who was already halfway up, not even glancing down at Didius.

Crastinus was two rungs from the top and Pullus about halfway up the ladder when, for perhaps the span of four or five heartbeats, the attention of the combatants on both side was arrested, the clamor of the shouts and curses in both the Roman and Lusitani tongue and the cracking sound of stone missiles striking the shields of the supporting Centuries drowned out by a single scream so shrill and piercing that, afterward, men claimed it made the hair on the back of their neck stand up, or they were certain that it was from an otherworldly source. Pullus' head snapped to the left, the direction from which the sound came, the sight that greeted him so disturbing that he froze in place, one foot still hovering in the air. He didn't really understand what he was seeing at first; obviously, it was the figure of a man, and because it was on the second ladder, it was clearly a Roman, but aside from that, there was nothing familiar about it. It looks, Pullus unconsciously referred to whoever it was as an object, like a fly that got trapped in thick honey and in its struggles, covered itself with the substance, the difference being that honey didn't smoke like that, and it didn't turn every inch of exposed flesh into blackened, charred meat. This was the instant that Pullus' gaze shifted, to a spot on the ladder up above this Roman on the ladder, and not seeing anyone, he suddenly realized that it had to be Optio Vinicius who, still the object of everyone's attention as every witness regarded him with varying levels of horror, and with what would have been a comical slowness, still was lifting one leg to place on the next rung. Finally, and perhaps mercifully, what had been Aulus Vinicius, the man who had taught him a better way to fight, toppled over backward, but Pullus was only vaguely aware of the manner in which his comrades at the base of the ladder shouted in alarm and scrambled away from what was now a Lusitani weapon, as Pullus remained frozen in place, seemingly unable to move his leg up to the next rung.

Chapter Two

Aulus Vinicius had been looking upward and saw the smoking cauldron hoisted by two Lusitani suddenly thrust into his vision just above him...and that was when he understood. Even if he had had the time to begin the leap off of the ladder, in that instant, he knew that he would be horribly burned regardless, and he had seen men who spent the last watches of their life in an agony that he couldn't imagine, nor did he have any desire to experience it himself. Despite this, it was typical of him that his last thought was, with a certain amount of grim humor, I'm about to find out how they felt. Mercifully, while his body continued to function, after a brief shock of a pain that, if he had been conscious for another heartbeat, would have driven him mad, Vinicius no longer knew he was doused in boiling pitch.

Crastinus had been like Vinicius, intent on what was waiting just above him when, responding in the same manner as Pullus, his attention was caught by the scream, temporarily forgetting the danger he was in from a few feet above him. Unlike Pullus, however, he had understood instantly what he was seeing, and he also knew that it was his Optio. His next immediate thought was one that he would never divulge to anyone other than another Centurion, not about Vinicius and what he was going through, but that he needed a new Optio, and there was someone on his mental list that every Centurion kept in their head who, if the gods were kind, would survive the day to replace a good man. Nevertheless, he found himself seemingly frozen like the men below him, and judging from the sudden cessation of shouting and slingshot, like the Lusitani, unable to tear his gaze away as he watched a corpse continue to at least attempt to ascend the ladder in fulfillment of his orders, like a true Roman, and even with his detachment, Crastinus felt a surge of pride that he would never be able to articulate. His momentary trance was broken when, from above him, he heard a shout in a foreign tongue, then a Lusitani suddenly appeared, leaning out between crenellations and armed with a long spear that he was drawing back to plunge right into Crastinus' face. Because of the warning, Crastinus was able to dodge out of the way by essentially throwing his upper body away from the ladder while still holding on to the shield he had borrowed from the Legion stores, leaving him clinging to the ladder with just his right hand as the blade plunged down into the now-empty space between his body and the ladder. If any of his men would have been asked, they would have unanimously sworn on Jupiter's black stone that what Crastinus did next was impossible, because he reversed his backward momentum of his upper body back towards the ladder while scrambling up the last two rungs, and with a speed that was not only an astonishing sight, it meant that his foe went from being certain that he was about to easily kill or incapacitate a Roman by at least shoving him off the ladder to suddenly having that same snarling Roman, wearing a helmet with a transverse crest, directly in front of him on the parapet.

As Crastinus expected, his opponent focused his attention on Crastinus' *gladius*, which he had drawn in the same motion as his foot launched him from the last rung up and over the parapet, so he was completely unprepared for the metal boss of Crastinus' shield to smash into his spear arm, snapping the bone and wrenching a shriek of agony from the man, while the pain distracted him just long enough that he never saw Crastinus' thrust that punched into his chest just above the small round shield in the Lusitani's left hand. With a brutal second blow of his shield, Crastinus sent the dying warrior staggering backward on the ten-foot-wide parapet to block the path of his comrades who had turned to address this newly arrived threat. Crastinus dropped into a crouch, while out of the corner of his eye, the huge bulk he knew was Pullus suddenly appeared, immediately pivoting in the opposite direction. Being the veteran that he was, Crastinus' gaze never left the men in front of him who, as he intended and hoped, had been temporarily delayed as they disentangled themselves from their mortally wounded comrade, but he didn't need to see what was happening with Pullus to know that the young Gregarius had blocked a blow with his shield, the hollow report that was unique to Roman shields because of their curvature telling him what was taking place. However, there was no noise following it, the flatter cracking noise of a flat shield being struck, or the cry of pain that signaled Pullus had countered; instead, there was another, identical noise. *What is that idiot doing?* Crastinus wondered, even as he was preparing to parry the first thrust from a war spear that one of the two men facing him was drawing his arm back to launch.

Taking the spear thrust on his shield, Crastinus expertly twisted his wrist just before it struck so that instead of striking his shield squarely, the iron point slid off of it, then without taking his eyes off his opponents, he bellowed, "Pullus, you stupid bastard, draw your *gladius* and kill that *cunnus*! Quit messing about!"

For Pullus, the first several heartbeats of his first engagement was a combination of confusion and fear, along with a healthy dose of embarrassment. Oh, he had essentially copied what he had seen Crastinus do, except that he actually leapt from the second rung of the ladder and had managed to clear the wall to land neatly on the parapet, something that his comrades would be talking about that night, among other things. The confusion came from the unfamiliar sight of what had to be well more than two hundred men, some arrayed on the parapet, while others were down on the ground but hurrying in his direction, although it was the dizzying array of weapons, armor, and shields that, to his Roman eyes, made these warriors look like a completely disorganized rabble who should be easy to defeat that made the deepest impression. There were even men with hoes and sharpened sticks, Pullus noticed, although these men were down on the ground and didn't seem all that eager to come rushing forward to scramble up one of the three ladders that were within his range of vision.

Anything else he might have noticed in that single heartbeat of time was interrupted by the sudden burst of movement to his right, and he pivoted just in time to raise his shield to catch the shoulder-high thrust from a *gladius* that Pullus was certain was more than twice as long as his own. He did take some solace in the certainty that, given how the Lusitani put his entire weight into the thrust, any of his comrades would have been sent reeling backward. Only later did he realize that the moment he spent gloating to himself could have been better spent, because his hesitation gave the Lusitani a second opportunity, this time by swinging his arm back so that, for an instant, his right hand was behind his head, before bringing his *gladius* down in a sweeping, and powerful, overhead blow, although again, Pullus caught it on his shield by lifting it above his head while simultaneously tilting it so that it was roughly parallel to the ground, thereby spreading out the impact of the heavy iron blade. The only real damage was that it turned his arm numb, and to his pride, because it was this second blow that Crastinus had heard and prompted his order to Pullus to draw his *gladius*. Which, Pullus instantly realized with horror, he had forgotten to do. He did respond instantly, the *gladius* suddenly appearing in his hand, although unknowingly copying his Pilus Prior, Pullus' first offensive move wasn't with his blade but with his shield. Unlike Crastinus, however, Titus Pullus was one of the very few men who could move his shield arm almost as quickly when it was holding a heavy shield as when it was empty, and with perfect aim, he smashed the boss of his shield into the small round shield of his foe. It carried so much force behind it that the Lusitani was lifted off his feet and sent reeling violently backward to a degree that the Lusitani instinctively moved his left arm out and back behind him, away from his body in the unconscious manner of all people when they're falling backward. As understandable as it was, it was a fatal error, something that Pullus saw in the man's eyes that he knew, but this time, Pullus didn't hesitate, twisting his hips as he drove the point of his *gladius* into the Lusitani's ribcage in a third position thrust, the man's eyes instantly rolling back in his head, followed by a spray of frothy blood from the mouth as he fell backward.

I did it! I've made my first kill, and it was perfect! This last thought had barely crossed Pullus' mind when he realized that, in fact, he had been anything but perfect, which he learned by the weight of the falling man jerking him off balance and towards the body because the blade had gotten trapped in the cartilage of the man's ribs. It was one of the first things taught to new *Tirones*, and from Pullus' perspective, he had even less of an excuse, because he had learned that every thrust should be made with the blade parallel to the ground when he was twelve or thirteen, taught by Cyclops, for this very reason, because you could find your blade trapped by the cartilage instead of it sliding in between the ribs.

When he put his foot on the corpse to yank the blade from his first victim, a second Lusitani, armed with the same kind of shield but a long spear, launched a lunging attack, but again, while Pullus was able to block the thrust, the blade remained stuck in the first mam's body. As Pullus frantically tugged at his own *gladius*, the Lusitani counterattacked, then attacked again, but on the fourth thrust, Pullus' blade finally came free, and this time, he used it to knock the point of his foe's spear down and away from his body, while at the same time, he stepped forward with his shield, putting his weight and strength behind the blow, the boss crushing the man's nose and cheekbones. Although he was essentially dead on his feet, Pullus, angry at himself and embarrassed, hit him again, and again, before the man's legs finally collapsed, unrecognizable as a human being except for his form. And, suddenly, the next Lusitani facing this large Roman didn't seem as eager as they had a moment before.

Calienus ended up ascending the ladder sixth, behind one of the half-dozen rankers who was a veteran like he was, and was why he was in the First Section, but the Sergeant was still shaken by what he had just witnessed with one of his closest friends in the Legion in Vinicius' death. This wasn't noticeable by anyone, and as they were trained, when Calienus reached the top of the ladder, he turned in the opposite direction of the man immediately above him, thereby ensuring that the numbers facing in both directions were even. This meant that he was behind Pullus and another veteran named Blaesus, and he was in time to see Pullus end a Lusitani then get his blade stuck in the ribs, but while he thought about chastising the Gregarius, after watching Pullus kill his second man in such a brutal fashion, turning the Lusitani's face into nothing but jellied meat, he decided that it could wait.

Instead, he reached out and grabbed the back of Pullus' harness, and when the large Roman glanced over his shoulders, his eyes widened in surprise at the sight of Calienus grinning up at him as he said, "Let's go get these bastards."

Now that they were two abreast, Pullus and Blaesus had a couple feet on either side of them, and they were each bolstered by a comrade behind them holding on to the back of their harness. Taking care as they stepped over the bodies of Pullus' first two kills, they advanced slowly down the parapet, while the Lusitani facing them, no longer as enthusiastic as they had been a mere moment before, started shuffling backward, one of the three men in the front row occasionally making a half-hearted lunge with their weapons as they retreated.

Calienus, who was still behind Pullus, had managed to get a quick look around the large Roman, and he saw that the retreat of these Lusitani would be short-lived because of the presence of three large vertical columns that bisected the wall just a few paces behind the rearmost warrior. Although there was a ladder there, even an inexperienced man knew that trying to descend it would only be possible if at least one of his comrades bought them time to do so, and almost inevitably sacrificing himself in the process. Calienus didn't see the moment when one of the Lusitani looked over their shoulder for the first time, but he felt the result through his arm, when a warrior that was almost Pullus' size came rushing forward with a bellowed cry that Calienus supposed was a Lusitani curse or war cry, swinging his Gallic-style long *gladius*, which had a slightly rounded point since it was used as a slashing weapon, down onto Pullus' shield. The next several heartbeats were spent with Calienus bolstering Pullus, while Blaesus, the veteran next to Pullus, was supported by another man of the First Section, a new Gregarius named Numerius Vulso, and the Lusitani warrior alternated between slashing down at Pullus then Blaesus, both of whom easily blocked the blows.

Somewhat curiously to Calienus, it didn't appear as if this warrior's comrades intended to take advantage of what he was certain would be this man's sacrifice to escape because, inevitably, the Lusitani was forced to stop, panting from his furious exertions. In the gap between Blaesus and Pullus, Calienus saw that, while he took a step backward to give himself some breathing room, in his fatigue, the Lusitani dropped his shield slightly, a common mistake. Blaesus saw the same thing, and like a striking serpent, launched a second position thrust as he stepped forward, the point missing the top of the man's shield by less than a finger width to punch into the man's chest, while Blaesus' blade was back behind the shield, half its length dripping with blood, even before the Lusitani collapsed to his knees.

Slowly but methodically, with Pullus and Blaesus leading the way in one direction, and Crastinus and another First Section man in the other, these Romans moved down the parapet, cutting down those Lusitani who made the same error of their fallen comrades. This first engagement, as Crastinus and the other Centurions had hoped, proved to be instructive, not just for the new men but for the veterans as well, because very few of them had faced native tribesmen of Hispania, and what they were learning now would be to their advantage in the years to come. Unlike the Legions of Rome, tribes who originated from the people that future generations would call the Celts viewed warfare as a means for personal glory, meaning that it was considered unmanly for an individual warrior to work in more than a rudimentary fashion with a fellow warrior because he viewed that man as a rival as much as a comrade. What this meant in a practical sense for the men of the First Century, Second Cohort, and all of the assaulting Centuries was that, while they worked as an integral unit, their enemies were content to assail them one or at most two at a time, and that was how they were cut down, as individuals, leaving a litter of bodies behind the Roman war machine.

The signal that the part of the First Century containing Pullus had cleared their part of the wall was when they found themselves at the columns, and it was to Calienus, who was the senior man of this group, the other men looked to for their next orders. While their part of the wall was now clear, that didn't mean their day was over, because down on the muddy strip that

served as the road that ran parallel to the wall were more
Lusitani, the bolder of them shouting up at their enemies,
gesturing to them to come down to the ground and continue the
fight.

"Now that we've cleared our section, we could go down the
ladder and," he used his *gladius* to point down the wall to where
they could see Crastinus' transverse crest at the front of his
assault group, "come back up behind them farther down the
wall."

Pullus tried to hide his dismay, unable to keep his eyes off
the Lusitani men down there waiting for them, and he was
consoled by seeing that, when he glanced at the other faces, they
were of a same mind as he was, but to their collective relief,
Calienus shook his head.

"But I think that while we could take most of those bastards,
there are just too many to make it a sure thing. So," he turned
and pushed his way through his comrades, "let's go help the
boys over there."

Moving at a trot, they were forced to hop over the fallen
Lusitani, all of whom had been checked by the men at the rear
and, if they were still alive, had been dispatched with a quick
thrust.

Reaching the end of the double line, Pullus was delighted
when he grabbed the harness of one of the men at the rear, who
turned his head in surprise, and saw that it was Domitius, his
friend, returning his grin and asking, "Well? How many have
you done for so far?"

"Three, and helped with a couple others." Pullus didn't even
try not to gloat. "You?"

He got his answer before Domitius opened his mouth by the
look of embarrassment, but his friend pointed up ahead of them
to complain, "Those bastards up there won't give me a chance.
They won't even rotate through like they're supposed to!"

For a brief instant, Pullus considered telling his best friend
that he had done the same thing, although Blaesus had been
perfectly happy to relinquish his spot, but decided against it. He
had to stand on tiptoes to do it, but he saw that not only was
Domitius right, there were only another three or four Lusitani
who were now caught between the assault teams of the First and

Second Centuries. In fact, it was perhaps another thirty heartbeats later that Crastinus blew on his bone whistle, giving three short blasts that was the signal for the rest of the Century who had been waiting at the base of the wall to ascend the ladders. This took a few more moments, but it was impossible for the men who were already on the parapet to ignore the fact that their enemy wasn't idle, and even those like Pullus who had wet their blade nervously eyed the growing mass of Lusitani down in the muddy strip between the wall and the first line of huts.

Once Crastinus was satisfied the bulk of the Century was there, he pointed down at the waiting warriors and shouted, "Let's sort those bastards out." Pausing briefly, Crastinus searched the faces around him, then pointed with his left hand at one of them. "Rufio, you're the acting Optio. If you don't completely fuck up in the next little while, maybe you'll be Optio for real." Crastinus saw in the expressions of his men that they were expecting him to say something about Vinicius, but he ignored that as he waited for Rufio to push through the crowd to join him. Once Rufio reached him, Crastinus continued briskly, "Half the Century is going to go down that ladder," he pointed to the ladder that was nailed to the parapet just behind him, "and the other half is going down that ladder." He pointed back to the ladder next to the columns. "So, Sections One through Five on me, the rest on Rufio. We go when I give the signal. And," he indicated the parapet, "look around to see if there are any *pila* that can be used lying around here. We'll use them to keep those savages away from the foot of the ladders while the rest of us go down. I go down first on my ladder, and Rufio goes first down his." Then, without thinking, he added, "Just make sure you don't end up like Vinicius." The instant the words were out of his mouth, Crastinus gave an inward groan. Gaius, you idiot! What were you thinking? As he feared, he saw that his men were affected by this callous mention of his Optio, so in a quieter but still firm tone, he finished, "Mourn him later, boys. We still have work to do."

The two groups split apart then, and as Rufio led his contingent down the wall towards their ladder, the men examined the *pila* that, along with the discarded or splintered shields, weapons and bodies, littered the rampart. Although they managed to gather up almost two dozen missiles, several of them were the short throwing javelins used by the Lusitani, although there were a handful of *pila* that, for one reason or another, hadn't had their wooden pins sheared because the soft iron of the shaft had bent on impact as they were designed to do. Thankfully, the Lusitani down on the muddy street had either experienced enough of a taste of the Roman missile that had been designed by the great Gaius Marius, or more likely in the opinions of many of the men, these warriors were more timid than their counterparts on the rampart. What mattered was that instead of lining up at the base of the ladder, they retreated to far side of the muddy strip of space between wall and huts, with many of them using the muddy side street that ran into the one paralleling this space, in between the double row of wattle and daub thatched huts that were the predominant type in barbarian towns, seemingly content to wait for their foes to descend to the ground. Rufio didn't take this for granted, and he assigned a half-dozen men to hold a javelin on their shoulder, ready to throw, then stepped to the ladder.

"Pullus, you were second up; you might as well be second down," Rufio ordered, ignoring the look of consternation on Pullus' face. To the men holding the javelins, he muttered, "Watch our backs on the way down."

Then, he took a breath, turned his back to the town and began to descend the ladder.

Rufio, Pullus, and two other men made it to the ground before whoever was commanding the Lusitani in this area decided that it was time to intervene, whereupon they began at a fast walk towards the four Romans who had moved away from the ladder several paces to give their comrades room to join them. Once they were within a handful of paces, the Lusitani broke into a run, all of them bellowing at the top of their lungs as they hurtled towards their enemy, emboldened by the paltry number of Romans on the ground. It was Calienus who shouted the order for the men on the rampart to hurl their missiles, just beating the Sixth Section Sergeant, every one of them striking a target, but while it didn't stop their charge, it did slow it as the stricken men either fell outright or were staggered, becoming obstacles to their comrades, with another volley happening once more with the same effect, which enabled another few Romans to join the men who had already made it to the ground. One of them was Domitius, who immediately stepped next to Pullus who, he noticed with grim amusement, had naturally made sure he was on one end, and they barely had time to grin at each other before the Lusitani recovered from the volleys to hurl themselves bodily against the Romans' shields, and even with his bulk, Pullus felt his feet sliding. Regardless, there was one benefit in this headlong charge, because the leading Lusitani were now effectively pinned against the shields of their enemies by the massive, crushing weight of their own comrades behind them, which meant that most of the men in the front rank couldn't employ their own weapons, yet neither could the Romans. It also meant their faces were literally inches away from each other, and even with their shields between them, every man in the front rank was able to smell the breath of a man who was as intent on killing their foe as their foe was on killing them, the resulting clamor almost overwhelming.

Domitius was fortunate that a comrade had made it down the ladder to bolster him, but as strong as he was for his size, it only took a quick glance at him to tell Pullus that his friend was close to the end of his energy, his face redder than Pullus could ever remember seeing it, his mouth open as he gasped for breath. In essence, this was nothing but a contest where the deciding factor was sheer, brute force. There were no tactics, there was no maneuver; it was a simple matter of willpower and weight, and Pullus wasn't alone in understanding that they were in real danger of losing this contest.

Even better than Pullus did, Domitius knew that he was on the verge of collapse, but he also had the added danger of his opponent, one of the few Lusitani who had managed to free his weapon hand. Thankfully, it was nothing more than a fire-hardened pointed stick, but Domitius was still forced to jerk his head one way, then another, as the Lusitani who, in some corner of his mind, Domitius noticed was no older than he was, kept jabbing it over their shields. As first Pullus, then Cyclops, and now his other comrades had learned, Domitius had the fastest reflexes of anyone he had met so far, which meant it wasn't particularly difficult to dodge and duck the repeated thrusts, but he also was exerting every bit of his energy at the same time, his knees bent to absorb the shock while he felt the hobnail soles of his *caligae* losing traction. However, in one of those quirks of battle that Domitius and his comrades would come to learn often played as much or more of a role in determining the outcome of a battle, it was the Lusitani who proverbially blinked first.

Becoming frustrated at his inability to stab this filthy Roman and with the impatience of youth, the Lusitani dropped both stick and shield to reach up with both hands to grab the top of Domitius' shield, and before Domitius could react, yanked it down and almost out of his grasp, exposing Domitius' upper body to the warrior to his opponent's left, who began drawing his right arm back, yet even with everything happening so quickly, Domitius had the time to see the man's lips peel back in a smile of savage anticipation of his almost certain kill. What happened next only made sense later, but from Domitius' perspective, there was a deafening bellow from someone to his right, temporarily forgetting that it was his best friend; most importantly, the Lusitani who had been about to slay him suddenly went reeling backward with enough force to knock two men behind him off their feet because Pullus had unleashed his tremendous brute strength by shoving the Lusitani with his shield. Less than an eyeblink later, the Roman to Domitius' left, who he had sensed but hadn't actually looked to see who it was, launched a thrust to the young warrior's throat, who was still clutching Domitius' shield with both hands, another sign of how quickly everything was happening. Instantly drenched in a spray of blood, some of which got in Domitius' eyes, he was still able to see the Lusitani immediately behind his dying opponent bringing his arm down, a long *gladius* in his hand, aiming for Domitius' head in an attempt to cleave his helmet and head. Because Domitius closed his eyes, hoping as he did that Titus fulfilled the wishes expressed in his will, he didn't see what happened, only knowing in the moment that the blow didn't land, though he did open them in time to see a hand and most of a forearm, still clutching the *gladius*, go spinning just above the heads of the combatants, then dropped his gaze to see a man, now exposed because the young Lusitani had just collapsed, staring dumbly down at the spurting stump of his right arm.

Once again, Domitius demonstrated his ability to move quickly, and he didn't hesitate, taking care to step over the corpse of the man at his feet as he launched a first position thrust that came from under his shield, which he had recovered to its proper orientation now that the young Lusitani had relinquished his grip on it, driving the point deep into the crippled man's belly just above his groin. It was not only a mortal wound—it was a painful one—but Domitius was now sufficiently angered that this wasn't enough, and as he'd been first trained by Cyclops, then Vinicius, he locked his elbow hard against his hip, then twisted his entire upper body, which caused the blade to slice across his foe's belly, cutting through the boiled leather, muscle, and intestines. Even before he recovered back to his proper position, he and the others around them could smell the stench of *cac*, leaving the Lusitani standing for a heartbeat as his guts fell out of his body before he collapsed on top of them.

With the death of two of the Lusitani, there was now a small pocket of space, not much, but enough for more men, and Rufio responded instantly, shouting, "Move forward, Pullus. Use your fat ass for something useful!"

His friend only replied with a nod, though he was stepping forward as he did so, requiring Domitius to hurry to move back in position next to his comrade, while the man on the opposite side did the same. The Lusitani who Pullus had shoved and prevented from stabbing Domitius had regained his balance, and Domitius didn't need to know the warrior to see that he was angry at his friend. More importantly, he had clearly decided that he wanted Pullus for himself, because the man who was now across from Domitius made a move as if to support the warrior, earning him a snarled rebuke. The other warrior clearly didn't care for it judging by the gesture he made, but he returned his attention to Domitius as Domitius did the same, thinking, Titus doesn't need any help. He was also sufficiently embarrassed that he had almost been killed, and he vowed to rely on his training, reinforced by the feeling of the hand bolstering him from behind as their comrades took advantage of the extra space they had created. What would have astonished all of those involved in this one small part of a larger battle for the town was that no more than a hundred heartbeats of time had elapsed from the moment Rufio hopped down onto the ground. It would serve as yet another lesson on this day, for all of the new men, that trying to measure time when fighting for your life was a futile endeavor.

In the immediate aftermath of his embarrassing lapse in forgetting to keep his blade parallel to the ground, Pullus had resolved to himself that he wouldn't make another mistake on this day. Despite this promise, young Titus Pullus learned another lesson, and it was one that would turn out to have long-lasting ramifications, not just for himself, but for his comrades and for the enemies he would face in the future. This lesson was at the hands of the man he had shoved away from Domitius, and as Domitius had observed, the Lusitani had obviously decided to mark Pullus as his personal adversary, a fact to which both Pullus and his comrades would become accustomed in the coming weeks. He was wearing mail, and his clothing was a quality that bespoke of a higher status than most of the men around him, while the spear he was holding had a broader blade than normal, with the lower half having barbed edges, making it a particularly cruel weapon designed to rip flesh apart. The manner in which he approached Pullus was different as well, first giving the large Roman a mocking bow before approaching with a shuffling step as he moved the spear point, using his wrist to demonstrate his dexterity and skill by making an intricate, weaving pattern with it. Pullus knew that this was by design, yet despite himself, he learned that he had been following it with his eyes, when, with lightning speed, the Lusitani launched what Pullus thought was a real thrust because it was simply an extension of the pattern the warrior had been making, and he reacted instantly, moving his shield farther away from his body than was wise. In fact, it had been a feint, made by a more experienced warrior who had seen Pullus for what he was, a large, powerful, but still inexperienced youth. And, the Lusitani was certain, anyone else would have been dead, but with a quickness that was astonishing for such a large man, the Roman managed to twist his body at the waist to his right just enough that, instead of the point striking him in the chest squarely, it slid along his ribcage, although it was with enough force for the barbed part of the spear blade to slice through several links and knock the breath out of his foe.

The Lusitani recovered his spear quickly then immediately launched another thrust, certain that this Roman had been lucky, snarling in frustration because, even before recovering his breath, Pullus was able to block this one effectively on his shield, whereupon the Lusitani struck another time before pausing for breath himself. On Pullus' part, he had been shaken for a second time, but this time, his error had been costly; while he didn't think the wound was serious, he could feel his side getting wet, and it felt as if someone had dragged a burning stick along his ribs. It was his state of mind more than anything that kept him on the defensive until the warrior took a step back, then began resuming the weaving pattern with his weapon as he prepared for another attack. Not this time, you *cunnus*; you're not going to fool me again, Pullus promised himself, and this time, when the Lusitani's arm shot forward, his shield didn't move, but he did. Timing it perfectly, Pullus took a large step forward at the exact instant that the Lusitani executed his move, and as he had expected, there was a space between the shaft of the man's spear and the edge of his shield. The point of his *gladius* landed exactly where he had aimed it, punching through the Lusitani's mail just under his breastbone, while this time, Pullus had kept the blade parallel to the ground, and he remembered to make a savagely powerful twist of his wrist before closing his stance back up, savoring the look of shock as the Lusitani stared up at him, then collapsed to his knees, whereupon the dying man was shoved roughly aside by one of his own comrades who took his place, launching his own thrust with a spear that was clearly made for hunting, which Pullus blocked easily.

"Relief! Relief!"

Because Rufio didn't have a whistle, Vinicius' being with him when he died, he was forced to bellow this, prompting every man on the front to either use his shield to shove his opponent backward a step, or make a lunge or some other offensive move that forced their foe to step back, then immediately take a single step to the side, while the man behind them stepped into his place at the same time. When executed well, it was practically impossible for an enemy to take advantage because there was less than a heartbeat of opportunity. Turning sideways, the relieved men sidestepped back to the rear, then grabbed the harness of the man in front of them, and Pullus and Domitius arrived at about the same moment, their first opportunity to speak about what had happened perhaps fifty heartbeats earlier.

Still panting, Pullus gasped out, "That was a close one, *neh?*"

Domitius didn't respond, nor did he look over at his friend, which irritated Pullus, but he was quickly occupied with shuffling forward as the fresh men up front battered their opponents, felling some, driving the rest back towards the line of huts. Reaching the perpendicular street, the Lusitani line collapsed together because of the narrowness between the huts, and Rufio wisely chose not to try and pursue, deciding instead to wait for further orders from Crastinus. The wall had been cleared, the next part of the battle was about to begin, and Rufio had only been Optio a matter of a few hundred heartbeats of time.

On his own, Pilus Prior Crastinus decided to order his Cohort to regroup rather than press their advantage by pursuing the withdrawing Lusitani. He knew that he was taking a risk by not waiting for orders from Favonius, who was somewhere off to his right along the wall that was about five stadia long on this side. Since the town was built atop the hill, the wall followed the contour so that it made a gentle curve that blocked his view of the Legion eagle, although he could see the Fifth and Sixth of the First. Before he made his decision, he watched them for a moment before telling his *Cornicen* to play the signal to his Cohort to regroup and wait for orders, and he felt somewhat confident that Favonius was doing the same, or was about to do so.

"All right, boys," he said, then turned and pointed down the perpendicular street that was closest to Rufio's group. "We head down that street. Keep tight, stay sharp, and by the gods, watch the alleys and spaces between these *cac*heaps! These bastards are regrouping somewhere, but they probably left some men behind to hold us up."

Unable to use their normal spacing, the men of the First Century walked shoulder to shoulder, and they had gone back to their normal spots in their formation, but while Pullus noticed that there were missing faces, the tension was too high for him to take the time to ask, nor did any of his comrades, even Calienus. Part of it was more sensory in nature; now that they were in the streets of the towns, the quality of the sound changed, having more of an echoing quality because of the surrounding huts, and before this moment, the human noises had been uniformly masculine. Now, they could hear shrieks that could only come from female voices, but more distressingly, at least to Pullus and most of the new men, the sound of terrified children crying now filled the air, and they all seemed to be coming from their right, where both the First Cohort and the 8th were located.

"Sounds like the boys in the other Cohorts are already having fun," Calienus muttered, then added, "the greedy bastards."

Crastinus proved he heard as well, and he held up a fist in the informal signal to halt, then turned to face his Century.

"If one of you *cunni* take so much as a crust of bread until you're told, I'll personally flog you until there's nothing left but a bunch of bloody meat, understand?" By this time, every one of his men knew when Crastinus used this tone of voice, this wasn't an empty threat, and in a ragged chorus, they assured him that they did; if some of them were disappointed, they were wise enough to keep their mouths shut about it. Satisfied, Crastinus finished, "Just because those bastards in the other Cohorts don't have any discipline, it doesn't mean that we're going to be like them. The Second Cohort isn't a bunch of fucking rabble, got it?"

Without bothering to wait for another response, Crastinus turned back around and they resumed heading for the center of the town. It had become obvious that, while there were alleys and nooks where there could have been men hiding, whoever was commanding the Lusitani had ordered them to forego any attempt to delay the Roman progress, and Crastinus quickened his pace, not wanting the Second to reach the town center behind the others. The first tendrils of smoke began drifting through the air, causing Crastinus to curse those men that every Century seemed to have who loved to see things burn, knowing that if it wasn't contained, there might not be a town left to sack. To his relief, when they emerged out into the large common area that essentially served the same purpose as the forum of a Roman town, he saw that not only was the Second ahead of the First Cohort, and although he saw that some of the Third was emerging onto the common area at the same time, the First Century was ahead of the rest of his Cohort, and he relished the thought of reminding his Centurions of this later.

"Section Sergeants," he heard Rufio shout, "give me a butcher's bill while we're waiting!"

This was the normal method, the Optio being responsible for taking a casualty count during a pause like this, but Crastinus was impressed that Rufio had acted without being told, which he took as a sign that he had made the right choice.

In each Section, it was the responsibility of the Sergeant to inform the Optio, and as they waited for Rufio to get to them, Calienus asked, "Anyone see what happened to Didius and Vellusius?"

It was Remus who said, "I saw Vellusius go down before we got to the wall."

"What about Didius?"

Atilius was the one who answered, but he was actually two ranks ahead in his file, calling over his shoulder, "I saw him fall off the ladder when we were coming down, but then I got busy."

This elicited some mirth, not just from the Tenth Section, but the other men who heard it then relayed it up to the men who hadn't, and fairly quickly, the entire Century was roaring with laughter, the veterans knowing that it wasn't because it was that funny but was a normal release of tension. The Lusitani who were now about a hundred paces away in a rough circle of some five hundred men, the last survivors now facing the First and Second Cohort of the 8th, and the First, Second and Third Cohorts of the 10th were understandably grim, and more than one of them was shaken at the sight and sound of their enemy enjoying something humorous at a moment such as this.

The two Primi Pili marched their men to a distance about fifty paces away before sounding the halt so that the Centuries could dress their lines. While the sounds of a town being sacked continued, the Lusitani warriors waiting for what was coming were no longer shouting or making demonstrations of defiance, making the large common area oddly quiet. Once things were to their satisfaction, the Primus Pilus of the 8th raised his *gladius*, instantly copied by Favonius, and whether his pause was intentional or not, it served to raise the tension, and the anticipation, the men on both sides beginning to quiver, some with eagerness, others with dread. The 8th's Primus Pilus' arm moved first, but Favonius reacted instantly so that they both swept their arms down almost simultaneously, while the *Corniceni* attached to every Century blew the long single note that sounded the attack at a run, although their calls were drowned out by the roar from almost three thousand voices as the final phase of the battle began.

Pullus and the rest of the First broke into a run as if they were launched from a scorpion, and once more, Pullus learned that if he wasn't careful, with his longer legs, he would run right up the back of Papiria. For a reason that men would be speculating about later, whoever was leading the Lusitani didn't perform the standard maneuver of the countercharge, which helped negate the speed of an attacking enemy when they made contact, choosing instead to remain standing to receive the charging Romans. It was universally agreed upon later that this had been an egregious error on the part of their leader, although the outcome was never really in doubt.

Didius hadn't actually meant to do it; at least, this was what he told himself later, it had just...happened. Certainly, he had been unhappy about being given the task of bracing the ladder, but Didius quickly realized that it had been a blessing in disguise, because he had an excuse for being the last man up the ladder. He should have been one of the last two, but Macro, the other man selected, had the misfortune of being struck by the flaming bunch of meat that moments before had been Optio Vinicius. Because of his vantage point, Didius had seen it all, not just the horrible moment the boiling pitch had been dumped on Vinicius, but the aftermath as well, forced to watch as the corpse burned for an obscenely long amount of time, giving off a black, greasy smoke that, to Didius, smelled like a haunch of pork being roasted and which caused him to vomit, his only consolation being that he was far from alone. Macro, unable to get out of the way because he was seated, suffered serious burns on his right leg and arm, not enough to keep him from marching, but enough to scar him forever, and to ensure that he suffered a painful recovery. That had been bad enough, but then Didius had been forced to sit there and listen as the fighting was taking place, above and behind him, and he was certain that this was much worse than if he had been with the other men still on the ground, looking up and able to see *something*, instead of being forced to keep track of what was going on with just his ears.

After what seemed to be a full watch but was probably no more a thousand heartbeats, the waiting men heard the whistle blast from their Pilus Prior. Obeying immediately, the men began scrambling up the ladder as Didius and Macro, despite his burns, held the ladder to keep the legs from slipping out from under them. As the last of his comrades ascended the ladder, the Princeps Posterior, commanding the Fourth Century, sent two men to replace Didius and Macro, but one of the freedmen attached to every Legion serving as a *medicus* stopped Macro, who had struggled to his feet in an attempt to join his comrades. Didius didn't say anything, although he did give a nod of acknowledgement when his replacement wished him good fortune, then he ascended the ladder, the last man of the First to do so. He wasn't opposed like Crastinus and the men of the assaulting element had been, yet Didius still tensed as if he expected some savage to be waiting, but the only Lusitani on the rampart were dead and he hadn't hesitated, much, to descend the ladder on the opposite side of the rampart. It certainly wasn't his fault that, just as he was climbing down, the Lusitani savages threw themselves at his waiting comrades, which was what caused him to panic. As every man had learned,

descending a ladder with your back turned to a larg‿
men who want to kill you is an extremely disconcerting‿
and he blamed the sudden explosion of noise as the reason ц‿
still several rungs from the bottom, Didius had leapt off the
ladder, actually jumping several feet to one side. He landed on
his feet, but the jagged bolt of pain in one heel caused him to
bellow in pain, though it went unheard because of the roaring
noise already present, and he collapsed, falling on his ass and
dropping his shield in the process to grab at his foot. A foot that,
he saw, had a board seemingly attached to the bottom of his
right *caligae*, and he saw the head of the nail that had clearly
attached the board to something at some point protruding from
the wood.

Oblivious to the fighting going on just a matter of paces
away, Didius had his own internal battle, desperately wanting
to yank the board from his foot, but afraid that this would be
even more painful than it was at that moment. Finally, he nerved
himself, took a breath, then tried to yank the board from his
foot. The only sign to Didius that he had fainted was that one
instant he had been sitting on the ground, and now he was lying
flat on his back, looking up at the bottom of the wooden
rampart. His foot still hurt, throbbing with a pain that brought
tears to his eyes, and his glance down at the foot told him the
board was still imbedded, although he would never admit that
he fainted, to anyone, even Atilius. Over the course of the rest
of that day and into the night, he convinced himself that he had
every intention of joining his comrades once he was able to
walk, although his heel hurt so much that it felt like Dis was
personally tormenting him. Nor did he intend to use not one but
two Lusitani bodies as a partial cover, yet he nevertheless found
himself reaching out and dragging the first one closer to him,
this man's eyes open and staring at him in such an accusing
fashion that he rolled the body over, followed by the second
man, who had died of blood loss judging from the pallor and
the huge stain on his lower tunic. What he *did* intend to do was
something that he never once asked himself, ever, but whatever
the intention was, the result was that he settled down and
remained lying on the ground, surrounded by death and with the
sound of the fall of the town and all that it meant filling the air.

For Pullus and his comrades, this was the last chance for action, and they participated with varying degrees of enthusiasm. Scribonius had acquitted himself well enough, certain that at least one of the wounds he had inflicted when he was facing one of the Lusitani warriors at the bottom of the ladder was mortal. In most ways, Scribonius was about as unlike the man next to him as he could be; thoughtful where Pullus was ruled by impulse, competent at feats of arms but not endowed with the same love of conflict; organized and naturally friendly, whereas Pullus seemed to be looking for the hidden insult or mockery in the comments of the other, older and more experienced men. And yet despite these differences, he had developed a deep regard for Pullus, and only to a slightly lesser degree, Domitius as well. Now, as he held on to the harness of his Ninth Section counterpart, Scribonius was one of the men of the Tenth who was still in the last rank, whereas Pullus was one man up ahead of him, but he didn't need to be standing next to him to see that Pullus was like a hound straining at the leash, begging to be released on its prey.

With the Century back together, Crastinus was now back in his role at the front, next to his *Signifer*, supervising his men but ready to intercede if one of them got into trouble. He kept the bone whistle in his teeth, and in recognition that many of the men had already exerted themselves to a substantial degree, he blew the whistle more frequently than he would normally, meaning shorter shifts at the front. It also meant that the respite was shorter, but this was one of the tradeoffs, and it was one of the many things that a wise Primus Pilus left up to his Centurions, each of them with a different philosophy. Nevertheless, Scribonius shuffled up a rank, along with both Romulus and Remus, Atilius, and Calienus. This put him in a perfect position to watch when it was the turn of the rank ahead of him, and Pullus wasted no time, taking advantage of the relieved man who had sent his foe staggering backward on the signal, killing that warrior with a quick thrust to the throat. Although he would never know, Scribonius assumed that the Lusitani who came rushing at Pullus, wearing a high conical helmet and the same kind of scale armor that the warrior who killed the Tribune was wearing, although it was badly tarnished and there were several scales missing, was related in some way to the man Pullus had just so casually dispatched, because there was a fury in his attack that Scribonius associated with a personal loss. He watched Pullus block the first blow, a sweeping attempt at decapitation with the Lusitani's long *gladius* that Pullus defended against with his shield well enough, yet Scribonius did notice that, for the first time he could ever recall seeing in training, the blow had enough power behind it that it actually made Pullus stagger, not much, but enough to notice. Pullus retaliated, but chose to employ his shield, using it as an extension of his hand, something that Scribonius had experienced enough times on his own in training with Pullus that he felt a surprise bordering on shock when the Lusitani didn't go reeling, although he did take a step backward.

What occurred next was the pair exchanging blows, although Scribonius' attention had become occupied elsewhere because the man he was bracing was now furiously engaged on his own, and it took all of his focus to maintain his grasp on his counterpart's harness as the ranker moved violently as he exchanged blows with his foe. This was the moment Crastinus blew the whistle for the relief, and his comrade behaved as expected, using his shield to shove his opponent back then stepping to the side as Scribonius moved forward. The foe across from him had staggered backward from the shove, although he recovered immediately, executing a thrust with his spear, which was of the shorter variety that could also be thrown. Consequently, Scribonius missed seeing Pullus refusing to heed the relief whistle, instead taking a step away from the front rank to maintain pressure on his opponent with the conical helmet, who had taken another step backward.

It was Crastinus who saw, and recognized what was happening, and he bellowed, "Pullus, you idiot! You're too far out in front!"

Scribonius suddenly found himself without an opponent as the spear-wielding warrior, seeing this huge Roman now isolated and alone, made a lunging thrust that, while Pullus blocked it, ended when the spearpoint embedded itself in the wood. The Lusitani gave a half-hearted yank before coming to his senses and realizing that, alone or not, this Roman was dangerous, prompting him to relinquish his grip as he retreated a step. This meant that Pullus had to dislodge the spear from his shield, which, predictably, gave his foe wearing the scale armor the opportunity he was waiting for now that this young, arrogant Roman bastard had taken his bait. With a bellow, he launched a horizontal, sweeping backhand slash aimed for Pullus' neck as the large Roman was momentarily occupied trying to shake the spear loose from his shield. Once more, Pullus' reflexes, and for the first of what would be many times, the grip taught by Aulus Vinicius saved him as he brought his blade vertically up across his body just in time to intercept the Lusitani's, the clanging sound of iron on iron ringing above the other crashing sound of this last, desperate fight. While he managed to hold on to his *gladius*, the force behind the blow knocked Pullus' arm aside, leaving him vulnerable, only for less than a heartbeat of time, but as Scribonius and the other new men had learned this day, that was all that it took to prevail, or to die. What happened next occurred so quickly that Scribonius only made sense of it in the heartbeats after it was over, as a figure flashed across his front at a sprint, coming from somewhere on his left, sliding to a stop only long enough to execute a thrust that caught the armored warrior in the throat, the point exiting the other side in a shower of blood, and it was only then that Scribonius saw that it was Domitius who had come to the aid of his friend. So quickly did it happen, and so surprising was it that Pullus, recovering quickly, was able to dispatch the man whose spear was still embedded in his shield as the young warrior stood, open-mouthed in shock. Domitius resumed his dash, except that it was back to the formation, while Pullus backed up until he was safely among their own, only then removing the spear and tossing it to the ground. As he moved to the rear, despite trying to avoid the attention of Crastinus by moving in between the ninth and tenth file instead of outside of the formation, it was a futile gesture.

Shouting his name, when Pullus reluctantly acknowledged his Centurion, Crastinus snapped, "We'll talk about this later."

Pullus only learned the identity of his savior when he reached the back of the formation to find Domitius there, a wide grin on his face as he said, "Now we're even."

"That was you?" Pullus gasped.

"I've always been faster than you," Domitius said smugly, yet as competitive as Pullus was, he didn't bother to argue, simply because it was true and he knew it.

Although it took two more rotations on the part of the First, the end was still inevitable, but it didn't mean the fighting was over. As the new men would learn, while many warriors chose to stand together in a heroic but doomed last stand, almost as many warriors with families to defend melted back into the town, returning to their own homes, choosing to die trying to protect those they loved. The men who had been involved with dispatching the last of the resistance in the town square were now allowed to sit on the ground for a respite, ignoring the bodies that were lying in clumps not more than fifty paces away from them, still in a rude circular mass. For the most part, if they were talking, it was in snatches of conversation as they caught their breath, mostly questions about comrades who were missing and their possible fate. As disorganized as it was to a Roman eye, the men were still sitting with the comrades in their Century, although without any regular spacing, their *Signiferi* jamming their standards into the ground as they joined their resting comrades sprawled on the ground. This was the scene that greeted Caesar and his command group as they trotted through the gates, both of them shattered, the remnants of them hanging from the iron hinges, while the gateway was littered with the detritus, both pieces of wood from the gates and the bodies of the Lusitani who had tried to hold it. Guiding his horse around the corpses, Caesar put himself in front of the town headman's hall, waiting until he was certain all eyes were on him before he began.

"Comrades!" Caesar used his public speaking voice, making it sound as if he was standing on the Rostra in the Forum of Rome. "For that is what you have become today! We have shed blood and had our own shed. Undoubtedly, you will have comrades who have been killed, or may Fortuna smile, have only been wounded, and that is a bond that can never be broken. Today, we become comrades in arms, the most precious connection any man can share, even more precious than the bonds of family." Making a sweeping gesture that encompassed the town, he finished, "As a salute to your bravery and as a gift, I give you this town and all that is in it, to do with it as you will!"

All the other sounds were drowned out by the roaring acclamation by the men of both Legions, and Caesar left them behind to ride deeper into the town to address the men of the other Cohorts who had participated in the assault and were now occupied in stamping out the last bit of resistance.

Crastinus, with a broad grin, bellowed, "All right, boys; you heard Caesar. The town's yours!" Naturally, this roused another cheer, then he continued, "Here's how it will work. You new *veterans*," he emphasized the word, pausing for the shouts of the new men at this acknowledgement, "will follow the older men's lead. Do what they do. And," he turned and pointed to the muddy street they had used to get to the town center, "you're going to do it in that area we just came through. You take what you can carry and that's it. And don't forget," Crastinus warned, "that you have to clear the houses before you can take anything. You can hear that the fighting's not over, and it looks like a fair number of their warriors are still about, so be careful. Remember," he reminded them, "the more you leave alive, the more slaves there will be for sale."

Dismissing the Century, Crastinus walked away, heading for the rest of his Cohort to check on them, leaving each section looking to their Sergeant for what came next. There was now an air of nervous anticipation that, while similar to the feeling just before battle, was subtly but noticeably different, because there was an eagerness, at least on most of their parts to experience the things the veterans had spent the off-duty watches telling them about around the fire at night.

"Let's get going before these selfish bastards take everything worth taking," Calienus was already walking, quickly, taking advantage of the fact that the Tenth Section was now in the lead because their designated area was behind them.

The rest of them, minus Didius and Vellusius, hurried after him, counting on their Sergeant's experience to guide them.

Domitius was completely uncertain about what to expect, but while, as he normally did, he was about to ask his best friend, he immediately realized that Pullus wouldn't know either, for the simple fact that they had both had the same tutor, and Cyclops hadn't ever mentioned what was coming, and they had always been together around the fire during training to hear the same stories from other veterans like Calienus. By the end of the day, both of them understood why Cyclops had been so reticent. It began in the first hut; Calienus kicked in the door, eliciting shrieks of terror from inside, then after a pause to allow a possible defender to come rushing out, the Sergeant stepped inside with his *gladius* in his hand, followed by Pullus, who, Domitius noticed with amusement, had essentially elbowed the others aside, silently daring them to challenge him for the privilege of being the second man inside. Nobody did, and Domitius followed Romulus and Remus, seeing for the first time who had been screaming, an older woman with a seamed face and iron gray hair, and three children, none of them appearing to be over the age of six, huddled against the far wall.

Along with the others, Domitius looked over at Calienus, but there was an expression on his face they'd never seen before, and he learned why when, in a flat tone of voice, the Sergeant told them, "The woman's too old to fetch a price, and the brats are too young." With a shrug, he said, "We may as well get rid of them."

The instant the words were out of his mouth, his blade was moving as he plunged it into the throat of the woman, who had fallen to her knees and was holding her arms out in a universal gesture of supplication. Shockingly, at least to Domitius, this actually stopped the children's crying, but he and his comrades would learn that this wasn't unusual at all, because they were suddenly too shocked to cry, despite the sudden brutality they were witnessing, or perhaps, because of it.

"Pullus," Calienus said softly, and when Domitius' friend looked at him, the Sergeant indicated the oldest of the children, a boy who, copying either his mother or grandmother, had fallen to his knees. Pullus shook his head, but Calienus' voice hardened. "This is part of it, Gregarius. When we're told the town is ours, this is what it means. If they won't fetch a price at the slave market, then we get rid of them."

The eyes of the other men turned to watch Pullus, who refused to meet their gaze, but while he was still shaking his head, he crouched down, grabbed the boy by the hair and drew his blade across the child's throat, closing his eyes as he did so. Burned into Domitius' mind was the image of the boy's eyes going wide as his best friend slaughtered him, and whether he was looking up at Pullus in a last silent plea, or his eyes just rolled back in his head, none of them would ever know.

"Romulus," Calienus pointed to the second child, a girl with a dirty face. "Your turn."

Not surprisingly, Romulus looked to his brother first, receiving only a resigned shake of the head, but whether the first child, now lying in a pitifully small heap on the dirt floor, the blood from his throat pooling around him, was related to her in some way, it did serve to rouse her from her stupor and she began screaming, the high-pitched shriek that only children are capable of producing making all of them wince, although not just because of the pain to their ears. Worse, she scrambled to her feet and darted for the open doorway, meaning that it was Atilius who was forced to stop her by snatching at her filthy shift, lifting her up and, while his *gladius* was in his hand, he didn't use it, bringing her back to where Romulus was standing with the same resigned expression as his brother, but he did as Pullus had, then there was the last, but before Calienus could say anything, it was Remus who stepped forward, joining his brother in spirit and in deed, not wanting Romulus to share that guilt alone.

"You never get used to it," Calienus said quietly. Then, before anything could be said, he continued, "Now, let me show you young things how to properly search a house."

By the time he was through, the two rooms had been ransacked, the thatch roof had been thoroughly examined, and the hearthstones in the center of the largest room had been pried up, yielding up a bag with a few coins, a gold necklace, a silver ring, and several pieces of silver that looked as if they had been hacked off of something larger.

Once he was satisfied, Calienus led them outside, then with his *pugio*, carved three numbers; a ten for their section, followed by a one for their Century, then a two for the Cohort, explaining as he did so, "This lets everyone know that this house has already been searched, and by who."

They turned their attention to the next hut directly across the muddy street, although they had to step over a body that was lying face-down in the mud, but this time, Calienus pointed to Scribonius.

"Your turn to kick in the door," he ordered, and as they had done with the first one, two of the others stood on either side of the doorway, ready to cut down anyone who might rush out.

It took Scribonius two tries to kick the door open, earning him some teasing, which he took with his normal good grace, but thankfully, at least as far as Domitius was concerned, it was empty, of people at least. As they waited to enter behind the others, Domitius reached out and grabbed Pullus' arm, his large friend having made it a point not to look in Domitius' direction.

Domitius opened his mouth, but Pullus shook his head and said, "Don't."

"You don't know what I was going to say," Domitius replied, but again Pullus shook his head, replying flatly, "It doesn't matter. I don't want to talk."

Then, he pulled his arm from Domitius' grasp to enter the hut. This time, their search didn't turn up anything, but Calienus said simply, "That happens sometimes."

It was with the third hut where, once again, the new men were faced with an unfamiliar situation. Calienus was the man to kick the door open again; this time, it was Scribonius and Romulus on either side, and an eyeblink after the door swung open, a bearded warrior came rushing out, a spear in hand, his arm drawn back to plunge it into Calienus' face when Scribonius and Romulus simultaneously thrust their blades into his body. He took one staggering step out of the hut before toppling to the ground, with just enough strength to roll over to stare at the Romans with accusing eyes, the blood pulsing from his mouth and soaking his beard as his lips moved, but he could only manage a gurgling sound that was almost as disturbing as the sight, and Domitius didn't meet the man's gaze as he stepped over him, thinking, Why won't you die already?

"Well, well," Calienus laughed, "I can see why he was so

keen to fight us."

Domitius entered to see, crouched in the corner, a young woman with black hair, but with a pale skin and high cheekbones, cheekbones that he was sure she had rubbed with dirt, as well as the rest of her face in a futile attempt to disguise her beauty. Instantly, the atmosphere in the room changed, as each of them stared hungrily at this woman who, by the rules of war during these times, was to be dealt with in any manner they saw fit. And, Domitius realized, he was not unaffected, feeling a stirring in his groin that couldn't be ignored or be dismissed as being for some other reason.

It was Scribonius who broke the silence, and Domitius heard by his comrade's tone that he was not the only one made nervous by her presence. "Maybe we should leave her be. She'll fetch a good price as a slave, won't she?"

Calienus laughed again, saying amiably, "That may be, but that doesn't mean we can't have a taste first. It's not like she's a virgin, right?" Jerking his thumb over his shoulder, he reminded them, "That was obviously her man we just did for, so there's no harm in taking a sample." Calienus began undoing his *baltea* and harness as he was speaking, then moved towards the woman who, from what Domitius could see, was certainly terrified, but he was certain he also saw anger, and a bit of defiance there, which ironically only made her more desirable. Ignoring her obvious unwillingness, Calienus turned to look over his shoulder, and with a grin said, "This is one time I'm pulling rank, boys. You can have a go after me, but don't mark her up because that will hurt the price. Got it?"

None of them spoke, although they all nodded their heads in agreement, while the woman, thinking that Calienus' moment of inattention gave her an opportunity, suddenly darted from the corner, and like the child in the first hut, made for the door. She learned the hard way that Calienus hadn't been fooled, and actually chuckled as he stuck a foot out, tripping her and sending her sprawling onto the dirt floor. Before she could react, Calienus had dropped down astride her and flipped her over with an ease and expertise that spoke to Domitius of a fair amount of practice. He had been moving to get in the line that was forming, but it was seeing her face clearly for the first time as it was illuminated by the light through the doorway that did it for him, the image of Juno thrusting into his mind, and before he could think about it, he spun about and hurried out of the hut.

Once outside, he made sure to turn his back to the doorway, and he learned that Pullus was joining him from Romulus, who warned, "You lose your place in line if you leave, Pullus!"

Domitius didn't glance over, sensing the presence of his friend looming next to him, and they stood there silently for a moment before Domitius said quietly, "I can't do something like that, Titus. I swore to be true to Juno, but it's not just that. When I looked at that woman, I saw Juno. How would I feel if that happened to her?"

Thinking that it would help Domitius, Pullus replied, "She's a Roman, Vibius. Nobody will ever beat us."

"I know," Domitius sighed, then looked up at his friend for the first time, "and that's what bothers me too."

Not knowing how to respond to this, Pullus didn't even try, and they stood there silently, listening as the woman in the hut behind them added her sobbing groans of pain and humiliation that were already in the air surrounding them, the panting and sudden moan of pleasure by their comrades climaxing not drowning them out.

It was Romulus who emerged, strapping his *baltea* and harness back out as he cheerfully called out to Pullus, "Your turn, Pullus. We left enough for your share."

For a span of a couple heartbeats, Domitius thought Pullus would remain outside, but then, without meeting his friend's eyes, he turned around and reentered the hut.

If anyone on the Roman side knew the name of this town, the men of the Tenth Section never learned it, but by the time the sun set, it essentially didn't exist any longer, although the fires that consumed the huts inside the wooden walls would be burning through the night. More than a thousand townspeople, including some warriors, had survived, keeping the ironworking *immunes* busy, hammering out the chains and cuffs that would secure these new slaves on the way to market. For the men of the Second Cohort, their short march back to the camp was one of the noisiest they would ever make, as men talked excitedly of what they had done, what they had seen, and what they had found in their sacking of the town. Pullus didn't participate in any of it, for a number of reasons, remaining silent despite Scribonius' attempts to engage him, and when they returned to their tent, for the first time and in the late afternoon light, he actually examined himself for the first time. He had assumed that he would look like his comrades; some of them had blood spattered on their arms, their legs, and on their *hamata*, but when he looked down, he saw with surprise that it was a matter of degree. Almost every inch of his bare skin was caked with both dirt and blood, although he deduced fairly quickly that what he thought was dirt was soot, but it was his armor that gave him the most concern, because the blood was caked in between the links from neck to the lower edge where his tunic showed. How long, he thought with dismay, will it take to get all that out? Along with the others, he stripped off his harness, but while he removed his *hamata* by himself, it was with more difficulty, the sharp pain in his side wrenching a groan from his lips. Dropping the armor on his cot, then the padded undershirt, for the first time, he was able to get a better look at the wound on his side, but the problem was that his tunic was stiff with dried blood and stuck to his side. Using his fingers, he tried to probe the wound, and it was his hiss of pain that attracted Calienus' attention, the Sergeant having just entered the tent after a chat with Rufio.

Seeing that Pullus intended to pull the tunic free from his side, he said quickly, "Don't do that. It will make it bleed even more."

Pullus turned, carefully, to face Calienus, a relieved expression on his face, a face that was still covered with blood, and Calienus gave himself a mental reminder to tell Pullus to clean himself up so that he didn't walk through camp looking like a victorious general in a triumph. Bending over, he chided the Gregarius, "I guess I have to teach you new boys everything, including how to take care of yourself." On his examination of the wound, his smile faded, replaced by a frown that betrayed a sense of worry that Pullus didn't miss. "This is more serious than I thought. You're going to need it cleaned up and stitched. I could do the cleaning part all right, but you'll have to go to the *medici* to get it stitched up." Pullus groaned again, not in pain but in frustration, although he managed to stand still while Calienus carefully peeled the tunic away, which as he had expected, caused the bleeding to begin again. However, when Calienus made no move to staunch it, when Pullus asked why, the Sergeant explained, "This will help clean the wound out." Once he was satisfied, Calienus held out a bandage, ordering, "Hold this against your side, and go to the hospital side of the *quaestorium*. Someone will take care of you there."

Pullus' walk to the *quaestorium* wasn't solitary; there was a stream of other men with relatively minor wounds who had been bandaged up to one degree or another while the fight was taking place, but he didn't make any attempt to talk to anyone, even men from the Second Cohort that he recognized. Instead, he spent the few moments excoriating himself over what, as far as he was concerned, was a disastrous first battle that he was lucky to survive. The fact that, once it was tallied up, Pullus had slain or wounded more Lusitani than any man, not just in the Century, but the entire Cohort, was meaningless to him, at least in this moment. All he thought about were the errors he had made, the pain in his side a stark reminder of the one that had almost cost him his life, although it was the last one against the warrior in the scale armor that was the most humiliating, because he now understood how it had happened. That Lusitani had seen a large, bumptious and inexperienced Roman and, most importantly, somehow sensed that the youth possessed an outsized pride in himself and his prowess. By the time he arrived at the open flap, he had vowed that he would devote a part of every day, whenever possible, working on his forms and skills, never again overestimating his abilities while underestimating his opponent's. So deep was he in thought that, when he stepped into the tent, he came to a stop, completely unprepared for the assault of sights, sounds, and smells that was an integral part of the aftermath of a battle fought by the Legions.

When Vellusius regained consciousness, he was alone, or so he thought, staring up at the wall, the two ladders in place, but it was when he turned his head to the left that wrenched first a gasp of pain, then one of horror at the sight of a charred corpse, still smoking, at the base of the ladder. Without thinking, he tried to roll over to his right while attempting to put weight on his right arm, but the shock from the jagged bolt of agony was such that he fell back onto the ground, gasping for breath. Deciding it might be time to take stock of himself, he was relieved to find that he could use his left arm without pain, which he used to run down the front of his *hamata,* praying that it did not come away wet, then moved his legs, one at a time. He had a horrific headache, and the back of his head was wet and throbbing, but after a few heartbeats, he determined that the major damage was to his right shoulder.

"All right, Publius, you have to get up," he muttered. "The boys will be worried about you."

This time, he was more prepared for the pain, but it was still a struggle to get to his feet, then the wave of dizziness came on so suddenly that he barely managed to sit back down, and without thinking, he reached up with his right arm to untie the chin thongs that secured his helmet. His next memory was peering up into a brown face, a man perhaps slightly older, with black curly hair and a neatly trimmed beard.

"Where are you hurt, Gregarius?"

The man's Latin was barely understandable, but Vellusius pointed to his right shoulder, then his head, mumbling, "I got hit by a sling bullet, then I fell backward and hit my head."

The man crouched, swinging the large leather bag around in front of him, then swiftly untied Vellusius' helmet, but while Vellusius braced himself for the *medicus* to simply yank it off, he instead lifted it gently off his head, leaving just the felt liner that fit snugly like a half-cap on the head. It was soaked, although Vellusius knew at least some of it was sweat, and while he was groggy, he was aware of his surroundings, noticing other men hurrying past, all of them wearing the same kind of tunic cut in the Greek style that identified them as *medici*. Peeling the cap off, the *medicus* grasped Vellusius by the jaw and turned his head to examine the cut.

"The edge of the helmet cut you, but it is not deep, Gregarius," he assured Vellusius. "You will not require stitches." Vellusius sighed with relief, but then the *medicus* added, "But you also might be bleeding inside your skull, which is why you are dizzy." Without warning, he turned his attention to Vellusius' right shoulder, frowning at the hole in the mail as big around as his thumb as he unfastened the hook that secured the outer flap, saw that the second layer was punctured as well, then gently inserted his hand under the other layer of armor, his fingers immediately covered with blood. Vellusius knew the man was trying to be gentle, but this wrenched a yelp of pain, which became louder because he instinctively jerked away from the other man's touch. "Your collarbone is broken, Gregarius, and the stone is lodged under the skin against the bone, which stopped it from going deeper," the *medicus* pronounced, but he was looking away over Vellusius' shoulder back down the hill, and he gave a shout in what Vellusius assumed was Greek, raising his hand. Returning his attention to Vellusius, the *medicus* explained, "Normally, you would be expected to return back to camp on your own since it is just your shoulder, but because of your blow to the head, I am having you taken by stretcher. So," he rose, "wait here and someone will be coming to pick you up."

Striding off, he left Vellusius to watch the *medicus* move towards the ladder where the smoking corpse was, but the man didn't even glance at it, which angered Vellusius before he reminded himself that whoever it was, they were obviously dead. He spent part of the time trying to guess who the dead man might be, but quickly stopped himself once his mind started going places that he didn't want it to go. Finally, two men carrying a board between them came puffing up the slope, and Vellusius shifted himself onto it, but just before they lifted him off the ground, he stopped them.

Pointing down to it, he said, "I need to bring my shield with me."

"You can have one your tentmates come and get it, Gregarius," the older of the two said, his Latin much better, but Vellusius shook his head.

"No, they might forget, and the Pilus Prior told us that if we lose our shield, we have to pay for it," he said stubbornly. "So," he lay back down, "just lay it on top of me."

Muttering under his breath, the stretcher bearer did as

Vellusius asked, then they carried him down the hill, joining a line of men carrying the other wounded, most of whom were more seriously injured than Vellusius. The bouncing as he was carried over the rough ground was painful, but Vellusius had glanced over at a man being carried from the area where the rest of the Second had been, and he recognized him as another new man from the Third Century who was missing his right arm above the elbow, the stump of arm having been tied off by what Vellusius assumed was the man's own *baltea*. He had turned his head, and seeing Vellusius, raised his left arm in a greeting, igniting in him a sense of shame that he had been moaning because he had a broken collarbone. It was when he was carried into the large tent that shamed Vellusius even more, because it was a nightmare of suffering.

There were lamps providing the illumination that the camp physicians used to tend to the most seriously wounded, and Vellusius was unceremoniously dumped off the stretcher and told to lie down on a table, next to an identical table where an older, bearded man in a physician's robe was sniffing the belly area of a Gregarius that Vellusius didn't recognize. The man's midriff was covered by a cloth, stained with blood, which the physician lifted out of the way, giving Vellusius a peek of what he initially thought, nonsensically, was a coil of eels, and he wondered if this man had somehow fallen into a tank of them and they had attached themselves to his belly. It was the smell that drifted across to him after the physician lifted the cloth that informed Vellusius that it wasn't eels, and he felt the bile rising up, caused by the smell of *cac* and what it meant, and he quickly turned his head in the opposite direction, missing the slight shake of the head by the physician, who then beckoned a *medicus*. Whispering something, the *medicus* acknowledged with a nod of his head and disappeared, while Vellusius quickly learned that the view on the opposite side, while better, was only marginally so, as another physician was examining the deep slash down the outside of another Gregarius' thigh, and as he probed at it, Vellusius saw the dull white of the man's thigh bone. This wounded man had a leather-wrapped dowel between his teeth, and was panting from the pain, but if he was groaning, Vellusius couldn't hear it over the low chorus created by the other men who were in agony to one degree or another.

"What is your injury, Gregarius?"

Vellusius turned his head again to see that the physician who had been sniffing the other man's belly was now standing next to his table, and not knowing how to address him, Vellusius decided to be safe. "It's my right collarbone, sir. I was hit by a sling bullet."

"Well, before we can look at you, we have to get your *hamata* and tunic off," he replied briskly, then snapped his finger to get the attention of the *medicus* he had whispered to, who at that moment was administering the contents of a stoppered bottle to the man with the belly wound, and Vellusius wondered if it was some sort of magic potion.

As he would come to learn, syrup of the poppy *was* something of a magic elixir, dulling a man's pain, or in this case, sending him across the river in Charon's Boat as painlessly as it was possible to make it. Finished, the *medicus* stepped around to the head of the table, and helped the physician slide the *hamata* off, then his padded undershirt, followed finally by his tunic, and this time, Vellusius couldn't help himself, crying out at the effort of raising his arm above his head. This, however, was the easiest part of the examination, but before the physician started probing in his shoulder, the *medicus* poured a small amount of something into a cup, lifting it to Vellusius' lips, who grimaced at the bitter taste as he drank it down. He was left on his own for a few moments in order to allow the concoction to work, the physician moving on to examine the wounded man who replaced the mortally wounded Gregarius, and Vellusius very quickly became drowsy. The pain hadn't gone away, but it turned out that he didn't mind it as much as just moments before, and the physician returned, picking up a bronze rod with one end curved into a hook and began to probe the wound, which did hurt quite a bit.

For some reason, Vellusius felt somewhat disconnected, so that the idea that this stranger was jabbing a hooked bronze stick into his body was more interesting than terrifying, and while he was clenching his teeth, he had shaken his head at the offer of a leather-wrapped dowel, which enabled him to ask, "What are you doing?"

"Lie still," the physician said sharply, then in a more conversational tone, he said, "I am checking to make sure that the only thing inside you is this stone. Which," he maneuvered the end of the hook so that it was behind the stone, then pulled his hand back, "I am removing now."

Vellusius gave a shout, and he jerked upward, but this time, the physician didn't admonish him, although he did press him firmly back down. "And now," he continued, "I need to make sure that none of your tunic is in the wound." Glancing up at the *medicus*, who was examining Vellusius' armor, he demanded, "Well? What's taking you so long, Praxis?"

The *medicus* wasn't flustered; he had worked with this physician when they had been with the 4th Legion, and he wasn't going to be rushed in his job of drawing the separated links of iron back together to see if there were any missing. This didn't necessarily mean that they had been driven into the wound; it was equally possible that they had simply fallen out and were trapped between the armor and padded undershirt, and while they always were careful to look for such things when they removed a man's *hamata,* the system was far from perfect. He was initially satisfied, and was about to assure the physician that it was intact when he noticed something.

"We're missing a rivet," he said with a frown.

This prompted the physician to reexamine the area around Vellusius' tunic, which he had draped across the man's lower body, the area around the hole stiff from the dried blood, but after running his hands along the fabric, he muttered a curse.

"Bring the lamp closer," he ordered. "I just want to check the wound to make sure it's not in there."

Vellusius was awake for this, but he was finding it difficult to make sense of what was being said, although he knew that it had something to do with his armor and his shoulder. It just seemed to be too much trouble to try and pay attention. Until, that was, the physician stuck that rod back into the hole, but the *medicus* was experienced and ready for what he knew was coming, pressing Vellusius back down on the table by pushing on his head and left shoulder at Vellusius' involuntary reaction of trying to raise his upper body, while the physician used his body to pin Vellusius' lower arm against the table. The physician made a sound of triumph, then snatched a pair of bronze tweezers with his left hand, and very delicately inserted the ends into the wound, clamped down, then extracted something that he dropped into a bowl sitting on the lower table holding the equipment, making a barely audible sound that Vellusius still heard. Things moved quickly after that; Vellusius was sat up, a wad of cloth shoved into the wound, then a linen bandage was wrapped around his shoulder, the final piece tying a long strip of cloth around his wrist that then looped around his neck to immobilize his arm against his chest.

"There," the physician said. "As long as the wound does not corrupt, you will recover fully, but you will need to keep your arm completely immobile for three days, then come back for a check of your bandages. You are going to spend the night here to make sure that your wound does not corrupt."

"Why would that happen?" Vellusius asked, although if he was being honest, at this moment, he didn't care all that much.

"Because," the physician answered simply, "I might have missed something and it is still in the wound. Or," he shrugged, "Febris turns her face away from you."

These weren't consoling words, and Vellusius knew that it should bother him, but it didn't, although he told himself that he might change his mind later. With the *medicus'* help, Vellusius was escorted to a cot where the other treated men were lying, and before he could ask, his equipment was brought and shoved under his cot, leaving Vellusius in a fog that helped shut out the sounds and smells as the wounded continued coming in.

For Pullus, the experience wasn't as painful, but it was more tedious, and in a way, more traumatic. After a quick examination, he was ordered to sit with a group of lightly wounded men, and he didn't have anything to dull his senses to the immense suffering all around him. The most unpleasant part was when a man's wounds were cauterized, not because of the screams, but the smell that instantly made him think of Vinicius, the scene coming back to him despite his determination to block it from his mind. Sitting on a series of benches, he and the other men didn't make much attempt at conversation, each of them more intent on what was going on, and with every stretcher brought in, they all studied the face of the fallen man, searching for someone familiar. In Pullus' case, of the two missing men from his section, he was worried about Vellusius, although he did feel a pang of guilt that he didn't feel the same way about Didius. While those who could be helped were more numerous than those who couldn't, there were still men who had survived long enough to be brought into the *quaestorium* but wouldn't live much longer. And, as Pullus and his fellow unfortunates learned, they were placed directly next to the path that led to the quarter of the tent that was curtained off with leather partitions.

"What's that?" he finally asked the man sitting next to him, pointing in that direction.

His question wasn't aimed randomly; the man was several years older than Pullus, and he didn't recognize him, so he guessed he was from the 8th, and a veteran.

"That," the man answered after glancing to see where Pullus was pointing before looking away so quickly that Pullus noticed, "is Charon's Boat."

"Charon's Boat?" Pullus repeated, not understanding the reference.

"It's where men who aren't dead yet but will be soon are taken. They don't like keeping them out where the rest of the wounded can see them suffering." He gave a bitter laugh. "It's bad for morale."

That, Pullus thought, was understandable, though he didn't say as much, and he returned his attention to the larger part of the room. While they were sitting there, Pullus only saw men being taken into Charon's Boat, but then, shortly before he was finally called, a pair of slaves who were given the duty of removing the dead emerged with a man who had succumbed, his mouth hanging open with a slackness that Pullus, and his new comrades, would learn was a sure sign of death.

As they carried him past, a ranker two men down from him muttered, "Well, that makes our tent roomier. Poor bastard."

A *medicus* arrived and summoned Pullus, but rather than taking him to a table, he was put on a stool and told to lift his arms above his head. The bleeding had stopped, but it had dried the tunic to his side again, and when the *medicus* pulled the tunic off him, the bleeding began anew; it also hurt to have the fabric yanked from the wound, but Pullus had decided he wasn't going to whine about something as inconsequential as this, not when he had just seen men offer no more than a muffled groan as their wound was cauterized. Dipping a rag into water that had long before turned red from the blood of his previous patients, the *medicus* scrubbed the wound, and the only way Pullus didn't cry out was by clenching his jaw so hard that it ached. Surprisingly, the cleaning was more painful than the actual stitching, then once he was finished, the *medicus* wrapped his chest, complaining that it took twice as much bandage as a normal man, telling Pullus indifferently that he was to come back in three days for the bandage to be replaced, and the stitches would be removed in a week.

"The only reason you need to come back before that is if the wound starts to smell, or if you start running a fever."

This alarmed Pullus even more than it had Vellusius, and he asked, "What does that mean?"

"That your wound has turned corrupt," the *medicus* said as if this were obvious, but Pullus wasn't satisfied.

"Why would it turn corrupt?"

"Oh," the *medicus* shrugged, "there might be a thread or a scrap from your tunic that we missed. Or," he gave the large Gregarius a grin that was tinged with mischief, "maybe the gods don't love you anymore."

Laughing at his own joke, he left Pullus alone to struggle back into his tunic, unaware that he had just heard a jibe that would be repeated more times than he could count, and he looked at the stained hole, wondering if it should be patched or sewn, and whether the blood would come out, not that it mattered all that much since the tunic was already red. Concerning the color, it was accepted as an article of faith that this was the reason for dying the tunics red, so the enemy would never know when they had made men of the Legions bleed.

It was as he was leaving that he heard someone call his name, and it took a moment to pick out the man from among the row of cots, but when Pullus saw the black hair sticking straight up from the man's head, he felt his lips form into a smile of true pleasure, and he hurried over to his wounded comrade.

"Vellusius," he said happily as he knelt down next to the cot, "I thought we'd lost you, old son."

Vellusius indicated the bandage with his left hand, explaining, "I got hit by one of those cursed missiles, right on my collarbone. It broke it, but it also slowed the damn thing down so it just lodged in my shoulder."

Offering a sympathetic wince, Pullus asked, "Did they get it out?"

Vellusius nodded, making a face as he said, "And it hurt like Dis, I can tell you, but I'm feeling all right now. They gave me some wine with some sort of herb mixed in that tasted like the butt end of a mule, but I'm feeling pretty good now." He stopped suddenly then said, "Wait, I already said that," and began laughing, which caused Pullus to laugh as well, wincing at the stab of pain in his side, and it reminded him of something.

"What about your wound? It's not going to put you on disability, is it?"

"No," Vellusius assured him, "they said I should be as good as new in a few weeks, as soon as the bone knits." The woozy smile returned. "You know what that means, right, Pullus? No digging, no guard duty, no marching about. Yes," he gave a contented, drowsy sigh, "I could definitely get used to that."

Pullus chuckled, then stood up to leave; when he was heading for Vellusius, he had debated telling him about Vinicius, but decided against it, and he felt certain he had made the right decision, believing that Vellusius would find out soon enough and didn't need to know at that moment.

"I'll be sure to tell everyone you're going to be all right," he said over his shoulder.

He was almost to the exit when Vellusius called to him again.

"Tell those thieving bastards to stay out of my things. Especially Didius!"

For Didius, the humiliation of being examined, then instantly dismissed as being seriously injured enough to warrant a stretcher was just the beginning, the *medicus* who examined him not doing a good job of hiding his amused disdain.

"Why didn't you pull it out yourself?" he demanded, and, for the moment, Didius' normal belligerence was nowhere in evidence.

"I tried," he answered somewhat sheepishly, "but it wouldn't come out. I think it's lodged in the bone."

This caused the man's expression to alter, not much, but he was more sober as he squatted down and commanded, "Stick your leg out, Gregarius. I need to examine your foot."

Didius complied, tensing himself for what he was sure would be an agony as this butcher fiddled with the board while he tried to decide how to get this cursed nail out of his foot, because he had convinced himself that it was indeed lodged in the bone of his heel. What happened was, in many ways, worse, because the *medicus* had no intention of wasting his time, so he grabbed Didius' ankle with one hand, and with the other pulled the board away from the sole of his *caligae*, the nail sliding out easily, although it was dripping blood. It happened so quickly that Didius let out a yelp that was more from being startled than from pain. The *medicus*, still on his haunches, didn't say anything immediately, holding the board out so that Didius could see that the nail protruded barely two inches from the board.

With a heavy humor, he announced, "I do not believe that this nail is long enough to lodge in your bone, Gregarius."

Didius' face grew hot, but he stubbornly insisted, "You don't know that for sure, do you?"

"Between the thickness of your sole and the distance between the bottom of your heel and the bone, I would say it is highly unlikely."

The *medicus* stood, no longer willing to devote any more time to a man he was certain was a malingerer, of which every Legion had their share, but before he turned away, Didius stopped him by pointing to the blood oozing out between his foot and the *caliga*. "At least give me a bandage so that I can stop the bleeding!"

More to get away than anything, the *medicus* reached into his bag, withdrew a rolled bandage and tossed it to Didius, not bothering to say anything more, turning to rejoin the handful of *medici* as they followed behind the advancing Cohorts in search of more of their men to treat. Didius did notice that they would stop over a Lusitani body, but his lip curled at the sight of them searching the corpses, clearly looking for any valuables.

"Stupid *cunni*," he muttered. "If you think that hasn't already been done, no wonder you're freedmen."

He was unlacing his boot as he said this, wincing when he pulled it off. Looking at the bottom of his foot, he was about to clean the blood away then thought, the more blood that shows through the bandage, the better. Wrapping his heel and ankle, he put the boot back on with some difficulty, took a couple of exploratory steps, and realized with a sinking feeling that it didn't hurt enough to make him walk with more than a slight limp. It certainly hurt, but there was enough of an honest man in Didius to recognize that it was something that wouldn't have hindered his ability to participate in the battle. I'll just have to play it up a bit, he thought as he picked up his shield from where he had dropped it earlier, noticing that the bodies were already starting to stink. The fighting was still going on, and for a long, torturous moment, Spurius Didius stood there, part of him longing to travel up that muddy street that he had seen his Century travel on their push into the center of the town to rejoin the group of which he had become a part, if grudgingly. If I just showed up and took my spot, they might not even notice I've been gone, he thought. And, he actually did start taking a tentative step in that direction, but then something happened, an image popping into his mind, one of Pullus on the day that he had humiliated him in their sparring bout, standing over him with a sneer that was as lacerating as the physical damage.

"No!" He said it aloud, almost shouting it. "I'm not going to go help that *cunnus*!" He lowered his voice, muttering to himself, "He thinks he's Hercules, let him prove it."

Instead, he turned about and walked, with a barely noticeable limp, to the ladder that led up to the rampart, then walked down the rampart over to the ladder that Crastinus and Pullus had ascended, swinging his legs over the parapet while avoiding looking to his left, where the corpse of Vinicius lay at the base of it. To his relief, both for himself and for the man, he saw that Macro was gone; he didn't know him that well, but Didius had seen the burns and knew that they were far more painful than his own minor injury, and he didn't bear the man any ill will. Walking back towards the camp, he began practicing a heavier limp, so that by the time he reached the *Porta Praetoria*, he did look as if he could barely walk. Aiding his cause was the fact that walking had kept his heel bleeding to the point that it soaked through the bandage, and the men who had been left behind to guard the camp gave him a sympathetic glance as he limped past. He wasn't the only one; men were streaming back, by themselves, or in some cases two's, with one man helping another, but while these genuinely wounded men headed for the *quaestorium*, Didius headed for the Second Cohort's area. Nobody was around, and he was struck by an awful temptation that he attributed to the *numen* of his father Aulus, who he knew wouldn't have hesitated to plunder the belongings and valuables of not just his own Century, but the entire Cohort. He successfully resisted that impulse, entering his own tent instead, and in an act of spite, dropped down onto Pullus' cot, suddenly realizing that he was extremely tired. I'll just rest a bit, he told himself, then I'll get up and he'll never know, he thought as he pulled off his helmet, then his *hamata,* which he dropped onto the dirt floor before collapsing back on Pullus' cot. More than once, his hand dropped down to finger the flap of Pullus' pack, but again he resisted the temptation, this time by reminding himself of what Pullus had done to him and would undoubtedly do if he was caught with any of Pullus' belongings. His last sensation before dozing off was a feeling of relief that he had survived his first battle.

Didius jerked awake at the sound of men talking, his heart immediately racing as he lifted his head to listen for a moment. Someone was coming back to the Second Cohort; whether it was his Century or one of the others, or the entire Cohort, there was no way to tell, and he didn't want to be discovered, not just because he had used Pullus' cot, but because he still hadn't worked out an explanation. He did take the time to carry his equipment over to his pack, still consigned to a corner of the tent, something that infuriated him every time he saw it, dumping them on top of it, then hurried to the tent flaps, which were hanging closed. Peeking out, he was relieved to see that the street was still empty, but judging from the sound, someone would be rounding the corner from the *Via Praetoria* any moment, and he slipped out, moving in the opposite direction then ducking into the space between the tents of his section and the Eighth's, the tent next to theirs, because the odd numbered sections were on the opposite side of the street. He had used this method of travel more times than he could count, eschewing the regularly spaced streets for what was, for all intents and purposes, alleys just like in regular cities like Gades, and even hampered by his heel, he skillfully navigated his way between the guy ropes and stakes, moving from the First Century street to the Second, then the Third, finally emerging on the street that was the border between the Second and Third Cohort. One of the advantages of a Roman military camp for all of the men, but especially for men like Didius, they were always laid out the same, and it didn't take long to learn the spots that gave a modicum of privacy. Near the latrine trench was one spot, but that stank, so instead, he headed to the area where the horses of the officers and spare mounts were kept, knowing that there were also water barrels, sacks, and crates kept there for the maintenance and feeding of the animals along with other sundry supplies. Settling down in between a pair of barrels and a stack of feed sacks, Didius tried to calculate just how much time it would have taken him to be seen at the *Quaestorium*, then return to his own tent. He was counting on the sight of his bandage to quell any questions that Calienus, or whoever was the new Optio, unaware that it was Rufio, might have about his absence for the fighting in the town. The noise level inside the camp increased, informing Didius that the two Legions were returning, but he still waited a bit longer. Just before sunset, he decided that it was time, and after taking a quick peek over the barrels to make sure he wouldn't be seen, he rose and began a slow, hobbling walk back towards the Second Cohort area. This time, he used the streets; as he had learned, being caught in another Century's area between the tents signaled ill intentions, and he was largely ignored by the men of the other Centuries. Turning the corner to his street, he saw that the section slaves had already started the fires, and men were beginning to settle down in their customary spots around it, including his section comrades. Taking a deep breath and reminding himself to limp, Didius hobbled down the street, only acknowledging the few men from the other sections with whom he was on speaking terms with a nod, and he was almost to the tent before Calienus, who had a neckerchief spread out on the ground in front of him and was examining the pile of items strewn across it, looked up to see Didius approaching.

"You got back early," the Sergeant said, which alerted the others, although it was just the Mallius brothers, Atilius, Domitius and Scribonius, all of whom were engaged in essentially the same thing as Calienus, with neckerchiefs in front of them, but each of them with only a couple of things on them.

He was about to ask how Calienus knew this but caught himself when he remembered he had left his equipment inside the tent, so instead he lied, "I was at the *Quaestorium*."

This earned him a frown, and Calienus pointed out, "You're coming from the opposite direction of the *Quaestorium*."

"I...I took the long way," was all Didius could think to say.

Calienus didn't say anything, regarding Didius with a cool gaze from those gray eyes that Didius, for one, found unsettling, but then he shrugged.

"We're dividing up the spoils," Calienus explained, then hesitated before adding, "so come get your share."

When he thought about it later, Didius would be hard-pressed to decide who was more surprised, his comrades or himself when he answered, "I didn't do anything. I got...hurt when I was coming down the ladder inside the walls." The looks of a surprise bordering on shock caused Didius to change the subject. "Where's Vellusius?"

"He was wounded," Atilius said quietly. "He took a sling bullet to the shoulder." Before Didius could ask, he assured him, "He's only in the hospital for a night, then he'll be on light duty for a week or two."

It was Domitius' steady gaze that prompted him to ask about Pullus, hoping that his tone didn't give away the fact that he was hoping to hear that the big bastard was dead, but he saw nobody was fooled.

Taking the glance from Domitius as his cue, Calienus informed him, "He was wounded...but not badly. Right now, he's at the baths getting a scraping."

Didius' response to the news was a grunt, but he couldn't stop himself from adding, "What, is he so sensitive that he can't stand a little dirt and blood and he has to go to the bath tent?"

Domitius came to his feet at this, although he didn't make a move towards Didius, but his fists were clenched, as was his jaw as he said tightly, "First, Didius, he was wounded and he needed to get his blood off."

"He was bloody," this came from Scribonius, and Domitius shot him a furious glance at being interrupted, until Scribonius continued quietly, "but most of it wasn't his, Didius. He had..." for this, he deferred to Calienus, who shrugged as he thought for a moment.

"I'm not completely sure, but he killed at least five of those *cunni*. Gods only know how many he wounded," he chuckled, "or just scared to death."

To Didius' consternation, this made the others laugh as well, and Domitius sat back down, giving Didius a triumphant smile, but it was Romulus who had another surprise in store for Didius, one he wouldn't care for at all.

It started innocently enough, when he pointed to Didius' bandage and asked, "How did that happen?"

"I told you," Didius answered evasively. "I jumped down from the ladder." Seeing this wasn't enough, he added, "I landed on a fucking nail that was so long, it got lodged in my heel bone. At least," he tried to imbue his shrug with an air of bravado that he hoped sufficed, "that's what the *medicus* told me."

"That's not what we heard," Remus shot back, a broad grin on his face.

Suddenly, Didius didn't feel very well, his stomach twisting into a knot, but he had to know.

"What did you hear?" he asked, then demanded, "And from who?"

"From the *medicus*." Romulus answered the second question first, and now Didius thought he might vomit.

Deciding that the best course of action was to cut his losses,

Didius fell back on his usual mode of address when challenged, blustering, "Well, if he said anything different, then he's lying!" He turned towards the tent. "And he said I need to be off my feet."

With as much dignity as he could muster, and with an exaggerated limp, he entered the tent, ignoring Romulus' cry, "Don't you want to know what he said?"

Throwing himself down on his pallet, cursing the fact that it was his turn to sleep in the dirt and not Atilius, who, as his close comrade, he was now sharing a cot with, Didius hoped that this was at least the last he would hear about this.

It turned out to be a forlorn hope, because Pullus finally returned from his stop at the bath tent, but while he was physically clean, he didn't feel that way, and he wondered if this was a common feeling after you killed your first man. A more unwelcome thought was, what if that was the way he felt after every battle? The fire was going, the section pot hanging from the iron tripod, and he was pleased to see that Domitius had taken care of baking his *castra paneris* as well as his own, and for a moment, he stood there, next to the Eighth Section tent, content to watch his comrades alternating between bickering and teasing each other about something that had happened on this eventful day. Then, he resumed walking, and Scribonius noticed him approaching, alerting the others, prompting them all to cry out his name with what, to his ears, was genuine happiness, which he acknowledged with an embarrassed wave.

"Calienus is dividing everything up," Domitius told him, then pointed to the neckerchief that lay in front of his empty spot. "See? I was taking care of your share."

Instead of dropping to the ground as he normally did, Pullus lowered himself more carefully; seeing Domitius' expression of concern, he assured his friend, "I'm just sore, that's all. When the stitches come out, I'll be fine." Turning his attention to his neckerchief, he gave a mock frown. "It doesn't look like you're taking care of me very well." He gave Domitius a shove.

As he intended, this ignited a new round of bickering, Domitius pointing to Calienus, saying indignantly, "Don't blame me, blame him. Calienus is the one deciding what everything's worth, not me!"

"That's how it's done," Calienus spoke up, but while he sounded patient, it was difficult since he had already gone through this when Pullus was gone. "The Sergeant decides the value, and just because you don't have as many things," he pointed to Pullus' pile consisting of a ring, what looked like a cloak clasp but made of finely worked silver, and two coins that weren't Roman and larger than even an *obol*, "that clasp is worth more by itself than three of Vellusius' pieces. And," he reminded them, "we're not finished."

Chastened, Pullus nodded his acceptance of Calienus' judgment, feeling a stab of guilt for doubting his Sergeant in the first place, so more to change the subject than anything, he finally asked, "So, what about Didius?"

The atmosphere around the fire instantly changed, which seemed to confirm Pullus' suspicion, and he struggled with himself, knowing that he should feel badly, but he was still secretly happy that the man would no longer be around. And, he noticed, the way his comrades suddenly became more interested in their new belongings than looking at him seemed to be confirmation.

"I'm in here. Why, Pullus? Did you miss me?"

He instantly recognized Didius' voice, and he tried to hide his disappointment, waiting for someone to explain, yet none of them seemed inclined to do so, and from Pullus' viewpoint, they were behaving quite strangely.

"Pluto's cock," Calienus muttered, seeing that none of the others had any intention of speaking up, and with a sigh, he explained, "Didius was injured on the way down the ladder. He took a serious fall."

It was Remus who coughed, or that was what it sounded like to Pullus. It turned out to be a futile attempt to avoid bursting out into laughter, but the instant he let out a guffaw, he was joined by everyone, except for Pullus, who was completely bewildered, and Calienus, although he was smiling.

From inside the tent, Didius, sounding like his normal self, roared, "*Quiet, by the gods, or I'll come out and gut every one of you!!*"

Instead of silencing them, it made them laugh harder, and Pullus, still not really understanding, couldn't stop himself from joining in, the humor proving too contagious.

This prompted Didius' appearance, hopping on one foot, the other bandaged one dangling in the air, and he held on to the tentpole for support, trying to sound threatening as he shouted, "I told you to be quiet or all of you will pay! I'll wager that if any of you had happen to you what happened to me, you would have done the same thing!"

His comrades, rather than being threatened, continued laughing, and finally, Pullus caught Calienus' eye, giving him a bemused shake of his head, and Calienus waved at the others to quiet down enough so that he could explain.

"It seems that our dear Didius, when he jumped off the ladder, landed on a nail that went into his foot."

Pullus had to raise his voice to be heard, asking what to him was the obvious question, "Why didn't he pull it out?"

The mirth had been gradually settling down, but this unleashed a fresh round of laughter, and Romulus, holding his stomach as tears came from his eyes, shouted, "Because he couldn't; he was too squeamish!"

Now that he knew the cause, Pullus joined the others, while an enraged Didius actually hopped away from the tent to come to the fire, bellowing, "It was in too deep, I tell you! None of you would have been able to pull it out if it had been in your foot!"

Again, none of his comrades were intimidated in the slightest, but Remus decided that a reenactment was in order, and he stood, miming descending a ladder, then made a hop up into the air, except the instant his feet touched the ground, he collapsed, holding his foot and howling, "By the gods, I've been shot! I'm dying! Oh gods, the pain...pain..."

By this point, none of them were upright, except for Didius, who stood there in mortal embarrassment, but he couldn't stop himself from insisting, "I tell you, it was all the way into the bone! By the gods, you'll all pay for your insults, I swear it! I'm..."

Calienus cut him off, tiring of this no matter how amusing it was, telling him, "Oh do be quiet, Achilles. Go rest your foot."

For the rest of his days, Didius would remember this moment, but while he initially viewed it as a humiliation that was in some ways worse than what he had suffered at the hands of his nemesis Pullus, over the years, he would gradually come to accept that, like Romulus and Remus, he would be known as Achilles for the rest of his time under the standard. He would have been shocked, and disbelieving, if he had been told that he would come to treasure the name, even when it no longer applied.

Caesar and his army spent the next three days in place, as the Legate allowed his two Legions who participated in the battle to rest, recuperate, and to send their fallen comrades on their way across the river Styx, releasing their *animi* to do so by the purifying fire that burned away the fleshly casing that kept the soul trapped within. There were other practical reasons, namely that a shuffling of the ranks was necessary, with men being promoted into spots that were now empty, like the position of Optio of the First of the Second, where Crastinus informed Rufio that he hadn't fucked up badly enough to lose the job. As a result of Rufio moving up, Crastinus also promoted a new Sergeant of the Fifth Section, naming Tiberius Macula as his successor, along with the Second Section, whose Sergeant had had his elbow shattered, requiring an amputation. There was one other post he needed to fill, and for this, Crastinus showed that, in his own way, he was like his Legate Caesar, disdaining long-held traditions when he viewed them as hurting the effectiveness of his Cohort.

This was what found him standing outside a tent of the First Century. The flaps were pulled back so that he could see that it was partially occupied with three men from the section, but he was only here for one of them. He didn't have to go far into the tent, the man occupying the first cot on the left being his target and who was sound asleep, but without thinking, he used a boot to kick the man's bare feet, and while the Gregarius responded immediately and leapt to his feet, it was with a gasp and a wince that reminded Crastinus that the man had been wounded, and he felt a pang of guilt, though it was not that strong.

"Side still bothering you?" he abruptly asked Pullus, who wasn't standing at a full position of *intente,* because if he did, his head would poke up against the roof of the tent.

"Not much, Pilus Prior. Only when I move."

This elicited Crastinus' version of a laugh, and he was pleased to see that Pullus didn't seem to be irritated at his thoughtlessness.

"Well," Crastinus informed him, "you'll be doing plenty of that. I've decided to make you our weapons instructor in place of Vinicius. Rufio agreed that you're the best choice," he added needlessly, because while it was true, Crastinus' mind had been made up when he broached the subject with his new Optio.

He knew that Pullus would be nervous at the idea, but he was surprised when Pullus shook his head.

"That's a great honor, Pilus Prior..."

"I don't give a fucking brass *obol* if you think it's an honor," Crastinus snapped, his anger only partially feigned. "It's an order, and the only response I expect is, 'Yes, Pilus Prior' or 'Yes, sir'."

There, Crastinus thought, that puts this matter to bed, and his mind had already moved on to the next item on his mental list of tasks for the day, but he quickly learned Pullus didn't see it the same way.

"But, sir," Pullus said quietly, and with a hint of nerves, "why me? I thought after what happened on the wall when I forgot to draw my *gladius*, you'd realize that I'm not ready for this. Maybe someday..."

This was more serious than he thought, Crastinus recognized, but he was also now truly angry, and he took a step closer to the large Gregarius, completely unintimidated even now after he had seen what the man was capable of, glaring up at him, although he didn't raise his voice, knowing that this made him sound more menacing and not less.

"Are you doubting my judgment, Gregarius?"

As he was speaking, Crastinus had begun leaning forward, a trick passed down from one Centurion to the next, while Pullus, despite their size difference and as Crastinus had been certain he would, started leaning backward, trying to keep some distance between them.

"N-n-no, Pilus Prior," Pullus stammered, in a manner that hearkened back to the first week of their association. "I just...I just..." Pullus searched for the right words, but then shrugged and finished, "...nothing, Pilus Prior. I'll do my absolute best, sir."

This was what Crastinus had been looking for, the sign that Pullus fully accepted his fate; that it reinforced that, as large and strong as he was, Pullus was still terrified of his Centurion was just a bonus as far as Crastinus was concerned.

Smiling suddenly, Crastinus clapped Pullus on the shoulder, saying, "Good, it's settled then. You won't be expected to start training the others until you're completely healed. And," he added in a warning, although he was still smiling, "that also means you can't be smashing anyone's nose flat anymore. Understand, Pullus?" Not surprisingly, Pullus assured him that he would do no such thing again, and Crastinus turned to leave, then stopped at the entrance, turning back to face the Gregarius, who was still standing with a stunned expression. "I know you can do this, Pullus. I have faith in you, which is why I picked you. I know you won't let me down."

Then, he was gone, leaving Pullus to mull over this shift in his fortunes, wondering if it was a good or a bad thing.

The 10th Legion was now blooded, and overall, Primus Pilus Favonius was quite pleased with the performance of his Legion. This wasn't saying that things had gone perfectly; while his First Cohort performed well, as had the Second, Favonius had some concerns about his Tertius Pilus Prior, Gnaeus Cornuficius, whose Cohort had been what Favonius viewed as a bit too timid in moving through the town. His artillery crews hadn't been as accurate as Caesar demanded either, and now that Favonius was beginning to get a sense of their general's style, he was beginning to recognize just how much his new commander favored, and relied on, artillery. Favonius had served under Lucullus first as a ranker, rising to the rank of Centurion, then had transferred over when Pompeius Magnus had called for a new *dilectus* in the 1st Legion, although this had been to serve as the Tertius Pilus Posterior, second in command of the Third Cohort. Lucullus had been a good Legate, if something of a prig, and never tried to hide his feelings about the other men of his class who he believed refused to give him his due, especially the Roman who usurped Favonius' own loyalty to Lucullus, Pompeius Magnus. That, at least, was how Lucullus viewed it, but for Favonius, when offered the chance of a promotion, going from the post of Octus Hastatus Posterior, commanding the Sixth Century of a third line Cohort to Tertius Princeps Posterior, it had been an easy choice and had nothing to do with a lack of regard he held for Lucullus. As Favonius quickly learned, as competent as Lucullus was, Pompeius Magnus was in an altogether different class, and unlike Lucullus, when he had informed Pompeius that he had been approached by the new *Praetor* Gaius Julius Caesar and offered the post of Primus Pilus, Favonius learned that, not only did Pompeius not hold it against him, but he was the one who had recommended Favonius to Caesar.

While grateful for the endorsement, Lucius Favonius was no fool; he knew that, while he had no doubt in his own abilities to run a new Legion, Pompeius was also putting a man he thought would be more loyal to Pompeius than he would be to Caesar into this new Legions. Yes, they were friends, and he understood that Caesar played a unique role in what later generations would call the First Triumvirate, serving as a buffer between Pompeius and Marcus Licinius Crassus, who loathed each other because they both harbored ambitions to be the First Man in Rome. And, while Caesar's bloodline was certainly eminent, and for the patrician and high-ranking plebeians who paid attention to such things, was actually superior to that of Crassus, and certainly that of Pompeius Magnus, who was a *homo novus*, not even from Rome but from Picenum, he had also had something of an undistinguished career to this point. At first, Favonius had been perfectly happy to keep his former Legate apprised of the events in the province now that Caesar was *Praetor*, and he didn't think that he was betraying any kind of confidence when he also reported on the progress of his new Legion as they underwent training...at least at first. Now, however, it was different, in a way that, while Favonius couldn't put his finger on, he was nevertheless acutely aware was troubling to him. If he had been pressed, Favonius would have ultimately said that he was beginning to feel disloyal to Caesar, but it was only partially due to the fact that the nature of Pompeius' questions had subtly changed, becoming more pointed, as if he was fishing for information that could potentially be used against Caesar. And, with almost every passing day, Favonius had become more impressed with Caesar, not only with his style of command and his easy rapport with men of all ranks, something that Lucullus never had, and Pompeius only possessed in a superficial sense, but with the man's tactical acumen.

Caesar had only been the most junior of Tribunes when serving with Thermus, but had distinguished himself at the siege of Mytilene, winning a Civic Crown in the process. His only other military experience had been as a Tribune during the uprising by the slave Spartacus, but he hadn't done anything distinguishing enough to be mentioned. Even with this seeming lack of experience, from the first day, Favonius had been impressed with Caesar's sheer competence in command, but more than anything else, it was Caesar's attention to even the most minor details that was, frankly, something that Favonius had never witnessed before. While Pompeius was similar in this regard, taking an interest in how many chickpeas there were in a barrel, it was a matter of degree, and Caesar was not only interested in such things, he retained an astonishing amount of this arcane information. Perhaps most importantly to a man like Lucius Favonius was Caesar's utter lack of regard for the customs that played such an outsized role in how a Legion was run, if those customs interfered with what Caesar viewed as the proper running of a Legion, and while at the beginning Favonius, along with most of the other Centurions, had been quite uncomfortable with Caesar's clear disdain for established customs, that had changed.

"Because this is how it's always been done," Caesar had memorably said at a meeting of all of the Centurions of his new Legion, "doesn't mean it's the best way now. Yes," he had allowed, "back when we were a four-line Legion, and campaigns only lasted a season, some of these things made sense. But," he had continued, "that was before my uncle Gaius Marius made his reforms, and now, they hamper our ability to operate as a Legion." He had finished by asking, "Does anyone disagree?"

By the time he had asked this question, barely a month into the training of the 10th, because of his closer contact with Caesar, who was still conducting business as *Praetor* of the province, Favonius knew that this question wasn't rhetorical, that Caesar not only allowed but encouraged input from his officers. He also, Favonius and his subordinates were to learn, acted on some of the suggestions and criticisms offered by the officers. For almost all of the men wearing the transverse crest in the 10th, this was highly unusual, even for those who had served Pompeius, who Favonius had learned through experience, albeit secondhand by witnessing the eruption of the great man's famous temper, was particularly sensitive to anything he viewed as criticizing his tactical decisions. Caesar, at least to this point, had never displayed his temper to his Centurions; the Tribunes, Favonius thought with some amusement as he sat in his tent, thinking about it, were a different matter. While this first assault on this town that, even now two days later, was still smoldering, had been a crucial first step towards turning the 10th into a truly veteran Legion, Caesar's dismissal of Doughboy had been almost as important a sign, not just to the officers, but to the rankers, which from what his spies in the *praetorium* told him, was taking place at this very moment. The fact that his Primi Pili had been informed of Caesar's decision even before the hapless Tribune sent a clear signal to them that what Caesar valued more than anything was competence, and even in his very limited role, Doughboy had caused more problems than any other Tribune attached to the Legion.

Deciding he had spent enough time ruminating on Caesar and what kind of general he was, Favonius turned his attention back to the more mundane but crucial task of managing the Legion. To that end, sitting before him was a stack of tablets, each containing the names submitted by the nine Pili Priori to be promoted into slots that had been vacated by men who had either fallen, or were so seriously wounded that they were unable to fulfill their duties, either in the short-term or for long. Knowing what his master liked, his chief clerk had placed the tablets in numerical order, so it was natural that the first one he examined was for the Second Cohort. While Favonius would never say as much aloud, if only because of the furor it would cause among his Centurions of his Cohort, the Primus Pilus considered Gaius Crastinus as the most qualified man to step into his *caligae*, despite his relative youth. His reasoning was based in two parts: the first was his own observation, and, while this was another thing he would ever divulge, especially to Crastinus, Favonius grudgingly acknowledged to himself that his Second Cohort was at least equal to the First in its deportment, conduct, and most crucially, fighting ability. Regardless of this regard, when Favonius got to the bottom of Crastinus' list of men he was putting forward for promotion, he was given pause. To that point, the list had been straightforward; he had assumed that the man Rufio would be put forward for the post of Optio, instead of the more normal *Tesserarius*, a man named Aulus Cordus in the First of the Second. Or sometimes, a Pilus Prior would cast a wider net, looking at the other Centuries of his Cohort for a suitable candidate, but not only had Crastinus informed him that, while Cordus was a good, solid man, he was neither suited nor interested in serving as an Optio, once Crastinus had alerted him, Favonius had made some quiet inquiries of his own that seemingly confirmed Crastinus' judgment. So, he thought, Rufio it is, nor did he have any issues with the other names, if only because of the remaining slots to be filled, *Signifer* and *Tesserarius*, it was traditionally left up to the Centurion in command of that Century.

It was this last name, however, that made Favonius pause. Yes, he had certainly heard good things about the Pullus boy, and even in training, Favonius had observed firsthand that the youth had more than just brute strength working to his advantage, and he had been told by Crastinus why this was the case, that he had been tutored by a former ranker, and not just a normal *Gregarius*, but Quintus Ausonius himself, who was something of a legend among Favonius' generation of men under the standard. Nevertheless, while the post of weapons instructor was a less formal post, and in fact was only operational during the formation of a new *dilectus*, it *was* an important post, and like Crastinus, once he had witnessed what Aulus Vinicius was capable of, he had held the belief that Vinicius would never be bested, especially by some barbarian. And, Favonius thought with the kind of grim humor a man had to have, Vinicius wasn't felled by a blade but by a vat of boiling pitch. But Pullus? A man just beginning his enlistment, and who had just been blooded himself? Then, unbidden, a recent memory came to him, just two days before, when his First and Second Cohort, along with the 8th, had finished the last stand of the Lusitani in the town center.

As Primus Pilus, Favonius' role was more to supervise his own Cohort, and the other Cohorts involved in the assault. Consequently, he had actually been with his own Hastatus Posterior, which was positioned next to the First of the Second, when this last fight was at its heaviest, and not surprisingly, his eyes had been drawn to the largest Roman in the area. Even as he was speaking to his Centurion, speaking at almost a shout to be heard, Favonius' eyes had stayed on Pullus because this had been his first opportunity to watch the large *Tiro* in something other than a training setting. As all veterans knew, being able to dole out punishment to a wooden stake with a *rudis* held no comparison to facing a flesh and blood opponent, and even sparring against another man, while more instructive, was a shade compared to the moment when the stakes were life or death. Watching Pullus, Favonius missed nothing; even without speaking a word of the Lusitani tongue, he could see by the gestures that what was likely a high-ranking noble Lusitani, given his armor and weapons, had challenged Pullus, luring him away from the safety, parlous as it was, of the Roman formation. It was the kind of rash move that some young *Tiros* made, but whereas most of them paid for their hubris, believing that the months of training they had just received was sufficient to vanquish a foe who had spent years honing his craft, that hadn't happened with Pullus.

Momentarily distracted by a question from his Centurion, Favonius had shifted his gaze away from Pullus, so he didn't see that it was actually Pullus' close comrade Domitius, who, in effect, saved Pullus' life, so when he returned his attention back to Pullus' fight, he saw the *Gregarius'* foe already supine and twitching in the manner that told the Primus Pilus the warrior was in his last heartbeats of life. He also noticed another body at Pullus' feet that hadn't been there a matter of heartbeats before, and unaware of the circumstances, Favonius decided to endorse Crastinus' choice of the youngster to help his comrades hone their skills with the *gladius*. If Pullus can kill two of those barbarian *cunni* that quickly, Favonius thought as he incised his initials into the tablet, which would be taken back to Crastinus and was the sign that the Primus Pilus had no objection to the choices, then I'll trust Crastinus' judgment. There was another thought in Favonius' mind, one that hadn't yet fully formed, but over the course of this campaign, it would harden into a conviction. In the moment, however, he thought that marching with Caesar would afford his new Legion more opportunities for honor and glory than just was on offer now, here in Hispania. Caesar, he knew by this point, was an ambitious man, and he suspected that, as Pompeius and Crassus were vying for the unofficial but extremely powerful title of First Man of Rome, Caesar had his own plans. Who knows? he mused wryly, maybe Caesar will supplant those two. It would be a thought that Favonius would have cause to remember.

Chapter Three

On the day before the army was scheduled to resume their march northward to find more rebellious Lusitani after the first assault on a native town, the name of which none of the army ever learned, and which saw the 10th Legion blooded for the first time, the Tribune Marcus Creticus Appius Piso, who had been given the unfortunate but apt appellation Doughboy, received a summons to the *praetorium*, delivered to the tent he was forced to share with another Tribune, Gaius Antistius Vetus, who wasn't a bad sort but certainly not from as distinguished a family as his. In fact, in his mind, Doughboy was quite cordial to the other man, who was a couple years younger than he was; if he had ever deigned to ask Vetus his opinion on the matter, he would have been shocked to learn what Vetus really thought of him, because Vetus hid his loathing well, and would have called Doughboy a condescending, pompous fool. Responding to the rapping sound on the piece of wood hanging outside the tent, when Vetus opened the flap to find a clerk from the *praetorium*, Doughboy was irritated that Vetus actually let the man into the tent, but when the clerk extended the tablet to him, he saw that it wasn't a parchment scroll, which meant that it wasn't anything important, so he pointed to the table with a sniff.

"Leave it there," he sniffed. "I'll attend to it shortly."

If it had been Vetus or any other Tribune, the clerk would have informed them that this wasn't a matter of a routine message, like announcing the orders for the day or who would be named the commanding Tribune, although it was meaningless, but not this one, so Doughboy completely missed the smirk on the clerk's face as he hurried out of the tent.

Vetus didn't, and once the clerk was gone, he turned to Doughboy and suggested, "Shouldn't you read that now, Piso?"

"Why?" Doughboy answered indifferently, his nose already back into the scroll that he had told Vetus was some epic poetry, but Vetus knew was one of the pornographic stories that were popular with the upper classes. "If it was important, there'd be a scroll and a seal on it."

Sighing, Vetus debated with himself about letting this lie, thinking that if it was more important than Doughboy thought, learning the hard way might be a good thing. Immediately on the heels of that thought was the recognition that he shared a tent with the fool, and he could easily envision the ramifications falling on his head as well.

He had learned the nickname that had been given to him by the rankers, which he thought both amusing and appropriate, but while he was always careful, he almost slipped this time when he asked, "Piso, would you mind if I took a look at it?"

Frowning at the interruption, Doughboy, clearly annoyed, asked, "Whatever for?" Before Vetus could answer, he used one hand in a shooing manner, saying, "Do as you please. But I know that it's not important."

Despite his suspicion that this tablet was more important than Doughboy thought, Vetus still had to suppress a gasp when he opened it, although it wasn't what it said.

Clearing his throat, Vetus' tone was as bland as he could make it, "Er, Piso?" Doughboy didn't look up, and Vetus sharpened his tone, repeating, "Piso!"

Heaving an exaggerated sigh, Doughboy only reluctantly looked up, but instead of saying anything, Vetus simply turned the tablet around to show the other Tribune what was incised in the tablet. When he thought about it later, and as he told the other Tribunes later that evening to their shared contemptuous amusement, it was the absolute fastest he had ever seen Marcus Creticus Appius Piso move. Which, he allowed to himself, was understandable when the seal of the Legate and *Praetor* Gaius Julius Caesar was impressed into the wax.

"You took your time," Caesar commented, leaning back in his folding chair to gaze up at Doughboy, whose quivering was so severe that it made his three chins ripple in such a comical fashion that Caesar had to make an effort not to show his amusement.

"I-I apologize, sir," Doughboy stammered, then in desperation, threw out, "I was detained by an important matter."

This elicited a raised eyebrow from Caesar, although this was the only flicker of expression.

"More important than a summons from your commanding officer?" he asked, rhetorically as it turned out, because he had just devoted almost all of the time that he was willing to spend on this miserable specimen.

Although, he thought waspishly, maybe if I tell him that I know the men call him "Doughboy," he might drop dead from mortal embarrassment and save me the trouble, but he did no such thing; what he did have in mind was so much more fitting.

Aloud, he told the Tribune, "The reason for my summons is that I've made a decision that concerns you."

"Oh?" Doughboy replied cautiously, and with good cause since the few words he had earned from Caesar had never been particularly positive. Still, he reasoned, perhaps Fortuna was finally smiling on him as she should. "And may I ask what that is, sir?"

"Of course," Caesar replied genially. "I've decided to give you an independent command."

While Doughboy was trying to be optimistic that this meeting might turn out well for him, this was beyond his wildest imagining, and he felt his mouth drop open, but he couldn't help himself.

Even worse, he clearly heard the squeaky quality to his voice when he repeated, "An independent command, sir?"

"Yes." Caesar nodded, his face grave now. "It's a very important task, and I've decided that you're the man for the job."

"What is it?" Doughboy almost clapped his hands together, actually bringing them up from his side before stopping himself. Then, out of the recesses of his mind came another thought, and he had to swallow before he asked, "Is it...dangerous?"

"It could be," Caesar nodded, expression still grave. "But, if you perform the way I know that you can, it shouldn't be."

Not completely reassured, Doughboy also knew what was

expected of him, and he said earnestly, "I'll do my very best to live up to your belief in my abilities, sir."

"That's good to hear." Caesar nodded. "I am assigning you the task of escorting these new slaves, along with the wounded who have either lost a limb or aren't likely to recover soon enough to return to duty for this campaign back to Scallabis."

"The slaves?" Doughboy repeated, his expression blank as his mind tried to absorb this information, because it certainly didn't sound like any kind of a promotion or honor. "You want me to do what?"

"Escort them under guard," Caesar answered him crisply, his patience wearing thin with this dullard. "You will have a Century of auxiliaries, and I can only afford to give you a *turma* of cavalry."

"But that means we'll have to go back through Lusitani territory!" Doughboy exclaimed, temporarily forgetting himself and to whom he was speaking. "There could be barbarians lurking all along the way!"

"There may be," Caesar agreed. "Which is why I'm giving you a Century of auxiliaries. The slaves have all been chained, and they'll be roped together so that they shouldn't cause you trouble. And," he pointed out, "as long as you use your cavalry wisely as scouts, you shouldn't be surprised."

"But a *turma* is only thirty men!" Doughboy protested.

"Which is why you need to use them wisely, Tribune Piso," Caesar replied coldly, his patience now completely exhausted. "Instead of thinking of all the things that can go wrong, your time would be better spent thinking of how to obey your orders and do your duty to Rome in a manner that I find acceptable."

To his credit, Doughboy recognized that further argument was not only futile, it could be dangerous to his career, a career that suddenly didn't seem quite so bright. As dull as he may have been, Doughboy recognized this for what it was, which was why he wasn't altogether surprised with what came next.

"When am I to leave, sir?" he asked listlessly.

"Tomorrow at dawn, when we depart," Caesar replied evenly. "We're going to be destroying the camp, of course, so you wouldn't have any protection anyway."

"Of course," the Tribune said as he nodded.

"Also," Caesar stood, and extended a scroll with his seal on it, "you're to deliver this to the *Quaestor*, who I left in charge of the civil administration in Scallabis. Do this immediately upon your entry into the city, because he'll tell you which slave traders I've contracted with for this campaign, then take our wounded men to the camp outside the city. By this time, there should at least be tents for the *praetorium* and *quaestorium* erected. The men who will eventually return to full duty will be cared for there, and the amputees will receive their discharges and stipend."

Caesar was actually surprised that Doughboy had nothing more to say, instead stiffening and offering a salute before executing his about-turn, and while he tried to march, he was weaving slightly. Once the Tribune was gone, Caesar dropped back into his seat with a satisfied smile. He had briefly entertained the idea of informing him that the scroll he was carrying to Fufius, the *Quaestor*, contained more than what Caesar had said. Along with those orders, there was also a report from Caesar that would effectively destroy the career of one Marcus Creticus Appius Piso, for which he held not a shred of regret, and for whom he held not a shred of pity. Men like Doughboy had, unfortunately, become more the norm than the exception among the men of the patrician class, and if Caesar was to achieve all that he intended for Rome, he'd need men who were the opposite of the fat Tribune. And, he thought, tomorrow, I resume the march on a campaign that's just the first step in my plans, with a harder, rested army at my back. Things were beginning to come together quite nicely.

Just as he intended, while Doughboy did fulfill his duties, mainly because he refused to do anything but sulk all the way back to Scallabis and it allowed the auxiliary Centurion and the Decurion in command of the cavalry to make the decisions, none of the men in Caesar's army ever heard of him again, and Caesar's army continued to move inexorably north, like an unstoppable tide of flesh, iron, and a grim determination that was in stark contrast to the frenzied, furious passion of the Lusitani tribes that still awaited them. It was, they assured each other in their tribal councils as they awaited the Romans, one victory for the invaders; there would be no more in their future; of this, they were certain.

The army of Caesar departed on the third day after the town was taken, and which now only existed as a smoking ruin, with the newly blooded 10th Legion in the vanguard. Marching with a newfound confidence, those sections, Centuries, and Cohorts who had lost comrades were learning to cope with what they were learning was a grim reality of life under the standard, that there was not much time to grieve fallen friends. All the empty leadership slots had been filled, with Rufio the new Optio of the First of the Second, and Titus Pullus the new weapons instructor, not just for his Century, but his entire Cohort, and the young Gregarius felt the enormous pressure of expectations on his shoulders that, while broad, were still only sixteen. The fact that Pullus was illegally enlisted in the Legion was a secret that only his friend Vibius Domitius knew, and it would be one they both guarded for some time to come.

Vellusius, his arm still bound to his chest, had been given the option of riding in one of the wagons for the wounded, but his only concession was to put his pack on the Cohort wagon so that he could march in the ranks with his section. Didius, however, despite his claim that he was still in pain and forced to carry the fiction by limping around the camp, hadn't even been given that option by Rufio. And, as he quickly learned, pretending to limp guaranteed that before the first few miles, he didn't have to play at it, but he knew better than to complain, and in doing so, divulge that he had been feigning to be more injured than he really was. At this moment, he was tolerated by his tentmates and nothing more, and he resolved to himself that he would lay low, keep his mouth shut and not even try to scare up a game for the next few days. The other difference with the new veterans was that, while they chattered as they had during the previous days, there were more topics, mainly about all that they had seen and done. It would take them time to recognize that the stories that they told on the march would differ from those told in the immediate aftermath, when men were coming to grips with the terror and loss of friends. Marching stories, as they were known, were almost always humorous, and Didius' fate was to provide one of those stories, as the "Tale of Achilles," which was what Remus had named it since he was the most eager purveyor of the yarn, had become very popular. To Didius' embarrassment, it proved to be popular not just in the First Century, but through the entire Cohort, and as tended to happen, the story transformed a bit with every telling to, as far as Didius was concerned, his detriment. All this added up to the fact that the next few days on the march were a misery for Spurius Didius.

When native tribes in provinces claimed by Rome rebelled, it was considered not only an accepted but expected practice to despoil the farmland, which meant that the men of Caesar's army spent a fair amount of their time in fields, uprooting and destroying the crops that were still growing. It was boring, dreary, and surprisingly tiring work, bent over at the waist in a line and moving slowly, pulling the plants out of the soil, where they would be gathered up in the wicker baskets that they had learned served many uses by their comrades who hadn't drawn the dirty end of the sponge. They were too green to burn, so they were used as forage for the animals; regardless, for many of the men, it brought back unpleasant memories, and it was Romulus who summed up the sentiment one day.

"I joined the Legions to get away from the farm," he complained, something with which his brother, Vellusius, and men of the other sections who came from farms within earshot heartily agreed.

While Pullus felt the same way to a degree, it was more because he associated the pursuit of farming with his father Lucius, who carried the dubious distinction of being considered the worst farmer in the Astigi area. It was, Pullus had learned at a relatively young age, a well-deserved one, and it was based in the fact that Lucius Pullus hadn't been born and raised in Hispania, coming to the province from a part of Italia where wheat was the primary crop grown. The land around Astigi was much drier and much rockier, making it suitable for grapes or olives, but rather than learn the methods that a grape or olive farmer needed to know, Lucius Pullus stubbornly attempted to grow wheat, with the predictable results. By the time young

Titus was five, and mostly due to the hard work of Phocas and Gaia, the male and female slaves that had been the wedding gift to Lucius from his father, the Pullus family was able to at least eke out a subsistence, and in good years, they would have just enough surplus grain to sell that provided their cash.

On the subject of Titus' grandfather, while Lucius never said as much, his children had deduced that he had essentially gotten rid of his son, something that Titus completely understood because, even sober, Lucius Pullus was a thoroughly disagreeable man. He was locally known for one distinction, something in which he was inordinately proud, and that was based in the fact that his was the only farm in the area that was enclosed by a stone wall. Titus loathed the wall, both because he had been put to work on it when he was six, when Phocas had suggested that there was a use for all of the rocks that they had been forced to dig out of the ground to save the plow, serving as brute labor, and also because rather than being viewed with admiration, it was just another thing that gave his fellow farmers something to mock his father for, along with his obsession with growing wheat. By the time Titus was old enough to join the Legions, he had actually come to appreciate the work his father had forced him to perform because he understood that it had greatly contributed to his prodigious strength, something that he had acknowledged not to his father, but to Phocas, who he viewed with far more familial affection than the man who sired him.

Now, to Remus, he offered, "Look at the bright side. At least you're not planting crops; you're pulling them up."

"Like that's a big difference," Romulus scoffed, answering for his brother as they usually did for each other, and instead of tossing the plant he had just uprooted into the basket held by his brother, he threw it at Pullus.

This triggered a furious mock battle as these young men, who were still mostly boys, hurled things at each other, starting with plants with the dirt clinging to the roots before quickly escalating to clods of dirt.

"If you *cunni* have this much energy, I can think of ways to put it to good use!" Crastinus bellowed after momentarily turning his back to have a conversation with his Pilus Posterior, which quickly ended the horseplay.

It was just a normal day on campaign when battle was not imminent, but while crops were destroyed, all forms of livestock were seized, and as the army's supply of grain lowered, the amount of meat fed to the men grew, much to the dissatisfaction and complaints of most of the men in the ranks. It was a peculiarly Roman trait; if a ranker was presented with a choice of a nicely roasted haunch of pork or joint of beef, fresh off the fire with the fat still sizzling, or a flat pan of *Panera castris,* steaming from the oven, the vast majority of men would refuse the pork, or any kind of animal flesh, in favor of the bread. Not all of them, however; another oddity about Pullus was his fondness for meat, which he actually preferred over bread. The fact that it came from his poverty, and that sometimes the only food they had to eat was what Phocas could put on the table thanks to his hunting skills, which were as prodigious as Titus' appetite, was something Pullus never shared with his new comrades. Phocas' ability was a matter of great curiosity to young Titus, but the one time the slave had started to talk to the boy about his life before he became a slave, Lucius had caught them and beaten Phocas severely for it. Now that he was in the Legions, Pullus took the teasing about his peculiar tastes in stride, although Domitius not only knew why his huge friend preferred meat, but that the cause for this bothered him a great deal. Nevertheless, Caesar's army despoiled and ate its way north, deeper into Lusitani territory every day.

Their progress wasn't unhindered, but for this period of the campaign, the Lusitani began to favor a delaying tactic, in the form of small bands of warriors, using their intimate knowledge of the land, suddenly materializing, seemingly out of nowhere, striking at either stragglers or smaller groups of Romans who had been sent out to scout or forage. While it didn't slow the Romans in any measurable way, it did serve to heighten tensions, and the men began to learn how fatiguing it was to be constantly on the alert as they marched, waiting for the sudden call of a *cornu* from somewhere along the column. A week after resuming, the army reached the Muna (Mondego) River, at a spot where just north of it was a Roman colony, Conimbriga (Coimbra), which had gone over to the Lusitani. It was the first sizable town since the first one, but unusually, the transfer of power to the Lusitani from the Roman occupants had been bloodless, and almost as soon as the eagle standards of Caesar's army were within sight from the town walls, a deputation of Lusitani noblemen hurried out under a flag of truce. The army had barely formed up in the same manner as they had the first time when they were informed that the town had surrendered to Caesar, which served as the occasion of another lesson for the new men.

That night around the fire as they were waiting for their meal to cook, Scribonius addressed Calienus, "Sergeant, I heard someone in the First Section talking about something." When Calienus indicated for him to continue, he asked, "Is it true that we don't get anything from a town that surrenders?"

"That's true." Calienus nodded. "If we take it by assault, then we get a cut of the slaves, and we split the loot we take just like we did at the first town. But," he yawned, "if the town surrenders, the Legate gets everything that comes from that."

"But Caesar didn't take any slaves," Domitius pointed out. "He only took hostages."

"But he levied a fine against the town," Calienus replied. "And he gets the money."

"But how is that fair?" Domitius demanded, not seeing Pullus roll his eyes, knowing already where this was headed, having learned long before of his friend's obsession with the ideas of fairness and justice.

However, if he expected support from Calienus, he was mistaken, because the Sergeant replied calmly, "Because that's the way it works, Domitius. That's the way it's always worked, and that's the way it always will work."

This did not appease Domitius, and as Pullus had feared, he turned towards his large friend expecting support, but it was actually Scribonius who spoke up.

"I think it makes sense," he said quietly. "If the Legate, Caesar in this case, is able to talk the rebels into surrendering without bloodshed, shouldn't he be rewarded for it?" Domitius opened his mouth to argue, but Scribonius continued, "And remember, when we take a town like we did that first one, it's not just the Lusitani who die." With a shrug, he finished, "I don't mind trading some gold and silver for my blood."

This was met with a ragged chorus of assent, and not even Domitius could argue this, while Calienus studied Scribonius with a thoughtful expression, although Scribonius was unaware of the scrutiny.

Fortunately for Calienus, none of his tentmates remembered his phlegmatic acceptance of this custom more than three weeks later when he complained, "How are we supposed to make any money on this campaign? When I marched with Pompeius, we took a pirate town or city a week almost, and they were all taken by storm so we had a share of the spoils. And," he smacked his lips at the memory, "those pirates were *rich*!"

The cause for his comment was due to the fact that, over the course of the previous three weeks, one town after another had surrendered to Caesar and his army; the accepted wisdom among the men was that enough time had elapsed for word of what had happened at the first town to spread a couple hundred miles north, so one after the other, delegations of Lusitani would hurry out and, just as at Conimbriga, offer their surrender.

By the time Calienus complained, he had a more receptive audience, particularly when it came to Domitius, who agreed, "He's the only one getting rich." Ignoring Pullus' look of surprise, he went on, "He uses his skills as an orator to talk them out of putting up a fight, just so he can keep all the money!"

While Pullus was disposed to argue the point, he saw that most of his tentmates were nodding in agreement, so he held his counsel. And, if he was being honest, Pullus was getting a little itchy for something besides what was still happening, ambushes and skirmishes that rarely involved more than a Cohort, and to this point, never the Second of the 10th.

Caesar left the 8th Legion behind at Conimbriga, charging them with holding the town and the surrounding area, so that he was now leading an army of three Legions, and in a sign that he was not deaf to the complaints, three days after the last town surrendered, when they found themselves arrayed outside another town that, unlike Conimbriga, was only composed of native Lusitani, Caesar's terms were so outrageous that the town elders had no other choice but to refuse, and he designated that the 7th and 9th conduct the assault, with the 10th in reserve with five Cohorts behind each assaulting Legion. Unlike the first town, this one did not have the natural advantage of being situated on a hilltop, there being a defensive ditch instead, twice as wide as it was deep, with large sharpened stakes driven into the town side of the ditch. Because there wasn't a hill, the walls were actually taller, almost fifteen feet, although as they all observed and many of them commented on, there were no trees of a sufficient size anywhere in the area. Since they were in reserve, Primus Pilus Favonius gave the men permission to sit on the ground, and very quickly, men were spreading out someone's *sagum* to use as a makeshift surface for dice to roll, while others began wagering on things related to the coming assault. Almost nothing was off limits; some men wagered on how many times the ram, manned by the 7th, would have to strike the gates before they were breached, others on which Legion would be the first either over the wall in the case of the 9th, or through the gate in the case of the 7th. One thing that was forbidden, although it was never spoken of, was any kind of wager based on how many of their comrades would fall. The stakes involved weren't money or valuables; these had all been deposited with the Century's *Tesserarius*, in this case Cordus, who refused to relinquish any of it to the men of the Century, ignoring their most urgent pleadings and importuning.

What occurred during this assault was another lesson, a sobering one, in what it was like for men not involved in the fight being forced to watch those wearing the same uniform absorbing the same kind of punishment that they had been subjected to during their assault. Inevitably, it also brought back memories of that assault, and for the men of the First of the Second, it was especially graphic, the memory of Aulus Vinicius being burned to death something with which they were still struggling to cope, mostly by refusing to think about it. Sitting there watching forced the men to relive that moment over again, which served to smother the happy chatter and festival atmosphere, a silence descending on the seated men watching the men of the 9th scaling the ladders as the Lusitani defenders hurled missiles, and in a gruesome reminder, dumped the boiling contents of iron kettles down on the heads of the men the gods had fated to suffer like Vinicius.

Because of their position supporting the 9th, the Second Cohort had to track the 7th's progress by a man, on his own initiative, getting up and trotting a hundred paces away so that he had a view of the gate, something that was technically forbidden but was ignored by Centurions and Optios for the simple reason they were as curious as their men how the 7th was progressing. The only commotion in the ranks of the 10th came when the ram, manned by the 7th, finally broke through the gates, with men howling in anger or shouting with joy, depending on their wager, followed by the sight of the first man of the 9th who managed to land on the enemy rampart, eliciting an identical response. With the Romans now atop the walls and storming through the battered gate, a new line of wagering began about when the town would fall, signaled by the *Cornicen* of either Primi Pili playing the distinctive set of notes that announced to all that Rome had conquered again. As it would turn out, nobody won, or lost, because it wasn't until well after dark that those notes were sounded, and in fact, there came a point where Caesar ordered Favonius to rouse the 10th and make ready to lend their support, although it wasn't needed. Being forced to watch their comrades fighting, bleeding, and dying to take a town without participating in the assault was another lesson for the young veterans of the 10th, and as time passed, they would no longer be as vocal in their disappointment at not being selected for the honor of taking a town.

As they had done after the first battle, Caesar's army stayed in place while the 7th and 9th recovered and reorganized, and it fell on the collective shoulders of the 10th to help with a task that was growing in importance with every passing day, replenishing the food supplies for almost twenty-five thousand men, counting the slaves, freedmen and clerks, although their rations were meager compared to the Legionaries'. On the second day after the battle, it was the turn of the Second Cohort to range over the countryside, and Pilus Prior Crastinus split the Cohort into three groups, consisting of two Centuries apiece, with the First and Second Century together. After coming across a good-sized farm, which they ransacked then put the buildings to the torch, Crastinus and his men began marching back to the camp. They hadn't run into any Lusitani, but Crastinus still took the precaution of sending a section ahead to act as scouts, and had a section lagging behind as rearguard, just behind the men who were occupied with driving the half-dozen cattle they had seized, along with the men given the task of carrying the few dozen freshly slaughtered chickens, while men in the column carried sacks of seized grain on one shoulder. It was far from ideal, Crastinus knew, and it had been a complaint by the Centurions for the entirety of the campaign, because as well equipped and formidable an army composed of four Roman Legions was, there was a dearth of cavalry. Ideally, it wouldn't be a section of infantry on foot serving as the advance guard, nor would they be the rearguard, but the few horsemen Caesar had were dedicated to more far-ranging scouting, scouring the countryside for towns or large bodies of Lusitani warriors. Combining this with the fact that the Lusitani knew the surrounding terrain better than the Romans ever would, Crastinus had been especially vigilant, and was growing increasingly nervous, although none of his men had any sense of this.

Just as they approached a heavily wooded tract that Crastinus had noted on their morning march, he pointed to it and bellowed over his shoulder, "All right, you bastards! This is a good spot for these barbarians to try an ambush, so keep your eyes open!"

It wasn't that his men didn't heed him; in simple terms, their Lusitani enemy were not only skilled warriors, they were excellent hunters, and they used that stealth to spring the very thing that Crastinus had warned about. The ambush began with the soft, barely audible swishing sound created by a dozen spears slicing through the air, and while not all of them hit their target, a man of Crastinus' First Section in the front rank was transfixed by one, dropping to the ground, wearing the expression of shock from what was the last surprise of his life. Simultaneously, the air was pierced by the alarmed shouts of men who suffered a near miss and the shrill screams of other men being struck, although their cries were almost overwhelmed as the waiting Lusitani leapt to their feet from their hiding places, bellowing their war cries as they came rushing at the Roman column. In the aftermath, there would be much discussion and disagreement over the events that were about to transpire, but it was the unanimous view of both Centuries that it was the quick reaction of Crastinus that enabled those men who survived to see another day.

"*FORM SQUARE! FORM SQUARE! QUICK NOW, BOYS!*"

Just as had happened when forming the *testudo* under enemy fire the first time, this was the moment when all the watches of grueling repetition bore fruit, the men reacting instantly and without thinking. This was especially important because, given their order of march and with two Centuries marching in one column, it meant that the men found themselves all mixed together, so that instead of being on the end of one side of the square, Pullus found himself in the middle, with Domitius to his right, and a ranker from the Third Section, Aulus Plautius, to his left. Even as quickly as they moved, they were barely set when the Lusitani, some armed with spears and others with *gladii* and all bellowing their war cries, literally threw themselves against the Roman shields, a tactic that had evolved from having learned that their best and only chance to defeat these invaders was to break their formation.

Over and over again, a warrior would hurl himself against a man's shield, doing it with such fury and so quickly that the Roman under assault never even had a chance to make an offensive move, consigning them to desperately endure the onslaught while hoping for a lull that would enable them to retaliate. The square was twenty men, or two sections, across per side, but with only one comrade bolstering those under the direct attack, meaning that it was practically inevitable that the Lusitani were successful somewhere. Although it was on Pullus' side, it was closer to the end of his rank and at the outer range of his peripheral vision, where he saw one of his comrades suddenly fall to his knees, but before the man to either side or his bolstering comrade could react, he was seized and dragged a few paces away, just out of reach of the Romans, whereupon his body was obscured by what Pullus guessed was about ten Lusitani as they surrounded the man who was thrashing about in a desperate but ultimately futile attempt to avoid being hacked to death. While they certainly wouldn't view it this way, because Pullus and his comrades farther down the line were too busy defending themselves, they were spared the sight of one of their own butchered. Finally, whether it was through fatigue or carelessness, the Lusitani who had obviously selected Pullus as his personal foe was too slow to leap back after another futile attempt to knock Pullus' shield from his hand, and he never even saw the thrust that shot out from the side of the big Roman's shield in a gray blur that took him just under his sternum, the force of the blow sending him reeling backwards, his eyes wide as he dropped his own weapon and protection to clutch his chest as it blossomed with frothy blood. Pullus' last sight of his foe was the man being brutally shoved aside by one of his fellow warriors, who followed the example of the first man, with his feet leaving the ground as he threw himself at the giant Roman's shield. However, there had been just enough of a pause between these assaults that, instead of his body slamming into the wooden shield, he was instead met by the iron point of a *gladius* from a thrust which Pullus had timed perfectly so that the man essentially ran himself through. With this man, Pullus was actually forced to lift one foot off the ground with the intention of kicking him off of his blade as the warrior sagged towards Pullus, staring at the Roman with the disbelief of a man who didn't expect to die, but the effort required Pullus to move his shield slightly to do so. It certainly wasn't planned, but the Lusitani immediately behind his impaled comrade, who had seen what he was certain was a perfect opportunity with the sight of the dull gray links of the Roman's mail shirt momentarily visible and not obscured by the shield, came rushing forward. To his misfortune and ultimate demise, what he didn't account for was the power in that Roman's leg, as Pullus kicked the now-dead warrior away from him, so that in something of a reversal of what was taking place up and down the line, the corpse actually came hurtling in the opposite direction directly into the path of the third Lusitani, the dead weight slamming into the onrushing warrior just below the knees and taking him off of his feet. The result was that he wasn't even able to look up and see the thrust that punched down between his shoulder blades, so that within the span of perhaps fifteen heartbeats, Pullus had dispatched three attackers, which didn't go unnoticed.

"That's three, you greedy bastard!" Domitius had to shout this over the other noise, but his eyes never wavered from the warrior who was now making another attempt to rush at his shield. "I've only done for one!"

While this complaint by Domitius would be one of the first of what would be many odd comments in the heat of battle that would make him somewhat famous throughout his Century, it was far from the last, but as Pullus had already learned, it was also Domitius' way of letting his friend know that, as Calienus had instructed him when they celebrated their finishing training, he was just watching out for his large friend.

The same, or similar, things were happening on all four sides of the square; private battles between two, three, or perhaps four men, none of whom in the moment were aware of anything but what was directly in front of and around them, and it would serve as yet another lesson for all of the new veterans, because when arrayed in a formation like a square, or the formation of last resort known as the *orbis*, that same kind of death struggle in which you were engaged was taking place directly behind you, meaning that your fate was in the hands of the men on the opposite side of the square. It required absolute faith and confidence in your comrades so that you could keep your focus on the most direct threat in front of you, something that Pullus and the rest of the men were learning this day. Once it became clear that their attempt to shatter the square wouldn't be successful, the Lusitani seemed content to drop back just out of javelin range, dragging their wounded with them but leaving behind those warriors who were obviously dead, whereupon they immediately began to taunt the Romans with curses none of the Romans knew, or making gestures at their foes that needed no translation. They weren't completely passive, however; small groups of no more than six or seven men would suddenly come dashing forward as if they were intent on renewing their assault, then dance away just before they were close enough that the Romans could retaliate.

It was actually Calienus, in the second rank behind Pullus who noticed it first, and now that the noise had died down somewhat, Pullus could hear him mutter, "Something isn't right."

Without saying anything more, Calienus turned to face inward, where Crastinus was located in the middle of the square, and he called out to the Pilus Prior as Crastinus was bent down examining one of the four wounded men who had crawled into the middle.

Irritated at the interruption, he did respond by snapping, "What is it, Calienus?"

"Does this seem right to you?" Whether it was the words themselves or Calienus' tone, this served to get Crastinus to straighten up and start paying closer attention now to one of his veterans, who went on, "Do these bastards seem like they're just trying to hold us in place more than they're trying to kill every one of us?"

Even before Calienus was finished, Crastinus had turned his attention to the surrounding Lusitani, performing a slow rotation while observing everything that was happening, so that by the time he was facing Calienus, he was nodding.

"You're right. They're trying to keep us pinned here while they wait. I don't know what they're waiting for, but I don't want to find out." Before saying anything more to the two Centuries, Crastinus returned his attention to the wounded men, keeping his voice low so that only they could hear, informing them of the situation and what their choices were, which prompted three of them to struggle to their feet, while the fourth man could only offer a mute shake of his head. Before he did anything else, and raising his voice back to his command volume, Crastinus called out, "Right. We're not going to wait around for whatever these bastards have planned for us, so everyone stand ready. When I give the command, we're going to march out of these woods and try to find some better ground."

He expected the ripple of anxious murmurs from the men, particularly those on both flanks and those who would have to spend most of their time and attention facing the rear and walking backward, so he reminded them, "Remember your training, boys. This is no different from on the drill field, except we have these little bastards as a nuisance. Think of them as you would a rock or a log in the way."

This was met with muted and nervous chuckles, while in the rank Pullus was in, the sight of his big friend's expression caused Domitius to actually laugh.

When Pullus looked over at him in bafflement, he teased, "By the gods, Titus, did you just swallow a bug or something?"

Completely unamused, Pullus shot back irritably, "No, I just don't like logs that are waving a *gladius* at me."

As much to needle Pullus than from any real amusement, Domitius laughed again, knowing how it would affect his friend. "You're not turning into an old woman, are you, Titus?"

This earned him the kind of glare that Domitius knew was a warning that he was dangerously close to rousing his friend's temper, so he decided it would be prudent to relent in his torment.

Furthermore, the Pilus Prior chose that moment to give a sudden blast on his bone whistle to get their attention, then shouted, "We're going to be going back the way we came, boys! We're less than halfway through these woods, and I saw a hill back there that we're going to move to and take up our position there!" Putting the whistle back in his mouth, Crastinus didn't hesitate, giving the three short blasts, followed by one long one that was the signal to begin moving.

As they had learned during their training, moving in square meant that the pace was less than half of their normal, even slower than when in *testudo*, it being one of the more difficult maneuvers when it came to maintaining the cohesion of the square. Adding a sizable force of enemy warriors meant that the tension and strain was beyond anything they had imagined or experienced before; nevertheless, step by step, the men of the two Centuries returned back in the direction from which they came, while the Lusitani, in a much less organized fashion, shadowed them. They were leaving behind their dead, including the man from the Second Century who had been too grievously wounded to move with them and who Crastinus had just dispatched with a quick thrust of his *gladius,* down into the space between left collarbone and shoulder blade, the preferred method for a quick death. As they had been doing once they retreated, small groups of Lusitani still made lunging rushes, aiming at the junctions where two lines met, the most vulnerable part of this kind of formation, but after they lost a handful of men, they subsided, contenting themselves with hurling insults at their foes, along with whatever rocks came to hand. Inside the square were the Centurions; Crastinus, and Pilus Posterior Vetruvius, their Optios, their *Signiferi* and the two *Corniceni*, with all but the Centurions occupied with helping one of the wounded keep up and remain within the parlous protection provided by their comrades. Not every man in the front rank had a man behind him, probably the most potent sign that the First and Second had sustained losses even before the start of this day. Somehow, like a lumbering, many-legged being, the two Centuries continued their progress in a slow two-count movement that accommodated the men on the two sides who had to sidestep, and it was Crastinus who called out the count.

"One!" The men on the sides extended the leg in the direction of travel, spreading their legs apart. "Two!" The second leg joined the first, while the men at the front and rear essentially mimicked the action.

Over and over, they moved one pace at a time until, finally, they emerged from the woods and out into the clear area, whereupon several things became evident. The first was that they could now see the hill towards which Crastinus was marching them; the second was a large plume of dust that, while still several miles away, was moving with a speed that could be tracked by the eye, but it was the third thing that would prove to be more than a nuisance as, without the shade, the sun beat down relentlessly, heating up the iron helmets and *hamatae* of the men, so that less than fifty paces from the woods, men began cursing from the perspiration that was running down into their eyes. This put them, especially in the front rank, in a dilemma, not only because their hands were full, but there would be an instant, not long but perhaps long enough, where their eyes would be closed or at least obscured by their hand as they used the fingers of their right hand, still holding their *gladius*, to wipe the sweat away. Most of the men decided to endure the discomfort of the salt stinging their eyes and the blurring, with the comfort that at least it did not completely obscure their vision, but some didn't, and it was the fate of one of the men at the rear of the square to take the risk of wiping his eyes, for which he was about to pay. Nobody, not even the men on either side or behind him knew why, but he suddenly stumbled and lost his footing, falling on his ass and momentarily moving his shield away from his body in the process. Before he could scramble back to his feet, an alert Lusitani who had snatched up a rock hurled it with all of his strength, smashing the man in his face, causing the Roman to drop both shield and *gladius* to grab the injured area, his hands muffling his cries of pain and for help.

The shouts of alarm from the men around him alerted Crastinus, who spun about, but when he saw one of them begin to move as if he was going to aid his wounded comrade, he bellowed, "You take one step towards him, I'll cut you down myself! He's a dead man! Leave him to his fate!"

He had raised his voice, not just to be heard by those at the rear of the square, but so that all of his men would hear this. The reaction from some of the men was shared by Pullus and his comrades, who had been blessed by Fortuna to be in what was now the front rank, but while Pullus didn't do so, both Domitius and Plautius cursed Crastinus, not loudly, but loud enough to be heard by Calienus, who was still in the second rank.

"*Silete!*" the Sergeant snapped, showing real anger for the first time in their association that shocked the younger men into silence.

The progress continued, while behind them at the rear of the square, there was a sudden uproar, over and above the shouting that was still taking place, but none of the men in the front rank could afford to look over their shoulder. Regardless, they discovered the cause quickly enough when, from their rear, a Lusitani came sprinting up the side of the square, holding a spear aloft vertically, and affixed to the point was the head of the newly slain man, his nose crushed and still dripping blood, while his helmet was still securely tied around his chin, with open eyes that bore the shocked expression of a man whose time had unexpectedly come. The reactions were roughly equal, albeit with opposing sentiments as the Lusitani roared their approval and promise that the Romans still alive would be suffering the same collective fate, with the Romans bellowing in rage and making their own promises to avenge their comrade. Just when the front rank was about a hundred paces from the base of the hill, a Lusitani inflicted the first casualty with the front rank, when a rock hurled by a man in the ragged line of Lusitani in front of them skipped off the ground and struck the man directly behind Plautius with enough force to shatter the man's shin bone. Dropping to the ground with a shrill scream, and while Calienus, who was bolstering Pullus, was still within arm's reach, he reached out and snatched the edge of Calienus' tunic, clutching it with the kind of strength that comes from a man who knows his life is hanging in the balance.

"Don't leave me! For the sake of all the gods, don't leave me with those savages!"

Rather than answer, Calienus tried to pull away from the doomed man, but when it became clear that he couldn't, he twisted at the waist and without any hesitation, performed the same kind of thrust that Crastinus had administered to the wounded man.

He had to lengthen his stride to return to his spot immediately behind Pullus, but as he did, he said loudly, "If we break ranks, we'll all die. I'll do the same to you, and I expect you to do the same to me if it's needed."

In a small consolation, the punishment was not all one way, and with what the men who witnessed it thought was an example of justice from the gods, one of the warriors made another quick dash to bring his long *gladius* down in an overhand blow when he thought he had caught a man near the end of the front rank in a moment of inattention, but when the blow was blocked, he danced backwards and away again. At least, this was his intention; instead, his feet became tangled, and just as had happened to the man at the rear of the square, before he could scramble to his feet, he was dispatched with a quick thrust, and in his last moments of life endured being spat on or kicked by the passing Romans marching up the hill. Once it became obvious that they would be unable to keep the Roman square from achieving the crest, the Lusitani retreated, choosing to regroup down at the base of the hill, which suited Crastinus and his men perfectly.

Without even allowing his men to rest or even drink from their flasks, Crastinus ordered, "We're going to use the tools we brought to make a ditch and wall." He was moving as he issued his orders to Vetruvius and to Rufio, confirming that the Optio would be responsible for the First while Crastinus supervised, outlining a roughly circular position that followed the contour of the hill. Knowing how unpopular it would be, he nevertheless informed Rufio, "The First digs while the Second stands watch."

Somewhat to Crastinus' surprise, his men only offered a few muttered complaints, immediately breaking out the reduced set of tools that they brought with them on foraging parties, each section responsible for a segment of the ditch, half of them using their picks to break up the rocky soil before standing aside to let the men with the shovels scoop up the loosened dirt. There was no talking from the working men, while the men of the Second were arrayed a short distance away, dividing their attention between watching the Lusitani at the base of the hill and the dust cloud that was growing larger as a mounted force approached at a rapid trot to reinforce the warriors now gathered at the base of the hill. Even before the new party arrived, something happened that provided both Centuries of Romans, the guards and those working, with an astonishing sight, as what was presumably a meeting of the Lusitani who had sprung the ambush to discuss strategy almost immediately turned into an argument between what appeared to be two factions. While it began with shouts that drifted up the hill to alert those who couldn't see the Lusitani that something was happening, the Second Century was in a perfect spot to watch as the arm waving turned into finger pointing, then was quickly followed by a shoving exchange. Nevertheless, the men of the First worked frantically, creating a ditch that was wide enough that it couldn't be leapt across, and deep enough that it couldn't be crossed without slowing down as the attackers dropped down into it.

"Keep it up, boys. The deeper you dig, the safer we'll be."

Crastinus repeated this with every section as he made a circuit, alternating his attention between his men and the Lusitani. It was a compact position, barely fifty paces across, the wounded already in the center, which was marked by the two Century standards planted in the ground and a makeshift breastwork consisting of the sacks of grain and forage, along with the discarded packs carrying the tools they had brought with them. It was just when Crastinus had come around to the side where the Second was standing that what had been a Lusitani argument turned into a brawl, with punches and men throwing themselves at each other in a manner strikingly similar to their attempts to break the formation. So astounding was the sight that, not only did the working men who could see it stop working, Crastinus didn't notice they had done so because he was standing open-mouthed like them at the sight of their enemy bashing each other in seeming ignorance that they were now being watched by their foes.

Finally, Crastinus shook his head, and when he turned away, he saw his men standing in the ditch that was now more than knee high, prompting him to growl at them, "All right, that's enough of the show. Put your backs into it you *cunni*, or I'll stripe you good."

Despite the words, the men had learned by now that their Pilus Prior's tone was the best indication of his true mood, and they grinned at each other as they resumed the work.

By the time the mounted Lusitani reinforcements arrived, the brawl had petered out, and it was already late afternoon by the time the men of the First had completed their work to Crastinus' satisfaction and were allowed to rest, if standing at their new dirt wall counted as such, but they at least were able to drink something. The wall was up to the lower chest of most of the men, which meant that it was at waist level for Pullus, but it was also fairly wide at the base, which they hoped would bolster the protection it offered. While they were all fatigued, the men of the First Century were exhausted, essentially asleep on their feet, and Calienus did what he could to keep his section alert, giving them the task of counting the Lusitani now that the forces had combined. It was a decision he would quickly regret, since the estimate offered up by his comrades was somewhere between eight and nine hundred men, against the one hundred eighty men of the two Centuries who were still standing. Before Calienus could say anything to soothe them, Crastinus called for all Sergeants and the two Optios to meet with him, requiring Calienus to leave the Tenth Section to their own devices, and worse, to their collective imagination.

"So, if they have more than eight hundred men," Romulus wondered, "how many of those *cunni* would we each have to kill?"

"About five," Scribonius answered immediately, his tone leaving no doubt that this was the correct answer.

"Well," Atilius spoke up, pointing to Pullus, "he can do that in his sleep."

"He already killed three," Domitius proudly informed the others.

This prompted a snort from Didius, which in turn earned him a glare from his comrades, and he quickly looked away from them to stare down the hill, his face burning.

Ignoring Didius, Pullus cleared his throat and said, "I don't know about you boys, but I'm fucking tired."

This was met with a murmured chorus of assent, while Vellusius added, "And I'm hungry enough to eat meat like Pullus."

"I remember hearing someone from the 8th say that these barbarian tribes in Hispania don't like fighting at night," this came from Remus.

"I've heard that too," Atilius agreed, adding hopefully, "so maybe we'll get a little sleep."

Their conversation was interrupted by the sound of laughter, and they all turned to see that it was Calienus and Rufio, the pair walking in their direction, although the Optio kept going to speak to the others.

It was Pullus who, in consternation at their levity, burst out, "What in the name of the gods could be so funny at a time like this?"

This surprised Calienus, mainly because it came from Pullus.

"Time like this? What do you mean?" Pullus didn't say anything, choosing instead to look pointedly down the hill at their enemy, but if he thought this would sober Calienus, he was wrong, because the Sergeant laughed again, asking mockingly, "Oh, you mean this bunch? Do you really think we're in that much danger, Pullus?"

For Pullus, it was an odd and extremely uncomfortable sensation, because he had become accustomed to the fact that, when he was singled out, it was usually for praise.

Despite this, he clearly didn't see why Calienus had cause to be so unconcerned, so he pointed out, "We're outnumbered five or six to one, Calienus. Are you saying that's not cause for worry?"

While Pullus was speaking, Calienus noticed something; their fellow tentmates were of a like mind with the large Gregarius, so instead of mocking him, he nodded in seeming agreement. "You're right, Pullus. We are outnumbered, but numbers don't tell the tale." Rather than pointing, Calienus used his head to indicate the Lusitani within their line of sight. "Do you notice anything, Pullus?"

Turning to gaze down at the Lusitani, Pullus considered, then with a shake of his head said flatly, "What I see are a lot of men down there who want to kill us."

Forcing himself to be patient, Calienus countered, "Yes, but look carefully. They've encircled us, correct?" Pullus didn't answer, and Calienus could see that the others had no intention of speaking, so he went on, "You want to know why I'm not worried? Because they have us surrounded." While this got Pullus' attention back on him, Calienus also saw the puzzlement on the dirty faces of his comrades, the only skin showing from where lines of perspiration had run down their cheeks. Deciding this was best conducted squatting down, Calienus dropped to his haunches and indicated the others to do the same for his explanation. "Now," he admitted, "if they were in one big bunch, I'd be very worried. See, I know that each of us can handle five or six of those bastards each, right? I mean, how many kills did you have in the attack on the town, Pullus?"

Calienus knew the answer, but decided to soothe Pullus' ego a bit, because as young as Pullus was, Calienus had recognized that he was the most important man in the Tenth Section for his comrades.

"More than that," Pullus admitted.

"Their problem is that they're thinking like warriors, not like an army. Not," he emphasized, "like us. I promise you that each one of them has picked one of us out that he's sworn to his gods he's going to kill personally." The Sergeant paused, heartened to see the nods, although they were slight, but they were going in the right direction. "And like I said, each one of us can handle a half-dozen of these bastards. Now," he acknowledged, although he made sure to smile, "what would scare me out of my wits is if they were down there, in a formation like we use, and focusing their attack on just one part of the defenses. And if they had a leader half as smart as the Pilus Prior, that's exactly what they would be doing right now, so thank the gods that they don't. Because," his smile vanished, "if they hit one area, they'd take a lot of casualties, but it would be a matter of moments before they'd overwhelm that point in our defenses, and that's when our lack of numbers would really show. No," he shook his head as he finished, "this isn't going to be that difficult to handle."

He was beginning to stand when Scribonius spoke up to ask him, "But how long are we going to have to hold this hill?" Using his head to nod in their direction, he continued, "I see that you're right about the way they're going to attack, but I have to believe that it's a good chance that there'll be other Lusitani showing up before too long."

Calienus hid his chagrin at being reminded, instead nodding. "You're right, and I forgot, that's what I was supposed to tell you before I got off course patting Pullus' ass for him." The men erupted in laughter, and while it was with a red face, Pullus joined in. Once they subsided, he explained, "The Pilus Prior wanted us to pass the word that we'll probably have to hold this hill through the night and the first couple of watches tomorrow, but since we weren't sent out on an overnight patrol, Caesar will know that we're in trouble. The command group also knows where we're assigned, so they'll send aid immediately." With a shrug, he finished, "My guess is that it will probably be the rest of the Cohort."

They stood up, just in time for someone to shout a warning, and they turned their attention to the Lusitani who, finally, were advancing up the hill. The attack was beginning.

Pilus Prior Crastinus divided the position into four parts, giving himself and Vetruvius one part each, Rufio another, and Vetruvius' Optio, Lucius Petrosidius the last, leaving it up to them to direct the men under their command, and while Crastinus had tried to array both Centuries so that Vetruvius and Petrosidius would be in command of Second men, there was some overlap, but that couldn't he helped. And now, the Lusitani had finally roused themselves, with the sun perhaps two fingers' width above the horizon, to come try and destroy him and his men.

As he was taking his spot, he heard laughter, looking over to see that it was the big oaf Pullus and his friend who, for whatever reason, found something to laugh about; despite the fact that Crastinus took this as a good sign, he still growled as he passed by, "I wonder if you two laughing boys would find it funny if I pitched both of you on the other side of the ditch?"

He did not stop to see how they reacted, and they weren't in position to see his grin as he took his spot.

Just as he did so, one of the men who was at the wall with their shields set on the parapet to protect the upper halves of their body bellowed, "*Slingers!*"

Like most of his comrades, both in the Centurionate and in the ranks, Crastinus loathed slingers and all form of missile troops, but also like most of his comrades, if he had to choose between facing archers or slingers, he would have chosen archers every time for the simple fact that in most cases you could at least see an arrow coming towards you unless it was at extremely close range, but between their small size and the speed with which they moved, the first hint a man might have that he was in danger was when he was struck by the sling bullet. At least these barbarians use rocks instead of lead like we do, Crastinus thought, marking the last moment where it was not hard to concentrate because of the sharp cracking sounds of sling bullets striking wooden shields. Thankfully, the hilltop was relatively flat so that Crastinus and the other officers were sheltered from the effects of the missiles as long as they maintained a crouched position, and as he watched, he saw that his men were absorbing the punishment calmly enough, hunched down behind their shields, with the exception of Pullus, who had to drop into something that was between a crouch and a squat. That has to be hard on his legs, Crastinus thought fleetingly as he was moving his attention back and forth, checking the men under his direct command, while occasionally glancing over his shoulder at Vetruvius on the opposite side, and whose men were weathering the same punishment. Like Calienus, Crastinus appreciated the fact that whoever was commanding these barbarians had chosen to spread his slingers out in the same fashion as his warriors, encircling the Roman position, thereby making it easier for his men to absorb the punishment. Within a heartbeat of the opening volley, another sound was added to the sharp but distinctive crack of stone on wood, one with more of a ringing sound as a stone missile struck the iron boss of a shield. In moments like this, it was impossible to keep track of time, but Crastinus would have guessed that they had endured this barrage for at least a hundred heartbeats when he heard something that, if possible, was a cross between the two sounds; it had a ringing quality to it, but it was instantly followed by a deeper, meatier sound, and he turned his head sharply in that direction to see who had been hit.

He wasn't helped when the Mallius brother that he had finally learned was called Romulus by his tentmates shouted, "Achilles is down!"

Where had he heard that name in relation to his Century before? It *was* familiar for some reason, over and above his status as a mythical hero, but he couldn't place it in the moment, snapping, "Who in Hades is Achilles?"

Crastinus had dropped into a crouch to duckwalk over in that direction as, over the noise, Romulus apologized, "I meant Didius, sir. Sorry."

"You will be, trust me, you little *cunnus,*" Crastinus snarled, but he was already turning his attention to the man in the second line from the First Section of the Second Century who was now kneeling by the fallen man. "I don't care if you call each other Aphrodite; next time, use his proper name so that I know who it is. I don't have time to learn all your pet lovers' names." Addressing the Second man as he examined Didius, whose eyes were closed, he asked, "Is he dead?"

Despite the fact that he had recognized Didius as a problem, he was still relieved when the man answered with a shake of his head, "No, Pilus Prior. It looks like it deflected off his shield first, then his helmet and then hit his forehead. He's out cold, but he's breathing, and it doesn't look like his skull is broken." The man paused, then added, "In fact, there's not much of a bump at all."

It was only later that Crastinus would learn that the reaction of Didius' tentmates was significant, because to a man, their heads all turned sharply, even as missiles slammed into their shields, but while he noticed them looking at each other, he was too preoccupied to think anything of it.

Addressing the Second Century man, Crastinus ordered, "Then drag him over to the middle behind the breastworks. Maybe he'll come to and be of some use."

Watching just long enough to see that the ranker remained in his crouch as he used Didius' harness as a handle to drag him to safety, such as it was, Crastinus quickly returned his attention to where it belonged, not on one man but on all of them. He was debating risking standing up to see how the Lusitani attack was progressing; fortunately, he didn't have to because, as suddenly as it started, the slingers ceased their barrage, instantly understanding that it could only mean that the warriors who would be conducting the actual assault were now in between the slingers and his own men, forcing the slingers to cease loosing to avoid inflicting casualties on their own men.

Recognizing this, it enabled him to stand erect to see the line of warriors, mostly armed with spears but with a fair number of men wielding *gladii*, and it now became a matter of timing. This was the moment where Crastinus cursed the flat crest of the hill because it was difficult to see between the bodies and shields of his men, although he managed to catch enough of a glimpse to see what he needed.

"Prepare javelins!" He shouted the preparatory order, pleased to see that he didn't have to repeat it, the sign that the men had already anticipated the command. The trick, Crastinus knew, was in timing the first volley so that there would be enough time for a second, each man carrying two of the deadly missiles.

Deciding it was time, he bellowed, "Release!"

Instantly, the air filled with blurring black lines of missiles as the men of the front rank on the wall hurled their javelins high into the air with all of their strength, counting on whatever force it was that made things come back down at speed. A high arcing angle, especially for a first volley, accomplished two purposes; it forced their foes to look skyward and perhaps be blinded by the sun as they raised their shields higher than usual, and it allowed for the javelins to pick up speed to plummet down. Even from where he was, Crastinus could hear the moment the javelins landed, a combination of a hollow wooden sound that signaled a successful block of a missile with a shield, and shouts, or better yet, screams of pain, when they were unsuccessful.

Crastinus used the noise as his guide, commanding, "First rank, kneel; second line, prepare javelins!" A pause of barely a heartbeat, then, "Release!" This time, Crastinus didn't pause at all, bellowing, "First rank, stand! Prepare javelins! Release!" Then, as soon as they hurled them, the Pilus Prior ordered, "Front rank, kneel and draw *gladii*; second rank, prepare javelins...Release!"

With their supply of missile weapons exhausted, the last command Crastinus gave was the order for the front rank to stand, and he took advantage of the short interlude before they did so and placed their shields on the parapet so that it would obstruct his view to survey the enemy to assess what damage had been done. He was heartened to see that the leading edge of the Lusitani, who were now moving at what was just a bit more than a trot, no longer presented an unbroken line of shields, and while he couldn't see them, Crastinus knew those shields that had been punctured by the Roman javelin were now useless and discarded. There would also be bodies strewn in the wake of the oncoming enemy, but he couldn't see how many there were because of the Lusitani who were still upright and approaching. He had been curious about the delay in the Lusitani assault, but he quickly learned why, when, instead of breaking out into a sprint in order to try and get across the ditch as rapidly as possible, they actually slowed as they reached the opposite edge to allow men who had been obscured by the front rank to push forward in order to toss what were nothing more than bundled sticks of a roughly uniform length bound together down into the ditch.

"Hurdles," Crastinus said aloud, though not loudly enough to be heard by anyone but himself. "The *cunni* are using hurdles."

The use of these devices, thrown down into the ditch, created a makeshift bridge so that the attackers didn't have to contend with clambering up out of it, which meant that the warriors weren't as impeded by the ditch as Crastinus had hoped, and in fact, by the time he had finished muttering this to himself, those Lusitani who were the boldest were already throwing themselves at the shields of his men at the wall, creating a cacophony of noises that made everything before it seem as if it was a quiet conversation. Now, Crastinus knew, he would find out what his boys were really made of, and he offered up a prayer to Mars and Bellona that they perform in the manner that he expected.

Didius *had* been knocked cold by the stone missile so that, since he was unconscious at the moment the man of the Second made his guess, he didn't hear it, because it was exactly what had happened. And, once he came to and gathered his wits, Didius had to acknowledge to himself that it had been his own fault, because he had tilted his shield slightly so that he could get a peek at the oncoming warriors in an attempt to get a better idea of what to expect. While he remembered moving his shield, this was all that he recalled, at least until he was roused to consciousness by the sensation of being dragged across the rocky ground, which was just painful enough to bring him back to his senses. Certainly, opening his eyes was a natural reflex, but in another sign to him that the gods hated Spurius Didius, it happened at the precise instant the bastard Pullus was glancing over his shoulder as he watched Didius being dragged away, and their eyes met. Only for an instant, because Didius immediately closed them again and feigned his unconsciousness, allowing his body to be handled like a slab of meat, which took an effort of will. The Second ranker let go of his harness, while Didius made sure to fall back limply to the ground as the man turned and hurried back to his position. Didius' intention at the moment was to gather his wits, that was all; it was what he told himself later anyway. He didn't plan to pretend to remain unconscious, yet somehow, it just happened, much like what had occurred in the town, when Didius hadn't planned to play up the nail in his foot to the point that he missed the entire battle. Now, much as had happened the last time, albeit from a different cause, Didius was consigned to listening to the sounds created by a furious fight, although this time, he was aided by hearing the commands of the Pilus Prior when he ordered the men still in the fight to prepare their javelins. Because of his position, the sounds created when the javelins landed amidst the attackers was slightly muffled by the bodies of his comrades, but he clearly heard several piercing screams originating from all around him. More than once, he had the urge to get up and join his comrades, yet for some reason that not even he could fathom, his body refused to obey his command to rise, to the point he actually almost convinced himself that he had been seriously injured and had lost all sensation in his limbs. After the last javelin volley, followed by Crastinus' order for the men along the dirt wall to stand, there was something of a lull in the noise, most of the din now in the form of men shouting in his tongue and in theirs, and he desperately wanted to open his eyes but managed to refrain.

Then, he heard Crastinus, who by the sound of it was only a half-dozen paces away, say, "Hurdles. The *cunni* are using hurdles."

This was an unfamiliar term to Didius and he wondered what it meant, but then the lull ended with a crashing sound of wood on wood, metal on wood, and metal on metal, although the piercing screams that had been muffled before were now much closer, and much shriller.

It was an agonized cry of "*Bona Dea save me! Mama!*" from the area where the Second Century was defending that caused Didius to open his eyes, suddenly worried that maybe the barbarians had managed to breach the defenses already. He didn't move his head, not initially at least, instead checking first to see that the men at the wall within his range of vision were too occupied to notice if he did before he risked raising his head to take a quick look around, relieved to see that, contrary to his fears, the position was still intact. Returning his attention back to his comrades, he was just in time to see Pullus in difficulty because he was forced to crouch lower than the others, thereby giving Didius an unobstructed view of the top of his nemesis' shield where he saw a hand appear, or at least the fingers belonging to a man attempting to grab Pullus' shield and either yank it out of his grasp or at least pull it downward. Despite his feelings towards the man, Didius felt a grim humor, thinking, you stupid *cunnus*, none of you are strong enough to yank that bastard's shield out of his hand. Even before the thought was finished, the first hand was joined by two more, and Didius saw Pullus' body jerk forward, but it only happened once before Pullus reacted by lifting his *gladius* then bringing it down onto the top of his shield, severing several fingers, three of which Didius saw flying up into the air as what sounded like three men shrieked in pain. The gods, Didius thought disgustedly, surely do love that bastard, but once again, the thought wasn't completed when he saw a spear point skid off the top of Pullus' shield and strike the Gregarius' helmet. It was a glancing blow, but it still made Pullus stagger backward into the man behind him whose identity Didius was unsure of and who shoved Pullus back towards the wall as the giant Roman shook his head several times in an attempt to clear it from the blow. That would have knocked anyone else on their ass, but not *him,* Didius thought bitterly. And yet, there was also a part of him, a secret part that as far as he was concerned would never see the light of day, that not only admired Titus Pullus, but was comforted knowing that he was standing there on the wall, knowing that it would take a lot of those barbarian bastards to bring him down.

Didius became aware of the sound subsiding almost too late, but he managed to shut his eyes just in time as the Lusitani retreated back across the hurdles to regroup, giving the Romans a chance to catch their breath, meaning that he was unaware that at their first opportunity, Pullus, Domitius, and Scribonius had all immediately turned to watch him. The lull didn't last long, the Lusitani renewing their attack, enabling Didius to open his eyes again to watch, and almost immediately, he could tell that his comrades would be able to repel this assault, and with the light fading, he felt certain this would be their final attempt of the day. He was right, and in fact, it didn't last very long before the Lusitani fully withdrew, dragging their wounded and as many of their dead as they could manage with them back down the hill. Even before they did so, Didius also realized that he had a dilemma on his hands; should he continue to feign unconsciousness or pretend to come to and just hope that he wasn't questioned too closely? Opening his eyes just a slit, he gauged the light, then decided that he would be unable to pretend for much longer, but he would at least wait until dark before he sat up, shaking his head and pretending he was still groggy.

For Scribonius, who was standing to Pullus' left on the wall, he never really felt under threat, knowing that he was protected by his large comrade's shield, and more importantly, Pullus' skill at killing. While he was under no illusions that he could match his giant comrade, he had undoubtedly slain one Lusitani with a thrust to the throat, and sent two more warriors reeling backward, one with an arm wound that issued a bright red spray that signaled a major vessel had been severed, and a thrust to a man's side that, if he had plunged it deeply enough, he was certain had punctured the man's bowels, which was a veritable death sentence, and even if he survived, he was out of this battle. He was also as exhausted as his comrades, so that once it became dark, when Crastinus finally sounded the relief to allow the men who had been standing at the wall to finally get some rest, he was staggering just as much as the other men at the wall, all of whom collapsed on the open ground, what there was of it, in the center of their position. The Pilus Prior forbade the use of fires to cook rations, but they were now experienced enough to have secreted pieces of bread, salted pork, and hard round balls of cheese somewhere, usually rolled up in their Legionary *sagum*. As had become a habit, the men tended to gather by section and with pairs sitting together, almost always their close comrade, but while Scribonius liked Vellusius and was happy that they had paired up, there was something bothering him, something that he had seen during the fighting. Actually, it was Didius' return to consciousness, sitting upright in the darkness, then slowly climbing to his feet, that spurred him to act.

"I need to talk to Pullus and Domitius," he whispered to Vellusius, who was more concerned with inspecting his piece of bread and only gave an absent nod.

Despite the fact that there was no need now, Scribonius still maintained a crouch as he moved the couple of paces away where Pullus' bulk loomed up in the dark. The other two were engaged in a quiet conversation, which Scribonius didn't feel comfortable intruding on, so he waited for there to be a lapse in their exchange.

Clearing his throat, and seeing Didius walking unsteadily in Atilius' direction, he whispered, "Did either of you happen to look at Achilles at all when we were fighting?"

They both shook their heads, which actually relieved Scribonius, and he was prepared to let it drop when Domitius spoke, "Why do you ask?"

Taking a deep breath before he began, Scribonius answered, "It's just that I could have sworn that I looked his way and he was watching the fighting, just like he was lying on his bunk."

It was Pullus who reacted most strongly, turning to look at Scribonius to exclaim, "I saw it too! I thought I must have been imagining it, but I swore I saw him peeking at us, right before they attacked us the first time!"

The three of them lapsed into silence for a moment, the import of what they had now confirmed hitting each of them, and it was Pullus who broke it by asking, "What do you think we should do?"

While he felt better now that his own opinion had been confirmed, Scribonius also had no desire to make this known to the officers, which was why he shook his head. "I don't think there's anything we can do." Both Pullus and Domitius reacted strongly to this, opening their mouths with what he was certain would be objections, but Scribonius had thought things through before he even brought it up, and he held up a hand as he explained, "Think about it, Pullus. It's well known that you hate him, and he you. And it's well known that he threatened you. I went and got Vellusius to split with him as close comrade, so there will be suspicions about me as well."

He was heartened to see, mostly by the sudden sagging of Pullus' shoulders and the manner in which Domitius sighed that they clearly accepted his reasoning.

Nevertheless, Pullus clearly wasn't willing to set it aside, saying disappointedly, "There has to be something we can do."

To Scribonius' surprise, it was Domitius who said firmly, "There is. But we can't do it now. We'll have to wait until we get back to the main camp."

With this settled, temporarily at least, and having finished what rations they had brought with them, the trio stretched out where they were sitting, with Scribonius on one side of Pullus and Domitius on the other. Within a matter of a couple heartbeats after untying his helmet, pulling it off and followed by the felt liner that he dropped into the helmet, Scribonius was already dozing off. He then was jerked awake when, without any warning, Pullus suddenly sat bolt upright. This was odd enough, but what he did next was even stranger, as he knelt, leaned over and pulled his *hamata* away from the padded undertunic.

"What in Dis has gotten into you?" Domitius demanded from the other side, but Pullus didn't reply. Scribonius couldn't see anything in the darkness, but he did hear a soft sound of something drop to the ground, and he saw Pullus pick up whatever it was, turn to Domitius and thrust it in front of his friend's face. Since he didn't know what it was, it seemed to Scribonius that Domitius' reaction was a bit extreme as he copied Pullus by sitting bolt upright as he gave a loud, gasped "You bastard!"

Pullus began laughing, and Scribonius was curious enough to ask, "What's so funny?"

Rather than answer, Pullus turned to him while holding something out for Scribonius to see. Because of the darkness, it took a moment, but then Scribonius realized what it was, echoing Domitius' gasp. "Is that a finger?"

This amused Pullus even more, but it also earned a rebuke from Calienus, who said irritably, "You three need to shut your mouths so we can get some sleep."

Pullus hurled the finger out beyond the parapet, then lay back down, still chuckling, leaving Scribonius to wonder about his large comrade and his sense of humor.

Crastinus had resigned himself to not getting any sleep this night, nor would Vetruvius, who, like his Pilus Prior, was pacing back and forth behind his Century's part of the position. It was quiet now, save for the sounds of snoring, and the occasional murmured exchange between the men standing on the wall as their comrades snatched what sleep they could. By Crastinus' estimate, it was close to midnight, the time to rouse the men on relief drawing closer, when the relative quiet was shattered by a sudden eruption of noise from shouting coming from the Second Century's area.

Even before he could turn about, he heard someone that he knew wasn't Vetruvius shouting, "To arms! To arms!"

It was the last understandable thing he heard, and without hesitating, he moved in that direction, relying more on his ears than his eyes to tell him what was happening, which was clearly an attack by an unknown number of Lusitani warriors who had managed to crawl up close enough to their position before leaping to their feet and rushing across the ditch, undoubtedly using the hurdles that had been left from the earlier assaults. The sharp cracking sound of Roman shields being battered by spears and *gladii* competed with the noise of alarmed Romans and determined Lusitani, but it told Crastinus what he wanted to know, that this wasn't an all-out assault, not yet anyway; there simply wasn't enough noise for several hundred warriors.

"The wall has been breached!"

Later, neither Crastinus, Vetruvius nor their Optios could find the culprit who shouted this, which wasn't true at that moment, but it served to get the formerly sleeping men who had come to their feet and put on their helmets to start moving. While it was almost impossible to determine the identity of his men in the dark, there was one exception, and while he wasn't surprised to see the dark shape that could only be Pullus moving in the direction of the fighting, he hurried to intercept him.

Grabbing Pullus by the arm, even in the moment, Crastinus was amused by the yelp of surprise from the big Gregarius, but he only asked, "Where do you think you're going, you big oaf?"

"To the fighting, Pilus Prior," Pullus replied in surprise.

"And what if this is just a diversion? That's just what the *cunni* want us to do," Crastinus said scornfully.

"But I thought the wall was breached."

Crastinus feigned a laugh. "That's just some woman posing as a Legionary saying that. They attacked, all right, but they haven't breached anything yet and aren't going to unless you fall for a trap like that."

He shoved Pullus then, back in the direction of the First Century, but he noticed that instead of going back to the spot his tentmates had claimed as their own as their half of the Century rested, he headed for the wall instead. If he doesn't want to get more rest, Crastinus thought as he turned away, that's his business. Returning his attention back to the sounds coming from the far side of the position, he decided that it might be time to go check with Vetruvius because while he didn't *think* the wall had been breached, the fighting still sounded furious, causing Crastinus a stab of doubt that perhaps he had made a mistake. After a span of perhaps two hundred heartbeats, during which Crastinus hurried to find Vetruvius, only finding him by calling his name and following the sound of his subordinate Centurion's voice, to Crastinus' relief, Vetruvius informed him that this attack was being easily contained, assuring Crastinus that it had been a diversion. The assault in earnest occurred behind him in the area defended by his Century, and this time, the noise was much louder, telling him that the several hundred Lusitani he had feared were now making their bid to destroy his two Centuries.

Understanding this, he snapped to Vetruvius, "Come with me. Let Petrosidius handle this. This is the real attack!"

He was already moving as he said this, and while it wasn't a run because of the darkness, it was as quickly as he could move. Once he got close enough that he could make out some details, he felt his stomach clench, accompanied by the loose, watery sensation deep in his bowels that he had learned as a young Gregarius was the sign of true fear. While he could not tell how, the Lusitani had managed to pull down a large enough section of the dirt wall to feed what at this moment was more than thirty Lusitani warriors into the position, forming a pocket inside the dirt wall several paces deep. Despite the fear, Crastinus didn't hesitate, drawing his *gladius* and arriving just in time to catch one of his men reeling backward from a powerful thrust by a Lusitani spear that the man had blocked with his shield, but while he stopped the man in his tracks by grabbing on to the back of his harness, Crastinus instantly saw the danger to the man he now recognized as one of his Second Section.

"Carbo, get your shield...!"

He was too late; before Carbo could obey, in an understandable but fatal instinctive reaction that occurs when someone is suddenly shoved backward, he moved both arms away from his body, and Crastinus felt the failure by the sudden spasm of Carbo's body transferring up through his left hand grasping Carbo's harness. In something of a blessing, the wind was driven from Carbo's lungs so that his last sound was only a breathy moan as he went limp, the Lusitani recovering his spear while Crastinus was suddenly confronted with the dead weight of Carbo's body falling back against him. He reacted by yanking Carbo's harness with all of his strength, effectively throwing the body aside to his left to give his *gladius* room, but he barely managed to parry the next thrust by the warrior with his blade, making a frantic sweeping blow that guided the thrust over his right shoulder. It was in this eyeblink of time that the Roman *gladius* proved its worth, because it took less time to recover for another thrust with the short blade than a spear, an unwieldy weapon when the fighting was so close. Whether or not the Lusitani was slow, or because of the dark he didn't see it coming didn't matter to Crastinus; what did was the point of his blade plunging into the warrior's body, midway between sternum and navel. Unlike Carbo, the Lusitani's lungs were unimpaired, his cry of pain turning into an almost feral shriek as, with a savage force and Crastinus thinking, This is for you,

Carbo, the Roman violently twisted his hips while locking his arm against his side in move that disemboweled the warrior. Just as with Carbo, it was the fate of this Lusitani to see the face of the man who had just killed him, Crastinus' features contorted with the kind of rage and hatred it took to gut another man. From Crastinus' perspective, he felt and smelled his success rather than see it as his hand, perhaps six inches away from the Lusitani's belly, was suddenly drenched with warm liquid and offal, the stench of *cac* filling his nostrils, but the Centurion didn't pause, using his free hand to do essentially what he had done to Carbo, shoving the dying man aside as he took a step forward, barely noticing the slimy feeling underfoot that were the man's intestines. It was a good thing that he behaved in this manner, because this time he saw the attack coming, although it was from a *gladius* wielding warrior who, as the Romans had learned in their first clashes with these tribes, favored a high overhead downward swing, usually aimed for the junction of neck and shoulder of their foe's body, and it was deadly effective if performed successfully.

Hampered without even his *vitus*, which every Centurion trained with, using it in a similar manner as a blade when used defensively, Crastinus' only choice was to bring his *gladius* parallel to the ground and across his body, swinging it up as his enemy's blade came slicing down, and while Crastinus was successful in his block, the blow sent a shivering shock down his arm, turning it numb in a tiny shower of sparks as iron collided with iron. It wasn't much illumination, but even in this moment, Crastinus saw the orange glow reflected in his opponent's eyes, making them gleam as if he was some otherworldly creature from the bowels of Hades. Without a shield, Crastinus was at a serious disadvantage, but he was aided by the fact that these barbarians only viewed their shields as a defensive weapon, because in the bare fraction of time before he recovered his blade back to position, the warrior could have used it to bash Crastinus in the face with the iron boss. The fact that he did not do so was costly, because Crastinus took advantage by lashing out with one hobnailed foot, striking his enemy on his knee with enough power that he felt the man's kneecap shatter, the sensation underfoot feeling like he had stepped on a cup that fragmented under his weight. This Lusitani's scream was every bit as shrill as the first man's, and he didn't even see the thrust that ended his life as he dropped both shield and weapon when his leg collapsed from under him. With this man dispatched, Crastinus wasn't under direct threat for perhaps four or five heartbeats, and he took that time to try and make more sense of the overall situation. Despite the gloom, he saw that it was desperate, although by this time, Vetruvius had arrived, rushing to support a man who was in much the same straits as Carbo, being forced to give ground, although in the glance he took, it appeared that the ranker had survived for the moment by disengaging by shuffling backward a pace.

What Crastinus didn't see was what would have been the familiar shape of Pullus, only learning later that the Gregarius had disobeyed Calienus' orders to stay at their post. However, what he did see was that there was only a single line of his men fighting desperately, unsupported by even one bolstering comrade, as the Lusitani, all of whom were shouting at the top of their voices, materialized in ever larger numbers in their attempt to rupture this single line of Legionaries, while his men were mostly silent, save for their gasping because they were unable to spare the breath. He was about to put his bone whistle to his lips when his short-lived respite ended, in the form of another spear-wielding warrior who had just arrived inside the breached wall. Realizing that he could either sound the relief or bend over to snatch up Carbo's shield, but not both, his decision was made for him by the speed of his foe, who was hurrying towards him, causing Crastinus to fumble blindly for the handle before finding it and bringing it up in front of him just as the warrior executed his first thrust, which he caught on his shield immediately below the boss. Along with the hollow thudding sound, Crastinus heard a splintering noise that he knew meant that the spear point had penetrated his protection. Using a move that he had been taught as a young Gregarius by his first Centurion, rather than pulling the shield back towards his body to extricate the spearpoint, he instead yanked downward with all of his power, which in turn served to jerk the Lusitani forward just as Crastinus executed his own thrust. To his frustration, the warrior blocked it with his shield, the *cunnus* actually laughing, then shouted what had to be a curse while managing to yank his spear free. When blows were exchanged that didn't score, it was customary for the combatants to pause for perhaps a heartbeat or two before renewing their attack, but Gaius Crastinus didn't give a fart in a *testudo* about customs, which was why as his opponent closed his stance back up, giving up perhaps a half pace, Crastinus pressed forward to make another thrust, this time from the third position around the side of his shield. It wasn't a killing blow, but he felt the point of the blade bite into the meat of the warrior's left arm, earning a sharp bellow of mostly anger from his enemy, followed by a poorly aimed thrust from the warrior's spear that Crastinus didn't even need to move his shield to block, the point going wide to strike nothing but air. Instead, he swung the shield as a weapon, taking advantage of the opening presented by the warrior's briefly extended arm, the metal edge of the Roman's shield striking it midway between elbow and wrist, breaking both bones with a clearly audible wet, snapping sound.

This time, there was no defiance in the man's voice as he screamed in agony, the spear dropping from a hand that was suddenly dangling downward at a place it wasn't supposed to, and while he did retain the presence of mind to keep his shield up, with a feint from Crastinus, followed by a first position thrust, another Lusitani warrior was down. The problem, Crastinus saw with dismay, was that they simply weren't killing enough of them quickly enough, and while his men were accounting for themselves well, he could see the inert forms of at least a half-dozen helmeted men lying among the steadily growing pile of bodies, some of them moving as a wounded man tried to crawl towards his respective comrades, the Lusitani wounded dragging themselves towards the breach while his men were moving in the opposite direction, and now that he had the chance, he didn't hesitate.

"All those on relief on me, at the double!"

The words were barely out of his mouth before he was under attack again, this time by two Lusitani who, by spreading out slightly, forced Crastinus to turn so that his back was essentially to the ranker next to him in the line, a Fourth Section man named Flaccus, who was himself engaged with a Lusitani spearman. Both of his opponents carried *gladii*, but while one of them was the longer style blade, the man who had moved a bit to his shield side was wielding a blade that was shaped identically to the one in Crastinus' hand, but perhaps a few inches longer. They were also both wearing armor, although only one of them was wearing a high, conical helmet, and Crastinus dropped into a crouch when the Lusitani to his left moved first. It was, Crastinus thought, predictable, but the reason for this was because it was effective, except that Crastinus didn't take the bait, and instead, he moved suddenly, not towards the closer Lusitani to his left, but towards the man on his right, and not directly at him but slightly to his foe's left. By doing so, he effectively placed one Lusitani in the path of another, something that they could correct quickly, but Crastinus was about to lunge before they could when, from behind him, there was a bellow of what could only be called rage that was, frankly, the loudest Crastinus had ever heard from human lungs. So startling was it that, despite his own peril, he couldn't stop himself from looking over his shoulder in surprise. What he saw was a Roman, a huge Roman who had violated the maxim of never leaving one's feet to leap up and forward into the air to get within arm's reach of a Lusitani whose spear arm was drawn back as far as it would go in the eyeblink before plunging it into Crastinus' back. It was a moment that would be burned into Crastinus' memory for the rest of his life, something that, although it happened over the span of less than a full heartbeat, still seemed in slow motion, enabling Crastinus to see the warrior's arm moving forward as a bizarrely calm voice inside his head told him, "You're dead, Gaius."

That he did not die was due to the massive power of an underage giant who, ignoring the training that taught him that the point was always better than the edge, swung his *gladius* in the kind of sweeping move usually favored by the barbarians. Somehow, despite being in midair, despite the darkness, despite everything that was happening, Titus Pullus' aim was unerring, his blade not even perceptibly slowing down as it bit into the warrior's neck with enough power that not only did it decapitate him, it sent the warrior's head tumbling up at least three feet in the air. A fraction of an eyeblink later, Crastinus felt the blow to his back from the dead man's spear, but it was with less than the force of a punch, and he heard the spear clatter onto the slain man's dropped shield. Although it was the first time, it would not be the last when Crastinus would witness Pullus doing something that was so astonishing that even their foes were shocked into immobility, and this proved to be the case with the Lusitani he had been about to attack. Although both Crastinus and his foe recovered, Crastinus was quicker, stepping forward to execute a second position thrust right over his shield, and over that of the Lusitani's, catching the warrior at the base of the throat, showering Crastinus' already filthy arm with fresh blood. Somewhat understandably, the second Lusitani suddenly didn't seem quite as eager, and in fact, he went sidling along the wall back in the direction of the breach as if he might be considering withdrawing, which enabled Crastinus to turn his body enough to face Pullus. The decapitated corpse had collapsed to its knees before toppling over, but the dead man's heart was still pumping, the ichor catching the light from the stars and partial moon just enough to glisten in the darkness.

Despite knowing already, Crastinus was still recovering from the surprise, and asked, "Is that you, Pullus?"

Once he had time to think about it later, Crastinus decided that it was the smile more than the words themselves that ignited his rage as Pullus grinned and said, "Yes, Pilus Prior, and you're welcome."

"Welcome, am I?" Crastinus snarled. "We'll see how welcome I am once I've striped your back, you *cunnus*! I seem to remember telling you specifically to remain at your post."

Even in the dark, Crastinus saw the surprise on Pullus' face as he protested, "But..."

Still in the grips of his rage, Crastinus cut him off, "But nothing. Those were your orders and you disobeyed them. Your ass is mine."

Just as he finished, Crastinus saw movement out of the corner of his eye, turning just in time to parry a thrust by the second Lusitani who had either had a change of heart and was back in the fight, or had been pretending to withdraw, and the

Centurion knocked the blade aside with his own, creating another shower of sparks. Consequently, he missed the expression on Pullus' face as it transformed from hurt surprise to rage, and he was only vaguely aware that the Gregarius had stalked off. What happened next would certainly capture his attention, but it would do much more than that, because Titus Pullus was about to embark on the real beginning of the legend he would become to men under the standard, and in the process, almost singlehandedly destroyed the Lusitani attack.

Titus Pullus would learn of his exploit solely from others because he had very little memory of it, although he did recall his shock, and the anger it created, from Crastinus' harsh words. No, he hadn't expected the Pilus Prior to fall all over himself in praise, especially in that moment, but Pullus was completely unprepared for clearly enraging his Centurion. And, when he had turned to walk away, he did remember that he hadn't headed back to his spot on the wall, but instead, directly into what was nothing more than a vicious brawl where there was no real order or tactics. He also recalled that, for some reason, Crastinus' words had triggered in him other memories, similar moments of pain and humiliation; how much his father hated him, how Juno had chosen his best friend and not him, and how Domitius had beaten him at dice a few days earlier, and it was these memories that were actually the last thing he could clearly recall. He did have a few fragments that were more sensations than images, like the feeling he got from the look of shock on the face of a bearded Lusitani at the sudden appearance of a giant Roman who was about to take his life. He could recall the taste of blood in his mouth, and how it felt on his face even as he knew that it wasn't his own, but more than anything, it was the memory of reveling in this moment that, perhaps more than anything, shook him. It was as if one moment he was walking towards a knot of men, some of them Roman but mostly Lusitani, then the next he was standing, alone with his *gladius* hanging down by his side, panting as if he had just sprinted up this hill, and he was more tired than he could ever recall. He was only vaguely aware that the cacophony of the fight had died down, though not completely, and he was confronted with what seemed, at least in his current condition, to be an insurmountable problem.

Essentially, he was hemmed in by a pile of bodies that completely surrounded him, to a height that made him certain he didn't have the strength to lift his legs high enough to step over them. If those bastards come back, he thought dully, I can't even lift my *gladius*, let alone my shield, and I'm trapped; such was his fatigue that the prospect of dying right then wasn't particularly unpleasant. As slowly as his mind seemed to be working, he understood that simply standing there wasn't an option, and he finally lifted one leg to straddle the heap of bodies, his lack of strength compounded by how there were men who weren't quite dead, making the pile shift as those on the bottom struggled to crawl out from under the dead men lying on top of them, yet somehow he managed to do so without falling. Remembering the Pilus Prior's promise of a flogging, Pullus knew the right thing to do would be to seek Crastinus out and hope that he had changed his mind, but like the prospect of death, the idea of a flogging wasn't all that terrifying, and all he wanted to do right now was to lie down, so he staggered back to where he and his comrades had been resting before the attack started. He gave no notice to the sounds of metal on metal, followed by a shout of pain at the same instant someone else gave a victorious bellow, nor did he even glance up to see that everyone around him had stopped what they were doing to watch him pass by. Finding his spot, Pullus dropped his shield, pulled off his helmet and liner then collapsed to the ground, more unconscious than asleep by the time his head touched his bunched up *sagum*.

"Did you see it?"

"Not all of it," Crastinus replied to Rufio's question, "but enough to know I've never seen anything like it before."

"If you haven't, I certainly haven't," Rufio agreed.

It was still dark, but the fight was over, the Lusitani gone, and the men of the First and Second Century were in the process of checking on their fallen comrades, helping those that they could, and carrying those that they couldn't to the center of the position, where they were gently laid side by side. Crastinus had put Vetruvius in charge of this, ignoring the look of irritation on the man's face, but while Crastinus wasn't as fatigued as Pullus, he was certainly near the end of his strength, not having gotten any sleep at all. It was more than that, however; the truth was that Gaius Crastinus had been shaken, not just by the desperate nature of this battle, but by what he had observed. Crastinus hadn't been entirely truthful with Rufio; the truth was that he had seen almost everything with Pullus, but because he had never witnessed something that extraordinary before, he was still struggling to come up with a way to define what he had witnessed. In the back of his mind, there was the glimmer of a foolish idea that he might have been watching the demigod Hercules himself, while another, larger part of him, the professional Centurion in him, had actually watched with disapproval. The truth was that Pullus had violated every single rule Roman Legionaries were taught from the first day they began weapons training. Pullus' recoveries were sloppy, if they could even have been called that, he had basically ignored his shield as a defensive weapon, using it instead to bludgeon his opponents, he had done at least as much slashing as thrusting, and more than anything, he had shown absolutely no regard for his own life. At first, the Lusitani had eagerly swarmed around this huge Roman who had walked alone into almost the exact middle of the pocket that was growing larger by the heartbeat, immediately surrounding him and cutting Pullus off from his comrades...and yet Pullus had clearly not cared.

Intruding into his thoughts, Rufio asked quietly, "What do you plan to do with him, Pilus Prior?"

While it startled him, it was also an appropriate question. Yes, Crastinus had been enraged by what, in the moment, he had seen as Pullus' impertinence and lack of respect with that fucking grin, and yes, he had meant it when he said he was going to have Pullus flogged. The problem was, that while Crastinus had watched what happened, he hadn't been the only Roman who saw at least part of it, and even before the fighting was completely over, he could hear men talking excitedly about all that Pullus had done. Judging from the buzzing conversations around him, a consensus was quickly building that Pullus had almost singlehandedly stopped the breach from expanding to a point that the numerical superiority of the Lusitani could tip the balance, and it was one with which Crastinus, albeit grudgingly, agreed. Regardless of his actions, however, as a rule Centurions of any grade didn't like reversing themselves, and this was especially true with Pili Priores.

Rubbing his chin, Crastinus finally answered, "I'm not sure yet. I'm going to think about it. But first," his tone turned brisk, "I need the butcher's bill for us, and go get the Second's from Petrosidius."

Rufio saluted, then left to make his count for the First, leaving Crastinus to stare in the general direction of where he had seen Pullus stagger off, although it still was too dark to make out much of anything. Slowly, a thought began to form that at least partially answered what he had been asking himself, about how he would describe what he had seen. It's as if, he realized, there's some...beast within Pullus that, when it gets loose, enables him to do what we just saw him do, become a perfect instrument of death, a machine that, like a *ballista* or scorpion, was built with the only purpose of killing Rome's enemies. While this was satisfying, it was also troubling, and before he could stop the thought, Crastinus worried, I hope whatever it is inside him doesn't turn on him and destroy him, or his comrades.

By the time Crastinus was ready to deal with Pullus, the sun was fully up, and the large Gregarius had been allowed to sleep while his comrades worked, collecting the discarded weapons and broken shields. While every able-bodied man was busy, there was one exception as Pullus slept on, completely oblivious to the activity around him. After speaking with Crastinus, Rufio had sought out Calienus, who informed him of the events that led up to Pullus' exploit.

"I tried to stop him, Optio," Calienus said frankly. "I told him that I knew the Pilus Prior was deadly serious about not leaving his post and that it was too dark to tell exactly what was happening."

"What did he say?"

"He said," Calienus sighed, "he was going, and that if I wanted to write him up for a flogging, that was fine."

Rufio nodded, informing the Sergeant, "And that's what the Pilus Prior promised to do, flog him."

"*Gerrae!*" Calienus exclaimed. "How can he do that now after what Pullus did?"

At this, they both glanced over to where Pullus was lying, but the large Gregarius' eyes were closed, and he didn't even stir at the sound of the conversation.

"You know how the Pilus Prior is, Lucius," Rufio said quietly. "I don't think he wants to stripe Pullus, but he said it in front of others." Suddenly, Rufio gave a short laugh. "Poor Flaccus was down and lying there between them. When he fell, he pulled his shield over him, and he told me that he was about to ask them to drag him out of the way, but he heard the Pilus Prior and decided it was safer under his shield."

Calienus joined Rufio in laughing, although he asked, "How bad is it?"

"For Flaccus?" Rufio shook his head, then realized by the Sergeant's expression that Calienus had taken it the wrong way, adding quickly, "He'll be fine. He took a spear thrust to the left thigh, but it's a clean wound and it was on the outside of his leg."

Relieved, Calienus returned to the original subject, unknowingly asking the question that Rufio had posed to Crastinus, "Did you see any of it?"

"Some," Rufio replied. "And you?"

Rufio didn't notice the subtle change in Calienus' manner, the Sergeant suddenly looking away as he answered, "No, I didn't. I stayed put until we were called." More to change the subject away from himself, Calienus asked, "Any idea when the Pilus Prior is going to make up his mind?"

Rufio opened his mouth to answer, but before he could, Crastinus shouted, "Optio and Sergeants, attend to me!"

As Rufio turned away to head to where Crastinus was standing next to the wounded, he murmured, "Maybe we're about to find out."

It started out with Crastinus demanding a report on the state of each section; the butcher's bill had already been tallied, and it was disheartening, but now Crastinus needed to determine how many men were still fit to fight and whether their equipment was serviceable.

After listening to each of them, all Crastinus could think of was to say wearily, "Well, at least we have enough spare shields to go around." Turning to Rufio, he ordered, "Go get Pullus and bring him to me."

He continued talking to the Sergeants, but he was watching as Rufio stood over Pullus' prone body, calling the Gregarius' name. When this did not work, Rufio kicked Pullus' foot, which succeeded in rousing him, and he climbed slowly to his feet like a much older man to follow the Optio back to where he was issuing orders.

"Gregarius Titus Pullus, reporting as ordered, sir," Pullus said while offering his salute, which Crastinus pointedly ignored.

It was a common game, this, making a man whose fate might be uncertain to wait, but it probably would have worried Pullus more that, in fact, Crastinus wasn't playing a game; he simply hadn't yet decided what to do. Dismissing the Sergeants, while Crastinus turned to bark at some men who were loitering instead of turning to face Pullus, out of the corner of his eye, he watched as Pullus' Sergeant walked by the Gregarius, and while nothing was said, he saw Calienus shake his head. Rufio had already relayed his conversation with Calienus, which Calienus reluctantly confirmed when Crastinus pressed him, so Crastinus knew that Pullus had been fully aware of the possible consequences of his actions when he chose to disobey. What that meant, however, was what Crastinus was having a problem determining. With the section leaders returned to their sections, and Crastinus having run out of men to tongue lash for imaginary misdeeds, he realized he could put it off no longer, and for the first time, faced Pullus in broad daylight. It wasn't anything Pullus said that made Crastinus' mind up; it was the sight of the man standing before him that did, because more than anything he had glimpsed in the gloom a matter of a couple watches earlier, it was seeing Pullus looking as if he had literally been dropped into a huge tub of blood and gore that brought home the reality of what the Gregarius had accomplished. There's not an inch of bare skin showing, Crastinus thought to himself, and as hardened and accustomed as he was to seeing what *gladii* and spears could do to a body, the small chunks of what was essentially raw meat clinging to his *hamata* caused Crastinus' stomach to do a queasy flip.

"You know," he finally broke the silence, "if I were to abide by the regulations, I should have you scourged at the very least, and scourged and crucified at the very worst." Frankly, it was impossible for Crastinus to tell how his words were registering with Pullus just going by his expression since the blood caked on his face obscured his features, but he did see Pullus' body stiffen, then Crastinus softened his tone. "But it wouldn't be very gracious to kill a man who saved my life. Besides," he almost allowed a smile to appear, "it wouldn't help morale, seeing as how you saved the lives of the rest of the Century, not to mention the Second's as well." He briefly considered offering his account of what he had witnessed, completely unaware of the fact that if he had, it would have been the first time Pullus would become aware of it, but instead he shook his head and said, "What you did last night, boy, was one of the stupidest things I've seen in all my years under the standards, but it was also the bravest. I told you once that I thought you might have a future in the Legions, and last night didn't change my mind." Now it was impossible to miss Pullus' broad shoulders sagging in relief, which prompted Crastinus to cross the distance between them so that there was barely a hand's width between them. Making sure to pin Pullus with his gaze, despite having to tilt his head up, Crastinus' voice lowered, which only enhanced the menace. "But if you ever disobey me again, I don't care how decorated or famous you are, I'll gut you myself, and I'll make it look like you were killed and nobody will ever know. Do you understand me?"

"Yes, sir," Pullus answered quickly, nodding as well.

"Good." Crastinus' voice returned to normal. "And we'll speak no more about it. I know I won't have to."

This time, when Pullus saluted before executing his about turn, Crastinus returned it immediately, then stood and watched the Gregarius walking away, back towards his tentmates, all of whom had now gathered together, watching their comrade approach as they sat on the ground eating. Once again, Crastinus noticed that all but one of them looked concerned, which reminded him of Didius and what he suspected was a case of cowardice with his injury the day before. That, he thought, can wait.

Watching Pullus standing at *intente* in front of Crastinus was hardest on Domitius, and it took a real effort not to betray his concern in front of the others, especially Didius. Once again, their section had been blessed by Fortuna; of the nine bodies now lying side by side and covered with a *sagum*, none of the Tenth Section was with them, although they were short a man because Romulus was with the wounded but, thank the gods, he wasn't the man whose guts were covered by a linen bandage as he moaned away the last moments of his life. Before Pullus got to them, Domitius climbed to his feet to hurry to greet his best friend. Like Crastinus, he saw the caked gore covering Pullus, but it didn't stop him from rushing up to embrace him.

"You mad bastard. If the Lusitani hadn't killed you, I swore I was going to for scaring me so badly," he whispered, aware that because of their height difference he looked like a son hugging his Tata, but he didn't care. "But now when I see you, I'm just happy that you're still alive."

"Me too," Pullus replied simply, returning the embrace, and he was surprised to find that he meant it, a far cry from his state of mind not long before.

Domitius' actions had spurred the others to come to their feet to surround their comrade, with two exceptions, although Pullus expected it of one of them with Didius, but seeing Calienus still seated and looking in the opposite direction surprised him. And, although Pullus was gratified by the reception, he was also somewhat mystified, asking why the fuss, thinking that only Crastinus was aware that anything unusual had happened.

It was Scribonius who informed him, "Everyone in the Century is talking about it. You singlehandedly saved both Centuries last night. Those bastards had broken through and it was you who stopped them and saved all of us."

Escorting him back to their gear, they took turns informing him of all that had occurred while he had been in his stupor.

"After you sent the Lusitani running off, once the sun came

up, they came back under a flag of truce asking to retrieve their wounded," Domitius told him.

Remus broke in, "We made a count, and there's almost three hundred of them dead, and of the rest, it didn't look like more than a hundred didn't have some kind of wound."

"What about your brother?" Pullus asked, having spotted him sitting with one eye obscured with a bloody bandage.

"He got nicked by a spear right above his eye," Remus answered, then assured Pullus, "but it didn't hurt his eye. He'll be fine."

"Is there any word on relief?" Pullus asked, and they all pointed off to where he could see a dust cloud rising high up into the air.

"They're almost here," Calienus spoke up for the first time, though he still refused to meet Pullus' gaze.

"Here," Vellusius thrust a flask out, along with a neckerchief, "at least get all that blood off your face and hands."

Pullus was embarrassed because he had forgotten his condition, but once he was reminded, he felt how the skin on his face felt tight from the dried blood, and he glanced down at his hands to see that the only spots where he could see his own flesh was where the gobbets of matter had finally dropped off.

"Thank you, Vellusius," he mumbled, taking the flask, but he shook his head at the neckerchief. "I've got my own spare. I'll use that."

Retrieving it, he doused it with the water and began scrubbing as the others returned to their original conversations, which suited Pullus perfectly since he wasn't in the mood to talk. Just as he was finishing, Rufio approached, his expression unreadable, and they quickly learned why.

"The Pilus Prior is ordering us to dig a pit to get rid of these bodies," he informed them, saying it loudly enough to be heard by all of the First.

"What? Why?"

"We're leaving here! Let the crows take care of these bastards!"

Rufio allowed the men to vent their displeasure, but only for a few heartbeats before he snapped, *"Tacete!* Now," he extended one hand to point to a spot just the other side of the ditch, "he said you can start there and just enlarge the ditch. So, get your tools and get to work." Still grumbling, the men climbed to their feet, but when Pullus followed suit, Rufio stopped him. "Not you, Pullus. The Pilus Prior excused you from duties for the day."

Now that his face was relatively clean, they could all see the broad grin on his face as he dropped back to the ground, and while he was jeered by his tentmates, Rufio could tell that it was good-natured, at least for the most part. Like Crastinus, Rufio tucked that away, thinking of Didius as a problem for later.

Pullus' inactivity only lasted a few dozen heartbeats before he got to his feet, although he did hesitate as he thought, If the Pilus Prior told me not to work, will he be angry if I do? Deciding that if he took his spade he could at least drop it and pretend that he was just chatting in the event that the Pilus Prior showed up, Pullus grabbed it and walked over to the wall, then dropped down into the ditch, startling his comrades, whereupon Pullus learned that Atilius had been giving his own account of the night before.

"Yes, boys, I thought we were well and truly fucked," he said as he tossed a spade full of dirt out of the growing hole, "because I couldn't see a fucking thing and all I could hear was that abominable screeching they do when they attack."

"I was angry because I'd just gotten off light duty," Vellusius spoke up. "I thought, by the gods, if I get wounded again and put back in the hospital, I'll go mad."

"You know that your arm's not healed," Scribonius reminded his close comrade. "You probably shouldn't be doing this."

"I've been lying about long enough," Vellusius countered. "I need to pull my weight just like everyone else." Straightening up, he nodded towards Pullus. "Look at him. He was given the day off, but here he is along with us."

What happened next was that, as a group, instead of looking at Pullus, all eyes turned towards Didius leaning on his spade, who went red, and while he glared at Vellusius, silently blaming him for this, he kept his mouth shut and resumed work. The bump on his head was noticeable, but it hadn't even turned colors, and his comrades had pointedly refused to ask him about it.

More to take their attention away from his close comrade, Atilius pointed down to the massive bruise on his thigh where a stone sling bullet had caromed downward off his shield.

"I got knocked down, and I knew I had had it. 'Atilius, old son,' I said to myself, 'if you get out of this one, it'll be because of the divine intervention of Fortuna herself. You better show her how grateful you are.'"

This prompted Domitius to ask, "Well, she obviously did, so what kind of sacrifice are you going to make?"

Atilius straightened up, pausing in his work. "You know, I've been thinking about that. I don't know what's appropriate. What do you boys think?"

"What about a dove?" Vellusius suggested, but Atilius dismissed this.

"That's not enough," he scoffed, but Vellusius had proven to have a stubborn streak when he got an idea that he thought had merit, prompting him to insist, "Then you can make it two doves, or even three."

To forestall a dispute, Scribonius suggested, "How about a lamb?"

"It's not the season for lambs," Remus pointed out. "They're only in the spring."

"What about a white kid goat?" Domitius offered, and Atilius nodded.

"That might do it," he allowed. "How much do those cost, I wonder?"

Nobody volunteered anything, then finally Scribonius guessed, "I shouldn't think more than twenty *sesterces*," causing Atilius to gasp, "*Twenty sesterces*?" Shaking his head, he said, "By Dis, I'm not *that* grateful. She'll have to do with something less than that, then."

Their laughter at this prompted a visit from the Pilus Prior, who had been walking past, and he stood up on the dirt wall with his hands on his hips, staring down at them as they came to *intente*.

"If you *cunni* have enough breath to laugh, then it means you're not working hard enough," Crastinus pronounced.

Pointing down at them with his *vitus*, he warned them, "Get back to work and don't let me catch you fucking off again."

Hopping down, he strode away, leaving the section behind and unable to see the broad grin on his face.

As they resumed working, Vellusius said smugly, "I *told* you doves were a good idea."

As the men under his command were learning, the relief column Caesar sent out was prepared not only to rescue the stranded Centuries, but they brought the necessary items to enable the men of the First and Second Century to send their fallen comrades to the afterlife in the Roman manner. One of the slaves belonging to the camp priests drove a wagon loaded down with cages for birds and small animals, along with the jars of scented oils that were part of the funeral rites. Since the First Century had labored to dig the pit, the Second Century had the task of dragging the Lusitani bodies into it, while some of the relieving Centuries had been sent the half-mile back to the forest to gather the wood necessary for the funeral pyres, the rest of the Second and the full Third Cohort had been sent by the Legate, along with enough wagons to carry the wounded. The pyres were built on the top of the hill, the dead men in just their tunics, their bodies cleaned by their surviving comrades and the ritual coin placed under each tongue. Each pyre was attended by the men of the section to which the dead man belonged as prayers were offered, the priests walking around each pyre while intoning the supplication to the gods for the dead as they sprinkled the holy oils on the wood that, while pleasantly scented, also worked as an accelerant. Standing in formation, their comrades watched silently as the flames did their work, burning away the flesh to release the spirits inside each fallen man, and while it was never spoken of, every man of the Tenth Section, even Didius, thanked the gods that none of them was on one of those pyres, each of them remembering Crastinus' counsel about how they would feel this way, that they would experience a combined sense of relief and guilt. The ashes were allowed to cool before being put into the urns brought by the relief, during which the wounded were loaded on wagons, then once the ashes were collected, the First

Century of the Second Cohort, given the vanguard while followed by the Second Century in a sign of honor, marched away from the hill. It would mark a turning point, especially for the men of the First Century, who began to carry themselves with a swagger that announced to not just the 10th, but the other Legions, that they were new men no longer in any sense of the word. And, although he was unaware of it, the name Titus Pullus began to be known outside the Second Cohort.

Chapter Four

Gaius Crastinus thought about not mentioning Pullus' exploits in the official report that he knew would ultimately end up on Caesar's desk, but there just seemed something petty about it and he couldn't justify doing so. Therefore, he wasn't particularly surprised when a runner came from the *praetorium*, summoning him to meet with Caesar. Although the Pilus Prior had certainly been around Caesar on numerous occasions, a personal audience where he was the only attendee was much rarer, so he was slightly nervous when he strode into the headquarters tent to announce to the duty Tribune that he was reporting as ordered. Because of what had happened to the First and Second, Caesar had ordered that they remain in this camp an extra day, so they would be breaking camp in two days instead of the next one. Crastinus didn't have to wait long, nor did Caesar behave like so many patrician officers did, pretending to be busy with other matters while their subordinate stood there and waited.

After the exchange of salutes, Caesar got down to business. "I've read your report, Pilus Prior Crastinus. And," he offered a slight smile, "it sounds like it was quite an adventure."

Sensing it was the prudent thing to do, Crastinus gave a polite laugh, agreeing, "That's one way to put it, sir."

Caesar's smile faded, and he replied soberly, "And I owe you and your men an apology, Pilus Prior. As you know, we've been plagued by a lack of cavalry on this campaign, and I take full responsibility for this, although I did try, but not enough native tribes friendly to Rome offered up their horsemen." Grimacing, he admitted, "I should have gone to Corduba or even Nova Carthago to hold a *dilectus* from the eastern tribes, but I didn't want to lose any more time than we already had."

What, Crastinus thought, am I supposed to say to that?

Aloud, he cleared his throat before answering awkwardly,

"There's so much to think about when planning a campaign, sir." Slightly inspired, he added, "And when has there ever been a campaign where the army had everything it needed?"

"That's true," Caesar granted. Then, he abruptly changed the subject, picking up the tablet that Crastinus recognized as his report, studying it with a frown for a moment before he said, "But what I wanted to talk to you about was your report. Specifically," his eyes narrowed as he scanned the text; finding the name, he provided, "this *Gregarius* Pullus." He looked up and directly at Crastinus, who suddenly felt uncomfortable as he realized that he had never been subjected to the commanding general's piercing gaze, with blue eyes that were the color of the deep ice that could only be found on the highest mountaintops, but his tone was neutral as he commented, "If this is accurate, he must be quite formidable."

This was when Crastinus understood something, that to Caesar, Pullus was just a name that he hadn't yet associated with the biggest man in the 10th Legion.

Understanding this, Crastinus assured Caesar, "He is, sir. And, I'm sure you've noticed him."

He stopped, waiting for Caesar to make the connection, and he was rewarded by the Legate's eyes slightly widening.

"Of *course*!" he exclaimed with a rueful tone. "Only someone as big as that *Gregarius* in your Century could have done something like this. I should have made the connection immediately."

Crastinus could have left it at this, but he felt compelled to say something.

"No doubt that his size and strength help, Caesar, but there's more to him than that."

"Oh?" Caesar asked with a raised eyebrow. Crossing his arms, he said, "Can you explain that?"

How, Crastinus wondered, do I explain what I saw? And why did I open my mouth? Nevertheless, Crastinus did his best, while Caesar listened without interruption. When the Pilus Prior was finished, Caesar didn't hesitate.

"Bring him to me, Crastinus. I think I want to meet this young *Gregarius*."

After the morning formation was held, Pilus Prior Crastinus dismissed his Century, turning them over to Rufio, but called Pullus to stay behind.

Without saying why, Crastinus snapped at him to stand to *intente* as he walked around him, visually inspecting the *Gregarius* before grunting, "Follow me."

He turned towards the *praetorium* and was walking so quickly that Pullus was forced to trot to catch up. Crastinus watched Pullus out of the corner of his eye as they drew near the headquarters tent and observed the play of emotions that crossed the young Gregarius' face as Pullus began to comprehend what this might mean. Given that Pullus hadn't been in the *praetorium* since his first day of training, Crastinus completely understood the suddenly nervous expression on the younger man's face when Pullus realized their destination.

"Right, now listen up." Crastinus dropped his voice just as they approached the entrance. "I turned in my report to the Legate, who forwarded it to Caesar, who interviewed me himself. He wants to meet you."

This caused Pullus to come to an abrupt halt, and it took an effort on Crastinus' part not to laugh at the sudden look of alarm and real fear on the *Gregarius'* face as he thought, You weren't this afraid on that hill.

"So," Pullus swallowed twice before he could get the words out, "what do I do?"

"Do?" Crastinus snorted. "You don't do a damn thing. You answer his questions with a 'Yes, sir' or 'No, sir,' and otherwise, keep your mouth shut. Got it?"

Rather than assure Pullus, he looked even more worried.

"What if he asks me a question that doesn't have a yes or no answer?"

Stifling a groan, Crastinus just snapped, "Then you answer the damn question, but use as few words as you possibly can."

Not wanting to delay any longer, Crastinus informed one of the men standing guard, "Secundus Pilus Posterior Crastinus with *Gregarius* Pullus, reporting to *Praetor* Caesar as directed."

The guard ducked inside, then quickly returned and held the flap aside, whereupon Crastinus took off his helmet to put under his arm, which Pullus copied despite not knowing if this was what he was supposed to do. For his part, Crastinus was accustomed to the inner workings of the *praetorium*, so he weaved confidently around Tribunes who seemed to be totally absorbed in talking to each other in hushed tones, while clerks hurried back and forth in front of their path as Pullus followed Crastinus to the far side of the tent. One of those Tribunes caught Pullus' eye, if only because he seemed to be the exact opposite of the absent Doughboy, with an air of quiet confidence about him. Before he could ask his Centurion who it was, Crastinus had reached the leather flap that had lead weights sewn along the bottom that served as a door, thrusting it aside as he entered the private office of the man commanding the entire army.

"Ready?" Crastinus murmured under his breath, but Pullus could only nod, earning him a glare, then the Pilus Prior was striding towards the desk that belonged to Caesar, who was standing behind it as he dictated something to a scribe. Stopping at the exact pace from the edge of the desk, Crastinus paused only long enough for Pullus to step to his side before saluting, "Secundus Pilus Prior Gaius Crastinus, of the 10th Legion, reporting with Legionary *Gregarius Immune* Titus Pullus as ordered, sir."

As Crastinus spoke, they both saluted, and in a show of the kind of vanity that he would come to learn he shared with Caesar, Pullus made sure to flex the bicep of his saluting arm, unaware that Caesar saw the gesture and understood what Pullus was doing. His expression, however, was solemn as he dropped the scroll he had been holding and returned the salute in the same manner in which it had been offered. This done, he didn't speak immediately, preferring instead to examine the pair, although almost all of his attention was understandably focused on Pullus. Naturally, and as he had indicated to Crastinus, he had certainly noticed the man who stood almost a head above than even the taller men like Caesar, although it was his musculature that was most impressive. Caesar was suddenly struck with an amusing thought: I'd love to see Marcus' reaction at seeing Pullus, thinking of his relative Marcus Antonius, who was considered by the women, and most of the men, of Rome to have the most impressive physique, not just in the city, but in the Republic. None of this showed in his face as he continued his silent inspection. He is, he thought, even bigger than I imagined. But it wasn't just his size and bulk that caught his attention. Despite Pullus having his eyes fixed on a spot above Caesar's head as he had been trained, Caesar was certain that he saw...*something* there in those brown eyes; call it a spark of something that indicated that there might be more to this youth than just raw, brute strength. It was this thought that got him to do something he hadn't intended, moving around the desk to extend his arm, not as an officer, but as one Roman man greeting another.

"*Salve, Gregarius* Titus Pullus. The Pilus Prior has told me of your valor in your engagement, and I wanted to offer you my hand in thanks."

This clearly flummoxed Pullus so that he didn't respond immediately, although this actually amused Caesar, understanding that no doubt Crastinus had never mentioned this as a possibility. Thankfully for both of them, the habits of courtesy got Pullus to thrust his arm out, but in another technical breach, the *Gregarius* actually dropped his gaze to look Caesar in the eye, and while Caesar could feel the power in the younger man's grip, unlike Antonius, Pullus clearly didn't feel the need to apply enough pressure to prove who was the strongest. However, it was the expression in Pullus' eyes that confirmed Caesar's first impression, that there was something deeper going on there.

Aloud, he said, "It's good to know that Rome will be served by young men such as you in the coming years. I feel that she will have more need of your services than either of us would like."

Caesar saw Pullus' eyes dart over to Crastinus, and while he was unaware of the Centurion's specific instructions, he intuited that this wasn't something that had been covered on their walk to his office.

It wasn't much of a pause, then Pullus answered earnestly, "And I'll be ready, sir, whenever Rome needs me and wherever I'm needed."

This was exactly what Caesar had hoped for, and he said as much. "This is what I wanted to hear. I must confess," he glanced at Crastinus, "when I was told that a young *Gregarius* was being selected as the weapons instructor for their Cohort, I was a little hesitant to approve. But the judgment of the Pilus Prior has been confirmed in a way that leaves no doubt." It was easy to see that this pleased Pullus, but Crastinus looked almost as satisfied, which was understandable. Caesar concluded the meeting. "Well, I just wanted to meet the young *Gregarius* I had heard so much about in the last couple of days. I will be keeping my eyes on you, Pullus. I expect great things in the coming years."

Offering a salute in dismissal, Caesar stood and watched the pair as they marched out with a thoughtful expression, and while it would be the first time, it would be far from the last that what crossed his mind in this moment was the thought, If I had a hundred men like that boy, there would be no limit to what I could accomplish.

Pullus wasn't surprised when he received a warning from Crastinus as they returned to the Cohort area.

"Don't go getting a big head now, boy. I'll knock the *cac* out of you if you mess up."

Despite the words, Pullus could see that Crastinus was almost as proud of him as he was of himself, and he had to smother a grin as he answered, "Yes, Pilus Prior."

Not surprisingly, he was surrounded by his tentmates, who plied him with questions about Caesar, which Calienus allowed for a bit before reminding them that they needed to resume packing. As pleasantly as his day began, later that evening, Pullus was reminded that such moments were fleeting. After the meal and sensing that he wasn't wanted, Didius had gotten up, using the excuse that he wanted to find a good dice game, while Calienus, knowing what was coming, also excused himself, telling them that he was going to have a cup with Rufio. Domitius waited only long enough for their comrades to be out of earshot before he broached the subject that had been on all of their minds.

"I'm not willing to see Didius scourged and crucified," he began. With a shake of his head, he continued, "But we can't let this kind of thing go unpunished."

"What do you have in mind?"

Domitius didn't immediately reply to Scribonius' question, but he finally responded, "I've been thinking about it, and the most obvious solution would be to beat him so badly he would never consider doing something like that again." He paused again, gauging the others' reaction, then added, "But I don't think we can do that."

"Why not?" Remus demanded indignantly, and with a heat that the others understood since his brother was still in the hospital tent. "What else will work with that bastard? You know how he is! That's the only thing he understands, brute force."

"And are you ready to answer all the questions that will come when he shows up on the list?" Domitius countered quietly. Shaking his head, he said flatly, "Because I'm not."

Remus opened his mouth to argue, but then shut it; after a heartbeat, he muttered, "No, I suppose not. But it's just...wrong."

"Which is why I don't think he should go unpunished," Domitius assured him. He paused to see if anyone else had a suggestion, and when they didn't, he offered, "But if we shun him, and," he warned, "I mean we don't even allow him in the tent and force him to look for someplace else to sleep, I think..." he stopped, shook his head and amended, "...no, I *hope* that that will be enough of a message for him not to do it again."

Stopping again, he watched the others absorbing this, heartened to see that the heads of his tentmates were nodding up and down.

Not surprising any of them, it was Scribonius who got to the heart of the matter, asking simply, "How long?"

This, Domitius was prepared for, so without hesitation, he answered, "A month."

He ignored the sudden intake of breath from the others, but Pullus' gasp of surprise caused Domitius to glare at his friend.

However, it was Vellusius who spoke up, asking doubtfully, "A month? I don't know about that."

Irritated at what he viewed as a lack of support, Domitius shot back, "Anything less than that isn't going to work, I know it!"

"I don't think there's any way to know if it will be or not,"

Scribonius interjected, although he used the tone that always seemed to soothe the fraying tempers of the moment. "And," he said with quiet confidence, "I think a month is going to draw the attention of Rufio at the very least, and most likely Crastinus. Then there are going to be the kind of questions that we didn't want coming up in the first place."

Domitius felt the scrutiny of everyone else, and his first instinct was to argue, but then he relented, grudgingly.

"Fine," he grumbled. "So how long do you think it should be?"

"I think no more than a week," Scribonius replied.

Once more, Domitius was disposed to argue, but a quick glance at the others told him that he was alone, with even Pullus siding with the others.

"All right," he muttered. However, it wasn't in Domitius' nature to acquiesce without a fight, and he warned the others, "But when that turns out to not be nearly enough, don't forget who told you that!"

Pullus beat everyone else, assuring his friend, "Don't worry. I know you; you'll never let us."

As Pullus had hoped, the others erupted in laughter, and while it irritated Domitius, he had never been able to stay angry at his best friend, and after a heartbeat, he joined in.

Didius had certainly sensed the mood of his tentmates, and for the first time, he was frightened by the coldness and disdain they were showing him. He realized that he had gone too far, and while a part of him yearned to at least try and explain what had taken place, at least with Atilius, the only man who would have anything to do with him at all, and that was reduced to grunted responses to anything Didius said, he also was too ashamed to do it. As the raw fear and horror evoked by that nighttime stand receded as the predominant emotion, Didius had been forced to confront the fact that he had exaggerated the severity of his condition for the second time. How, he thought miserably, can any of them trust me after that? In at least one slight blessing from Fortuna, it had become clear to him that his tentmates hadn't mentioned anything to the other sections in the First, or in any of the other Centuries, which at least enabled him to spend time at other fires, where he had adopted what he considered the wise policy of losing more than he won at dice, for the time being anyway.

What compounded Didius' shame was Pullus' exploits of that night, because they were the talk of everyone in the Second Cohort, so that no matter where he went, he was plied with questions about what he had heard from Pullus himself. Because he had followed his plan of rousing himself once it got dark, Didius had been standing on the wall a few paces away from Pullus, witnessing the confrontation between Calienus and Pullus, and had heard the Sergeant's warning about a flogging. This put Didius in a good mood throughout the night, and he was happy that it was dark so that his comrades couldn't see his broad grin at the thought since he was certain they would guess the cause. But that had been before everything else happened, and although he hadn't personally witnessed it, by the time the sun came up, while Pullus lay stretched out more unconscious than asleep, Didius had heard more than he ever wanted about what that big bastard had done. Nevertheless, there was also the part of him that was happy about Pullus' exploits, because it meant that he hadn't been forced to confront a screaming barbarian charging at him out of the darkness. Although he didn't know exactly what was happening on the evening after their return to the main camp with his tentmates, he was certain that it had to do with him, but when he returned to the tent when the *bucina* sounded the preparatory command before the call to retire, he was confronted with a sight that, while not quite as terrifying as facing the Lusitani, was close to it. Arraying themselves in a manner that blocked his path to their tent, it was their manner, most of them with crossed arms as they regarded him coldly, that gave him a presentiment of some sort of catastrophe. He was expecting that it would be Pullus who would speak; instead, it was Domitius, which he instantly understood made more sense, and who he implicitly understood was speaking on behalf of the entire section.

"You know what this is about, Didius," Domitius began; Didius' first instinct was to argue, and he actually opened his mouth, but he quickly read in the expressions of the others that this would just make whatever was coming worse. Seeing that

Didius was at least not going to argue, Domitius continued, "You chose to take yourself out of the fight...again, and we've decided that this is unacceptable. By regulations, we should have reported this to the Pilus Prior." While Didius was cognizant of what the regulations stated, the true import of what this meant hit him for the first time, making his legs suddenly feel so weak that he worried they might collapse. Domitius went on, his voice still hard and unyielding, although his words gave Didius a sense of hope. "But while we don't approve of what you did and won't tolerate it, none of us want to see you scourged and crucified for cowardice in battle." Instinctively, Didius' eyes went immediately to Pullus, expecting to see an expression of disappointment at his close comrade's temperance, but to his surprise, Pullus' face was unreadable. Now, Domitius did pause to take a glance to either side, and Didius could see each of them give a faint nod before Domitius turned back to him. "We've decided that you're going to have to find another tent to sleep, and another fire to eat at for the next week."

Didius felt the blood drain from his face, but what was most astonishing to him was that, instead of raging at them, and threatening them, what he heard come out of his mouth was to ask meekly, "May I go get my gear?"

Domitius actually looked embarrassed, mumbling, "Of course," as he and the others stepped aside.

He was truly surprised that at least one of them didn't follow him inside to make sure that he didn't do anything to their property out of spite, but Didius was so shaken that it never occurred to him. Keeping his head down, he exited the tent, and taking the shortcut between his former tent and that of the Eighth Section, he only stopped once the tent blocked their view of him so that they couldn't see him blinking away the tears.

"Do you have any idea where you're going to go?"

The sound of Atilius' voice made Didius jump, and his hands were full so he couldn't wipe his eyes, so he remained with his back to his close comrade.

"Did you vote for this?" Didius demanded without looking back at Atilius.

"No," Atilius answered quietly, but while he could have left

156

it at that, he added, "but I didn't vote against it either. I just didn't vote."

"I bet that bastard Pullus is happy," Didius said bitterly; he was surprised, almost shocked in fact when Atilius disagreed.

"I don't think he is, and I know nobody else is happy about this, Didius," Atilius replied. "But they felt like they had to do give you a warning." Since Didius didn't know what to say, he didn't respond, but Atilius wasn't through. "I talked to Plautius," he said quietly, "and you can eat and sleep with his section at least for tonight."

"T-thank you, Atilius."

When there was no answer, he glanced over his shoulder, but Atilius was gone, so Didius made his way to the Third Section tent.

Calienus' dilemma was similar to Didius', yet despite the fact that it was for a completely different reason, Calienus didn't feel that way, and he assiduously avoided Pullus as much as possible, the only exception being meals and when they retired for the night. It was the evening of the second day of their resumed march when Pullus, finally having grown tired of Calienus' behavior, asked to speak privately with the Sergeant as the meal was being prepared. Calienus was sorely tempted to say no, but he also recognized that he couldn't put this off forever, so, while he made it clear he was reluctant, he rose and followed Pullus out into the Century street, the pair walking far enough away not to be overheard.

Rounding on Calienus, Pullus demanded, "Why are you angry with me? What did I do wrong?"

While Calienus hadn't been sure what to expect, the way Pullus automatically assumed that it was something that Pullus had done surprised the Sergeant.

More to stall for time, Calienus asked, "Who says I'm angry?"

"I do," Pullus retorted. "You haven't said more than two words to me since the other day."

"That's not true." Calienus knew how lame the words sounded, yet he said them anyway. "It's been more than that."

This didn't deter Pullus in the least.

"Fine. You've said three words. Is that better?"

Calienus recognized this as Pullus' attempt at humor, but under the big man's scrutiny, Calienus was still unwilling to discuss the matter, something that Pullus clearly sensed because, without another word, he turned about and began stalking away.

Before he could stop himself, Calienus called out, "Wait, Pullus."

For a moment, it didn't seem as if Pullus would do so, taking a couple more strides before stopping. Calienus saw Pullus take a breath, then turn and walk back to him, while Calienus tried to think of what he would say.

"Believe it or not," he began, "I'm not angry with you." Pausing, he copied Pullus by taking a breath before admitting, "I'm angry with me."

Now, it was Pullus' turn to be surprised, yet he was also confused to the point he shook his head as he repeated, "With yourself? But why? You're not the one who disobeyed an order."

This was the moment Calienus had been dreading, although he was surprised that it didn't feel as painful as he had thought it would when he replied, "But I should have." Shaking his head, he couldn't keep his disgust with himself from his voice. "I knew it then, that you were doing the right thing." Unable to look Pullus in the eye, Calienus studied the dirt street as he admitted, "But instead, I chose to hide behind the fact that we were given orders to stay where we were, rather than jump into a fight where I was needed."

Calienus hoped this would be enough for Pullus, but it wasn't, although not for the reason Calienus expected.

"But why?" Pullus seemed genuinely bewildered. "You were doing what you were supposed to do, but if you knew what I was doing was right, why didn't you come with me?"

Growing angry at Pullus' seeming obtuseness, Calienus shot back, "Why do you think?" Once again, his hope that Pullus comprehended what he was confessing without saying the words was a vain one, because the *Gregarius* was still obviously mystified. Closing his eyes, Calienus' voice dropped to a near whisper. "I was too scared to, Titus." He was surprised that now that the words were out, the next ones came more easily. "I didn't know what was going on, that's true, but I've been in enough fights to know that this was a bad one. And," he looked back down at the ground, admitting, "my nerve failed me."

Pullus' reaction deeply surprised Calienus, because the large *Gregarius* took a step closer to Calienus so that he was towering above his Sergeant, and to Calienus, it looked as if Pullus was angry.

"No," Pullus snapped. "That's a pile of *cac*. Your nerve didn't fail you. You did the smart thing." Sneering, Pullus argued, "What Didius did? *That* is someone whose nerve failed. If," Pullus' tone altered slightly, "he has any to begin with." Pullus put a hand on Calienus' shoulder, and it was an oddly comforting gesture as the Sergeant thought, this should be the other way around. "Calienus, you did nothing to be ashamed of. By the end of the night, you got your *gladius* as bloody as any man there."

"Not as bloody as yours," Calienus replied with a rueful laugh.

Pullus grinned down at him. "That's true. But nobody has ever accused me of being smart." Suddenly, he thrust his arm out, which Calienus accepted with a lump in his throat, neither man speaking for a moment as they clasped arms. Pullus broke the silence. "Well, at least I'm happy to know that it's not me you're angry with." Turning back in the direction of their tent, Pullus said as he walked away, "Now, let's get back before those greedy bastards eat all the chickpeas."

Before he moved to follow his comrade, Calienus called to Pullus.

When he turned, Calienus asked anxiously, "You won't mention this to any of the others? Even Domitius?"

Without a flicker of expression, Pullus asked blandly, "Mention what?"

He didn't wait for Calienus to answer, reminding Calienus that filling his stomach was a matter of utmost importance to Pullus, and with a smile, he followed behind. Although he didn't know it yet, Calienus' secret would be safe for the rest of his days.

Chapter Five

Caesar and his army continued north, entering the territory of a tribe that, to that point in time, the Romans had had little contact with, meaning that they were known more by reputation than any real experience, which in turn meant that rumors ran rampant about these warlike people called the Gallaeci. And, not surprising to the veterans like Calienus and Crastinus, the more lurid tales about the Gallaeci and their barbarity were immediately considered the most credible by the *Gregarii*, meaning that stories of blood drinking, or the consumption of their enemies' flesh soon dominated the fireside conversations at night. More worrying to the experienced men was the information, confirmed by the *exploratores*, that unlike the other Lusitani tribes they had faced to this point, the Gallaeci used horses to a much larger extent, although it was the manner in which they did so that created a practical challenge.

"It looks like they've gone mad, just galloping their horses in a big loop, round and round and round," Crastinus explained at the meeting of the Century officers he had called in his tent after coming from the *praetorium*. "But when they're passing closest to their enemy, that's when they launch their missiles. Between the movement and all the dust they churn up, they're almost impossible to see, and they're moving too fast for us to hit with our own javelins."

As the Romans would learn, hearing about it was one thing; experiencing it was altogether different. Fortunately, over the previous weeks, Caesar had at least partially corrected his deficiency in cavalry, and once the army had endured a handful of this type of attack, the men learned that the trick was to react quickly, dropping their packs and raising their shields in a defensive position, then endure the onslaught until the Roman cavalry arrived to drive them off. As Crastinus and the other

Centurions were quick to point out, because of their reliance on missile weapons, the Gallaeci horsemen were more of a nuisance since they didn't have heavily armored mounted troops to exploit any kind of advantage they created through their shower of missiles. The only real gain on the part of the Gallaeci was in slowing the Roman advance, but inevitably, they neared the southern bank of the Durius (Douro) River and the northernmost Roman colony, Portus Cale (Grando Porte, Portugal), which was now occupied by the enemy. Normally, the Bracari and Lucenses, the two largest branches of the Gallaeci tribe, hated each other, but in a sign of how much more they hated Rome, they had formed a confederation and it had been these two branches who had assaulted and taken Portus Cale.

The day before, the army, now consisting of three Legions, arrived at the Durius, the Gallaeci burned down the wooden bridge in an attempt to forestall the Roman advance. It was a desperate, and ultimately futile move because Caesar wasted no time in building a pontoon bridge, but by the time it was created, there was only time for the 9th Legion to cross, whereupon they immediately created a fortified camp, settling down to wait through the night for the rest of the army to join them. Around the fires that night, there was much speculation about what the men considered to be the most likely act by their foes, a nighttime attack on the lone Legion separated from help by the river. Certainly, if the situation for the 9th became extreme, Caesar would not hesitate in ordering the men of the 7th and 10th to cross the pontoon bridge in the dark, but it was highly unstable because of its construction, which was nothing more than boats lashed together, with planks thrown down to serve as a makeshift roadway, and there was little doubt that men would lose their footing and pitch into the swiftly running river and sink to the bottom because of their armor and equipment, especially in the dark. There *was* an attack that night, but not against the 9th; instead, the enemy sent a number of fire rafts downriver so that, by the time the midnight watch was starting, the pontoon bridge was a fully involved, raging inferno, each boat burning down to the waterline, while the cables lashing them together were incinerated, separating the burning hulks, which went drifting downriver and out to the sea more than a mile away.

While it was successful, it was also a desperate attempt that only forestalled what every man marching for Caesar knew was inevitable, and as usual, he wasted no time. With the 9th in their fortified camp on the same side of the river as the town, Caesar sent the 7th to scour the countryside for raw materials to construct another wooden bridge, which was found a half-day's march away. Time was of the essence because, when the 9th had crossed the river, they only had three days' rations, and once the 7th returned with the timber, both Legions were put to work. Even so, it was a close-run thing; on the fourth day after the pontoon bridge was destroyed, the 10th marched across the new bridge, relieving the 9th, while the defenders in the town could only watch helplessly. The one event of note was that, on the second day, the Lucenses tribesmen chose to abandon Portus Cale, leaving their Bracari brethren behind to defend the town. However, rather than stopping to reduce Porto Cale, Caesar chose to leave the 7th Legion behind to conduct the siege. With only one Legion, it would take longer, of course, but the general decided that it was worth being able to continue their pursuit of the Lucenses at the same time.

Because the Lucenses had a two-day head start, Caesar set a blistering pace, but by this point in the campaign, his men were inured to the hardship, even with the undulating terrain that was a feature of the northern part of the province. Finally, two days into their pursuit, they drew within sight of the tail end of the Lucenses column, and for a brief period, it seemed as if the Lucenses had grown tired of being harried, because they came to a stop atop a hill just a mile north, which prompted Caesar to sound the halt to change from their marching column into their battle formation. It was during this process, as the 9th moved up from their spot at the rear of the column to align alongside the 10th that one of the Roman scouts came galloping back to the column to report the likely reason for the Lucenses choosing to fight. Since the 10th Legion was the leading Legion of the two-Legion column, the men of the Second Cohort were fairly near Caesar and his command party; not close enough to hear, but able to see that the rider's horse was heavily lathered, while the man was obviously excited about something. It was when he turned in the saddle and pointed to the northeast that it caused Crastinus to follow the pointing finger with his own eyes, and before he could stop himself, he swore aloud.

"It looks like those barbarian *cunni* are being reinforced," he commented bitterly, but he used his head to nod in the direction the scout had indicated, trying to keep his voice down but not enough so that every man in the Century heard.

As usually happened, the men of the Tenth Section relied on Pullus and his height to see above his comrades in the leading ranks, although it took a few heartbeats as he strained his eyes before, finally, he informed his comrades, "I *think* I see a dust trail, a big one."

This, in fact, was the case; whether by accident or by design, as Caesar and his men watched, the pursued Lucenses were joined by a second column that almost doubled their numbers. They outnumbered the Romans now, not significantly, but it did preclude Caesar from pressing his attack, and instead, he ordered the army to retreat back to a hill that they had just traversed, following the ancient adage that a defender should always take advantage of the high ground, where they awaited developments. Despite the reinforcements, just as Caesar had, the Lucenses chieftain ultimately decided against pressing an attack, although once the two columns joined, they did array for battle, spreading out along the hill across the narrow valley separating them as the barbarian leaders presumably talked matters over. Not unexpectedly, the atmosphere was tense at first, but as time dragged by, the sun seemingly crawling across the sky more slowly than normal, the Romans began to relax as it became apparent that the Lucenses were not particularly eager. Then, with perhaps a full watch of daylight left, there was a flurry of movement on the opposite hill, except that, instead of advancing towards the waiting Romans, the Lucenses turned about and descended the far slope, heading north. There would be no battle that day...nor the next, or the one after that. Instead, the combined enemy force resumed their march north, paralleling the coast, with Caesar's army following, leaving his men, of all ranks, speculating on why their general did not seem to be in much of a hurry to close with them.

The previous days of Didius' banishment had been hard on
him, not only because of the inconvenience of being forced to
find a new place to sleep, but the frequency with which he had
to do it as he learned that his unpopularity was not just with his
tentmates. On some level, Spurius Didius had always been
aware that others considered him disagreeable, but the truth was
that he had not cared all that much; at least, before he was under
the standard that had been the case. Now, however, it was
different, and there were practical considerations, the most
important being because his life depended on the men around
him. Of his tentmates, only Atilius had anything to do with him,
and more than once, Didius almost blurted out how much it
meant to him that Atilius was willing to be seen with him; not
until later did Didius learn that Domitius, Romulus, and Remus
had expressed their objections that he was doing so. Still, while
he almost did so on numerous occasions, he never actually
adequately expressed his appreciation, although he would offer
a muttered thanks whenever Atilius handed him a hunk of
bread, or occasionally, sneaked a bowl of soldier's porridge to
him. What surprised Didius the most was that Pullus had not
done like his close comrade and the brothers, choosing to
remain silent about what Atilius was doing; in fact, it would not
be for almost two decades that Didius would learn that it had
been Pullus who quietly urged Atilius to maintain contact with
Pullus' nemesis. It was his relationship with the men of the
other nine sections of the First Century and how they really
viewed him that proved to be an eye-opening experience for
Didius, and while he did not have an understanding of the term,
it drove Didius into a dark depression. Once, that is, his initial
reaction, a feeling of deep anger, wore off, and he was forced
to recognize and accept that one reason why he fell back on
being angry as his usual first response was because he was more
comfortable with this emotion than any other feeling.

Never prone to introspection, this period of time found
Didius thinking about his life more than he ever had previously,
and there was one realization that stuck with him. He had been
angry for most of his life; he woke up angry and went to sleep
at night angry, and in the intervening watches between those

two, most of that time was spent in a state of heightened irritation at the very least. And, as he was learning, his sour disposition wore on his comrades to a point that he could count on spending no more than a single night curled up in a corner of a tent not his own. During the day, of course, he was in his normal spot in the marching column as they continued their pursuit of the Lucenses, where he was largely ignored by his tentmates, except for Atilius, who now marched to his right, in between Didius and Scribonius.

Thankfully, as far as Didius was concerned, large part of their focus, and ire, centered on the fact that they spent virtually no time on level ground; they were either struggling uphill or trying to avoid careening downhill, reduced to catching just a quick glimpse of their enemy if they happened to crest one of the never-ending hills at the same time as the Lucenses, still no more than two miles ahead of them, occupying most of their attention and the resulting complaining. Then, after three days of this, the monotony was broken when, instead of a vista of an unbroken series of ridges stretching across their line of march, they were confronted by the gleam produced by sunlight on the water of a river that emptied out into the great sea off to their left that they had never been out of sight of for days. Compounding matters was the presence of a good-sized fortified town on the opposite bank, built on a hill that offered a commanding view of the river, although there was no bridge. Instead, as the Romans increased their marching pace in a vain attempt to reach the southern bank to stop them, the Lucenses used dozens of flat-bottomed boats to ferry their warriors, livestock, and supplies across the river, called the Minus (Guadiana) River. Even without the presence of a town where the southern rampart was close enough for archers positioned on the wall to rain missiles down on their heads, a pontoon bridge like the one they constructed at Portus Cale was out of the question because of the proximity to the sea, creating a current that was too swift and strong for the boats that would be required for construction. Consequently, Caesar marched the army inland in search of either a fordable spot, or barring that, a suitable site for a bridge. To forestall the possibility of the enemy rowing back across the river and falling on their rear, once they were upriver far enough to be out of sight of even the part of the town on the uppermost slope of the hill, the Eighth, Ninth, and Tenth Cohorts of the 10th were left behind and ordered to construct a fortified camp on the opposite slope from the town, but with an outpost that would be constantly manned at a spot where they had a view of the town. The rest of the army ended up marching ten miles inland before a suitable spot was found for a bridge, and to nobody's surprise, they were followed by their enemies on the opposite bank, meaning that what the Romans were up to was no secret. Their presence made the first order of business for Caesar to have wooden platforms constructed in a line along the southern bank, upon which were placed their artillery pieces.

"We may not be able to keep them from watching," Crastinus had said with grim satisfaction, "but by the gods, they'll do it from a fucking distance or we'll skewer the *cunni*."

The other challenge was that Caesar's army, and the labor each man provided, had been substantially reduced, even since Portus Cale, with the 7th still besieging that town, while the 8th had been left behind even before that, and finally, with only seven Cohorts of the 10th available for labor. Accordingly, it took five full days to build the bridge rather than the two it would have taken with all four Legions present, although they were only harassed by the enemy on the first day, the Lucenses suffering heavy losses from the Roman scorpions in the process. For Didius, however, what was most important was that, it was at the end of the first day, after working all day with his section in what he now accepted as the customary silence from his comrades, and without any indication beforehand that circumstances had changed, Calienus grabbed the sleeve of his tunic as they were heading back to the camp.

"Where's your gear?" the Sergeant asked him.

Caught by surprise, Didius was forced to think for a moment, then he said, "With the Third Section."

This clearly startled Calienus, and Didius understood why when, with some evident embarrassment, Calienus muttered, "Oh. I thought that you and Glabrio had a...disagreement."

"We did," Didius admitted, then explained quietly, "I meant the Third of the Second."

"You've been staying with the Second Century?" Calienus gasped, suddenly feeling ashamed that he had allowed matters to get to this point, where Didius had been forced to go outside the Century.

"Only last night." Didius shrugged, but he pointedly looked away in what might have been a quiet rebuke.

"Well," Calienus said, more harshly than he intended, "go get it and come back to our tent." He paused, then added, "Where you belong."

Even if Didius had known what to say, he could not have done so because of the sudden lump in his throat, but it was the sudden stinging of his eyes that caused him to spin about.

Before he had gone more than a couple steps, Calienus called out to him, waiting for Didius to turn back to face him before he said, "I hope you learned your lesson, Didius, because you're not going to get a second chance. You know that, yes?"

Didius nodded, then realized that Calienus was expecting more, and he answered tersely, "Yes, Sergeant."

There was a part of him that was angry at Calienus' words, but in what was a rarity for Spurius Didius, the happiness outweighed the anger by a good measure, and he was grinning broadly as he headed for the Second Century.

Once the bridge across the Minus was finished, Caesar led the 9th and 10th across, while the three Cohorts of the third line of the 10th were forced to hurry upriver to attach themselves to the end of the marching column. Once across the river and reversing their direction of march back towards the coast, Caesar's army had traversed five of the ten miles back to the enemy town when the Lucenses attempted an ambush of the Fifth Cohort of the 9th, the leading element of the column, but the attack was repelled with minimal losses. While it was not enough to stop the Romans, it was enough to delay them, and they arrived outside the eastern wall of the town too late in the day to begin preparations for a siege. For what many of the men swore was the hundredth time, they found themselves constructing another fortified marching camp within sight of enemy walls which, as usual, were lined by the occupants of the town, watching the Romans working. As the Romans labored, it gave them the opportunity to perform their own examination of what they were facing, and none of them, from the hoariest veterans to the men like those of the Tenth Section, were encouraged by what they saw. Unlike the other towns they had assaulted to this point, the walls of this one were made of native stone, while the buildings of the town occupied a shelf of relatively flat ground, although there were a couple blocks that occupied the slope just above the shelf that were clearly of more recent construction. The rest of the slope, however, above the northern wall that bisected the hill, was bare, although this earned nothing more than a cursory glance from the rankers. Calienus summed it up that night as they sat around the fire, with Didius now back in his customary spot next to Atilius.

"That's going to be a real bastard to take," he said disgustedly, earning nods and murmurs of assent from the rest of the section.

They were interrupted then by the appearance of Rufio, who dropped to his haunches before he began, and while they had been expecting a visit from either the Optio or the Pilus Prior, none of them were prepared for what came out of his mouth.

"We're looking for volunteers," he began, ignoring the muttered comments that were essentially identical to what he had heard from the other sections already. Honestly, he was not irritated, he was amused, thinking, You boys have no idea what's coming. Continuing, he explained, "Caesar is looking for men with experience in..." twisting at the waist, he pointed up at the dark, looming bulk of the top of the hill above the town, "...climbing something like that."

Just as had occurred with the other nine sections, the initial reaction from the Tenth was thunderstruck silence; it was broken by Domitius, who asked, "Why?"

"I don't know," Rufio admitted with a shrug. "Just that Caesar wants about two Cohorts worth of men if possible." Thinking of something, he added, "Oh, and they need to be experienced in carrying a load while they're doing it."

"But...why?" Domitius persisted.

"It doesn't matter why," Rufio snapped. "What does matter is that Caesar has ordered us to find volunteers."

"How many of us have volunteered?" Calienus asked, more

to divert Domitius than for any real interest.

"Just seven," Rufio answered, his tone betraying his unhappiness at what he clearly thought of as a paltry showing by the First Century.

"I'll do it," Atilius spoke up, but despite the low number of volunteers, Rufio asked doubtfully, "I thought you grew up in Corduba. What do you know about climbing mountains?"

"Among other places," Atilius agreed, but he was not particularly eager to explain that his skill at scaling heights was limited to climbing up the outside of an *insula* to take advantage of a carelessly open window he had spotted when he was passing by, then descending with whatever he managed to steal. Consequently, he was deliberately vague, but he lied, "I can climb while carrying some sort of load. That's what Caesar is asking for, isn't he?"

That was not something Rufio could deny, so he did not try; instead, he stood up and said briskly, "Good. Get into your armor, but you won't need your shield. Just bring your javelins and come to my tent as soon as you're ready."

That was when it happened.

"I'm coming too."

Rufio had already begun walking back to his tent, and he whirled about in a state close to shock, but he was far from alone, as the rest of the section were gaping up in astonishment at Didius, who had come to his feet.

"You? You're...volunteering?"

The firelight was sufficient for Rufio to see that his question affected Didius, but not that he was angry at being questioned, which was as much of a surprise as the fact that Spurius Didius was volunteering for something in the first place, although Rufio did see a trace of defiance in the man's swarthy features.

"Atilius is my close comrade," Didius offered with a shrug. "I'm going with him."

Not knowing what else to say, Rufio nodded at the section tent and muttered, "Then hurry up and get your armor on."

As soon as they entered their tent, Atilius turned on Didius, demanding in a whisper, "Why are you doing this? You never volunteer for anything!"

It was not something that Didius could argue, so he did not

even try, but neither was he willing to divulge the real reason, that he wanted to repay his close comrade for the kindness Atilius had shown him.

What he came up with was a shrug, followed by a lame lie. "I'm bored. Besides," he changed the subject, "we both know I can carry more than you can."

"We don't know what we're going to be carrying," Atilius pointed out, his voice muffled by his armor as he dropped it over his head.

"It doesn't matter," Didius replied as he followed suit. "Whatever it is, I can carry more of it."

They strapped on their *baltea*, but Atilius had to remind Didius to leave his shield behind, then the pair emerged where their comrades were still sitting around the fire. Nobody said a word at first, until Atilius and Didius began to head for Rufio's tent, when Calienus called out, "Don't do anything foolish and get back here in one piece." After a pause, he added, "That goes for both of you."

The others echoed Calienus, perhaps with differing degrees of genuineness, but for once, Didius chose to believe that their comrades were all sincere.

Caesar had immediately spotted the weakness in the layout of the town, and he wasted no time in exploiting it. Once it got dark, and under the command of one of his Legates and the Octus Pilus Prior of the 9th Legion, more than a thousand men slipped out of the camp, moving north and using a ravine that separated the hill upon which the town was located from a lower hill to the east that paralleled the Minus. The pace was slow, deliberately so, both to minimize the noise and because the human eye is drawn by movement, even in the dark, and what Caesar had planned required complete and utter surprise. Before they had traveled a few furlongs, Didius was chastising himself, albeit ruefully, both because of his impulsive decision to accompany Atilius, and his constant boasting about his strength meant that he was carrying one of the heaviest pieces of equipment, the lower frame of one of the four *ballistae* that they were carrying with them. Along with the *ballistae*, they were carrying more than half of the two remaining Legion's complement of scorpions, with Atilius carrying a leather bag containing the iron-tipped wooden bolts for the smaller weapon. There was no talking, of course, so the only noise was the creaking of leather bits of gear, punctuated by the cracking sound of hobnails on the rocks of what was a dry watercourse, although this was quickly joined by the harsher breathing as the slope steepened. About a third of a watch after they departed, the head of the column reached the top of the ravine, and a brief halt was called before they turned back in the direction of the coast, which was a bit more than a mile away. They were now on the back side of the hill, shielded from view from the town, even if it had been daylight, by the bulk of it towering above them.

While talking was forbidden, it was also next to impossible to keep men from whispering to each other, having long before perfected the art of making sure their officers were out of earshot, and it was Atilius, who, staring up at what looked to him more like a mountain than a hill, whispered, "That looks a lot steeper from here."

Didius had been thinking the exact same thing, but he tried to sound unworried.

"It's probably because of the dark, that's all."

As they all quickly learned, it was *not* because of the darkness, but this too was something Caesar had foreseen and for which he had planned. It had escaped the pair's notice that the burdened men were not all carrying pieces of artillery, ammunition, or extra javelins. More than a hundred were carrying lengths of rope, looped around their upper body, while about half as many men were loaded down with leather bags filled with iron stakes that had loops at one end, and they all had iron hammers in their *balteae*. Unnoticed by almost every other man in the party, these men had been placed at the head of the column, and had been handpicked by their Centurions, exclusively from the last three Cohorts of the 9th, because of their arcane skills. Like the 10th, the men of the 9th came exclusively from Hispania, and like the 7th, 8th, and 10th, were referred to as the Spanish Legions by the rest of the Roman army. What made the men of the Eighth, Ninth, and Tenth Cohorts of the 9th different was that a large number of them came from around the Mons Pyrenai region, south of Lugdunum, and they eked out a living as herders, miners, and more commonly, smugglers, using torturous tracks through the steep and rugged mountains of the region.

Wrapping cloth around the head of the iron stakes to muffle the sound, they hammered them into cracks in the rock, then threaded one of the ropes through the open eye of the stake, creating a handhold for the men struggling up the hill behind them. The going was slow, but both Didius and Atilius, like the rest of their comrades, were grateful for the extra security, grabbing the rope with their free hand and pulling themselves, one step at a time, up the hill. It did not go all their way; very quickly, it became apparent that they were in a race against the sun, and Didius found himself glancing to his left every few steps, trying to determine if the slight lightening he thought he saw on the eastern horizon was his imagination. Like many of the others, Didius also discovered something else; he could not switch hands between his load and the rope, and it became a question whether or not he would drop the heavy piece of wood before they reached the top because of the fatigue in his right arm, and the cramping of his hand. He would not have been the only one; ahead of him, and off to his right, where a parallel set of ropes had been strung up the slope, he heard a crashing noise, although the cry of frustration from the unfortunate ranker who had lost his grip was quickly stifled. His vision was blurred from the sweat pouring down into his eyes, and more than once, he cursed himself for his hubris, but he forced one foot in front of the other, trying to ignore the screaming pain of his thighs. Then, just in front of him, Atilius lost his footing, and Didius was forced to make a choice.

The rest of the army was roused two parts of a watch before dawn, though not by the *bucina* but by the officers moving from tent to tent, whereupon they broke their fast, although fires had been forbidden since the Lucenses could look down into the camp from the town walls. Fortunately, light was not necessary for them to make ready, and less than a third of a watch later, the bulk of the 9th and 10th, minus the men scaling the hill, exited the camp and marched out a short distance into the space between their camp and the eastern wall of the town. The artillery that had been left behind was moved into position, with the scorpions arrayed in front of the leading ranks, while their crews staked out the legs and set up their aiming stakes. By this point in the campaign, Caesar's army was accustomed to his habit of making certain that they were deployed and ready to begin their assault, and whenever possible, from the east, before the sun was fully up. They had learned the value of this tactic, both from the practical standpoint that meant the rising sun would shine directly into the collective eyes of the defenders, but also from the subtler aspect of what it did to the enemy's morale to see the neatly ordered ranks of the Legions of Rome, ready and waiting as the sun rose and illuminated them.

Because of the smaller size of the army, Caesar had the 9th and 10th arrayed in an *acies duplex* instead of the normal three lines, while the men were allowed to ground their shields as they waited for the sun to peek over the horizon. Naturally, the top of the hill was illuminated first, and while the Pili Priores had related what Caesar had planned, they had also given their men very specific instructions, and it just happened that Scribonius' attention was not on the ramparts but higher up to the part of the town built on the slope as he wondered what it would be like fighting from block to block, uphill. While his eye was caught by movement, it was not in the town, but he remembered Crastinus' admonition just in time and did not turn his head upward as Caesar's surprise began to unfold. They continued to keep their attention on the rampart as their comrades atop the hill began setting up the artillery, and what became apparent was that the Lucenses arrayed along the eastern wall were, understandably, completely absorbed by the sight of the two Legions before them and nothing else. As normal, Caesar was mounted, wearing his cuirass, *paludamentum*, and helmet with the black plume of the commander, surrounded by men of his staff. Seeing his men on the heights, Caesar nodded to the Tribune next to him, who lofted a javelin, upon which a square of white bandage was affixed, then nudged his mount forward, heading for the eastern wall.

"At least he's not going by himself this time," Domitius

murmured.

There was no need for him to make any further reference back to the occasion of the first town, when the Tribune performing the exact same task had been murdered. This time, the Tribune was accompanied by a party of ten, composed of some of Caesar's personal bodyguards that he had arrived with when he took the post of *Praetor*, and some of the cavalry troopers, but despite the protection, a hush fell over the ranks as they all watched tensely, waiting for, and expecting, another act of treachery. The Tribune's party arrived at the eastern gate, while a helmeted and armored Lucenses stepped up onto the crenellation in an almost identical fashion as the leader had the first time, which only increased the tension. Then, from atop the hill and behind the Lucenses on the rampart, one of the *Signiferi* began waving his standard back and forth in an exaggerated fashion because of the distance, which prompted the mounted Tribune to suddenly extend one arm to point upward in their direction. They saw the Lucenses turn, and even with the distance between them, they could see the man's shoulder's slump, his head drop, then he turned to face the Tribune, giving the junior officer a nod. There was not a cheer, but the sudden exhalation of thousands of men who had been holding their breath to one degree or another was clearly audible, and to Pullus' ears, it sounded equally divided between relief and disappointment between his comrades. He put himself in the latter group; there had been no action of any kind since the ambush, and he was discovering that this lack was making him irritable and anxious, something he had only divulged to Domitius.

"Tell me something I don't know." His friend had laughed, then added, "*Everyone* knows you've got an itch. And," he leered, "not for a woman."

That was not exactly true; he would have judged the itch for a woman to be commensurate with his craving for action, but Pullus also knew when Domitius was teasing him to get a reaction out of him, so he did not rise to the bait, taking satisfaction in the moment with Domitius' look of disappointment. But now, it appeared as if the battle for the town was over before it began, yet while this was more or less true, it did not mean that the excitement was over.

"What," Scribonius wondered with a yawn, "is taking so long?"

Pulled from his own thoughts, Pullus turned his attention to what was taking place at the wall, where the Tribune was now gesticulating furiously, jabbing a finger up at the Lucenses, who was still standing on the rampart and offering a series of vague gestures and shrugs. It was Caesar who, clearly sensing something was amiss, kicked his horse and cantered up to where the negotiations were taking place.

"Something's wrong, or else Caesar wouldn't be so worked up."

Scribonius' comment earned him a snarled rebuke from Crastinus, another sign that, suddenly, things were not as routine as they appeared. If anything, Caesar's gestures were even more emphatic than the Tribune's, but he was not in front of the wall long, spinning his horse about suddenly and coming back at the gallop, shouting for the *ballistae* to prepare to loose, aiming at the eastern gate. With every heavy piece focused on the gate, it did not take long to smash it into splinters, while the First Cohort, in a column of Centuries but in their battle spacing, went moving at a trot for the gateway, with the Second Cohort following right behind.

"Keep your intervals, you bastards!" Crastinus bellowed, over and over.

"Outer files, watch the wall as we enter the town!" Rufio shouted. "We don't need any of these *cunni* dropping rocks on our heads, so shout out if you see anything!"

Once through the gate, the First fanned out to the left, with the Second taking the right, but despite the tension arising from the knowledge that the Lucenses had some sort of surprise planned, once they entered the town, they found that it was almost completely deserted. The only able-bodied men had been the relative handful who had been manning the wall, all of whom had been rounded up and were now kneeling on the street. Crastinus led the First of the Second along the eastern wall until the street reached the point where the shelf ended and turned uphill, following the orders issued by Caesar to put anyone who could not fetch a price as a slave to the *gladius*. In further evidence that they had been duped, all they found were old people and the infirm who had been judged by their own people to be too much trouble to take with them, and they were all quickly dispatched. Meanwhile, a Cohort of the 9th who had been sent to the western side of the town solved the mystery of where not only the defenders but most of the townspeople had gone, finding a narrow street next to the western wall that dropped down to a small, sheltered cove.

For a second time, the Romans were treated to the sight of the last Lucenses ships disappearing to the north, though this time not crossing the river but putting out to sea, which the Romans learned was the sign that their foe had decided long before the sun came up that trying to defend the town was a forlorn hope. The one question asked around the fires that night concerned their force on the hill, and how they had missed what was essentially a fleet of enemy ships sailing away from the town; however, the explanation was simple, and for the most part was accepted without further question. The two Cohorts had been struggling up the hill in the dark, so even if they had been able to see the ships being loaded from their vantage point on the rear side of the hill, their attention had been on their own troubles. Then, once the sun came up, they had been occupied in setting up the artillery. Simply put, it was one of those things that happened in war, and while they were all angry, albeit to varying degrees, the Romans did have a grudging admiration for the guile of their enemy, even as they knew that it meant the pursuit would continue.

"He saved my bacon," Atilius said flatly that night, after their return from the hill. He saw, and understood, the looks of disbelief or doubt from most of his tentmates, which was why he had waited until Didius had gone to the latrines to tell his story. Ignoring this reaction, he went on, "I lost my grip on the rope on the steepest part of that fucking hill, and I fell backward and started sliding back down." He saw that they did not fully grasp the peril he had been in, and he realized that he would have had the same reaction; yes, it would be painful, but sliding back down over ground that you had already covered would not seem to be likely to get one killed, so he explained, "But I didn't slide straight back, but off at an angle because I grabbed at the rope and it swung me around, and there was a sheer drop off just a couple paces off to our left, and I was heading straight for it."

"How high?" Remus asked.

"I don't know exactly," Atilius admitted. "It was still dark, but it was high enough to kill me, because the same thing happened to another poor bastard farther down the column behind me, and he broke his neck."

"I heard we lost a half-dozen men in the 10th," Calienus interjected, "but none from the Second."

Atilius nodded in confirmation, then said grimly, "And I would have been one of them if it hadn't been for Didius."

"What happened?"

Atilius shrugged. "Honestly, I don't really know. Just that I was on my back sliding headfirst, and I heard some yelling, then I was hanging headfirst and upside down with nothing underneath me, but someone was holding on to one ankle with both hands. It turned out to be Didius."

"I thought he was carrying something," Romulus said with a frown, clearly unwilling to believe that Didius was the man responsible.

Atilius was normally slow to anger, but now he snapped at the brother, "He was, and he dropped it to keep me from going over the edge. And," he jabbed a finger at all of them, "he got thrashed for dropping it afterward!"

This was a surprise to all of them, but before anything could be said, Vellusius hissed a warning, having spotted Didius returning, who, sensing that something unusual was happening, slowed before reaching his spot.

"What?" he asked, suspicious, but also trying to hide his alarm as the thought came to him, *They're banishing me again!*

Calienus, sensing Didius' thoughts, stood, thrusting a stoppered jug into his hand as he said quietly, "Atilius just told us what you did for him, so you deserve this."

Taking the jug, Didius unstopped it, then without sniffing, took a swallow, his eyes widening as he coughed, then exclaimed, "This wine is unwatered! Where did you get it?"

"There wasn't much to pick over in this fucking town,"

Calienus replied, then with a grin, he added, "but you should know your Sergeant well enough by now. If there's something worth finding, I'll find it."

Didius knew, as did the others, that this was true, and he thanked Calienus. Dropping down next to Atilius, he did not say anything, nor did he demand to know what the others had been talking about before he arrived, though he was tempted. This was a marked difference from his behavior before his banishment; then, he would have belligerently demanded to know what his tentmates were saying about him. After taking a long draught, he handed the jug to Atilius, but when Atilius turned to extend the jug to Remus, who was sitting on the side opposite from Didius, Didius pointedly stopped him, taking the jug back, then glared at the brothers as he drained the jug. He was rewarded by a look of, if not shame, then acute embarrassment on the part of the pair who, save for Domitius, had been the most vocal about his banishment. A silence fell, but then the call to retire sounded, and they all got up to enter their tent, when the section got another shock, although Didius had not planned it that way. It was when he took his tunic off, and by the light of the one lamp that was kept lit inside the tent, until it was extinguished every night before the men slept, the raw, red and bloody welts on Didius' back were clearly visible.

"He had his armor on," Domitius whispered to Pullus, "so he must have gotten a right beating."

"And Atilius wouldn't lie about it anyway," Pullus replied. "It's true. Didius saved his life."

Didius heard it all, but he made no sign that he did; the sense of satisfaction he felt was enough reward, at least for now.

They did not spend any time at the town, nor did they leave part of the army behind to occupy it, setting out in pursuit of a trail that, because the Lucenses had escaped by ship, was a cold one. The terrain remained the same, so that they were either slogging uphill or forced to work to keep the wagons and carts carrying their baggage from hurtling downward, with the men using pulleys and ropes, and their combined weight, to act as a brake. On flat or slightly rolling terrain, Caesar's army had been conditioned to a degree so that they could cover between twenty-five and thirty miles in a day. Because of the hills, it took them four days to cover thirty miles, when the scouts came galloping back to the column to report that they had at last found the enemy. The Romans had reached a point where a bay cut into the coast directly north of their line of march, requiring them to turn east and move several miles inland before they could resume moving north. Out in the bay were a number of islands, with three small ones arranged from east to west, while beyond them and farther west was a pair of larger islands, which were in a north/south orientation. Following the contour of the bay that made a gentle curve inland, Caesar led the army along the coast, and as they advanced and drew even with the islands out in the bay, more details became clear. The larger of the two islands was shaped like a crescent, with the open end on the eastern side, and they could see the beach lined with ships, while some sort of fortifications had either been constructed a short distance inland from the beach, or perhaps they had already been there. While men were sent out to scour the area for usable boats, Caesar's scouts continued north, finding yet another island, this one even larger, with what was in essence a fortified town, obviously having been there for some time. Very quickly, it was also determined that there were not any usable ships to be found, and for an admittedly brief period, the men spent time speculating about their future, since none of them viewed crossing what they were told was at least five miles of open water with anything close to resembling eagerness.

It was an accepted belief, almost an article of faith that Romans were not meant for the sea, and there were conversations within every Century and Cohort that echoed the one Domitius and Pullus had, when Domitius said hopefully as the friends stared across the water at the barely visible smudge of smoke from the fires rising from the fortifications, "Maybe he'll call off an attack."

This earned him a derisive snort from Pullus.

"Not very likely. We've just marched across the entire length of Hispania; do you really think Caesar is going to be denied now?"

Domitius glared at his large friend...but he did not argue, knowing that Pullus was likely right.

The lack of available ships did not surprise Caesar, and he wasted no time giving orders for the army to build enough vessels to transport two Cohorts at a time, with their artillery, and once again, the men found themselves hard at work, moving inland and felling trees, then dragging them back to an inlet, where a narrow river flowed into the bay, making sure that they remained out of sight of the island. As they quickly learned, once done chopping down the trees that would provide the raw materials for the boats, building ships had little in common with constructing bridges. Fortunately, there were men in the ranks with some experience in shipbuilding, with the bulk of the men providing nothing but the raw labor, but inevitably, mistakes were made, resulting in delays, although this was not the only difficulty. Although the bulk of the Lucenses had fled to the island, a fair number had either chosen or been ordered to stay behind, and they did their best to harass the Romans, including one nighttime raid where they were successful in firing one of the barges. This forced a reinforced guard shift through the night watches, which inevitably meant that men lost sleep, and when combined with the unfamiliar work and the tension created by the idea that they would be using these ships to cross a wider expanse of water than most of them had ever been exposed to before, tempers were raw. In turn, this meant that the Centurions and Optios were more liberal with the use of their *vitus* than at any previous time once the campaign had started. Nevertheless, work progressed until, after more than a full week of work, a dozen flat-bottomed transports had been constructed, each of them large enough to carry two Centuries and one *ballista* or two scorpions. This did not mean that the assault was conducted immediately, which Crastinus and the other Centurions learned when Caesar summoned the Pili Priores for a briefing in the *praetorium* on the day the final boat was finished.

Without any preamble, Caesar informed them, "There will be no moon in three days' time, and we'll wait until then to assault the island."

This had been the rumor, certainly, but hearing their general confirm it still created a stir, and Crastinus, sitting next to

Favonius, exchanged a glance with his Primus Pilus, but there was something in Favonius' expression that warned Crastinus that the older Centurion knew something else as well.

He learned what it was when Caesar continued, looking at Favonius, Crastinus, and the Tertius and Quartus Pilus Prior who were all seated in a row, "And the 10th will go first, with the First through Fourth in the first wave."

"You knew," Crastinus murmured, and Favonius gave a barely perceptible nod, while Caesar continued to outline his plan.

Using a wooden pointer, he indicated a map of the island hanging on the wall, placing the tip on the southern end of the island as he continued, "The night before the main assault, I'll be sending a small boat, crewed by experienced men, and they'll spend the day in hiding in the stand of trees here at the southern end of the island. As soon as it's dark on the night of the assault, they will come out of hiding, and using a shielded lamp, they will guide us in to land on the stretch of beach they select once they get there."

It was, Crastinus thought, a good plan...as far as it went, but he was also an experienced officer, and he had learned that any plan with a lot of moving parts offered more opportunities for things to go wrong, and he gave Favonius a sidelong glance, trying to divine his thoughts on the matter. The Primus Pilus kept his eyes on Caesar, but Crastinus caught the almost imperceptible shrug that he interpreted as a tacit acknowledgement of Crastinus' own thoughts. Not, he understood, that it made any difference. Besides, he thought, so far, this Caesar has been one of the best commanders I've ever served under. In that moment, he decided to trust the man, and he returned his full attention to the briefing.

Surprising none of them, the next three days dragged by, yet at the same time, once the day came, they were all surprised at how quickly it had arrived. At first, it seemed as if they were blessed by the gods because there was a heavy cloud cover, which would make them even harder to see. Then, the wind began to pick up, blowing in from the sea, which in turn made it more difficult for the men who had been chosen to row the barges, all from the 9th, to move them from where the barges had been shielded from view during their construction, creating a delay that only served to increase the tension. Because Caesar had ordered the loading to go in Cohort order, it meant that the First and Second of the Second spent more time on their barge, which was rowed away from the beach to make room for the next one to be loaded. Bobbing about as they were, it did not take long for both low sides to be lined with puking Legionaries, and Domitius, Pullus, and more than half of the rest of the section were among them.

"By the gods, I *hate* the sea," Domitius groaned in between heaves, but Pullus barely heard his friend, grappling with his own misery.

"Pluto's *cock*, I don't have anything left to puke up!" he cried out. "So why can't I stop?"

Calienus, who by virtue of his rank, was actually sitting comfortably with his back against the side and legs splayed out in front of him, was not sympathetic in the slightest.

"This," he said scornfully, "is nothing. When I was with Pompeius, we were at sea with no land in sight, and it was a *lot* worse than this. And," he added, "it was like that for three days!"

"Well, remind me to desert if Caesar ever decides to chase pirates," Domitius gasped.

Calienus laughed, but his humor was not destined to last long because, before they were joined by the next barge away from the beach, it began to rain. Not, they quickly learned, a light rain, but one that lashed their exposed skin, stinging them, while the wind increased and, of course, created more of a chop that sent the barge bucking and pitching.

"Maybe Caesar will postpone the assault," Scribonius said hopefully, addressing Calienus, but while the Sergeant shook his head, there was a wistful tone to Calienus' voice as he answered, "I don't think so."

Calienus was correct, and while it was much slower than the plan called for, the half-dozen barges were finally loaded, followed by the *Bucinator* sounding the prearranged signal, prompting the men seated at the oars to begin pulling together at the command. Between both the load each barge was carrying—Crastinus and the Second Century were responsible for two scorpions and the bolts—and the ship design, with a flat bow that did not cut through the water, the barges moved with a ponderous slowness, yet somehow they did move, heading for the island. Their stomachs emptied, Domitius, Pullus, and the other afflicted men had slumped against the side, some of them using their shields as a makeshift shelter, thankful that they had been ordered to keep the leather covers on to avoid getting them soaked with water and rendering them next to useless, while resigning themselves to being miserable. They all lost track of time, and none of them were disposed to talk, the only sound the Legionary who had been named the master of the barge calling out the rhythm so that the oarsmen stroked evenly, competing with the howling of the wind and the crashing sound of the whitecaps smashing against the flat bow of the barge.

Then, out of the darkness and from the bow, they heard Rufio's voice saying, "I can't see the light!"

Not surprisingly, this elicited a response from the rest of the men, both those of the 10th, and the men doing the rowing, which prompted Crastinus to snarl at them to shut their mouths, although he was moving quickly to the bow. The gloom made it next to impossible for Pullus, or any of them, to make much out, but he got the impression of both Crastinus and Vetruvius leaning forward as if getting a matter of inches closer to the island by doing so, even while risking pitching overboard, might help them see anything.

Standing just a few spots away from them, with Atilius next to him, before he could stop himself, Didius cried out, "If we can't see the damn light, how can we know which way we're going? For all we know, we may end up twenty miles out to sea, then what'll happen?"

It was Calienus who answered, his earlier aplomb nowhere to be heard in his voice as he snapped, "Then we'll all drown, you idiot. What do you think will happen?"

They had all climbed to their feet by this time, and they stood there, staring ahead but, like their officers, unable to see anything resembling a light. Instead, all they saw was an inky blackness; all they heard was the howling wind, and the hissing of an angry sea.

"Titus," Domitius whispered, "I'm not going to lie. I'm scared to death."

Normally, whenever presented with an opportunity to demonstrate his bravery, even with his best friend, Titus Pullus never passed it up.

This time, however, all that came out of his mouth was, "Me too."

From one of the benches, one of their 9th comrades cried out, "Jupiter Optimus Maximus, protect this Legion, soldiers all!"

Chapter Six

It did not help Publius Vellusius at all that he overheard Pullus admit to Domitius that he was as frightened as Vellusius felt, even as the men assigned to the oars battled the wind, rain and battering of the waves against their transport, heading in what they could all only hope was in the right direction. Packed together as they were in the middle of the barge, Vellusius was at least able to keep his feet, although the men were swaying back and forth in the rhythm created by the heaving sea, and he soon realized he had one of two choices, both of them bad. If he faced inboard, he was slightly protected from the lashing rain and the spray from wind-whipped waves, but it made his seasickness worse. Facing outboard, however, was a more frightening prospect because there was nothing to see but the whitecaps of the nearest waves, and nothing resembling land, no matter how intently he tried to peer ahead, although he was slightly less seasick. All around him, the men of the First Century, loaded in the forward part of the transport, were either retching, silently miserable...or muttering prayers to Neptune, to Jupiter Optimus Maximus, and to every god they knew in the vast pantheon of Roman gods. Only later did he hear other men offer an estimate that a full third of a watch passed after Vellusius overheard Domitius' and Pullus' exchange, an interminable period that, for the most part, Vellusius spent in something of a daze, willing himself not to think about the likelihood that he, and all of his friends and comrades, would be sinking to the bottom of the sea in the near future.

Finally, from the bow of the transport, a voice shouted, "There it is, off to the right!"

Thanks to his spot closer to the starboard side of the transport, it did not take long for Vellusius to spy the flickering light, nor did it take him long to see that, given its position off their right quarter, if they had continued on their original course, their barge would have missed the island and headed out to sea and, he was certain, a death by drowning.

"By the gods, we almost missed the cursed island." He recognized the voice as a man in the First Section of his Century, but Crastinus cut off further conversation.

"Well, at least we found the damn thing." Raising his voice, the Pilus Prior continued, "Listen up, boys. You just saw how long it took us to get to the island. It won't take them half as long to get back because the wind is at their back, but it'll take them just as long, if not longer, to bring up the next four Cohorts. In fact, we'll probably be on this island for at least a full watch by ourselves, so keep that in mind. No heroes; make sure we stay together because it's darker than Pluto's bunghole out here. Hopefully, the boys on the island will be able to point us in the right direction."

To Vellusius' surprise, out of the darkness, a voice that he recognized as belonging to Gaius Surenas, the Sergeant of the Second Section of the First, asked, "Pilus Prior, wouldn't it make more sense to wait until the whole Legion is on the beach?"

"Someone's about to get thrashed," Scribonius, who was standing next to Vellusius, murmured.

Vellusius agreed with Scribonius' assessment, and he waited to hear Crastinus explode in a fit of temper, the prelude to him lashing out with his *vitus*, but to his shock, and in a sign that their Pilus Prior had been as shaken by their near miss as his men, he actually agreed, "Yes, it would make more sense, but that's not our orders. Caesar has commanded that we begin the assault immediately when the front line Cohorts land, and that's what we're going to do. The thing that worries me is that the artillery won't be able to use the combustibles to start a fire in their defenses to give us light, so we're going to have to be very careful and stay in formation. Make sure that nobody gets separated by keeping close enough to each other so that you're touching. If you lose contact with someone on either side, call out immediately so they'll know to close back in and regain contact, but by the gods, keep your voices down when you do it." Even as Crastinus was finishing, Vellusius felt the lurching of the bottom of the transport scraping the sand of the beach, and he fell against Scribonius, who caught him, but Crastinus did not hesitate. "All right, boys, let's go give these bastards some Roman iron. They escaped their fate once; we're not going to let them get away a second time."

Even over the sounds of the surf and the hissing of the rain, Vellusius heard the splash as the first man, he assumed that it was the Pilus Prior, leapt over the side, and the men at the front of the transport followed their Centurion immediately. Shuffling forward, Vellusius only had long enough to wonder how deep the water was before he found out, the shock of the waist deep surf immediately making his balls shrivel up and wrenching a gasp from his lips because of the cold water. Thankfully, he had made sure to hold his shield high enough so that it remained dry, but he lost his grip on his javelins, almost panicking at the thought of them being taken out to sea in the surf, forcing him to stop his progress to the beach as he blindly thrust his hand down into the water. He was hit from behind by another man, and while he roundly cursed whoever it was, it proved to be a gift from the gods because, as he stumbled forward, now in knee-deep surf, while he could not see, he felt his right hand strike the shaft of one of his javelins, and after scrabbling about, was able to retrieve the second, offering up a quick prayer of thanks as he staggered up onto the beach where the First Century was in the process of forming up about twenty paces from the surf line. He could barely make out the shapes of his comrades, but just as he passed the small group of men who he knew were responsible for assembling the two scorpions the First and Second had brought with them, he heard someone curse.

He recognized Pullus' voice asking, "What's the problem?"

"The torsion rope is completely soaked. That means it's completely useless."

That, Vellusius thought with dismay, is a bad omen, but he kept moving, the endless watches of drill enabling him to find his spot in the formation without trouble, whereupon he quietly relayed the news to Domitius and the others, creating a ripple of curses that prompted Rufio to snap at them to shut their mouths. All along the beach, the rest of the wave was assembling, and despite the orders for quiet, Vellusius was certain that they were making enough noise to be heard, especially if the Gallaeci had men watching the possible landing sites, yet there were no cries of alarm or any other sign that their presence had been noticed. They had been ordered to leave their cloaks behind, and were forced to endure the lashing rain without any protection, and it did not take long before Vellusius was shivering uncontrollably, though he took some comfort when he heard a rapid clicking sound from Domitius on his left and Remus to his right that he realized were their teeth chattering from the cold. Being in the first wave, they were forced to wait for the Third and Fourth Cohorts to arrive, and they were allowed to sit down and huddle together for warmth. Since Crastinus had had the foresight to order them to keep the leather covers on their shields, it protected them from being waterlogged, and smaller men like Vellusius actually used them as partial shelters by curling up underneath them. Even as he did so, he could hear Pullus, and Vellusius' own close comrade Scribonius roundly cursing the smaller rankers, and when he peeked out from under his protection, even in the darkness, he could see Domitius, doing the same thing, with an ear-to-ear grin.

"I'm never going to stop reminding him about how we were snug and warm," he whispered to Vellusius, "while he had to sit there and freeze his balls off."

Vellusius laughed, and while Pullus did not hear what Domitius said, he recognized his best friend's voice, and he growled that Domitius would pay for whatever he was saying, earning him another round of snickering.

As they were waiting, Crastinus went over to where Favonius and the Primus Pilus Posterior were standing, both seemingly impervious to the wet and cold, and Crastinus himself adopted the same posture, knowing that he and his men were just as cold, but setting an example by ignoring his discomfort, as this was what being a Centurion of Rome meant; they were men of iron.

Saluting, Crastinus reported the state of his artillery, earning him a sour grunt from Favonius. "So you're no better off than we are, eh?" He was silent for a heartbeat, then mused aloud,

"We've got no way to illuminate the walls now, nor to keep those savages' heads down when we bring the ladders up." Thinking for a moment, he spoke decisively, "Right, then here's what we're going to do." Turning to his Pilus Posterior Fulvius, he ordered, "Go to the beach and hold one of the transports bringing the rest of the Cohorts. Once the Third and Fourth Cohorts arrive, we'll see if Fortuna has been kinder to them with their torsion ropes. If not, we'll send them back to inform Caesar of the situation and tell him that we'll await further orders. Quickly now!"

Fulvius stayed only long enough to repeat his orders as required, then salute before he dashed off into the darkness, while Crastinus said, "I'll go tell my boys, Primus Pilus."

Then he saluted as well, and while he did not run because of the darkness and uneven surface, he moved quickly, returning to relay the situation. With this further delay, he allowed the men to break their formation so that they could huddle together, and as usual, the men gathered together within their section, usually next to their close comrade but also with other men they considered friends, although this was not the case with all of them, and then they settled down to wait.

Didius was never more thankful for Atilius than he was that night when, in a show of loyalty towards the man the Fates had deemed to be his close comrade, Atilius demurred when Romulus and Remus invited him to come huddle with them, where, using their javelins, they had propped up their shields to create a makeshift shelter, choosing instead to stay with Didius. His exile had been more painful than he would ever admit, and now, when the misery was completely physical in nature, having someone willing to share the ordeal with him brought Didius a great deal of comfort, especially knowing what was still to come. Naturally, he did not say as much, but Atilius never seemed to need his thanks for the small kindnesses he showed Didius, which suited Didius perfectly, his pride not allowing him to acknowledge his appreciation. They did not talk much, mainly because, as Vellusius had noticed, their teeth were chattering so much that talking was difficult, although at one point, Atilius made an observation that Didius would remember.

"I wonder if those *cunni* will be ready for us because they hear our teeth clacking together like this."

This had not occurred to Didius; while it was humorous, and it even made Didius laugh, something he did not normally do, he began to wonder if, in fact, this was a possibility, so he spent the rest of their time waiting intently watching in the direction of where the Gallaeci fortifications were located, though the wall was not visible. Ever so slowly, the rest of the first four Cohorts of 10th arrived on the beach, and while they were not told as much, Didius correctly assumed that, on the subject of the artillery and its utility, they were well and truly fucked.

This was confirmed when, well past midnight, they heard Crastinus' voice break the silence, informing his men, "The artillery with the second load is in the same shape as ours, so we've sent them back to inform Caesar of this and we're waiting for his orders now. Try and get some rest while we wait."

This, of course, was easier said than done, yet somehow, much to his surprise, Didius actually dozed off, although it was a fitful rest from which he kept jerking awake, either because of the noise created by the arrival of the next wave of Legionaries, or because of a dream of what was coming, and he could feel his heart pounding against his ribs as the terror came rushing up from deep within his mind. As miserable as he was, Didius was secretly thankful that time seemed to be standing still, and despite the miserable conditions, he offered up a prayer to Sol that the god chose this day not to rise, even as he knew it was a vain hope. It seemed to be a full watch later but was probably less than half that when Crastinus issued new orders.

"We're postponing the assault until first light," he announced. "The men who just arrived have brought assault ladders, and we'll be carrying them to the walls instead of creating a breach."

With these new orders, there was a low buzzing of talk as the men around them began speculating on who would be the first up the ladders, and Didius and Atilius were no exceptions.

"You know that the big bastard will volunteer to be the first up," Didius commented sourly, but he was not surprised when Atilius made no comment; he had learned that, when it came to criticizing Pullus, his close comrade was reticent and would never echo Didius' jibes.

In a subtle but unmistakable change of subject, Atilius said, "I just want this fucking rain to stop. After," he added hastily, "we get to the wall. If the Gallaeci are like us right now, they're more concerned with staying dry than watching for us."

Despite his irritation at what he viewed as the lack of support in his ceaseless enmity towards the man Didius blamed for most of his troubles, he murmured an agreement, hoping that this was the case. Finally, two events occurred: the rest of the Legion arrived, and even with the heavy clouds, the eastern sky began lightening, prompting Crastinus to order the men to stand and return to their spots in their formation.

"Get ready, boys," Crastinus spoke just loudly enough to be heard. "We'll be going in shortly."

He was correct; not long afterward, he gave the order to advance, and Didius stepped off with the rest of the First Century, telling himself that the reason his javelins kept slipping in his grip was because of the rain and not because of the sweat caused by his nerves. His Century had been given two ladders, a pair of men from the first five sections carrying the heavy ladder by looping their right arms in between the rungs so that one of the vertical supports rested on their shoulders. Very quickly, Didius felt the ground tilting upward slightly, telling him that they were climbing a low hill, and only then did he recall that the Gallaeci fort was perched atop this low rise, but there was a slight dip in between the wall and the Legion, and the halt was called, followed by the order to drop into a crouch to cover the last hundred paces before they reached the spot where the dip was located. Another wait ensued, although this one was not nearly as long, which to Didius was a mixed blessing; it delayed what was coming, but it meant that he had time to envision all the things that could happen to him once the wait was over. So absorbed was he in these thoughts that, when the *Cornicen* of the First Cohort sounded the long, single note signaling the start of the assault, he was a heartbeat late in standing erect and going to the run, something that Rufio, in his spot at the left rear of the Century, didn't miss. Despite this, Didius managed to catch up as the Legionaries rushed across the hundred paces of open ground, giving him time to see that, while the parapet was not empty of men, the Gallaeci who were present were spaced out in a manner that informed him that they were sentries, and that, somehow, the Romans had caught their foe completely by surprise. Everything happened rapidly after that; the ladders were thrown up, and by the time the Tenth Section scaled them, the parapet was clear, and their comrades had already leapt down into the fort. Didius paused for perhaps two heartbeats once he scaled the parapet, taking in the scene in the dim light of a gray dawn, which was one of utter chaos resulting from the surprise attack. Men were rushing in his direction as, down on the ground inside the wall, Crastinus and the other Centurions were bellowing orders, getting their Centuries into formation, while women and children were running in seemingly every direction, all of them shrieking in terror.

"Hurry up, Didius! Get down off the wall!"

He obeyed Rufio's snapped command, just in time for Crastinus to bellow the order to charge at the ragged line of Gallaeci warriors who were the only protection for their families, and Didius did not even have the opportunity to launch his own javelins, as the volley from the first five sections slashed down and removed either a warrior's shield or the warrior himself before Crastinus bellowed the order to go to the *gladius*. After that, it was not a battle but a slaughter as the Romans unleashed their anger over the misery and fear of the previous watches, and in this respect, for once, Spurius Didius was of a like mind as his comrades. While he did not keep count, along with men he dispatched several women with his own blade, nor did he spare any child who had the misfortune to be a step too slow, but he was far from alone, and it took Crastinus wading in and using his *vitus*, slashing it across the one vulnerable spot on the armored men, the backs and sides of their thighs to stop the slaughter.

"The more of these bastards you kill, the less slaves there will be, and the less money for you, you idiots!"

He bellowed this repeatedly, and while it did stop the

killing, it did not, nor did he try all that hard, stop the rapine, and for Didius, this was the real reward. There was something about taking a woman against her will that excited Didius much more than paying for her services, and he was far from alone in this proclivity. By the time of the noon watch, the fort was taken, Didius and his like-minded comrades had sated their lust, if temporarily, and the surviving Gallaeci were rounded up and under guard. It had been, all agreed, a successful assault with only a handful of casualties, none among the men of the First of the Second. Now, there was only one island left, but as they quickly learned, this one would be a much different, and more difficult, proposition.

The 10th returned to the mainland to prepare for the next, and what they were told would be the final, assault of the last bastion of the Gallaeci. Very quickly, however, the word had spread among the ranks that, unlike the fortifications on the first island, this island was much larger, and from what Caesar's scouts reported, what was waiting for them was what was assumed to be a permanent fortification that had been in place for some time.

"They probably have used it as a stronghold to fall back on whenever they're attacked by another tribe," Scribonius had guessed, correctly as they would learn. "So they've had time to improve it over the years."

In terms of numbers, the most often repeated estimate was that there were fifteen thousand Gallaeci located within what was, in effect, a town, with at least five thousand of them being warriors, perhaps as many as seven thousand. Consequently, Caesar ordered that this would require both Legions still with him, the 9th and 10th, which in turn meant that even more boats had to be constructed, though not nearly as many as the men feared because of the number of boats the Romans had captured. Nevertheless, once more, the First Century was part of the working party sent out to chop down the trees that would be used to constructed the flat-bottomed transports, dragging them back to the sheltered bay that was roughly midway between the two islands. The *immunes* responsible for the construction got to work immediately, but even with the superior organization of Rome's Legions, made even more efficient by Caesar, and now experienced in the building them, it still required another solid week of work before all was ready. That time was spent by the rest of the army, particularly the 10th, in repairing and replacing the equipment damaged during the first assault, most of it being the javelins that had been used to soften up the Gallaeci defenders. Otherwise, there was not much to do other than speculate on what awaited them on the last island, and of course, wagering with each other on the myriad things that might happen. Most prevalent as fodder for a bet was the weather, and the wagering was brisk, the more pessimistic men betting that it would be a repeat of the last time, while those with a more positive outlook equally adamant that on the day of the assault, it would be sunny and clear.

Much to Didius' dismay, it was the latter group who ended up winning whatever had been on offer as the stakes, usually a man's wine ration, followed by duties that were rotated among them but considered either tedious or downright unpleasant, like mucking out the cavalry enclosure, or worst of all, emptying the latrine pits. In another blessing from Fortuna, this time, the men manning the oars would not be Legionaries; there were now enough slaves to man the transports, making the Legionaries passengers. Unfortunately, at least as far as the men of the 10th were concerned, this was as far as the goddess was willing to go, because Caesar had deemed that this last assault would consist of two prongs, with the 10th approaching from the south, while the 9th would row the shorter distance directly from the east, across the sheltered bay. The distance for the 10th was estimated to be such that they would be on the water for two full watches, and that was not counting the time spent embarking, then bobbing about waiting for the rest of the Legion to load up now that there were enough boats between the new construction and the captured vessels for both Legions, without the need to shuttle back and forth. Not surprising to anyone, when the day of the assault dawned bright and clear, with only a scattering of clouds, there was much rejoicing, especially from those men who now could look forward to more wine or escape from unpleasant duties, and while Didius was unhappy, he acknowledged, grudgingly and only to himself, that he was secretly relieved to have lost this particular wager. As had happened the last time, the boarding process was done in numerical Cohort order, meaning that the men of the First of the Second were on the water for a fair amount of time even before the Cohorts set out. The Gallaeci were tethered to their benches not with chains but lengths of rope, while a long rope was looped around their necks and secured at both ends, and they sullenly obeyed the ship's master who, once the *cornu* notes used to order an advance sounded across the water, began calling out the cadence. These ships were not designed for speed, so men settled down as comfortably as they could, and Didius noted with anger how Pullus had managed to find a spot along the side, but when he pointed this out to Atilius, his close comrade was not sympathetic.

"Didn't you see him puking his guts out a bit ago?" he asked, and Didius had not. "He's just near the side because he's seasick."

This made Didius actually feel a bit better, and he had felt quite smug about the fact that, for whatever reason, he had not been afflicted with seasickness like so many of his comrades. The idea of Pullus suffering this malady made Didius happier than he would ever admit, if only because it meant the bastard was human and not the demigod the other men of not just his section, but the Century, and the Cohort, believed him to be. Otherwise, if it had not been for what lay in their immediate future, it was actually not unpleasant; the sun was shining, the breeze kept them from getting hot, and the men were occupied in the kind of activities that might have been taking place around the fire in camp. The Mallius brothers were carrying on the same argument that had been raging for weeks about a maiden named Livia Plautus back home they both insisted lusted after them, Scribonius and Vellusius were playing dice, while Calienus and Rufio were competing with each other to see who could balance their *pugio* on their finger the longest. Despite his feelings towards the men of his section, Spurius Didius realized that he missed the sense of belonging that these men felt for each other, and not for the first time, he felt a pang of regret that it had been his own actions that had resulted in his alienation. But then, he would look over at Pullus, his seasickness at least temporarily in abeyance and who was smiling at something Domitius was saying, and the sullen hostility and indignation came rushing back. His ruminations on the injustice of his treatment was interrupted by a call from the bow of the transport, and without being told, the men stopped whatever they were doing to pay attention. Standing on his toes, Didius spotted what he assumed had warranted the call, a small, barren and deserted island in between the transport and their target, which the ship's master steered around before making a slight right turn to align their transport on their assigned landing spot, giving Didius and the other men the first view of the large island. They would be landing on the southern tip of the island, about a mile away from the Gallaeci fortress, and they were close enough now that Didius could see the tops of what would turn out to be a line of trees that helped block the Gallaeci view of that part of the island. Then, one of their comrades in the First Section he had been told had had experience at sea, who was nearest to the bow, spoke loudly enough for him to hear.

"This isn't good."

Not surprisingly, this got everyone's attention, but because of his position, and the fact that he was not quite tall enough to see over the heads of the men closer to the bow, he had to hear Pullus' voice asking Calienus, "Sergeant, have you ever seen sand that white before?"

It was not Calienus but the man in the First Section who answered, "That's because it's not sand, Pullus. That's foam."

"Foam? What exactly does that mean?"

This was asked by Calienus, but while the experienced ranker didn't hesitate, there was no mistaking the grim tone as he replied, "It means that that's not a beach, Sergeant; it's rocks, and the foam is made from water striking the rocks. There's no way we can land there."

The ranker was moving as he said this, shoving his way through the packed men to get to the rear to where the master was standing at the steering oar to warn him of the danger, whereupon things happened very quickly after that. They had just passed the small island, and Didius could actually feel the transport fighting the change in direction as the master leaned against the oar, trying to turn the bow of thc unwieldy ship away from the rocks, which were now clearly visible, and even from where he stood, he could see were growing larger with every heartbeat. When it became clear the steering oar would not be enough, the master bellowed the order for the slaves on the right side to lift their oars while accompanying his words with a gesture, relying on the men on the left side, who he ordered to increase their rhythm. At first, it did not seem to have any effect, and there was almost total silence as the eyes of every Legionary were fixed on the rocks that, to the naked eye, seemed to be closing at an impossibly rapid rate. This was when it occurred to Didius that their collective fates were in the hands of men who, with good reason, hated them, and he glanced over to his right, half expecting to see that the slaves had ignored the order to ship their oars and were still rowing in an attempt to send the transport onto the rocks. To his surprise, none of them were, all of them leaning on their oar so that the blade was above the water. They want to live as much as we do, he thought, even as slaves; it would be a moment he would remember over the years, a symbol of the power of the will to live, no matter the circumstances. Finally, after what seemed to be a full watch but was only a matter of heartbeats, the flat bow of the transport began to swing to the right, and with less than a hundred paces to spare, the jagged, foam-lashed rocks slid by their left side as the transport steered for a better landing spot. What they found was not a sandy beach, but the master clearly deemed it to be safe enough to put ashore without damaging the transport, and Didius followed his comrades, leaping over the side, thankfully in just knee deep water, then waded ashore onto what was a beach composed of small, smooth pebbles and not sand. Because they had been forced to find a different spot, it meant they had to march a short distance to reach their spot in the long single line of Cohorts as the other Centuries were assembling.

"Right, it didn't take those bastards in the 9th nearly as long to get to their spot as it did us," Crastinus announced. "So we can't fuck about." He offered his men a wolfish grin. "We don't want to let them have the first pickings of the loot, do we, boys?"

He was answered in the form of a chorus of affirmation that this was not acceptable, and Didius' voice was among them, his thoughts less on pecuniary matters and more on sating his lust once again, the image of the look of terror and despair on the last woman he had raped at the fort on the other island serving to fan the fire building in his loins. It was his way of overcoming the fear of what had to be done in order to achieve this reward, the fear of the pain that would come if one of those barbarian savages got fortunate enough to get past your shield to plunge their blade into your guts so that your last moments among the living would be filled with an unspeakable agony. A gut wound was accepted as the absolute worst way to die around the fires, and there were men who seemed to be obsessed with the idea, talking about it incessantly, telling lurid stories of men they supposedly knew, or who some comrade, always unnamed, knew, and the shrieking agony as their guts spilled onto the ground, or even worse, they survived the initial wound, only to have their own body betray them when, inevitably, the *cac* in their punctured bowels leaked out and poisoned them. This was the image that Didius always conjured up before they went into battle, of lying on a cot in the hospital portion of the *quaestorium*, smelling the stench of his own rotting flesh, and as always, it proved to be almost impossible to dispel. Nevertheless, when Crastinus bellowed the order to go to the double quick, his body automatically obeyed, breaking into the shuffling run as the First of the Second hurried into position.

Not for the first time, Scribonius thanked the gods that, because of his height, he was next to Pullus, and protected by the giant Roman's shield, just as he protected Atilius to his left. Another advantage of being taller was in being able to have a better view of what lay ahead of them, although this was something of a mixed blessing.

"First Cohort, on line!"

The Primus Pilus bellowed the order, and as they stood watching, the First advanced towards the trees that screened all but the towers of the Gallaeci fortress, where he could just barely make out the figures of several men.

"They know we're coming," he muttered to Pullus, but he

only got a grunt in return, and when he glanced over, he saw the giant Roman's attention was fixed on the scrub forest ahead of them.

The rear ranks of the First Cohort were still visible when the noise erupted; first it was shouting, though it was impossible to determine whether it was in their tongue or Gallaeci, followed by the crashing sound they had learned signaled the collision of shields as the two forces rushed at each other. It was over quickly, and Crastinus gave the order to advance, and while they did not move at the double quick, to Scribonius, it seemed to be only a handful of heartbeats before they entered the forest, slightly darker, and cooler because of the shade provided by the trees. Within a few paces, they came across the first of the Gallaeci dead, but it was not long after that they came across a *medicus* from the First Cohort crouching next to a ranker, tying a tourniquet in an attempt to stop the spurting spray of blood from the stump of his severed right hand.

"Poor bastard," Pullus muttered, waiting until they were out of earshot. "He hasn't been in long enough to earn his payout and bonus."

This, Scribonius, as well as all of his comrades, knew; it was a harsh, and many men thought, unjust system, but this was the way of things. The only way to earn the full amount owed to men for serving was to make it the full sixteen years, although much also depended on the largesse of their general, and while it was early in their association, Scribonius was optimistic that Caesar would prove to be generous to men like the unfortunate ranker in their wake, perhaps giving him a stipend that would allow him to survive, if not thrive, for the rest of his days minus a right hand. He shoved this thought to the back of his mind as they exited the trees to confront the very first of the obstacles in their path in the form of a low wooden wall a bit more than two hundred paces away, as they stopped just out of range of Gallaeci bows. Once they halted, Pullus left his spot, having once more carried the heaviest part of the scorpion, the frame, moving to the spot a few paces in front of the long line of Centuries to help assemble the smaller artillery piece, while teams of men carried the pieces of the larger *ballistae*. It took perhaps a sixth part of a watch for the artillery to be assembled, while the Romans endured the taunts, jeers and challenges of the Gallaeci warriors lining the first, lower wall, their enemy seemingly undaunted at their first glimpse of Roman might. There was a brief wait as every man looked to the east, their right, waiting for the signal they had been told was coming, a fire arrow that informed the 10th that the 9th was in position and beginning their assault. They did not have to wait long, although it was not the flame but the thin trail of greasy smoke that Scribonius spotted. Less than two full heartbeats later, the *Corniceni* of each Pilus Prior sounded the long, single note.

"Prepare to loose!" He recognized the voice as belonging to Favonius, who followed a heartbeat later with the bellowed command, "*Loose!*"

Instantly, the *immunes* who served as the commander of each *ballistae* crew yanked the long leather cord that released the iron pin holding the torsion arms in place, the tightly twisted rope unwinding with a blinding speed as the leather sling shot forward to fling the rounded, smooth rock flying at the vertical logs of the first wall. All along the wall, there was a cascade of sharp cracking sounds, but it was the shards of bark and splintered wood exploding outward from the impact that mattered, although inevitably, not all of the crews were on the mark with this first volley, and Scribonius watched as one rock landed short and caromed off the ground before striking the wall, with negligible effect. Meanwhile, the men manning the scorpions had more success, having already selected an unfortunate Gallaeci as their initial target, and because of the flatter trajectory, the iron-tipped bolts moved too quickly for men to dodge out of the way. Unlike the *ballistae*, all of them continuing to loose now that they had the range, the scorpions did not waste their bolts after the first volley as the Gallaeci ducked down to deprive them of targets, and Scribonius and his comrades were consigned to watch as the Roman artillery attempted to create what they had been told would be a half-dozen breaches in the first wall, thereby saving the assault ladders for the second and higher wall.

What became apparent was that a single *ballista* would be unable to create a breach, and Scribonius, his eyes still on the wall, heard Pullus mutter, "All they're doing is taking the bark off."

Primus Pilus Favonius, seeing the same thing, quickly drew the same conclusion, and he had his *Cornicen* blow the notes that signaled a halt, followed by the order for the Centurions to assemble on the eagle. Scribonius hoped that the cessation would tempt the Gallaeci to stand up and give the scorpions a chance to inflict damage, but they clearly had learned their lesson, and while a warrior would lift his head to peek over the top of the wall, it was never long enough for a clean shot.

"What now?" Romulus wondered, but none of them had any ideas, at least none they were willing to offer aloud.

They got their answer when Crastinus came trotting back, stopped at the one *ballista* assigned to the Second, pointing with his *vitus* at a spot on the wall that was already scarred, and the crew immediately began turning the piece. It did not take long before the *Cornu* sounded the call to resume, and they quickly saw that every piece was now concentrating their barrage on one of two spots.

"With only two breaches, this first wall is going to be a right bastard to take," they all heard Calienus' comment.

"It's a good thing that it's not our turn then," Remus offered, and this was met with a chorus of agreement.

For a heartbeat, Scribonius thought of pointing out that the reason for their reprieve was because they were going to be assaulting the second wall, but he thought better of it, knowing the likely response. And, he thought, it's only right that it's the Fifth and Eighth Cohorts' turn for this first wall, understanding that one key to maintaining good morale was based in the idea that every man at one point or another got the *cac* end of the sponge, as the saying went. By spreading the misery and danger equally, it kept the men in the lower-numbered Cohorts from complaining, at least no more than normal. With their barrage concentrated, it did not take long for the logs in the two spots to be turned into splinters, leaving the shattered stumps protruding just a foot or two from the ground, looking much like an old boxer's mouth, with each breach the approximate width of a section in their battle formation. The dust had barely settled when the *Cornu* sounded the order that sent the Fifth and Eighth forward, whereupon the Gallaeci leapt to their feet and launched their own response in the form of a shower of arrows and sling bullets.

"Pluto's *cock!*" Scribonius gasped, shocked by the volume of missiles, realizing that there had to be at least two to three hundred invisible barbarian warriors armed with bows who were not standing on the wall, but were just behind it and arcing their missiles to rain down on the leading Centuries, with at least as many men standing on the parapet, swinging their arms over their heads before loosing their slings to send the small but deadly rocks streaking at the Romans.

The Romans retaliated, launching their scorpion bolts, but as quickly as a Gallaeci was swept from the rampart, usually in a shower of blood as the bolt passed through their bodies, they were immediately replaced by another man. As they had learned during the assault on the first town, the tribes of Hispania excelled in their use of the sling, but what made the Gallaeci different was their reliance on bows as well, and the combination of the two missiles, sling bullets with a flat trajectory, while arrows were plunging down from the sky, proved to be a potent combination, so that by the time they had closed half the distance to the first wall, the men of the Fifth Cohort, nearest to the Second, had been savaged, leaving a trail of bodies in their lumbering wake, although fortunately, most of the casualties had the presence of mind to pull their shield over their body. They absorbed the punishment nonetheless until, when they were no more than fifty paces away, the unseen commander of the Gallaeci on this first wall gave the order for one last concentrated volley, as the slingers were joined by the archers up on the wall now that the range was closed. From where they were standing, to Scribonius, it looked as if a giant but invisible hand made a sweeping, ruthless wave through the ranks of their comrades, their shields proving next to useless because of the short range.

A collective sound issued from the men of the First Century, a combination of gasps, moans, and curses at the scene, but it was Pullus who muttered what they were all thinking, loudly enough to be heard.

"They're getting slaughtered."

"Shut your mouth, Pullus!" Rufio snapped, glaring angrily

at the large Roman, who, for a heartbeat, appeared disposed to argue, and Scribonius braced himself for what would happen after that, but he managed to refrain from reaching out and grabbing Pullus' arm in a warning.

Both Cohorts had come to a shuddering halt, contracting into *testudo* formations as they stood there, absorbing the punishment that the now-heartened Gallaeci were subjecting them to, and it became immediately apparent to Scribonius that their comrades were now faced with an impossible choice. Continuing forward into the breach did not seem feasible because they had lost what he estimated to be at least a third of their numbers, although not all of these men were dead, yet while many of them would recover, they were out of the fight for now. However, trying to move backward, with so many of their fallen comrades in the way, was equally an invitation to disaster.

"Second Cohort, prepare to advance!"

At first, Scribonius was certain that he was hearing things, but he heard Didius' muttered curse, and he quickly realized that his Pilus Prior had in fact given the order.

Sounding eerily calm, Crastinus had to shout to be heard. "Boys, I know we're not slated to go next, but we can't let our brothers take that kind of beating. We're going to move at the double quick over there," he pointed to a spot immediately behind the nearest Century of the beleaguered Fifth, "stop when I give the signal to redress the lines and catch our breath, then we're going to show these *cunni* what happens when you fuck with the 10th!"

Men cheered at this, and Scribonius added his voice, but only because it was expected, and he could tell there was not much enthusiasm behind it, yet when Crastinus bellowed the order *"Procedite Ite Aciem...Mōve!"*, like his comrades, he did not hesitate to begin marching forward.

Once they were clear of the line of Centuries, Crastinus ordered them to march at an angle so that they could align themselves behind the stalled Fifth Cohort, which brought the First Century, followed by the rest of the Second Cohort near to where Primus Pilus Favonius was standing next to the eagle standard, and Scribonius saw him sprinting towards Crastinus, trailed by one of the Tribunes who, by this point in the campaign, was little more than a decoration, although thankfully, Doughboy had vanished, never to be seen again. They reached Crastinus, who stepped aside but gestured at the men to continue marching past, and while Scribonius did not hear the entire exchange, because he was next to Pullus on the outside of the formation, he caught the last words as they marched past.

Favonius' tone was harsh as he warned Crastinus, "All I can say is that this better work, Crastinus, or you know what's going to happen."

"It will work," Crastinus answered without hesitation.

"But what about the second wall? Your Cohort was supposed to assault the second wall, not the first. Who's supposed to do it now?"

As far as Scribonius and the other men who could hear the conversation were concerned, this was an excellent question, but again, Crastinus did not hesitate to answer Favonius.

"We'll do both."

They had just passed Crastinus, and he heard Pullus gasp, and he opened his mouth to say something, but Scribonius beat him to it, the bitterness overwhelming his normal sense of caution about speaking ill of any officer, muttering, "I heard the bastard. Well, Titus, it was nice knowing you."

For a heartbeat, Scribonius thought that Crastinus had overheard him because they heard his pounding footsteps from behind them where he left Favonius and the Tribune, but he passed by on his way back to his spot without a glance in their direction, and even with what was coming, Scribonius sighed in relief, not wanting to be thrashed just before he died. Meanwhile, the Pili Priores of both the Fifth and Eighth had independently arrived at the conclusion that the best of the two bad options facing them was to resume their advance, with the First of the Fifth just reaching the jagged maw of the breach, where the men were forced to spread out to fill the width of the breach in the wall to avoid being flanked by the waiting Gallaeci.

Just a few paces from the breach, above the noise of Gallaeci, the Romans of the Fifth, with a huge roar, broke into a run, rushing at the barbarian warriors who had arrayed themselves several rows deep across the mouth of the breach. Because the First had reached the beginning of the beaten zone, the ground now studded with arrows and littered with discarded shields, most of them with arrows protruding from them, along with the bodies of their comrades in the Fifth, they had to watch their footing, none of them wanting to tread on an already wounded man, so Scribonius missed seeing the collision, but he clearly heard it, the cracking of shields colliding together, the ringing sounds of iron striking iron, all of it punctuated by shrill screams of mortal agony and bellowed challenges and curses that were universal to every fighting man. Many of the stricken men had retained their wits after being struck by an arrow or sling bullet, curling up and pulling their shield on top of them, but among these men, who looked something like turtles with just their lower legs and the top of their helmets showing, there were others who no longer needed protection, sprawled out in the curious shapelessness of death, and it was at these men Scribonius refused to look, stepping over them when required without a downward glance. Crastinus called a halt then to dress the lines, but he also had something else in mind.

"Pullus, get your fat ass up here!"

"Pluto's cock," Scribonius' comrade muttered. "Now what?"

He did not hesitate, however, while Scribonius automatically sidestepped to take his friend's spot on the outside, as Atilius did the same, but for a moment, it appeared as if Didius had no intention of moving, then he was shoved by Calienus. Meanwhile, Crastinus was calling the names of the other larger men, yet for some reason, he did not call on Didius, who, Scribonius noticed with sour amusement, looked happier than he had ever seen the normally dour ranker. One small blessing was that, now that the Fifth and Eighth were fighting in the breach, the Gallaeci on the rampart had ceased their barrage of arrows and sling bullets, dropping off the wall to add their weight in an attempt to stop their enemy from exploiting this toehold with their spears and swords. And, Scribonius could see, that was all it was, a toehold; the men of the Fifth had managed to push their way into the breach, aided by the sheer bulk provided by the other five Centuries, where they formed a pocket no more than two dozen paces deep that was crammed with men, as the Gallaeci surrounded them, hacking, thrusting and slashing at the Legionaries. They could hear the shrill blast of the bone whistles of the Centurions of the Fifth Cohort sounding the relief, but men were staggering away from the breach, too many men, some of them limping, some staggering, and some forced to crawl away with the singlemindedness of a wounded animal whose only thought was to escape the slaughter just a matter of paces away. It meant that their own advance was made more difficult because of their comrades, and more than once, Pullus, who was now in the front rank next to Crastinus, was forced to shove some of these men out of the way, sending them reeling and more than one lost their footing and collapsed. One of these men fell to the ground, then gave a massive shudder, his entire body spasming as with his last effort, he rolled over to face the sky, but when Scribonius marched past, he saw that while the man's eyes were open, they were staring up sightlessly, the rent in his mail right over his heart still oozing blood. He offered a quick prayer to Dis, but this was all the time he could spend on the dead man's passage to the afterlife because, once again, Crastinus ordered the halt, just a matter of twenty paces from the Sixth of the Fifth, where Scribonius could see the men at the rear of their formation looking over their shoulder, and he was close enough to see the fatigue, the fear, and the hope at the sign of the Second Cohort coming to their aid.

Thrusting his *gladius* into the air, Crastinus bellowed, "Kill them all, boys! Kill them all!" Then, he swept his arm down and bellowed, "*Porro!*"

And, with Pullus and the other larger men of the First leading the way, they went rushing into the breach, where the men of the Fifth, with the last of their energy, used their shields to shove their Gallaeci opponent a step backward before turning sideways to let Crastinus and the First Century go rushing at the enemy. Even in a rank ten men deep, Scribonius could feel the collision as he grasped the back of his comrade in the Ninth Section's harness, and he offered up another prayer that Pullus' fortune held, seeing the huge Roman's *gladius* rise up in the air, and he saw there was already blood on it, then it went slashing down and out of sight. Within a span of heartbeats, what had been a pocket that spanned just a few paces more than the width of the breach on either side widened outward along the wall in both directions, as the men of the five ranks following the first five split evenly down the middle, with five men turning to face the enemy on the left, and the other five facing to the right, while the first half of the Century pressed forward to expand the pocket in the direction of the second wall. This put Scribonius hard up against the first wall, with the second wall to his left, and he added his weight to his file, widening the pocket, while the men of the Second Century arrived and pushed straight ahead, where Pullus and the first five ranks were pushing outwards and making it deeper.

Scribonius never drew his *gladius* for this part of the struggle, and within the span of perhaps a hundred heartbeats, the wiser Gallaeci, sensing that the fight for the first wall was lost, began streaming back to the second wall. Then, suddenly, they were all gone, rushing back to the second wall, where ladders made of both wood and rope were waiting, and they scrambled up them, leaving scores of dead and wounded behind, the latter being dispatched with a quick thrust, but Scribonius was thankful that he did not have to perform this task; killing a man in battle who was trying to kill you was one thing, but he derived no joy from thrusting his blade into the throat of a wounded and defenseless man, even if he had just heartbeats before been trying to kill him. Fortunately, there were other men, like Didius, who had no such compunction. The men of the Fifth who had remained in the breach withdrew to regroup, while the Second Cohort did the same, every man aware that they had only accomplished half of their goal; the second wall awaited.

Unlike the first wall, which did not have a ditch or any other impediment, the second wall was not only taller, but there was a ditch in front of it, with a series of sharpened stakes pounded into the opposite side, pointing outward in a bristling row that, in the headlong rush to get to the wall, were waiting to impale men who got shoved forward by overeager comrades. Scattered in the bottom of the ditch were caltrops, simple devices consisting of two iron spikes, sharpened at both ends and twisted together so that, when they were dropped on the ground, there was always a sharpened, and sometimes barbed point sticking up, waiting to pierce through the leather sole and flesh of an unsuspecting enemy. Compounding the difficulty was that, with the first wall cleared of Gallaeci, the surviving bowmen and slingers were now on the second wall, savaging the attackers in another shower of missiles.

"*Testudo* by Centuries!"

Now that Pullus had returned to his normal spot in the formation, the Tenth Section was once more intact, and Didius' arm moved up as he sidestepped closer to Atilius, although he heard a man shout in pain farther up the formation, and he saw the gap in the raised shields that signaled one of their comrades was down. Then it was the darkness and the deafening racket as their shields were raked with sling bullets and arrows, and twice Didius felt the jerk of his shield from the impact of the stone bullets. As they had discovered in their training, there was no way to hurry when in *testudo*, and as they had all learned in their first assault, this time, no man was tempted to move his shield aside to take a peek. Like a ponderous, many-legged beast, the First Century led the way in a line of six Centuries, while, farther down the wall, the men of the Third Cohort, who had originally been slated to go through the breach used by the Second Cohort behind the Fifth, had marched over to relieve the Eighth instead, both of the original assaulting Cohorts now in reserve. It was impossible to speak in a normal tone of voice because of the constant cracking sound of the bullets lashing the *testudo*, while the arrows striking the shields made a slightly deeper, more hollow sound. Occasionally, there would be a loud, metallic clang as a boss was struck, but the First absorbed the punishment, moving across the beaten zone, less than a hundred paces wide, heading for the ditch. Even with the noise, Didius recognized Rufio's voice, who called out from his spot at the left rear of their *testudo* where, as officers always did, he had snatched up a shield from a man who no longer needed it, and even over the noise, he could hear the excitement in the Optio's voice.

"Pilus Prior!" He had to call out twice before Crastinus snapped that he heard Rufio. "Did you notice anything strange about when those bastards left the wall?"

Like every man who could hear Rufio's question, Didius was mystified, and it became clear the Pilus Prior was equally in the dark as he bellowed, "What do you mean, Rufio? Spit it out, man; we don't have time for riddles!"

"What I mean is that they had to negotiate the ditch and obstacles just like we will, yes? But did you see how quickly they made it across? It's almost as if..."

"...as if they had a path across the ground that allowed them to move like the obstacles weren't there in the first place," Crastinus finished for him, his tone now matching the Optio's.

"Exactly!" Rufio shouted back. "There has to be a way where we won't have to worry about that damn ditch. It's further down that way."

"Good for Rufio," Didius heard Calienus say, the Optio being popular among the men, particularly the Sergeants, since he had been one until Vinicius' death.

Didius did not comment; what he cared about was the Optio being right, and almost immediately, Crastinus turned the *testudo* slightly as he dashed a short distance from the formation, also with a shield, which he held above his head as he ran forward to survey the ground and the ditch.

"There's stakes in the ground!" he heard Pullus call out, using his vantage point on the outside of the formation. "We're going to go between them!"

Shuffling along with his comrades, Didius' arm was aching, but he knew that he was not alone; besides, his mind was almost completely occupied on what was coming next, and he had also learned that complaining about it earned nothing but derision from the men around him. Now that they were at something of an oblique angle to the wall, the men on the right outermost file had the most important and the toughest task, because they were forced to switch hands with their shields, although some men, Pullus among them, possessed the ability to keep the shield in their left hand while reaching across and maintaining the shield in what was an extremely awkward position by lifting it a bit higher so that their shield touched the horizontally raised shield of the men in the next file. Not for the first time, Didius offered a prayer that his nemesis pay for what he viewed as Pullus' hubris in doing it this way, but he also knew that Scribonius would be assiduous in shifting his shield over to provide Pullus some overhead protection, which forced Atilius to do the same to protect Scribonius, and of course Didius to do the same for Atilius. He knew he should hate Scribonius because of his clear friendship with his most loathed enemy, but he could not summon that kind of hostility towards his tall but lean comrade, and there were times Didius found himself wishing that Scribonius was not just so...likable. Nevertheless, he moved his shield to close the gap created by Scribonius' shift to cover Pullus without hesitation because it was Atilius, while Calienus did the same for him, despite how he knew the Sergeant felt about him. Moving along the ditch, Didius was too far removed from the outer files to see the stakes, and he was forced to put his trust in Crastinus to guide them down into the ditch, in between the obstacles. Consequently, he was surprised when the leading ranks vanished from sight as they dropped down in the ditch, but Crastinus was prepared for the moment.

"Last five!" he bellowed, "Ready javelins! If any of those *cunni* lean out over the wall, put a javelin through their fucking face!"

Didius fumbled with his javelins, dropping the second, and he was forced to move his shield away from Atilius as he drew his arm back an instant later than the men around him. As Crastinus had warned, a Gallaeci directly above him had leapt up and was drawing his bow back when, from three ranks up, two of his comrades hurled their missiles. Despite the sharp upward angle, they both had enough momentum to strike the Gallaeci, one of the javelins punching through what Didius saw was a boiled leather vest to bury itself in his chest, while the second struck him just below one eye an eyeblink later. Then, he had to drop down into the ditch with his section, finally able to lower his shield as he did so, and he felt his shoulders involuntarily clench in expectation of a missile plunging down from the second wall, but it never came. The Second Century was now just on the opposite side of the ditch, and he sensed as much as he saw a flurry of javelins streaking overhead, but he could hear the cries of alarm and pain as some of them struck their targets. There was a space of less than fifteen paces between the ditch and the base of the wall, and now that they were at the base of the wall there was no longer a need for a *testudo*, while the two files carrying the ladders moved quickly into position. To his surprise, when Crastinus called for Pullus, it was not to be second up the ladder behind the Pilus Prior as it had been the first time. Instead, the large Roman was given the task that Didius had performed during the first assault, sitting with his back to the wall to brace the ladder as his comrades scaled it. Let's see how you like it, he thought with sour satisfaction, but he was completely unprepared for what came next.

"You there! Achilles!" Crastinus barked, and for a fleeting instant, Didius prayed that there was another man with that nickname, but his heart sank when he saw the Pilus Prior standing with his back to the wall, his *gladius* pointing directly at him. "We're going to see what you're made of and if you can live up to the name. You're going up first."

Didius' first instinct was to turn and leap back down into the ditch, but somehow, without willing it, he felt his body moving in obedience to Crastinus' order, and suddenly, he was standing where the six men, three on each side, were waiting for the command to lift the heavy ladder up and place it against the wall. His mouth was dryer than he could ever remember, and his legs were shaking so violently that, to his shame, he could tell by the expressions of his comrades that they could see his knees almost knocking together, but it was Pullus, already sitting there in readiness who Didius cared about the most. Then, from behind them, the Legion *Cornicen* played the note, and all down the wall, the assaulting Centuries raised their ladders, while the Centuries, in support, hurled the last of their javelins. Despite his terror, Didius noticed that, while the Gallaeci were still shouting, hurling curses and imprecations at the attackers, because of the Romans' position at the base of the wall, there was a muted quality to the noise, but then he felt a rough hand shove him forward, even before the top of the ladder touched the wood of the wall. Somehow, he felt his left leg lift to step up on the first rung, and for a brief moment, he was face to face with Pullus, who was holding the vertical supports so that his fingers were not smashed, and Didius saw the contempt on the large Roman's face...which was exactly what Didius needed. Suddenly, his fear, while not overwhelmed, was at least subdued by the hatred he felt for Pullus, and he remembered his own many boasts in the beginning of training how he would perform feats that would cement his status as the best Legionary in battle, not just in his Century, or his Cohort, but the entire Legion, making the name of Didius known to all men under the standard. The anger he felt was sufficient to get his right leg to raise, and he began climbing the ladder, holding on to a rung with his right hand while keeping his shield up over his head, although he was forced to turn it sideways to avoid getting caught by a rung of the ladder.

Didius was followed by Rufio, and while he heard the Optio, it did not register when Rufio addressed Pullus in an obscenely cheerful voice, "I think he *cac*ed himself. At least that's what it smells like."

By this moment, Didius' head was just below the parapet, and he could see the Gallaeci shields resting on the edge, with just enough of a gap between them for a spear or sword blade to punch out, and he dimly remembered Crastinus warning them of the danger of blindly ascending a ladder, only to get a sword in the face. Consequently, he straightened his leg, as if he was still ascending, but instantly dropped back down, and just as Crastinus had warned, an iron spearpoint shot out from the gap, though it hit nothing but the air above his head. It was when the Gallaeci warrior recovered his spear that Didius moved, scrambling up the last few rungs while using his shield, punching it out against the Gallaeci's. As much as he boasted about it, Spurius Didius *was* strong, easily the second strongest man in his Century, and even with the awkward position he was in on the ladder, there was enough power behind the blow that it sent the Gallaeci staggering back across the parapet, which was about five paces wide, giving Didius just enough space to land, and in one motion, he stepped up onto the parapet then quickly dropped down. He had pulled his shield back towards his body to protect his left side, which saved his life because the Gallaeci to that side made a thrust with a sword that was essentially identical to the one that, Didius realized in horror, he had yet to draw, and while he blocked the thrust with his shield, he saw the point of the Gallaeci weapon punch through the wood to protrude perhaps a half-inch before the warrior recovered it. Without having any memory of doing so, Didius drew his own *gladius* and, again without any thought, instinctively swept it upward from his body just as the Gallaeci to his right, also armed with a spear like the warrior he had sent staggering, executed his own thrust, aiming for Didius' throat, which was actually fortunate for the Legionary because, while he was an eyeblink slow, his blade managed to strike the shaft and knocked it up and out from his body so that the point shot past his face, no more than a couple of inches away.

With his blade now at shoulder level and across his body, Didius could not execute any of the thrusts that he and his comrades spent watches at the stakes perfecting, so he wildly swung his *gladius* at his spear-wielding attacker while lashing out with his shield in the opposite direction. He missed with the *gladius*, but it did force the warrior to his right to leap backward and out of the way, and he felt the shock of the impact running up his left arm as his shield boss struck his foe, the power of his own strength accentuated by the fact that the Gallaeci to his left had actually been stepping forward to make another thrust, sending him staggering backward as well. His original foe, the warrior he knocked back to gain his foothold, came rushing at him, this man eager to take advantage of the fact that, even if it was for the span of less than a normal heartbeat, Didius' body was completely exposed with his shield extended to his left, and his *gladius* out of position to knock this warrior's spear thrust aside. It happened so quickly, yet for Didius, it was as if his opponent was encased in honey, giving him enough time to understand that he was a dead man with his arms out and away from his body.

For the rest of his days, Didius could never recall exactly how he did it, yet somehow, and to his deep surprise, he saw his blade, starting from its position up at shoulder level, this time sweep down and back across his body, but with the flat of his blade striking the spear shaft just behind the iron head as it hurtled towards him, driving it downward so that the point, instead of burying itself in his body, shot in between his legs just below his balls to strike the wooden parapet, the point burying itself in wood instead of flesh; later, when he had time to examine it, he saw the hole through the lower part of his tunic where the spearpoint had sliced through the wool before striking the wall . And, while he certainly had not planned it this way, the pommel of his *gladius* was in a perfect position for him to use it as an extension of his fist, and he drove the iron point at the end directly into the mouth of his foe, feeling and hearing the Gallaeci's teeth shattering, the resulting scream showering his face with blood and bits of teeth as the man staggered back yet again, dropping his shield to clutch his face.

"Achilles, you lazy bastard, make us some room up there!"

Didius recognized Rufio's voice, but while he did not intend to answer, he heard someone replying with a voice that sounded exactly like his snarling, "I'm trying, damn you!"

Even as he heard himself respond, he was once again using his shield to block a third attack from the sword-wielding Gallaeci to his left, except this time, it was a glancing blow that did not move Didius' shield, the blade clanging off the boss, and Didius lashed out for a second time, still forced to use only the strength of his arm, although now, he felt the boss striking flesh with a meaty sound, followed immediately by a sharp cry of pain. Then, as if summoned by the gods, Rufio was suddenly by his side, arriving just in time to counter what would be the final thrust from the spear wielding Gallaeci to Didius' right, the Optio taking the thrust on his shield but then with a speed that was too fast for his foe's eye to track, the point of his *gladius* swept up from under the Roman's shield in a classic first position thrust to bury itself just above the Gallaeci's cock, whereupon Rufio, using his hips for power, twisted his body with his arm locked against his side to rip the cutting edge across the man's belly, opening him up so that his guts came bulging out through the gaping slit in his leather armor. The scream was so shrill that it made both Romans wince, but the Optio used his *caliga* to ruthlessly shove the man into the path of the Gallaeci defenders to their right, creating enough of an obstacle to slow them. Bolstered by the presence of his Optio to guard his back, for the first time, Didius went on the offensive, taking advantage of the sword-wielding Gallaeci's slow recovery from Didius' shield punch to execute his own first thrust, this one from the second position that came over his shield, taking advantage of his foe's involuntary reaction in lowering his shield as he recovered his lost breath. To his pleasure, and surprise, Didius' point struck at exactly the spot for which he had aimed before his foe could lift his shield, the soft hollow of his enemy's throat just above the man's armor, and he felt the grating vibration as the point struck the bones of the neck. However, it was the sudden look of shock and despair that Didius relished the most, and he heard himself snarling unintelligibly but with a savage satisfaction, reveling in his victory. It was his first kill of this nature, besting another man who was not wounded and either seriously hampered or completely helpless, and he relished the sudden rush of a joy that he had never experienced before. For the first time, he actually felt a kinship with Titus Pullus, finally understanding why the giant Roman seemed to enjoy this so much. Without waiting to be told by the Optio, Didius was already moving, even before his first victim had collapsed to his knees, and still snarling, he thrust his *gladius* down into the chest of his original foe, who died on his knees and still clutching his ruined mouth. When he spun about, his shield up and *gladius* ready, he saw that Scribonius, Vellusius, and Calienus were already on the parapet, and despite his feelings, Didius felt a rush of relief, and happiness, that his comrades were here.

For Pullus, it was a mixture of feelings that, even now as a veteran, he was having a hard time understanding, not realizing that, even with all that he had seen and done in a few short months, he was still sixteen years old. Watching his comrades clamber up the ladder rather than leading the way, he experienced a rush of worry as Domitius scrambled up behind Vellusius, though his close comrade stopped just long enough before he ascended the ladder to give his best friend a cheerful grin, then grabbed his crotch.

"You're blessed by Fortuna that I have to hold this ladder," Pullus called out to him, but Domitius was not intimidated in the slightest.

"You're blessed that you can't catch me," Domitius taunted. "It would be like trying grab lightning."

"Go piss on your *caligae*," Pullus called up as his friend scrambled up the ladder, earning him another laugh as Domitius leapt over the parapet and vanished from sight.

Then, it was finally his turn, although he waited long enough for his counterpart in the Second Century to come take his place, and since he was not leading the way, he drew his *gladius*, his hand large enough that he could grasp a rung as he climbed upward. The noise, even somewhat muffled as it was by the wall, told him that the fighting was taking place at a frenzied pace, and even in the span of the half-dozen heartbeats it took him to scale the ladder, he heard the shrill cries of men who had suffered some sort of wound; worst of all, he heard men crying out in his tongue, and he offered up a prayer to the gods to save them. What met his eyes as he reached the top matched what he heard, a scene of utter chaos as Gallaeci warriors came streaming from what he now saw was actually a town, in numbers too many for him to count. Even more distressing to him was that, while the men of the First had cleared a stretch of the parapet, with half of the men climbing up his ladder pressing towards where Crastinus had led men up the second ladder, and the other half was fighting their way towards the Sixth Century of the First Cohort, the cleared area was littered with bodies, most of them Gallaeci but a disturbingly large number of them were Roman. Most of them were moving, even if it was to writhe in pain, while some were sitting up with their backs against the wall, but it was a daunting sight nonetheless seeing so many of his comrades already down, although thankfully, he did not see anyone from his section. Turning his attention to the larger situation, Pullus saw where Calienus and Atilius had become isolated, their backs pressed to the wall and surrounded by a half-dozen Gallaeci warriors.

Pullus did not hesitate, rushing down the parapet, shouting, "Hold on, Calienus!"

It was, he realized in that instant, a foolish thing to do because he could have struck down at least one Gallaeci whose back was turned to him, perhaps two if he had kept his mouth shut, but one warrior, alerted by his shout, spun about and saw the giant Roman approaching. However, when another Gallaeci moved to join him, the warrior snarled something over his shoulder, the meaning made clear when, shouting something back that sounded like a curse, the second warrior returned his attention to Calienus and Atilius who were, just barely, keeping their foes at bay with a series of thrusts that kept these warriors occupied. The sight of this Gallaeci disdaining any help fired Pullus' ire at what he saw as a sign of hubris, and he made a beckoning gesture.

"Come to me, you *cunnus*," he had to shout this to be heard, but while the Gallaeci gave no sign he understood the words, he clearly comprehended the meaning, because he did come at Pullus with a rush.

Like Didius had earlier, Pullus saw that he was holding a sword that was, in most ways, identical to the one Pullus was holding, while his shield was significantly smaller and round and, as they had learned at the beginning of the campaign, which the tribes of Hispania only used for defensive purposes. This warrior proved no different, and while he did have skill, rushing at Pullus with a speed that impressed the giant Roman then launched a series of thrusts and slashes that, while Pullus blocked them, kept him on the defensive before the Gallaeci danced backward, somehow managing to avoid tripping over the bodies of the fallen, Pullus had seen enough, certain that he would vanquish this foe. Consequently, Pullus was content to reduce the gap between them without launching an attack of his own, not only because it narrowed the distance to his two comrades and the warriors surrounding them, but he was certain that his opponent would launch another attack as long as he was patient. In their first exchange, Pullus had seen that, while the man did have some skill, he was too aggressive on his thrusts, overextending his arm while taking too much of a lunging step, and he did not have to wait more than a couple of heartbeats when, once more, the Gallaeci came at him.

This time, Pullus did not stand his ground, instead feigning a retreat as his foe pressed his attack, sensing that he had this huge Roman on the defensive, which was exactly what Pullus intended. And, just as he expected, the Gallaeci overextended his arm on what would be his final thrust, and by leaning forward, he exposed his throat for less than a heartbeat, but that was enough because of Pullus' anticipation, and his own arm shot out, the point slicing into the Gallaeci's neck, severing the large vessel in a shower of bright red blood. Pullus, however, was already moving, using his shield to knock the dying Gallaeci aside to reach his own comrades, while these other Gallaeci clearly put their faith in the slain warrior, because Pullus was able to plunge his blade into the back of one of the dead man's comrades, then into the side of another who was just beginning to turn to face the new threat, and within a handful of heartbeats, all six Gallaeci who had been pressing Calienus and Atilius were dead or incapacitated, giving the pair a much needed chance to recover.

"Thanks, Pullus," the Sergeant gasped, while Atilius managed, "I was about done in!"

Pullus only grinned, then turned his attention back to the fighting along the parapet, pleased to see that, overall, the Romans were doing what they were trained to do, pressing the Gallaeci defenders who refused to leave the parapet into tighter and tighter groups from both sides.

Recognizing Scribonius and Didius, Pullus pointed in their direction, but he thought to ask Calienus rather than tell him, "Should we go over there, Sergeant?"

Calienus, still catching his breath, only nodded, but he did not hesitate to stride over and attach himself to the end of a file by grabbing the back of the harness, the ranker turning in surprise, and Pullus saw that it was a man from the Ninth Section. He and Atilius joined Calienus on either side of their Sergeant, both of them quickly settling into the rhythm of the Roman way of fighting, bolstering their comrades ahead of them in their file, which Rufio was directing, using his bone whistle to sound the relief. Inch by inch, step by step, Pullus' group shuffled forward as the men in the front thrust, slashed, and hacked down those Gallaeci who refused to recognize the inevitable, that the fight for the parapet of the second wall was lost. Finally, several of the warriors, now crammed together so tightly that they could not even employ their weapons, began to leap down from the parapet, some of them landing awkwardly and collapsing to the ground, usually clutching an ankle or knee before struggling to their feet to limp back towards the town, where the remainder of the Gallaeci warriors, seeing that the second wall was lost, were beginning to form themselves up across the muddy strip that served as a street. Some of the more quick-thinking Romans who were not otherwise engaged in the fighting snatched up the handful of javelins littering the parapet that had not struck a target and were intact, hurling them into the backs of several of the fleeing enemy in Pullus' part of the parapet. To his disappointment, the last resistance was either cut down, or they abandoned the parapet before he could take a turn at the front, but it did give him the opportunity to scan the rampart, looking for one man in particular.

"Have any of you seen Domitius?" he asked, trying not to sound concerned, but Scribonius shook his head, and none of the others remembered seeing him either.

Now that their part of the parapet was secured, he did not think he would run afoul of Rufio if he turned around and began searching for Domitius, his anxiety growing after he scanned what was roughly the other half of the First Century about a hundred paces down the rampart, where only Crastinus' Centurion's crest was visible in the crush of bodies, but not spotting his diminutive friend. Nevertheless, he began walking in that direction, but he had only gone about fifteen paces when he froze, looking down at a small pile of three bodies, two of them Gallaeci, but while the upper half of the body was obscured by their corpses, he recognized the Roman *caligae*. But, worst of all, he recognized the legs, despite the fact that they were covered in blood, he was certain of it, and with his heart suddenly pounding, he went rushing over, yanking the first, then the second body off, flinging them both off the parapet with brutal force before forcing himself to kneel so he could examine the fallen Roman. He was lying face down, but there was no mistaking it; it was Domitius.

Chapter Seven

For Domitius, being on the outermost file on the left side of the formation meant that he had the easiest job in the *testudo*, merely having to hold his shield up a bit higher than he normally would if they were marching. While nobody had ever said as much, he had deduced that this was one reason why their formation was arranged by height and size from right to left, so that smaller men like himself would not be overburdened by being forced to hold the shield above his head. Not that it mattered in the moment, and he moved with his Century, sheltering under both Vellusius' shield and the shield of the man in the Ninth Section ahead of him as they advanced towards the breach on their mission to rescue the Fifth Cohort. Given the angle of their approach, he was sheltered and no missile struck his own shield, although his comrade in the Ninth Section took an arrow above the boss that, if the shield had not been there, would have plunged down into his face. He could see the iron tip protruding through the back of the shield, but Domitius had developed the ability to not dwell on what might have happened; as far as he was concerned, he was still among the living and that was what mattered, and there was no point wondering what might have occurred had the shield not been there.

While most of his comrades commented about the darkness while in *testudo*, and their absolute blindness, especially those men packed into the middle of the formation, where their entire world consisted of the back of the man in front of them and their comrades on either side pressing against them, for Domitius, what he always remembered about this most famous formation used by the Legions was the smell. It was distinctly different than when they had been in training, and as he had learned, men who were afraid exuded a distinctly different and sharper stench than the normal sweat that came with the exertion of holding a shield aloft while moving at the required shuffling pace. One small blessing for Domitius was that, unlike Pullus and his longer legs, he did not have to concentrate nearly as much to avoid stepping on the back of the feet of the man ahead of him, and he always took delight in reminding his giant friend of the relatively easy time he had compared to Pullus. Now, as he moved with his Century, he kept his eye on Rufio, who was in his spot just behind and to Domitius' left, although now that he was carrying a shield, he had moved even closer than normal to the formation, taking advantage of the shelter provided by the upraised shields while adding his own to the protection. As Domitius had learned, Rufio's behavior and actions were always a good indicator of what was coming, and in this, Domitius was like every other ranker, all of whom were interested to the point of obsession about the larger situation, using every means at their disposal to get an idea of what lay in their immediate future. Consequently, Domitius was prepared for Crastinus' order to halt and break out of the *testudo* when they reached the ditch because of Rufio suddenly lowering his shield as he trotted up the left side of the formation, and along with his comrades, dropped down into it. He had to toss his shield and javelins up out of the ditch because he needed both hands to clamber up out of it, then scrambled to get back in his spot, and it was then he heard Crastinus ordering Didius up the ladder first, while somewhat unusually, the Pilus Prior had the sections going up in reverse order, in another example of how the danger was shared equally, even down to the section level, with the Fifth Section following him up one ladder, and the Tenth going up the other first. It was only fair, but while Domitius did not mind; he could see by the sudden pallor on Didius' normally swarthy features that his surly comrade did not care all that much about being fair.

Of all of the Tenth Section, it was Domitius who took exception to Didius' shirking and his attempts to avoid danger the most personally, and while they never spoke of it, he suspected that at least Pullus knew why. Being as small as he was; in fact, if he had not experienced a growth spurt the summer before, he wouldn't have met the height requirement for joining the Legion, Domitius had to work harder, not only to meet his own standard, but to prove himself to his new comrades when they began training. He was proud of what he had accomplished, and had learned to use his size, or lack thereof, to his advantage, particularly his quickness. Whereas his best friend could rely on brute strength, although he was exceptionally quick for a man his size, Domitius relied on his speed and nimble footwork, which he had been forced to develop to avoid being bashed by Pullus once Cyclops started pitting them against each other, back when Domitius was thirteen and Pullus only twelve but already taller than many adult men. Seeing someone like Didius who, while not as gifted as Pullus, still possessed considerable strength and better than average reflexes, doing his utmost to do as little as possible was bad enough, but what truly infuriated Domitius was what he viewed as Didius' cowardice. It was a feature of his character; even before Titus Pullus had rescued him from having his head dunked into a bucket of *cac* by the bullies Marcus and Aulus, Vibius Domitius had always despised injustice in any form, and he took it personally when someone abused their position, or in this case, the physical gifts that the gods had not seen fit to impart to him.

Now, as he watched Didius approaching the ladder on wobbly legs, the only surprise he felt was that his comrade actually began ascending the ladder. Standing behind Vellusius, he did keep a javelin in his hand, watching for an opportunity, but the Gallaeci within range presented an unbroken line of shields resting on the parapet, although he did see farther down the wall several missiles go streaking upward, and he heard over the shouting from both sides at least one cry of pain that signaled a hit. After a delay that was ended when Rufio, following Didius, finally lost patience and disappeared over the rampart, it was his turn, although he took a moment to taunt Pullus, who was sitting there bracing the ladder and looking unhappy about it, before scrambling up to join his comrades. There was no immediate danger, Didius and Rufio having cut down what he counted to be four enemy warriors to create enough space, but the Optio was already occupied, pushing his way to the right of the ladder with Scribonius and Atilius by his side, with Calienus and Romulus behind them, and without orders, Domitius instinctively followed Vellusius, who had turned to his left, joining Didius and Remus, who were already standing side by side across the width of the rampart. Didius was closer, but Domitius moved to stand behind Vellusius, who rushed to take up the spot next to Didius to block the rampart, as Domitius grabbed the back of his friend's harness, while the first men of the Ninth Section joined him, one bracing Didius, the other Remus.

Being second in line meant three things: he had to be instantly ready to step into the spot of the first man, either when someone sounded the relief or he fell, but also to bolster his comrade and finally, if necessary, use his shield to protect the man from an overhead blow. Vellusius was facing a warrior who, somewhat unusually, was wearing both a helmet and mail, which, unlike the Roman style of mail, was sleeveless but was also longer, and wielding a sword, not the shorter weapon like the one in his scabbard, but one with a longer blade and a slightly rounded tip. While he did not know it, it would be a weapon with which Domitius, and all of his comrades who survived this campaign, would become very familiar. Because it was not a weapon designed for thrusting, the Gallaeci swung his arm back, and while Vellusius' own blade shot out, the warrior caught it on his shield, then brought his sword arm forward in a powerful, sweeping blow that seemed meant to split Vellusius in two, right down the middle of his head. Domitius saw, and understood, the Gallaeci's intent an instant before Vellusius did, his left arm immediately moving to swing his shield up above Vellusius' head, while Vellusius belatedly lifted his shield up so that it was Domitius' shield that was in position first. The impact was tremendous, both from the heavier blade and the power behind the blow, driving Domitius' shield down where it actually touched his comrade's helmet, albeit not with much force. As he, and the other men, had learned, every battle provided a learning experience, and both Vellusius and Domitius saw that this kind of attack, while powerful, took more time to execute than a simple thrust.

Vellusius proved that he had been paying attention because, while he did not make a counterthrust, nor did he use his shield offensively this time, so that when, with a bellowed challenge, the Gallaeci drew his arm back again for another blow, this time, Vellusius did not hesitate. Leading with the boss of his shield, Vellusius' arm shot out in a punch that he timed perfectly for the moment when, as the blade swung down and relying on Domitius' shield to remain in place above him, he struck the Gallaeci's own, smaller shield just as the warrior was stepping into his blow. Domitius felt the double impact, his shield arm once more being driven downward, while he felt the shock up through his right hand and arm grasping Vellusius' harness, while the warrior reeled from essentially walking right into the shield punch. And, while it was grudging, Domitius had to admit that Didius, who was to Vellusius' left, had been paying attention and, most importantly, didn't hesitate, his own blade shooting out, parallel to the rampart to punch directly into the right armpit of the Gallaeci, and Domitius could see Didius' *gladius* penetrate several inches into their foe's body. He didn't scream; it was more of a breathy moan that was accompanied by a bloody froth from his mouth that Domitius knew meant Didius had punctured a lung. The Gallaeci took one staggering step backward, but the warrior behind him did not try to offer any aid, instead shoving his comrade with enough force that he toppled from the rampart as that warrior came rushing to fill the vacated spot. He was an instant too late as Vellusius, aided by Domitius pushing him forward, beat the Gallaeci to it, forcing him to slide to a halt, but he was unable to block Vellusius' thrust that, while not a killing blow, sliced into the man's upper thigh. Before Vellusius could follow up, his opponent, making the best of the bad choices facing him, threw himself off of the rampart, where his fall was at least partially broken by the body of the mail-clad warrior. Now, the Gallaeci who had been trying to kill Didius found himself essentially surrounded on three sides, and he was quickly cut down, earning the Romans another couple of feet of rampart. It was Roman efficiency at its best, where men didn't think and behave like individual warriors seeking glory, but as a team, working together and as one organic machine that methodically ground their enemies down with a dispassionate but ruthless economy. And, as was occurring behind them in the opposite direction, there were many Gallaeci who recognized that the battle for the second wall was effectively over, and their last option was to abandon the rampart to join their own comrades who were now trying to get organized for what would be not just the final phase of this battle, but the end of a rebellion.

With Rufio leading the effort behind them, and Crastinus on the opposite side of those Gallaeci trying desperately to stop Vibius and his group from reaching their Centurion, it fell to the *Tesserarius* Aulus Cordus to take command of their effort, and although he didn't have the bone whistle, he shouted out the order for relief. Domitius felt Vellusius tense, then after feinting a thrust with his *gladius* he used his shield, smashing it into his opponent's own small, round one that, while the warrior blocked the blow, made him take a step backward to maintain his balance. Since this was the goal, Vellusius didn't hesitate in taking a step to his left, away from the edge of the parapet as Domitius moved into his spot, all in one coordinated motion that, during their training, they had all vociferously complained about, albeit out of their officers' earshot, but which now paid off in a manner that none of them would ever argue. Because of the narrower spacing, Vellusius had to turn sideways to move between his and Domitius' file and the file in the middle of the three-man rank, and he was surprised to see that the lines behind the files had grown to a half-dozen men in each. Up front, the warrior Vellusius had forced backward rushed at Domitius, but Pullus' friend was prepared, taking the spear thrust the Gallaeci had aimed at Vellusius just as he turned sideways, when Domitius' comrade made the mistake of turning to face the parapet and thereby exposing his right side on his shield, the spearpoint glancing off of Domitius' protection. His own *gladius* was already moving, relying on his quickness to launch the third position thrust that came from roughly the middle outer edge of his own shield, taking advantage of the Gallaeci's upper body twisting from the impact of his own blocked thrust. It was not a killing blow, but it was almost as good, feeling the sudden resistance as the point of his blade bit into the flesh of the Gallaeci's bicep, slicing through the muscle and causing the man, who in one of those odd moments, Domitius saw was not much older than himself, to drop the shield as he screamed in pain, the blood spraying a bright red from a severed vessel. He was dead a heartbeat later from Domitius' second thrust, and just that quickly, the space between his group and that led by Crastinus pressing from the opposite side became smaller.

To this point, Domitius had not been challenged in his opponent, and later, he would conclude that this was the cause for what was about to happen; in short, he became overconfident. The resistance on the parapet had been reduced to no more than two dozen Gallaeci, roughly equally divided between those facing in his direction and those facing Crastinus with the first five sections, and it was now Domitius' second rotation at the front. Facing him was an older warrior, perhaps in his thirties, and Domitius reminded himself that this meant his opponent possessed some skill to reach that age, yet he was not particularly concerned. This Gallaeci was also armed with the same kind of short sword, although his shield was unusually large, and was rectangular, which Domitius assumed he had taken as spoils from another tribe. He also was cleanshaven except for a mustache that he had allowed to grow so that the ends hung down several inches below his chin, and he was wearing the high, conical helmet favored by these tribes, while his armor was a boiled leather vest with iron rings sewn in overlapping circles. Domitius observed all of this in the span of the perhaps single heartbeat he had before his opponent feinted a high thrust, which he blocked easily enough, though he took note of the power behind the warrior's blow. His foe clearly expected Domitius to retaliate with a thrust of his own, but, sensing that this was what the Gallaeci wanted, instead, Domitius lashed out with his shield, mainly to test his foe's reflexes. As he expected, the Gallaeci moved his shield over and cleanly blocked the blow with a metal clanging sound as boss struck boss, the shock of the impact traveling up Domitius' arm, and he was disquieted to see that, while he did not move backward, neither did his opponent.

Next to him now was a Ninth Section man, but he was occupied with his own opponent, a young warrior who was armed only with a spear that he kept jabbing at Domitius' comrade repeatedly, and so rapidly that the Legionary was kept on the defensive, meaning that, for the moment, Domitius was on his own. Even as he recognized this, his foe launched another attack, this time a low thrust but across the Gallaeci's body in an attempt to get past Domitius' shield, forcing him to move his protection in the same direction, taking the sword thrust on his shield. For the briefest instant, the Gallaeci's right arm was extended out in front of his shield, and relying on his natural quickness, Domitius executed a thrust over his shield, but with the point downward to stab his enemy's right forearm. He felt the blade bite into flesh, the sudden bellow of pain coming at almost the same instant, turning into a scream of a deeper agony when, in a reflexive reaction, the Gallaeci jerked his arm back while Domitius' blade was still embedded in his forearm, the sharp edge slicing through muscle, tendons and blood vessels from just below his elbow to a couple inches above his wrist. Once again, there was a bright red spray from the severed vessels as the Gallaeci dropped his sword onto the wooden parapet, reeling backward a step before he reflexively discarded his shield to clutch his ruined appendage. It was then that Domitius made his mistake, relying on his comrade in the Ninth Section to keep the spear-wielding warrior occupied as he pressed forward, intent on dispatching his now-defenseless opponent, whose face was twisted into a grimace of pain, and Domitius was certain he saw an expression of resignation in the warrior's eyes as he executed another thrust over his shield, but this time with the blade parallel to the ground and not perpendicular and aimed at the Gallaeci's throat. In doing so, he inadvertently stepped into a thrust from the young spear-wielding warrior, who took advantage of Domitius not returning his shield back to protect the left side of his body quickly enough. Piecing it together later, Domitius concluded that the point of his blade punched into the wounded Gallaeci's throat simultaneously with the spearpoint of the young warrior to his left piercing his thigh, plunging through the thick muscle, and because of his own momentum moving forward, the point exiting the back of his leg. The pain was instantaneous and excruciating, but most importantly, he felt his left leg collapsing from under him, and the thought that went through his mind was how many times he and the other new *Tirones* had heard Pilus Prior Crastinus, Optio Vinicius, and the veterans like Calienus stress what they said was the most important factor in surviving battle.

"If you lose your feet in a fight, you've got one foot in Charon's Boat."

Consequently, even with the agony that felt like someone had plunged a burning torch into his leg, Domitius' intention was to regain his feet as quickly as possible, but just as he hit the wooden surface of the parapet, he was crushed under the weight of something heavy that effectively pinned him. He was only vaguely aware of someone bellowing something in his tongue, followed immediately by a gurgling sound, and even if he had possessed the strength to push himself up off the parapet and dislodge what he dimly understood was likely the body of the Gallaeci he had just slain, there was another devastating blow, the weight on top of him seeming to double, crushing him and driving the breath from his lungs. It was dark, and he was trapped, while above him the fighting continued to rage, without him in it; this was his last memory as he slipped into unconsciousness.

For Pullus, dashing down the parapet, hurdling over the bodies of both friend and foe seemed to take twice as long as it should have, but then he was there, kneeling down as he grabbed the first body partially covering his friend, barely noticing that it was a young warrior around his own age, using his massive strength to fling the body with enough power that it flew off the parapet, the corpse's limbs flailing in a grotesque parody as if the dead man was trying to maintain his balance. The second warrior, wearing a helmet, with his right arm completely covered in blood and almost sliced in two parts from elbow to wrist, he slung off the parapet, barely noticing the slit in the dead man's throat that was the width of a Roman *gladius* as he did so, intent on checking his friend. His initial reaction was a gasp at seeing that Domitius' tunic below his *hamata* was completely soaked in blood, and it was his reaction that roused Domitius, his eyes fluttering open, and he moved his head slightly to squint up at Pullus.

He opened his mouth, but it took him two attempts to croak, "Wha...what happened? Where am I, Titus?"

"You've been wounded," Pullus began, and while he attempted to use a comforting tone, Domitius' eyes widened, but he also tried to sit up as his hands reached down around the area of his midsection, which Pullus stopped by grabbing Domitius' hands, saying firmly, "Don't do that. Let me see. I'm sure it's nothing," more hopefully than with any real conviction.

Pullus could see his hands trembling as he reached down to lift the hem of Domitius' tunic, hoping that his friend could not, but to this point, Domitius had not lifted his head, and he lay there as Pullus gingerly pulled the *hamata* and tunic up. While Domitius' *subligaculum* was similarly blood-soaked, he did not try to hide his relief when he saw that there was no wound, either in the groin or belly, and he heard Domitius' prayer of thanks, correctly reading Pullus' expression. Moving his examination down, Pullus found the wound, and while he did not want to and was as gentle as he could be, he lifted Domitius' leg, prompting a groan of pain from his friend, and he saw that there was an exit wound as well. It was a serious wound, but most importantly, it had not severed the large vessel that ran up the inside of the thigh, and in fact the bleeding, while still happening, had visibly slowed.

"It's a through and through wound," Pullus told Domitius, trying to sound matter-of-fact and not disturbed, "but it didn't cut a vessel or you'd already be dead." Standing up, he said, "Let me go get a *medicus*."

Without waiting for a reply, he left his friend, leaving Domitius to lie there, trying unsuccessfully to keep his hands from roaming over his lower body to probe the wound, only dimly aware of the sounds of the fight that was now raging down on the ground, just a matter of paces away. Like most wounded men, he couldn't summon much interest in the larger events going on around him, his mind occupied with all the questions that, up until this moment and like almost all of his comrades, he kept shoved into a cupboard in his mind. He was grateful that Pullus wasn't gone long, informing him that a *medicus* would be coming shortly, and despite the fact the Gallaeci were not subdued yet, rather than return to the fighting, the large Roman sat down next to his best friend, his legs dangling off the rampart.

Even if he hadn't known Domitius so well, he would have seen the worry on his face that was warring with the pain from the wound, and Pullus assured him, "Vibius, don't worry. I've seen enough wounds to know this isn't fatal."

Domitius didn't reply immediately, afraid to voice the fear that was now threatening to consume him, but he finally confessed, "That's not what I'm worried about, Titus. I'm worried that it won't heal properly, or even if it does, it will cripple me and I'll be dismissed from the Legion."

Domitius could tell by Pullus' reaction, who gave a sudden start, his eyes widening that this hadn't even occurred to his large friend, but Pullus shook his head as he scoffed, "*Gerrae!* Don't talk nonsense! You're going to be fine, I swear it! And," he warned jokingly, "if you keep talking like that, I'm going to thrash you." Suddenly, he seemed to understand how this could be construed, and added hastily, "After you're healed up, of course."

Saving them both further awkwardness, a *medicus* arrived, and Pullus stayed just long enough to get an assurance from the man that his prediction was true, but he wasn't completely satisfied with what he heard, and he saw that neither was Domitius.

"As long as it heals cleanly and doesn't corrupt," the *medicus* shrugged, "he should be fine. But," he warned, having had conversations of this nature more times than he could easily count, and he had been wrong before, "you need to make sacrifices to the gods, because it's up to them."

It wasn't the answer either of them wanted to hear, but they both understood this was all they would get, and after promising to come and check on him again, Pullus dropped down off the parapet, while Domitius, who was now sitting up with his back against the parapet, watched his giant friend race in the direction of where the fighting was the thickest and resembling the kind of brawl one would find in a soldier's *taverna* rather than on a battlefield, and he felt a twinge of guilt that he felt no desire to join Pullus.

For Scribonius, not only was this the hardest fight he, or any of his comrades, had ever faced, it was the first occasion where he spent a significant amount of time without Pullus' shield there to protect him, and on that day, he realized how he had come to take it for granted that the giant Roman would always be there next to him. Instead, he found himself on the outside, without the protection of a shield to protect his weak side, pressed by Gallaeci who were fighting with the desperation that comes from knowing that their defeat would spell the end of their rebellion against Rome, and expose their families who were huddled in the huts behind them to Rome's harsh and pitiless punishment where, if they were fortunate, a life of slavery awaited them. Crastinus, along with the other Centurions, had tried to get their Centuries organized once down on the ground, but because of the constant pressure from the Gallaeci, matters were hopelessly confused, so that the man to Scribonius' left was from the Second Section, while he was being bolstered by a comrade from the Fifth Section, who was also using his own *gladius* to keep at bay any enemy warrior with an idea to try and attack from the flank. The noise was deafening, but Scribonius, like most of the combatants on both sides, had learned to block out the din, though he listened for the calls and signals that were relevant to him, particularly the shrill shriek of the bone whistle sounding the relief, and the notes played by the *Cornicen* who, along with the *Signifer*, never left Crastinus' side.

When it came to this kind of fighting, where there were tactics in only the roughest sense and, as many of his more experienced comrades would comment, were more aligned with a brawl in a *taverna*, Scribonius couldn't seem to summon the kind of fury that seemed to be elemental in seeing another sunrise, so he was forced to rely on his skill, and while it wouldn't be until later, after this fight, Sextus Scribonius reached a conclusion, that facing Titus Pullus in sparring as often as he had had prepared him for this moment. Without any conscious thought, Scribonius would feel his shield moving in response to an attack, then his *gladius* would lash out even before his mind could form the idea, and while he didn't land a damaging blow every time, to his dull surprise, when the relief did sound and he moved to the rear, he saw that his *gladius* was bloody halfway to the hilt. Suddenly, the Gallaeci facing his

Century were either reinforced or found fresh reserves of energy because the entire formation was shoved backward and with enough violence that it rippled down the files and made Scribonius and the other men at the tail end stagger backward. Crastinus reacted immediately, blowing three short blasts on his whistle that was the signal that new orders were coming.

"Right, boys! We're going to back up a bit! Prepare to withdraw!"

It was, the new *Tirones* had concluded, because Romans never used the word "retreat" that the command to move backward was called a "withdrawal," and while they spent time mastering the technique, Scribonius and the others lost count of the number of times they had been told by Crastinus that as long as he was their Centurion, they would never be moving backwards. Regardless of his boast, Scribonius, and the other men, responded immediately, although his role at the back was limited to holding on to the harness of the man in front of him and keeping his feet clear when the move backwards began.

After another single blast, Crastinus then bellowed a single word command, "One!"

Instantly, every man on the front rank used either their shield to shove the Gallaeci pressing them backward, or in some cases, unleashed a thrust that was designed more to make the enemy recoil than with any hope of drawing blood while Crastinus watched, his eyes narrowed as he concentrated on what was, under these circumstances, a difficult maneuver.

In the eyeblink of time after his men responded, he shouted, "Two!"

This was the second part of the maneuver but instead of pressing forward, as one, the men on the front rank stepped aside then began moving back down between the files as if it was a standard relief, but instead of stepping into their place, the men of the second rank didn't move, bracing themselves for the renewed onslaught as the warriors came rushing into the newly cleared space. Not surprising to anyone, this sign that the Romans were retreating heartened them, but while he wouldn't have thought it possible, to Scribonius, it became clear that it also infused the Gallaeci with even more energy. By the time his Century had retreated so that the rear rank was within a pace of the second wall, Scribonius was back as the second man in his line, and he was forced to drop his shield and lean it against his leg to maintain his grasp of his comrade's harness, while simultaneously parrying a spear thrust from a warrior who had managed to get himself around the edge of the formation.

Under normal circumstances, Crastinus, *Signifer* Scaevola and *Cornicen* Poplicola would have been on the right side of the formation, but they were actually on the opposite side, forcing Scribonius and the man behind him, the Sergeant of the Second Section, to provide security from this threat to their right flank. Once more, Scribonius' arm had moved before he could think, sweeping down and away from his body to strike the shaft of the spear just behind the head as it punched forward so that it stabbed nothing but air in the space between his body and that of his comrade behind him. Somehow, he didn't know exactly how, Scribonius suddenly knew what was coming next so that, when the warrior didn't simply draw his arm back to recover for another thrust and reversed his direction in a backhanded slashing movement with the intention of slicing into Scribonius' outstretched arm holding his *gladius*, he was ready.

There wasn't time for him to move his arm out of the path of the spearpoint, but with what appeared to be a flick of his wrist, he managed to sweep his *gladius* up just enough to change the trajectory of the arc of the Gallaeci's attempt so that instead of slicing into flesh, the iron spear blade struck the iron of the shoulder of Scribonius' mail, the force of the blow breaking several links and leaving a deep bruise, though he wouldn't learn this until later. It also sent him reeling sideways, but he had the presence of mind to relax his left arm so that his momentum didn't jerk the man he was bracing on the front rank and send him stumbling along with Scribonius. It would have made sense, nor would he have been blamed for relinquishing his hold on his comrade's harness to at least be able to pivot to face his foe, but while he wasn't like Domitius, who was widely acknowledged to be the most stubborn man in their tent, Scribonius possessed his own streak of obstinance, so he maintained his grip on the harness, while the Gallaeci, a man of indeterminate age with a full beard, did finally pull his arm back after his second failed attempt. Scribonius' right arm was throbbing now, and there was a tingling sensation that ran down into his hand, which he ignored as he waited for what came next. He's going to kill me if I don't do something. It was the clarity of the thought that Scribonius would have cause to recall, as if he was sitting on a bench playing a game of tables and contemplating his next move, despite the fact that less than two full heartbeats of time had elapsed since the Gallaeci had initiated his first lunge. Immediately following this thought was his conviction that he again knew what was coming next, so that his arm was, for another time, already moving, anticipating that his frustrated foe would take a larger step than was wise as he launched another thrust, this one straight and aimed for Scribonius' exposed torso just under the Roman's ribs to avoid the spearpoint from lodging in the cartilage. The result was that the point of his *gladius* was essentially waiting to bite into the Gallaeci's arm, right at the elbow as the warrior executed his thrust, and Scribonius was rewarded by a simultaneous shriek of pain, accompanied by the solid impact running up his arm as the point struck the bone just above the elbow joint, and he didn't even have to move his blade to sever the large vessel running down the inside of the Gallaeci's arm, the warrior doing it for him when he instinctively recoiled, the spray from his rapidly pumping heart showering Scribonius' arm with blood. The Gallaeci did have the presence of mind to reel backwards a couple of steps, leaving his spear on ground that was already soaked with blood before spinning about and staggering back into the press of warriors, out of the fight. Scribonius didn't have any time to savor this victory, both because Crastinus again blew his whistle three times, and his original opponent was quickly replaced, this time by a warrior armed with a long sword, whereupon Scribonius snatched up his shield where he had leaned it against his left leg, bringing it up into position barely in time to stop the Gallaeci in mid-stroke, the warrior quickly recovering for a different attack now that his Roman foe was protected.

"Right! We've gone backwards as far as we're going." He could just make out Crastinus' words, though his eyes never left his foe, but while he didn't see his Centurion thrusting his *gladius* into the air, he clearly heard Crastinus bellow, "Kill 'em! Kill 'em all, boys! No mercy!"

And, with what was more of a guttural growl that, to his surprise, Scribonius added his own voice to, his men signaled their acceptance of their Centurion's order, and made a promise of their own. In the sudden rush back at the Gallaeci, Scribonius was right there with his comrades.

This battle was, by common consent, the hardest fight that the men, both the veterans from Pompeius' army and the newer veterans of the *dilectus*, had ever experienced.

It was Calienus who summed up the feeling as, still panting from the exertion required to finally crush the last embers of the Lucenses branch of the Gallaeci's attempt at rebellion, he observed, "If those fucking pirates had fought like this, we'd still be sailing around Our Sea."

Along with the nature of the fight put up by the Gallaeci, it had also proven to be the most disorganized battle of the campaign, one in which men from the Second and Third Century found themselves standing next to men from the First Century, while commanded by a Centurion from the Fourth Century. As seemingly hopelessly confused as it had been, once the fight was over and as men began to talk about what had happened, a consensus quickly developed among those for whom this had not even been a consideration before this battle.

"We won because of our training," was how Romulus put it, back at the camp that night. "I didn't know half of the bastards I was standing with there at the end, but when we heard the whistle blow, we all knew what to do and we did it as if we'd been together all the time."

This was met by a ragged chorus of agreement, and while there was a face missing from around the fire on this evening, Pullus had assured his comrades that Domitius was going to be fine.

"He's already trying to get the camp physician to let him out of the hospital," Pullus had informed them, laughing at the memory of his friend arguing with the man who, as was customary, was a Greek who was actually attached to Caesar's staff, that he should be released.

"Can he walk?" Scribonius asked, having taken a moment to check on their comrade when he was lying with the rest of the wounded who were waiting for the hospital tent to be erected outside the walls.

"No," Pullus replied, shaking his head. "But do you think that matters to Vibius?"

While Domitius was the only man of the Tenth Section who had been wounded seriously enough to require time in the hospital, none of them had escaped completely unscathed, though it was an assortment of minor cuts and numerous bruises. Ironically, aside from Domitius, Pullus himself had suffered the most serious wound, a long, deep cut running down the length of his right arm from just below the elbow to a couple inches above his wrist, which he had bound up by taking the neckerchief from Plautius, who had died from a spear thrust to his chest. Remus had suffered a puncture wound to his upper left arm from an arrow, which, when his brother had seen it and rushed to his side, was the first moment that Remus was even aware that he had been hit.

"I didn't even feel it," he kept saying over and over. "Having that fucking *medicus* rummaging around in it hurt more than the arrow did!"

"How deep was it?" Calienus asked, and Remus held up a hand to hold his thumb and forefinger less than an inch apart.

"Only that much." Remus shrugged, then glanced down at the bandage, which had a red spot on it. "The *medicus* said that Fortuna loves me, and I guess that must be true, because there wasn't any scrap of my tunic in it. At least," he shrugged again, "that's what he said."

"Keep an eye on it anyway," Calienus said quietly, although he was addressing Romulus, who assured him that he would.

Their conversation was cut short by a fit of coughing, caused by a momentary shift in the wind that sent the smoke from the still smoldering remnants of the Gallaeci fortified town drifting through their midst.

"We're blessed those bastards from the 9th didn't burn us all to death," Atilius grumbled, and this was again met with murmurs of agreement, while it also revived another common conversation.

"There are always *mentulae* who love to see things burn," Calienus commented, then added, "and that's as true for us as it is for the 9th. They," he concluded, "just got the chance to start it before any of us did."

None of his comrades had enough experience to know whether this was true or not, but they were all inclined to believe their Sergeant. Their conversation was interrupted by Rufio, who was walking with a heavy limp, a thick bandage just below his knee and above his greave, though he was otherwise not visibly marked.

"Boys," the Optio greeted them, although this time, he didn't drop into a squat because of his wound, waving them down as they climbed to their feet as custom dictated. "I just came to let you know what will be happening at first light tomorrow."

The men understandably listened attentively, learning that there was going to be a formation where Caesar would be accepting the formal surrender by the surviving elders of the Gallaeci, who had begged Caesar for mercy when, with their numbers whittled down to barely five thousand people of the fifteen thousand who had greeted the sun that morning, they had thrown down their weapons and surrendered. It hadn't been a popular decision by Caesar for many of the men who, again understandably, were grieving the loss of so many of their own.

It was with this in mind that Calienus asked, "What's the butcher's bill, Optio?"

"It's not good," Rufio admitted, but he did not provide numbers, which he explained. "It's still too early to tell whether some of ours who are in the *quaestorium* will survive, but with what we've already lost before this, we suffered twelve dead, and two men who will have to be cashiered out."

"How many men did we leave Scallabis with?" Scribonius asked, though he thought he remembered the number, which was confirmed when Rufio replied, "Ninety-one."

"So at best we're going to have, what, seventy-six men left?" Calienus frowned, but while it was a daunting number given their original numbers, Rufio did point out, "Which isn't bad considering the traditional eighty-man Centuries, so we're almost at full strength when you look at it that way."

It was, they all knew, a thin gruel, as they liked to say, but nobody challenged Rufio about it, knowing the words weren't his own but had been relayed to him, probably by Crastinus, although it could have come from the Primus Pilus.

With his news delivered, Rufio limped off, and there was a brief silence before Calienus looked over at Pullus, who was staring into the flames, and asked the question he had been debating on bringing up.

"Did you..." Calienus stopped, trying to search for the right words, before settling on, "...lose your head again? Like you did at the ambush that night?"

There was something in the giant Roman's reaction that indicated to the Sergeant, as well as to Scribonius, that he was either not surprised by the question, or perhaps he had been thinking about it as he stared into the fire.

Rather than answer directly, Pullus looked over at Calienus and asked, "What makes you ask?"

To Pullus' surprise, this made Calienus chuckle, and the Sergeant answered laconically, "Oh, I suppose it was because you were bellowing some sort of gibberish like you were possessed by a *numen* for one thing."

"And," Scribonius spoke up, "I saw you split one of those barbarian's heads open with your shield." He mimicked the action, lifting his left arm high above his head, then bringing it down. "You brought it down from above his head and split it open like a melon."

Pullus looked embarrassed; again, he had no real memory of anything other than, immediately after he had been wounded, the feeling of that...*thing* inside him suddenly breaking free and running rampant, so he could only answer with a shrug, "If you say so, Sextus."

"I saw him gut one of those bastards," Romulus spoke up, leaning on one elbow, his normal method of relaxing, "then laugh in the *cunnus'* face when his guts fell on his *caligae*."

That, Pullus thought uneasily, explained why his *caligae* and lower legs had looked like they had been dipped in a vat of blood and offal, and smelled as bad.

"All I know," Atilius said, "is it's safer being behind him than in front of him."

This was met with a roar of laughter, and even Pullus joined in, albeit reluctantly; only Didius, who had contributed next to nothing to the conversation, remained quiet, choosing instead to glower into the fire.

The next morning, as Rufio had informed them, the ten most senior men of the Lucenses branch of the Gallaeci tribe were subjected to the humiliation of approaching Caesar, who was seated on the curule chair that, for Romans, was the symbol of his authority as *Praetor*, which was perched atop a makeshift rostra made of wooden crates, while he wore a garland of laurel that, as importantly, marked him as the victor of this campaign. In accordance with custom, the Gallaeci elders were forced to kneel before Caesar, then, through an interpreter, offer their submission and total surrender of not just themselves, but all of the surviving tribespeople, who were under guard a short distance away, clustered together in family units, weeping as they clung to each other to watch their leaders throw themselves on the mercy of Caesar. One by one, they were ordered to rise to their feet, then approach Caesar, who offered them a baton of carved ivory, another symbol of his *imperium* and which signified the legal authority vested in him by the Senate and People of Rome, which they kissed. In a further humiliation, but one that the assembled Legionaries of the 9th and 10th enjoyed the most, the *Aquilifer* of each Legion, standing on either side of Caesar, lowered their eagle standards, which each man kissed as well, this action greeted by a roar that was more than a cheer. To the watching men who had sweated, bled, and watched friends and comrades fall for the previous months of this campaign, it was the most potent symbol of their victory, and more importantly, the sign that they were going home. They were less happy with Caesar's command that, while some Gallaeci were kept as prisoners to be sold into slavery, the proceeds of which the men would share, he ordered that others remain free, including the tribal nobility, who were ordered to give up hostages as surety of their good faith and promise to keep the peace. As time had passed, the men of the Tenth Section had come to rely on Scribonius to provide explanations for the actions of their social betters, and while nobody ever asked him, it was widely accepted that Scribonius' knowledge was not secondhand.

"He's at the very least from the Equestrian Order," had been Calienus' guess when he and Rufio had talked about it, not long after the campaign had begun and when Rufio was still a Sergeant like himself. "And I'd wager a month's pay that he's from Rome."

While it would have been a simple enough thing to ask Scribonius himself, neither of them, nor any of his comrades, Didius included, were willing to break one of the unwritten but most sacrosanct rules against asking a comrade about their past; with Didius and Atilius in particular, it was also because it invited questions about their own past they had no desire to answer. That night, as they made preparations to break camp and return south to retrieve the 7th and 8th Legions, it had fallen to Scribonius to explain to his comrades.

"The reason Caesar is leaving so many of the survivors free is because if he didn't, then it would be a practical invitation to the other tribes up here to attack them. And then," he pointed out, "we'd be coming back up here now that Caesar accepted their surrender and promised them protection."

"All the more reason to take them all as slaves," Romulus declared, then gestured at the countryside around them, hilly and dry. "Anyone who wants to live here can have it, that's what I say!"

"Once Caesar accepted their surrender," Scribonius explained, displaying a patience for which he had already become known among his comrades, "it became a matter of honor."

"Who cares about Caesar's honor?" Remus spoke up, as he usually did, in defense of his brother's point. "We worked hard for that money, and look how many towns surrendered before we got here! He's already rich, isn't he? I wouldn't be surprised if he's as rich as Marcus Crassus now!"

"I doubt that." Scribonius laughed, then he glanced around, lowering his voice so he couldn't be overheard by anyone outside the section. "One reason Caesar wanted a Praetorship so badly was because he needed to get out of Rome, and he needed a way to get out of debt, which was why he needed to leave. He has a *lot* of creditors."

"What are creditors?" Romulus stumbled over the unfamiliar word.

"People he owed money to," Calienus answered, just beating Scribonius.

"But Caesar is a patrician," Atilius spoke up, puzzled, and Scribonius could see that his comrade wasn't alone. "How can a patrician not have money?"

"A lot of patricians don't," Scribonius explained quietly. "They have ancestors, that's true, but think of Doughboy." The mention of the corpulent, inept Tribune elicited chuckles all around, and Scribonius asked rhetorically, "If you had an ancestor like Doughboy, how long do you think it would take him to piss away the family fortune?"

This, he saw, made sense to them when put that way, and they soon moved on to some other topic, and while Calienus participated in the banter, he found his eyes going to Scribonius, his expression thoughtful.

Domitius, over his strenuous protests, was consigned to one of the wagons, but after the first day, he was no longer of a mind to complain since he shared the conveyance with men who were in much worse shape than he was in. His wound, while painful and rendering him unable to bear weight on his leg, was still minor when compared to a man like Numidius, a veteran from the Third Century, who was missing his leg at mid-thigh after his knee joint was shattered by a sling bullet, then the wound corrupted. Pullus came to visit at every break, bringing him something to drink and to relate some humorous moment on the march, which was a more relaxed affair now that the whole region had been subdued. Caesar still ordered flank guards out, but they were marching through lands that they had already despoiled or subdued, and some men found it disquieting to see their handiwork now that the fighting was over.

It was Publius Vellusius, who, despite loathing the idea of being one, was still a farmer's son, commented, "It seems a shame that we had to kill all their flocks and herds," when they came upon a field filled with the remains of slaughtered sheep, their carcasses having been picked clean by the birds and carrion eaters.

Mile by mile, the men of Caesar's army made their way south and were confronted by their handiwork in despoiling almost countless *iugerae* of farm and grazing land, passing through the small, unfortified villages that were, for the most part, destroyed, the blackened timbers of the daub and wattle huts thrusting up from the ground in the only sign that this had once been a habitation. Not every man was disturbed by this potent sign of the destruction they had wrought; indeed, those who were constituted a distinct minority, and they all knew better than to say anything aloud, understanding it would bring nothing but mockery at what their comrades would view as a sign of weakness. Two of them were in the Tenth Section, and Scribonius was one of them; to his surprise, it was his huge comrade who shared his unease, although they were careful to speak of it only when none of the others could hear.

"I remember after the first town, Vibius said something to me that I keep thinking about," Pullus admitted one night as he and Scribonius headed to the latrine before retiring. Glancing over at the only other man in his tent he didn't have to incline his head to look in the eye, he asked, "It was when we found that warrior and his woman when we were clearing out our part of the town. Do you remember?"

"Yes," Scribonius replied shortly, but he didn't return Pullus' gaze, unwilling to give more than a bare acknowledgment since, as it had been with Pullus and the other *Tirones*, this had been his first experience with what the sacking of a town by Rome's Legions really meant.

Pullus took note of Scribonius' reaction, but didn't comment on it, instead continuing, "And remember, Vibius didn't go in and...you know," he said awkwardly. "But when I asked him why, he said he couldn't help thinking about Juno and what if that was her. When I told him that will never happen to Juno because of us and how Rome will never be defeated, he said that bothered him too." He gave a strained laugh. "I thought at the time he'd gone soft in the head." The smile faded, and he admitted, "But over the last few weeks, I keep thinking about what he said." Suddenly, he stopped, and there was an intensity in his voice that startled Scribonius, although it was the words he would remember, as Pullus asked, "What does that mean, Sextus? Does it mean that I'm not cut out for this?"

For Scribonius' part, he could only gape at his friend in astonishment, and without thinking, he blurted, "*Gerrae*! What kind of nonsense is that, Titus?" Seeing that his friend needed more, he went on, and while he didn't raise his voice, he matched Pullus' feelings, "Titus, of all of us, you're meant to be under the standard more than any man in this Legion, at least of us rankers. And," he added, "at least as much as Crastinus."

Pullus didn't answer immediately, but when he did, it was something that Scribonius would remember for the rest of his days, and it gave him a glimpse into his friend's soul that, while he didn't know it at the time, was the first step in entwining their destinies for all that was to come.

"That," Pullus said honestly, "worries me almost as much as if I wasn't, Sextus." Embarrassed now, he looked away, eyes fixed on something Scribonius couldn't see, and it was as if he was speaking to himself, "What kind of life will that give me, if I'm only fit to kill our enemies?" He laughed again, and Scribonius sensed the embarrassment there, and he finished, "I *have* gone soft in the head, I suppose."

Not knowing what else to say, Scribonius simply offered, "No, I don't think so, Titus. I truly don't."

They reached the latrine, and it was the last they spoke of it.

The army returned by the same route they had taken, retrieving the 7th from Portus Cale, which had been reduced and pacified, although in accordance with Caesar's orders, it hadn't been destroyed like the island fortress. Continuing south, they reunited with the 8th next, who had finished pacifying the Lusitani, and the army that returned to Scallabis, while reduced in numbers, was now a battle-hardened force that, although none of them, with perhaps one exception, knew, would serve as the nucleus for what was to come, and would go down in history as one of the greatest feats of arms ever attempted. In a foreshadowing of what was to come as far as the 10th was concerned, they were given the place of honor leading the army into Scallabis, where they were greeted by what seemed to be every inhabitant lining the *Via Praetoria*, the main thoroughfare into the capital. In accordance to Roman tradition, the standards of every Legion, down to the Cohort and Century standards, were garlanded with ivy, the symbol of victory that had originated in the misty past of Rome's history.

By this point in time, in late September and about two weeks after the island fortress had been captured, Domitius was back in the ranks, albeit still with a limp, one that would never completely go away, although it was noticeable only on cold, wet days, and like his comrades, he thoroughly enjoyed the adoration of the crowds, particularly the women who threw flowers in their path, but it was their offers of showing their appreciation in more tangible ways that, despite his determination to remain faithful to Juno, still had him grinning from ear to ear and thinking: She doesn't need to know what happens in Scallabis, after all. The return of the army was welcomed for other reasons, at least by those purveyors of the various vices that had seen their business drop off with the army's departure, but they were destined to only enjoy the largess that came from the return of men with bulging purses full of loot for a month, as Caesar gave the most seriously wounded men time to fully heal. Naturally, and as any experienced veteran knew, not all of the men who managed to survive their initial wound, followed by being transported in wagons across the rough terrain of Hispania, would survive the month, although almost all of these men succumbed to some form of corruption of their wound, or to an illness that they otherwise would have fought off but their weakened bodies couldn't resist. Their comrades who had either survived unscathed, or whose wounds were minor enough to have healed, were given only those duties required for the maintenance of the camp. The other activities that normally came at the end of a campaign; the repair or replacement of bits of gear, the reissue of javelins and replacing things like the torsion ropes of the artillery were postponed because the army would be relocating to Corduba, something that most, though not all of the men looked forward to since the city was larger and more established. There was still a raw, frontier quality to Scallabis that the more worldly Legionaries sneered at, reminding their less traveled comrades that the opportunities for debauchery there were a shade compared to what awaited them in someplace like Corduba. Their arrival there in late October was markedly different than it had been in Scallabis; there were no crowds, the news of their victories over the rebelling tribes now being considered in the past, but whatever disappointment the men of the army experienced was quickly forgotten, for a number of reasons.

"Caesar's being given a triumph in Rome!"

This bit of news was relayed to the men of the Tenth Section by Calienus, who always seemed better informed than almost anyone in the Century, a fact that had engendered a great deal of speculation, although it was Scribonius, who, while their Sergeant never confirmed it, correctly guessed, "He's bribed a clerk in the *praetorium*; that's how he knows."

However Calienus came by the information, he was far from alone in having a "little bird" in the headquarters, meaning that it was impossible for this to remain a secret, the word spreading through the permanent camp outside Corduba with the speed of a lightning strike. Unfortunately for the men of the 10th, their celebration at the idea of marching through the streets of Rome was short-lived, lasting a bit less than a full day, and this time, Calienus decided to let their Pilus Prior give the First Century the news at their morning formation.

"Right," Crastinus began, and while he wasn't hesitant, he certainly wasn't eager to inform them, "Caesar has decided that, given that we're a new Legion, he's only going to be taking the 7th, 8th, and 9th to Rome for his triumph." This was, understandably, met with a ripple of muttered dismay, and anger, and in a small sign that their Pilus Prior shared their feelings, Crastinus didn't chastise the men for this display, although he did add, half-heartedly, "I suppose it's because we're still in our first year, and we enlisted on a sixteen-year term while those bastards in the other Spanish Legions have already been in a while and they're on a twelve-year term, so we'll have plenty of opportunity for glory, boys, mark my words."

This, Crastinus saw, didn't appease the men, nor did he expect it to, but aside from a bit more grumbling than was normal for rankers, Caesar's decision didn't cause undue problems. Later that day, the men were dismissed to their quarters to prepare for the next day, a full dress formation marking Caesar and the three Legions' departure for Rome, culminating in the *Praetor*'s last official duty with the army, the awarding of decorations to men who distinguished themselves during the campaign, and this was what brought Crastinus to the hut belonging to the Tenth Section. As was customary, he rapped on the door with his *vitus* twice, then paused briefly, an old Centurion's trick to warn the men to hide whatever they were doing that might get them written up and put on punishment detail...or worse. When he opened the door, he was greeted by every man seemingly hard at work preparing for what was, in effect, a dress parade the next day, but he stopped where Pullus was sitting at the table, hunched over as he varnished his leathers.

Without warning, Crastinus whacked Pullus across the back with his *vitus*, not hard but with enough force to make Pullus squawk, but when he looked to Crastinus, the Pilus Prior pointed to the *baltea*, barking, "What if by some miracle you happened to be chosen to be decorated, eh, Pullus? Would you really embarrass the Cohort and Legion with that sorry job?"

In response, Pullus looked down at the *baltea*, but although he was certain that there was nothing wrong with it, he also had learned at this point there was one, and only one, response he could give that wouldn't get him bashed again.

"No, Pilus Prior," he answered, and made a show of adding another coat of varnish, only glaring at the door after Crastinus left, slamming it in the process.

"I think it looks fine as it is," he muttered, but he did complete the job, knowing by now that it was entirely possible that Crastinus would suddenly reappear, trying to catch him out.

"Do you think you're going to be decorated?" Scribonius was on his bunk, replacing the leather thongs that secured his *caligae* in place around his ankles.

"I have no idea." Pullus shrugged. "And why would I be?"

"That's what I was asking myself," Calienus said, with a touch of sarcasm. "It's not like you did anything the rest of us didn't do...like slaughter a couple dozen of those Lusitani *cunni* in one battle."

This was met with a ripple of chuckles and murmurs of agreement from all of his comrades, save one, but Pullus felt his face go hot, and he refused to look up as he mumbled, "I told you I don't remember anything about it."

"We do," Domitius said quietly, and Atilius, Romulus, and Remus chorused their agreement. "We all saw it even if you didn't."

Didius, who had returned to lounging on his bunk after sitting upright to appear busy fiddling with his scabbard when Crastinus entered after his warning knock, knew he should keep his mouth shut, but his anger at what he saw as the injustice of it all was too much.

"Did any of you forget that I was first up the ladder on the island?" he demanded, and while he saw the eyerolls the brothers shared, he ignored it. "That should qualify me for a set of *phalarae* at the very least, if not a *corona murales*!"

"Achilles," Calienus sighed, using his nickname mainly because he knew Didius hated being reminded of it, "you may have been first up *our* ladder, but that doesn't mean you were first on the wall. That was Optio Cornuficius in the Fifth of the First from what I heard."

"There wasn't a single Roman on that wall when I got up there," Didius snapped. "I know I was first!"

This was met as it had been ever since he had boasted of it the night after the fortress fell, with a ragged chorus of sounds that, at best, could have been considered noncommittal, and he knew that this was a battle he couldn't win, which only compounded Didius' frustration. And, the brutal truth was that, in this one thing, Spurius Didius was telling the truth; he *had* been the first man on the second wall of the Gallaeci fortress, which by rights should have earned him a *corona murales*. And, while he would never learn the truth, if it had been any other man of the First Century of the Second Cohort, Pilus Prior Crastinus would have aggressively pressed his case on the behalf of one of his men, but this was a case where Didius was reaping what he had sown during his months under the standard. In simple terms, there was too much evidence of Didius' duplicity, dishonesty, and outright shirking for Crastinus to justify making the effort to defend his man's claim, and over the ensuing years, Didius would often think of that moment when, for the first time in his life, he was actually robbed of an accolade that he deserved, and while it wasn't all that often, as he grew older, he would wonder how differently his life might have turned out because of it.

The final formation of what had been informally called the Army of Hispania Superior was, in the estimation of everyone present, a glorious affair, particularly for two men of the ranks.

"This," Vibius had said to Titus in the moment before the assembly to formation was called, "is why we joined the Legions."

"It is," Pullus agreed wholeheartedly.

Whose heart wouldn't be stirred at the sight of so many men, standing in perfectly aligned ranks, their black horsetail plumes moving slightly in the faint breeze, the dull gleam of *hamatae* that had been scrubbed with sand so that the links caught the sun, and above them all, the cloth banners of Century and Cohort, while the gilt silver outstretched wings of four eagles caught the sunlight? It was as potent a display of Rome's might as anyone present could imagine, but for the men of the ranks, it represented so much more, because, in their own way, each of them was part of that display. *They* were Rome, and all that it meant to their entire world, where there was no human being alive who didn't at least know of Rome's existence, and Rome's power. The actual formation was held outside the camp walls so that it could be attended by those citizens of Corduba who wished to be present could witness it, and they marched out, in Legion order this time, where they formed a three-sided box, with the 7th on one side, the 8th and 9th on the bottom, the 10th opposite the 7th, with Caesar, along with his staff and the Tribunes minus the unlamented Doughboy occupying the center.

Like his men, Caesar was wearing his armor, a muscled cuirass that was polished to such a high degree that it made men squint against the brilliance, while his general's cloak, the *paludamentum,* had either been freshly laundered, or perhaps re-dyed so that it was a striking scarlet. However, rather than a helmet, Caesar wore the garland of laurel leaves that signified his status as victorious general, and while he arrived on horseback, he quickly dismounted and took his place just in front of the hastily constructed rostrum from which he would address his men. To this point, everything had happened as it normally did, with the Legion *Cornicen* sounding the notes that were then repeated by the other *Corniceni*, followed by the bellowed orders of the Centurions that got the men marching into their positions for the award ceremony. There was a brief silence, and while Caesar only gave a nod, the Centurions, all of whom had been informed, knew what to do next, which was when Pullus learned that his Pilus Prior hadn't been asking about his leathers randomly.

"*Gregarius Immune* Pullus, *Gregarius Ordinarius* Norbanus, and Optio Rufio," Crastinus barked. "Attend to me!"

Pullus didn't move immediately, and Scribonius glanced over and saw his friend, jaw hanging open in surprise, so he nudged him and hissed, "Get up there, you big oaf! Do you want to get thrashed in front of Caesar?"

This got the large Roman moving, and he took a step to the side and out of the formation before moving at a trot to the front of the formation, falling in on the spot Crastinus pointed to that placed Pullus next to his Centurion. When the four men were formed in a single line, instead of moving, they remained there, which was a mystery for the new men, though it would be solved quickly. This scene was being repeated all along the formation, as all of the men designated for some sort of decoration left their spots, and there was a slight delay as they arranged themselves, then, again in Legion order, each group of men marched to stand in front of Caesar, whereupon one of the Tribunes, reading from a scroll, announced the name and rank of the man being awarded, what the award was, and the reason they had earned it. Not every Century, or Cohort, had men who had earned decorations, a fact that the members of those who had would make sure they never forgot, which almost always resulted in some sort of altercation, but it still took a fair amount of time before it was the turn of the First of the Second since the 10th was the last Legion to be decorated. Crastinus gave the order to march in a conversational tone, but they all stepped off at the same time, moving smartly towards Caesar as Crastinus expertly guided them so that they stopped immediately in front of the general, then executed a facing movement. For Pullus, there was a surreal quality to this moment because he was still unsure exactly for what he was being decorated. While Didius, and a fair number of other men, would have dismissed it as hubris, Pullus knew that he had performed well during this campaign, and there were several moments where he could recall either Crastinus or Rufio mentioning him for special attention. Before his turn came, however, Caesar, who could have delegated this task to a Tribune as so many generals did, stood in front of Crastinus first, while a second Tribune, standing behind and to Caesar's left, held a pillow, upon which rested a crown, but one with a crest designed to look like the crenellations of a wall, the sign that this was the *Corona Murales*.

"Pilus Prior Crastinus," Caesar was smiling as he spoke, in an almost bantering term, "I've been informed that this is actually the third *Corona Murales* you've earned. Is that true?"

"It is, sir," Crastinus responded, but while his voice was modulated, Pullus was certain he heard the pride there.

"It seems as if you're determined not to make old bones, Pilus Prior," Caesar chided, but still with the smile.

It was the turn of the Tribune holding the scroll to read from it, confirming that this award was for Crastinus' actions during the assault on the first town, whereupon Pullus and the others learned that they weren't the only men who never learned the name of the place. Once the Tribune was finished, Crastinus untied the thongs securing his helmet, taking it off and bowing his head slightly as Caesar, lifting the crown from the pillow then holding it aloft in the air so all could see it, ceremoniously placed it on the Centurion's head before taking a step back. By this time, Pullus and the others who had never been decorated before had watched and knew what was coming, as Crastinus, his helmet under his left arm, rendered a salute, which Caesar returned, making the *paludamentum* flutter before he took a single step to his right, placing him directly in front of Pullus. For his part, Pullus' heart was galloping in his chest as if he had just sprinted a hundred paces, and he could feel the sweat trickling down his back, but he kept his eyes above Caesar's head this time, determined not to make the same error he had made on the occasion of their first meeting.

Which, of course, meant that when Caesar spoke, he found himself once again looking down into his general's gaze, and again, Caesar didn't seem to mind as he said, a bit more loudly than he had with Crastinus, "*Gregarius* Pullus, I'm happy to see that you survived your first campaign. From what I have heard, that's an exceeding accomplishment, given your habit of always being in the front."

Pullus' first instinct in such moments was usually his worst one, and he began to open his mouth to point out that the reason he had been in the front so often was due to the man standing next to him ordering him to be there, but whether it was his imagination or not, he was certain he heard a warning growl from his Centurion. If it wasn't his imagination, Caesar gave no sign that he had heard, and then the Tribune was reading from the scroll that would become part of his permanent record, whereupon Pullus learned that it was for his actions during the ambush. His comrades had long since given up trying to get him to offer up his version of the events that night, not even Domitius accepting that he had no memory of it, but it was the truth. Now, hearing the Tribune, who he vaguely knew was named Trebonius and was one of the only men of that rank who weren't considered to be a waste of space, read in a flat, emotionless voice what was, in effect, the recollection of other men, like his Centurion, Optio, *Signifer*, and a handful of others, Pullus was assaulted by a wave of emotions, some of them conflicting. Personally, he found it hard to believe that, according to the citation, he had personally dispatched twenty-two Lusitani warriors in single combat, while singlehandedly being credited for blocking the breach of the makeshift wall that threatened the men of the First and Second Century with being overrun. Frankly, his most vivid memory of the event was after it was over, and how utterly exhausted he had been, while every inch of his bare skin was covered in blood and bits of flesh that, to his astonishment, was solely from his victims and not from himself. Then, the Tribune was finished, and this time on the pillow were three silver disks, perhaps three inches in diameter, each of them embossed with the head of a bull, the symbol of the 10th Legion, which Caesar carefully attached to his harness, one above the other. Somehow, Pullus remembered to salute when Caesar stepped back, and the general returned it, then made his next step to where *Gregarius* Norbanus, of the First Section, was waiting to receive his award.

In the case of Norbanus, it was in fact the simplest of all the decorations awarded by the Legions, but it was the most prized, and Pullus felt a stab of envy as Caesar, with a solemnity bordering on reverence, lifted up another crown, but this one was not made of hammered silver like the *Corona Murales*, but of plaited strands of dried grass. As Pullus, and every Roman knew, this was the Civic Crown, awarded to a Roman citizen for the act of saving the life of a fellow citizen. In Norbanus' case, it had been the Sergeant of his Section, who had been knocked senseless during the battle at the fortress and was being dragged away by a pair of Gallaeci warriors to almost undoubtedly be butchered. Norbanus had broken ranks and waded into a knot of Gallaeci warriors, dispatching two of them and, because of the fury of his assault, managing to keep the others at bay long enough for Norbanus to grab the Sergeant, still unconscious, by the ankle and drag him to safety. The last man of the Century was Rufio, who also earned a set of *phalarae* for his performance when he had been pressed into service as Optio during the assault on the first town. There was one last award, but this one was for the entire Second Cohort, the awarding of silver discs that, while the same size as the *phalarae,* were blank, and of which the Cohort was awarded two, more than any other Cohort in the army, which would be affixed to the Cohort standard, and were given to Crastinus. Once their part was done, as one, they rendered a final salute, then marched back to the Century, each of them returning to their spot in the formation, and since they were still at *intente*, his comrades only murmured their congratulations.

"Your head is so big already you're going to have to sell those to get a bigger helmet made," Calienus spoke just loudly enough for Pullus to hear, earning some snickers from his comrades, but Pullus was grinning broadly; besides, he was unable to think of a clever retort.

Once the last men of the 10th had been decorated, a bit more than a full watch had passed, which meant that most of the civilian onlookers had gotten bored and left, although there were a few hundred still present, and Caesar mounted the rostrum. Standing there silently for a moment, he spent that time surveying his army, his head moving slowly across the ranks of the four Legions, and while it may have been unintentional, the men of the 10th didn't believe that since he began speaking when he was still gazing at the 10th.

"My comrades," he began with what would become a customary method Caesar used to address his troops. "We have successfully conducted a hard-fought campaign, against a worthy opponent in the tribes of Hispania. The Lusitani, and the Bracari and Lucenses branches of the Gallaeci, while barbarian, were men of great courage, which makes our victory over them even more noteworthy!" As he obviously expected, this elicited a roar of agreement, because Caesar didn't try to continue immediately, waiting for the men to die down before he went on, "And each Legion under my command performed admirably, executing their duties to the utmost and performing with great bravery. And," his tone became somber, "each Legion now mourns lost comrades, men who fell doing their duty to Rome. Know this! I have made an offering to the gods on their behalf, beseeching them to accept each of these men into Elysium, as befits brave warriors who have fallen in battle!" While there was approbation at this, it was also muted, each man who had lost a friend remembering them even as they raised their voice in acknowledgement of their general's words, while silently offering up for another time their own prayer on behalf of the fallen. "But," Caesar's tone changed slightly again, and he returned his attention to his left, where the 10th was standing, "there is one Legion in particular who, by virtue of being a newly called *dilectus* with no battle experience, still exceeded even my expectations, and that Legion is," he extended a hand towards them, "your comrades in the 10th. And, if I ever find myself in a position where I need to summon a Legion, know this, you men of the 10th. You will be the first men I call on!"

Even if he had planned on saying anything more, the roar

raised, albeit by just one Legion, was enough to drown out his words, and with them, Caesar aligned the collective fortune of the 10th Legion to his own; they would be Caesar's Legion from this moment forward.

Chapter Eight

While most of the men of the 10th Legion welcomed the relocation to the larger city of Corduba, it wasn't unanimous. For Atilius, returning to the capital, where for an all-too-brief moment of time, his family had been happy until his father's scheming had gotten his brother Lucius killed by the *Praetor* at the time, Gnaeus Aufidius Orestes, brought up unpleasant memories. It wasn't just that; yes, he had been younger then, but he had spent watches of his time in the forum of the city, either acting as a lookout for his father, also dead and, he was certain, killed by his mother in an act of revenge that had been the direct cause for Atilius finding himself wearing the soldier's tunic or cutting the strings of purses himself. While he didn't think it was likely anyone would recognize him, given the curse that seemed to hang over all of those bearing the Atilius name, he felt he could be excused for thinking this way.

Once the other Legions were gone, the 10th had the run of the town, but more importantly for most of the men, over a period of the last few months of the year, they were allowed to return to their homes on a period of leave. While most of the men, especially the new veterans for whom leaving their homes had been just a matter of a few months before took advantage of this, Atilius wasn't one of them, for the simple reason that, as many bad memories as he might have had about Corduba, returning to Nova Carthago and his mother Domitilla was even more unpalatable. He understood that his return wouldn't put him in danger, if for the only reason that although he would be walking into their apartment with a coin purse carrying more money than he had ever seen in his life, even as assiduously he had tried to drink it away in Scallabis, he was now a hardened killer. In its simplest terms, Atilius didn't want to return to his mother because he was certain that he wouldn't like what he found. During their last day together, when he had discovered his father dead after essentially drowning in his own vomit, he had also seen that, at last, his mother's grip on sanity had finally been loosened. There had been too many betrayals, too many nights fearing the sudden pounding on the door, too many days of hunger and deprivation, and Domitilla had finally had enough of all of it. Seeing the son who, as she liked to remind Atilius, was exactly like his father walking through the door was an invitation to disaster, and he thanked Fortuna that he had survived his first campaign; the thought of being killed by his mother was not appealing in the slightest. Still, he didn't like the prospect of sitting in the camp watching his comrades, like Pullus and Domitius, who were going back to their town of Astigi, leave the camp, but he was still surprised when Didius approached him one evening.

He could tell that his close comrade was, if not nervous, then a bit unsettled, but he was completely unprepared to hear Didius say, "I'm thinking of taking some leave time to go to Gades."

"Oh?" Atilius was surprised, at least at first; once he thought about it later, he realized that he shouldn't have been. At that moment, however, he was sufficiently startled to ask, "What for? I mean," he added hastily, "given what your uncle told you."

It was a fair question, and a potentially troubling one, but by this point in time, Didius trusted Atilius completely, which was what prompted him to reply frankly, "It's *because* of what my uncle told me that I want to see Aulus one more time."

For an instant, Atilius was going to ask what Didius had planned, but what came out of his mouth, accompanied by a shrug, was, "If that's what you need to do, you should. The gods know that if the rumors are true and we're going to be marching somewhere else, you may not be this close to Gades again."

"Will you come with me?"

At first, Atilius didn't reply because he was so surprised, not as much at the question itself, but because of the expression on Didius' face, which for the only time in their association, betrayed an expression of a kind of anxious vulnerability that was decidedly at odds with the face Spurius Didius presented to the world. And, while he would never say as much, Atilius was moved, and touched, that Didius clearly wanted Atilius' company at what would undoubtedly be a trying moment, provided that his close comrade's nerve didn't fail him once they got there.

Consequently, Atilius answered without thinking, "Of course." Then, more to cover up his own emotions, he shrugged as he added, "I've always wanted to see Gades."

It was relatively rare for Didius to smile, but this was one of those occasions, and he clapped Atilius on the shoulder, laughing as he said with unfeigned pleasure and relief, "I'll show you where the best whorehouses are, and where the wine flows like water, Marcus, I swear it!"

Two days later, the pair departed, and like most of the new veterans, they carried their packs, though not with the *furca*, threading one arm through the loops by which the pack hung and loaded with, among other things, their *hamatae*, and with their helmet dangling from their pack, eager to show the citizens of their hometowns they were now men of the Legions. They were forbidden to carry their shields and weapons, but as they had been told by men like Calienus, it was a rule that was never enforced, at least for their *gladii*, provided they weren't wearing them when they left the camp.

"Nobody on the guard Cohort is going to search your packs," Calienus had assured them. "So just make sure that you've got the hilts wrapped up since they'll be the only thing sticking out."

It was more than a hundred fifty miles to Gades from Corduba, but both Didius' and Atilius' circumstances had drastically changed since their arrival in Scallabis, which meant they happily paid for passage on a barge that was floating down the Baetis (Guadalquivir) River to Hispalis, where they transferred to a coastal freighter that rowed across the bay and around the tip of the island to the port, arriving in the city shortly after noon on their fourth day. And, just as their other comrades did, although they wouldn't learn about this until later, they both put on their *hamata* over their soldier's tunics and donned their helmet, with the horsehair plume, not bothering with their greave, but with both *gladius* and *pugio* on their *baltea*.

"I just wish we were as blessed by Fortuna as that big bastard," Didius grumbled, "and were wearing *phalarae, neh?*"

By this time, Atilius had heard his comrade's complaint more times than he could count, and knew that a noncommittal grunt would suffice, although he would never express his true feelings to Didius. The truth was that he, like the other men of not just the Tenth Section but both the First and Second Centuries, with a few exceptions like Didius, credited the huge Roman with almost singlehandedly saving both Centuries from what would have been a much costlier battle atop that anonymous hill. Whether they would have been wiped out to a man only the gods knew, but Atilius didn't doubt in the slightest that they would have lost at least half their number, if not more. This, however, was something Didius simply refused to accept, and Atilius had recognized that it was not only a vain hope but was a source of conflict with his close comrade, and to Atilius, it simply wasn't worth the aggravation.

"At least our tunics aren't still so red," he offered instead, and it was Didius' turn to answer with a grunt.

Descending the plank down to the dock, both men savored the stares and, while Atilius wasn't quite as keen about it as Didius, he did appreciate the manner in which the civilians scrambled out of their way, taking it as a sign of respect. It was a far cry from his days as an anonymous face dressed in filthy tunic, battered sandals, and with an empty purse unless he had just stolen something. Since Atilius had never been to Gades before, he didn't mind when Didius took him on a tour of the city, showing him the temples, and the statue of Alexander that, unknown to either of them, had been a cause of heartache and disappointment on the part of their general.

"Do you think we'll ever see as much as the men who marched for Alexander did?" Atilius asked suddenly as the pair stood at the foot of the statue, gazing up at the startlingly lifelike figure, painted to look as they imagined Alexander did, down to the startlingly blue eyes.

Not surprisingly, Didius hadn't ever given this any thought, but he considered for a moment before replying offhandedly,

"You know what everyone says about him, that he's at least as ambitious as Alexander."

Then, with a shrug, he led Atilius away from the statue, heading across the forum, but Atilius noticed that Didius didn't seem to be in any hurry to head for the southwest quarter of the city, which Didius had informed his close comrade was where Didius' father and family lived, and served as the headquarters for the *collegia* his family ran. In fact, Didius was showing more interest in the temples ringing the forum of Gades than he had ever shown in Corduba, or even in Scallabis, although the latter was still a raw frontier town made of wood, including the temples. He didn't say anything at first, yet despite the fact that Didius hadn't said anything specific about his intentions, Atilius felt certain that he knew there was some sort of conflict coming between his close comrade and the *paterfamilias* of the family. Exactly what form it would take, he didn't know, and while he didn't dwell on it overmuch, Atilius did have a thought that he might end up ruing accepting Didius' invitation.

Nevertheless, he also didn't see the point in postponing matters, so after they exited the Temple of Hercules Gaditanus, the most famous of the temples, dating as it did back to the days when Carthage ruled in this part of Hispania, and who called Hercules Melqart, he casually asked Didius, "Where are we staying for the night? Any ideas?"

Didius wasn't fooled, but while he couldn't be described as jovial, with Atilius, he displayed an entirely different aspect of his personality, which was why he grinned as he countered, "Is that your way of asking if I plan on seeing Aulus today?"

Relieved, Atilius laughed, admitting, "More or less."

The grin faded from Didius' face, and he suddenly looked away, seemingly watching the passersby going about their business as he said awkwardly, "It's just that he said I could never come back."

"And," Atilius asked, and while he was smiling, his tone was serious, "what's he going to do now that you're here, eh?" When Didius didn't reply immediately, Atilius reached down and tapped the hilt of his own *gladius*, and said quietly, "You're not the same man who your Tata bullied, Spurius."

During their time together, they never spoke of it, but while it was the first time, it wouldn't be the last that Didius intuited that Marcus Atilius and he had more in common than sharing a tent, that perhaps they both had the same kind of father in their lives, although Didius did know that Atilius' father was dead; it would be some time later that his close comrade revealed how it had happened. Nor was it in his nature to thank or even acknowledge Atilius' words, but he did give a curt nod, then without a word, abruptly changed his direction and led Atilius in the opposite direction.

As usual, Aulus Didius occupied a corner table in Proserpina's Grotto, in which he was a majority, albeit silent, owner, forcing Vibius Pacula, a nice enough sort but with a bad gambling habit that, thanks to Spurius' skill with dice, gave Aulus the leverage he needed to make the hapless man sign over this *taverna* and brothel over to Aulus in everything but name, leaving Pacula to pay the fees and taxes levied by the *duumviri* of Gades. It was one of Aulus Didius' proudest achievements in his life of criminal enterprise, and he enjoyed reigning over his domain from this corner table, usually with one of the prostitutes who worked upstairs either next to him, or perched on his knee, which he assured his wife was strictly for business purposes.

"I have to set a certain example, *meum mel,*" he had assured Livinia, his second wife and the woman his son Spurius suspected of poisoning his own mother, Aulus' first wife, and while he never admitted as much to his son, Aulus was practically certain that she had. "A man of a *collegia* can't appear to be henpecked, can he?"

"A man of the *collegia* who doesn't want to sleep with one eye open for the rest of his days should know better," Livinia had shot back, but this was as far as her complaining went.

After all, she was living a life that she had never dreamed of when she had been the third daughter of a poor farmer in Baetica and had been forced out of her childhood home to fend for herself, making her way to Gades where, while she preferred not to think about it, she had once been the pretty young thing perched on the knee of Aulus' father, old Spurius.

On this day, however, all was well in Aulus' world.

Septimus had come to tell him that their theft of a few amphorae of olive oil from a cargo shop at the docks had been successful, costing only a few *sesterces* to bribe the guard assigned to that part of the dock to look the other way, which was a pittance compared to what selling the amphorae to his list of merchants who weren't choosy about from where the oil came, caring only that it was cheaper, would gain for him. It was late afternoon, and the doorway to the *taverna* was situated so that at this time of day, the sun shone almost directly above the doorway, throwing a long rectangle of light into the otherwise dim interior. What it meant in a practical sense was that, while it was easy to see when a person entered, framed in the doorway as they were by the sunlight, it also was next to impossible to distinguish the person's features. Consequently, while Aulus Didius could tell by the helmets the pair of men were wearing as they entered were Legionaries, which, while unusual, wasn't unheard of but fairly rare, his recognition was delayed by a few heartbeats. In fact, it was Pacula who responded the quickest, hurrying from behind the long wooden counter where trays were served up for the pair of women, his wife and daughter, who served their customers.

"*Ave,* soldiers!" he called out, passing Aulus to stand in between him and the pair of men, further delaying Aulus' identification. "Welcome to Proserpina's Grotto! Have you come for the wine? Or," Pacula chuckled, though it didn't fool anyone into thinking this wasn't a proprietor's customary attempt to broach the subject of the other sources of entertainment available, "were you thinking of...another form of entertainment, perhaps? Women? Or is it a good game of dice?"

This was instantly followed by Pacula's sudden gasp of recognition that indicated something was amiss, but it was the voice that alerted Aulus, and he felt a sudden chill, as if a *numen* had just passed by; fortunately for him, he had long practice in not showing surprise or fear.

"Spurius Didius?" Pacula, on the other hand, was truly startled. "Is that you?"

"It is," Didius replied shortly, but while the voice was familiar, there was something different in his tone that his father clearly heard but couldn't immediately identify.

For his part, Didius accepted Pacula's arm without even glancing down at the man, his eyes only on Aulus, who, gently but firmly, shoved the prostitute off his lap. She, clearly sensing something unusual and potentially dangerous was taking place, didn't protest, and actually got up and walked over to the counter, not far away but far enough to be out of immediate harm should trouble arise.

"*Ave*, Aulus," Didius said in a monotone, but just as he intended, referring to his *paterfamilias* by his *praenomen* and not as "Father" even, let alone "Tata," made the older Didius flush with anger.

Determined not to be thrown off balance, Aulus matched his son's tone and, sounding disinterested, grunted, "You're back, I see."

"It's good to know that you haven't gone blind since I've been gone," Didius countered coldly, but when Aulus didn't immediately reply, he challenged, "As I recall, you said something about what would happen if I came back here. Well," he held out both arms, "I'm here."

And, there it was, the naked challenge, and in public, with the half-dozen men who answered to him scattered around the room, none of them even trying to pretend they weren't paying avid attention. It's my own fault, Aulus thought ruefully. I shouldn't have told anyone what I said to Spurius, and now here he is.

Aulus wasn't frightened of his son, although he was cautious, acutely aware that Spurius was armed, as was the man standing just behind him, and Aulus used his presence to try and throw his son off balance, asking, "Who's this with you then, son?"

An expression of what might have been embarrassment flashed across Didius' face, but he didn't hesitate, nor did he look away from Aulus, using his thumb to indicate Atilius, explaining, "This is my close comrade, Marcus Atilius. We," Didius said with what he felt was justifiable pride, "are in the Tenth Section of the First Century, Second Cohort of the 10th Legion."

Since it was still early in their time under the standard and with the 10th, this didn't engender the reaction that it would in a few short years, and in fact, in the future, the men of the 10th would only need to use a nickname that they would earn, but on this day, it warranted nothing more than a few murmurs.

"So, you deserted already?" Aulus sneered, and the words were still hanging in the air when the mood in the room changed, just as Aulus intended, because in the span of heartbeats since his son's unexpected appearance, Aulus Didius understood what was happening.

Not the specifics, perhaps, but he knew that, given their last conversation months earlier, and his explicit warning, his son was back in a direct challenge to his authority and leadership, which in Aulus' view could only mean that Spurius had deserted.

He was surprised that, while this angered his son, Didius controlled it, but it was actually the other Legionary Atilius who answered, "No, we're not deserters. We were given leave because of our successful campaign against the Lusitani and the Gallaeci."

"We heard about that," Pacula spoke up, understanding something potentially bad was hanging in the balance and not wanting the place he still thought of as his torn apart. "We heard you boys taught them a lesson they won't soon forget! And," he added with only partially false sincerity, "we appreciate you keeping us Roman citizens safe." He turned and addressed Aulus, "Isn't that so, Aulus?"

"Oh yes," Aulus answered mockingly. "I couldn't sleep worrying that those barbarian *cunni* would suddenly show up here in Gades and slit our throats when we slept."

Before Didius could respond, once again, Atilius interjected, "That's actually not their style. They may be barbarians, but they prefer to look a man in the eye when they try and gut them and not while they're sleeping and helpless. Not," he finished cheerfully, "like some Romans I know."

"Are you implying I'm one of them?" Aulus challenged.

"Not at all!" Atilius shook his head, looking at Aulus with a wide-eyed innocence, then with a laugh, he added, "I was talking about *my* Tata, nobody else."

"Neither am I," Didius finally spoke, then added, "implying

it, I mean. I'm saying it, to your face...Aulus."

Whereas his father had been on his guard, now Aulus was uneasy, and he couldn't seem to keep his eyes from going to the *gladius* hanging from his son's hip, and how Didius just naturally seemed to have his hand resting on the hilt.

"I don't know what you're talking about, son," Aulus countered. "I've never murdered a sleeping man in my life! It's not my style!" For the first time, Aulus turned his attention to the half-dozen men who were part of his *collegia*, asking loudly, "Is it, boys? Eh? Aulus Didius isn't the type! If I need a man done, I'll face him!"

As soon as the words left his mouth, Aulus Didius knew that he had erred, had given his son an opening, and despite himself, he felt a flash of what was almost paternal pride when Spurius didn't hesitate, challenging his father, "What about having someone else do your killing for you, Aulus? You said that wouldn't do it yourself, but you'd have me killed if I ever came back, but here I am."

Even before he finished, Didius had pivoted slightly so that he was facing his father's men, and while they hadn't discussed it beforehand, Atilius hadn't hesitated, taking a step forward and to Didius' side so that none of the six men could move without the pair seeing it. Neither of them drew their *gladius*, but now Atilius copied his comrade, his hand on the hilt, while Aulus' men either looked confused or made it clear they wanted no part of any trouble. You little bastard, Aulus thought. You've boxed me, and done it neatly too.

Raising both hands above the table, palms out, Aulus said, "Now, Spurius, there's no need for any of this! I was just talking; I certainly didn't mean it. You're my son! How could I hurt you?"

"The same way you hurt your brother Gaius," Didius shot back, though his eyes remained on his potential adversaries. This elicited a sudden hiss as Aulus took in a breath, and Didius laughed. "Really? You didn't think Marcus Surenas would tell me who he really was? And," now he did turn and look down at his father, and Aulus saw nothing familial in his son's gaze, "what you did to him?"

"He's lying," Aulus replied, trying to sound calm.

Didius snorted.

"How do you know? I didn't tell you what he told me."

"It's obviously something bad if it's gotten you coming here like this," Aulus countered. "Gaius was always a liar, son. You shouldn't believe anything he told you."

"But I should believe you?" Didius scoffed. "No," he shook his head, "what you did to him is the same thing you did to me. You didn't want him challenging you, and you did the same thing to me."

"Is that what he told you?" Aulus laughed, but it was forced even to his ears, "Don't believe everything you hear, boy."

"I know the truth when I hear it," Didius shot back, although his eyes had returned to his father's men.

He didn't want to, but Aulus recognized that he had no real choice, because, while it was for different reasons, he didn't want bloodshed here any more than Pacula did, so he turned to the men, commanding, "Boys, go wait outside. I want to talk to my son, alone."

"What about the other customers?" Pacula squawked, but Aulus silenced him with a look, which the proprietor interpreted correctly, because he turned and, while he was clearly unhappy, he said in a loud voice, "Friends, Proserpina's Grotto is now closed for business for the next little while. I'm sorry, but you're going to have to go elsewhere." There was some grumbling, but it was muted; the people who frequented this place knew what was really going on and who really ran things at the *taverna*. That most of them benefited in some way from Aulus Didius' activities was no accident, and they got to their feet and began shuffling out. "Wait!" Pacula called out sharply, pointing to one man. "Leave that cup behind, Glabius! That belongs to me and I know when you come back, you'll *forget* to bring it back."

Glabius, who looked as if he was some sort of laborer, which he was, groused, "Who said I'm coming back? I don't like my drinking interrupted like this!"

"He'll be back," Aulus spoke up, staring at Glabius as he added, "won't you, Glabius?"

Even in the dim light, everyone saw the laborer suddenly pale, and he hastily assured Aulus, "Yes, Aulus, of course I will!" Giving a nervous laugh, he added, "You know when I'm in my cups sometimes I run my mouth, eh?"

"That's a bad habit, Glabius." Aulus' voice was cold, but then he grinned suddenly. "But you're a good customer, and I know you'll remember what I said." He paused. "Won't you?"

"Absolutely, Aulus," Glabius assured him, but he had set the cup down and was moving out the door as he said it.

One by one, the dozen patrons filed out the door, most of them averting their gaze from where Didius and Atilius still stood, followed by Aulus' men, one of whom lingered at the doorway.

"Are you sure, *Dominus*?"

Before Aulus could reply, it was his son who answered for him, "He's sure, Prixus," knowing this man since childhood, and that he was his father's longest serving man who wasn't related to the Didius clan by blood. The truth was that, in his way, Didius liked Prixus well enough, because he had shown the young Spurius more kindness than he ever got from his father, which was why he assured Prixus, "It'll be all right. I'm not going to do anything. I just want to talk to my father."

Still, Prixus was reluctant, but he did leave, pulling the door behind him, while Aulus addressed Pacula, "That means you, Pacula. Take your wife and daughter and go to the storeroom. We need to be ready for the evening rush."

Pacula flushed, not caring for the inference that he didn't know how to run his business, which had been thriving before Aulus Didius got involved, and for what had to be the thousandth time, Pacula silently cursed himself for his gambling habit. Nevertheless, he obeyed, satisfying his honor with nothing more than a curt nod, then muttering to the two women, who followed him obediently into the back of the *taverna*. An awkward silence ensued, as both of the primary actors in this small drama realized that they didn't know what to do next.

Extending a hand and gesturing to the pair of stools on the opposite side of his table, Aulus said, "Come, sit down, both of you. Let's talk."

Atilius continued to take his lead from Didius, glancing over at his comrade who, for a moment, didn't move, or even indicate his intentions, then gave a slight nod. The pair walked over, and Aulus noticed how the man Atilius used one foot to move the stool over, not much, but adequate for there being enough space between the two Legionaries in the event they needed to move quickly. More importantly, at least for Aulus, was that Atilius now blocked his best avenue of escape from behind his table in the corner, and Aulus experienced a flash of regret that he had made this a habit, and he reminded himself to rethink this later. As always, there was already a pitcher of wine on Aulus' table, as well as extra cups since this was where he conducted most of his business during the day, and he filled two of them, with his left hand, Didius noticed, then shoved the cups towards his son and friend.

Lifting his own, he said, "To Fortuna, Mars and Bellona for your safe return from campaign."

As he hoped, this startled his son, but it was Atilius who moved first, snatching up the cup, then touching Aulus' with it before lifting it to his lips, and there was something in the way he drank the wine down that told Aulus that this Atilius loved his grape. Although he hesitated, Didius followed his comrade's example, lifting the cup and taking a swallow, but his eyes never left Aulus.

Setting the cup down, Didius asked bluntly, "Did you set your brother up in order to get him out of Gades so that you could take over from Old Spurius?"

Aulus didn't reply immediately, preferring to appear to study the cup in front of him, but he finally said carefully, "I can see how Gaius would think that's what happened. But," he shook his head, "that wasn't why."

"Then, why did you do it?"

Be careful, Aulus, he warned himself. Spurius is cunning; he's your son and you taught him how to spot lying and cheating so that he wouldn't make the same mistakes.

Aloud, Aulus replied evenly, "Because it was either get him out of Gades or he was a dead man."

Of all the things Didius was prepared to hear, what he believed to be the truth was the last on his mental list, and he couldn't stifle a gasp at what he saw as the confirmation of his uncle's side of the story.

Within a span of a couple of heartbeats, however, he was more confused than ever, because when he exclaimed, "So Gaius was telling the truth! You were going to kill him if he didn't leave!"

"No," Aulus countered emphatically. "I had no intention of killing Gaius. It was...someone else," he finished weakly.

He wasn't surprised that Didius wasn't satisfied with this evasion, and he pressed, "If not you, then who? The *Duumvir's* family?"

It would have been so simple for Aulus to confirm his son's suspicions, but Aulus wasn't ever content taking the easy way out of things, and he shook his head.

"It wasn't them. They," he sneered, "were typical upper-class weaklings, and they were too afraid of what would happen to the rest of them if they did." He laughed then, but there was a bitter edge to it, "If Old Spurius had one quality, it was his ability to scare the *cac* out of anyone who crossed him." Aulus took a breath, then said, "And that's who wanted him dead, Spurius."

Didius stared at him, not wanting to believe that his grandfather would want one of his sons dead, but on the heels of that thought was another, as a cold voice asked him, Why not? Didn't your father promise that you'd be dead if you came back? So why wouldn't Old Spurius do the same? Your father learned from his father, after all.

Consequently, what came out of Didius' mouth was a simple question: "But why?"

"Because Old Spurius was scared of Gaius," Aulus answered immediately. "Because Gaius was, or is, very clever. And," he paused to take a sip, "I think Old Spurius knew that Gaius would push our father out of the business before he was ready to step down."

"So you were doing it to protect your brother?"

It was the first words uttered by Atilius, and since it came from him and not his son, Aulus was more honest in his reply than he might have been, admitting, "Yes...and no." He shrugged. "With Gaius gone, I was the only one left for old Spurius to rely on, and I won't pretend that it didn't work out well for me. It's also true that I wanted to run our business."

With this, he turned to look directly at Spurius as he said earnestly, "But I wasn't willing to kill my brother to achieve that. It was," he concluded, "the best way I knew to solve two problems."

Didius didn't respond, instead regarding Aulus with a long, steady gaze; even as he lifted his cup to take a sip, his eyes searched his father's face.

Then, setting the cup down, he asked Aulus, "What now?"

"What do you mean 'what now'?" Aulus frowned, not understanding, and Didius explained, "Now you know that Gaius told me a different story, and you obviously know where he is, what are you going to do to him?"

Spreading his hands, Aulus answered reasonably enough, "Why would I do anything? He's there in Scallabis, and I'm here in Gades. He's never caused me any trouble, and I've never caused him any. And," he nodded his head in Didius' direction, "he obviously did what I asked since you're in the Legions now."

"How did you know he would?" Didius asked, truly curious.

"Just because we haven't had anything to do with each other, it doesn't mean I haven't been keeping an eye on him," Aulus replied, then with a chuckle, he added, "just as I'm sure he's done the same with me. And, I knew that he'd done this before with other *dilecti*."

It was mention of this that prompted Didius to ask another question that, while not as important, still troubled him.

"He also said that he was the one who served under Lucullus against Mithridates and not you."

Now, Aulus did look embarrassed; at least, this was what Didius assumed the expression on his father's face meant since he had never seen it before, but most telling was how Aulus stared into his cup as he admitted, "That's true." He looked up and directly into Didius' eyes as he said, in almost a pleading tone, "I *wanted* to, but Old Spurius forbade both of us serving because it would be bad for the business." His mouth twisted as he performed a bitter impersonation of his father's distinctive nasal growl. "Rome will only get one Didius boy, not both of them." Resuming his normal voice, Aulus sighed, "That's what he said, anyway."

"Was Old Spurius really one of Marius' Mules?" Didius asked, but he was surprised when his father nodded, answering firmly, "Yes, he was. Which is why he didn't want both of us under the standard, because he knew what it was like." Using this as an opportunity to change the subject, Aulus became jovial. "But you know all about it now, *neh?*"

Despite himself, Didius did laugh, and he shared a look with Atilius, who was equally amused, then he admitted to his father, "There's a *lot* of digging."

"And marching," Atilius added with a grin. "And we're always in a hurry, until we get where we're going. Then," he held up his hands as he shrugged, "we sit there waiting for whatever comes next."

"So, did you get your blade wet, boy?"

"I did," Didius answered with what he felt was justifiable pride. "I personally killed at least a dozen barbarians, maybe more." Suddenly remembering who was seated next to him, and that his close comrade could offer up other details of his time that Didius had no desire to be known, he indicated his friend, adding hastily, "But no more than Marcus here. We," he finished with a modesty that was completely out of character, "just did our duty to Rome, that's all."

They continued a bit longer, with both Didius and Atilius offering anecdotes of their time, the training, and their comrades of their section, with one exception. That Didius never mentioned Titus Pullus didn't surprise Atilius, while for his part, he decided that discretion was called for during this moment, so he followed Didius' example, although he did mention Domitius, earning him a glare from Didius, reminding Atilius that it had been the shortest member of their section who was the most instrumental in banishing Didius from their tent for that week.

Finally, there was nothing left to discuss, which Aulus signaled by saying, "Yes, well, I think we've kept the customers' throats dry long enough, eh? Besides," he forced a laugh, "I'll never hear the end of it from Pacula as it is."

As if you care about what he thinks, Didius thought, but he kept it to himself, as eager to go now as his father was to be rid of him. It had been a supremely unsatisfying encounter, and in many ways, he was more confused now than when he had entered the *taverna*. Nevertheless, he understood that this was where things would be left, which he signaled by standing up.

"How long will you be in Gades?" Aulus asked, a perfectly reasonable question.

"Two or three days," Didius replied, informing Atilius for the first time of his plans. "I want to talk to some of my friends. Is Septimus around?"

"He's out on the docks," Aulus replied. "Come back tonight and I'll make sure he's here." Then, he gave a leering grin at the pair as he said, "And when you come back, I'll make sure you get first choice of our best girls upstairs. It's the least I can do for my son and his friend now that they're protecting us!"

Atilius naturally thought this was a splendid idea, and while Didius was not quite as enthusiastic, it was a tempting offer, and he said, "We'll be back tonight."

They departed then, stepping into the street to find that the occupants of the *taverna* had chosen to linger nearby, even Glabius, who went rushing back inside as the pair walked away.

Once they were out of earshot, Atilius asked, "Well? Do you believe him?"

"No," Didius said flatly. "I don't believe a word of it. But," he sighed, "I'm not sure it really matters." For the first time, Didius thought about Atilius and what he might like to do next, which was why he nudged his comrade as he grinned. "You know that Gades has more than one *taverna* and brothel, don't you? What do you say I take you on a tour of some of the places down by the docks?"

"I thought," Atilius answered fervently, "you'd never ask. One cup of wine is *not* enough for me."

They were laughing as they strode down the street, their *sagum* swirling behind them, two young warriors who could face any challenge with the confidence that came from no longer being green *Tiros*. Neither of them saw Aulus, who had stepped outside, staring at the pair, so they missed the expression on his face, a grim mask that communicated a man who had made a decision...a bloody one.

It was well past dark now, and both Didius and Atilius were

inebriated, though neither of them was falling-down drunk, yet.

"Should we head back to Proserpina's Grotto?" Atilius asked, only slightly slurring his words. "I," he grinned, "have an itch for something other than wine."

While Didius was far from sober, he wasn't in the same condition as Atilius. For some reason, he hadn't enjoyed the debauching as much as he normally did, but he put it down to still being unsettled from his confrontation with Aulus.

Regardless, he was sufficiently grateful for Atilius' presence that he tried not to dampen his comrade's enthusiasm, so he smiled and agreed, "You're not the only one, Marcus. Let's go see what new choice bits are upstairs since I've been gone."

It was an almost perfectly executed ambush, made possible because of Aulus' familiarity with his son, shrewdly guessing that Didius and his friend would head for one of two *tavernae* near the docks. And, from there, he knew the most likely route his son would take back to Proserpina's Grotto; the only complication was the presence of his friend Atilius, who didn't seem to be a bad sort. Aulus was acutely aware of the risk he was taking, murdering two men of the Legions, but just as Spurius didn't believe his father, the father didn't believe for one heartbeat that his son's reappearance in Gades was just to satisfy Spurius' curiosity about an old family matter. Corduba was a long way away, and it was common knowledge that the *Praetor*, Gaius Julius Caesar, had left the province and was on his way back to Rome with three of the four Legions, leaving his son's 10th behind, and if someone connected to the Legion came poking their nose around Gades, well, Aulus was certain that he wouldn't be a suspect given that one of the victims would be his son. Nevertheless, he instructed his men to wear hoods, and most importantly, attach them to their tunics with *fibulae* so that their victims couldn't snatch the hood from their heads, just one of the many valuable lessons Old Spurius had taught to his son. What he couldn't remember was whether or not he had passed this on to Spurius, and while he had taught Septimus this trick, Spurius' half-brother had nothing to do with this, and in fact, Aulus had kept him in the dark about it. For reasons that Aulus couldn't really fathom, despite Spurius' sour disposition and general surly attitude towards his half-brother, Septimus never seemed to begrudge his treatment from his slightly older brother, and by slightly, it meant that he was six months younger. Livinia's pregnancy had been what precipitated all that transpired, and while Aulus didn't have anything to do with his current wife and her role in Spurius' mother's demise, neither had he done anything to stop Livinia from pursuing her own plans to secure her status as Aulus' woman. It was, after all, flattering to have a woman willing to kill another woman just for the privilege of being with him, and it enhanced his reputation as a virile man who women desired. In the case of Spurius, this was also a matter of his *dignitas*; his son had openly challenged him, in front of witnesses, and Aulus had been seen to back down. Add to that the fact that Aulus had boasted of his promise to Spurius if he returned to Gades, it meant that, as far as Aulus was concerned, he had been given no choice in taking what, even with all that, was a drastic action. If anything, it was Spurius' fault, he assured himself; if the little bastard hadn't come back, none of this would be happening. Now, however, six men, including Prixus, were waiting in an alley that bisected the street that Aulus was certain Spurius would be taking to return to the Grotto, three of them armed with cudgels, their task to knock the pair senseless, Aulus assuming they would still be wearing their helmets since they were outside, while the other three were armed with *gladii*, which was forbidden by Roman law for civilians but was almost universally ignored, in recognition that the pair would be wearing their *hamatae*. Once subdued, then killed, their *sagum*, armor and tunics would be stripped from them and their bodies taken to a man who raised pigs next to the city wall who Aulus used whenever he needed someone to disappear. Of all of what he had planned, it was this that gave Aulus the most pause, it disturbing him that his son would be consumed by swine that, within a few months, Aulus himself would possibly consume, but once again, he reminded himself that this was, after all, Spurius' fault. Prixus hadn't been happy, and had asked Aulus to be excused from the party, but Aulus hadn't budged.

"I need someone I trust with this, Prixus," he had said flatly.

"And you've been with me the longest."

"Which means I've known Spurius since he was a tad, *Dominus*," Prixus had pleaded, but the habit of more than twenty years was ingrained too deeply in the man, which was why he was one of the six leaning against the wall of a building, waiting.

"Is there anyone you'd suggest?" Atilius was asking Didius as they made their way to the Grotto.

"If she's still there, I'd ask for Diana," Didius replied. With a grin, he added, "She does this thing with her tongue that..."

It was perfectly executed, three men leaping out of the deeper shadows of the alley on one side, three on the other, and it should have worked. The fact that it didn't rested in the fact that, just after they exited the *taverna* across from the docks, Didius had stopped Atilius.

"I think my father is going to try and have me killed," he told his friend.

He was expecting some sort of protest, so he was shocked when, instead, Atilius agreed by saying, "I think so too. Besides," he had shrugged and added without any emotion, "it's what my father would do if he thought I was a threat."

"It sounds like your father was a heartless bastard too," was all Didius could think to say.

Atilius didn't respond to this, asking instead, "What do you want to do? We could just not go there, then leave at dawn."

"No." Didius shook his head, but his objection was more practical in nature. "He knows me too well, Marcus. Any place I could think for us to stay tonight, he'd send men there." When he saw Atilius nod his acceptance, he thought for a moment. "If I was going to ambush someone between here and Proserpina's Grotto, I can think of a couple places to do it, although one is more likely than the other." He went on to describe the two spots, the second one being the bisecting alley two blocks away from the *taverna*, explaining, "It's far enough away so he can deny being involved, but it's close enough for him to have extra men in case we don't die as quickly as he wants us to. Which," he gave Atilius a grim smile, "I don't plan on doing at all, do you?"

"No, I've got more wine to drink and whores to fuck,"

Atilius replied, shaking his head vigorously at the idea of his demise, then he added, "Besides, if those Lusitani and Gallaeci couldn't do it, I'm not about to let some *collegia* bully boys have my head!"

Despite their inebriated condition, the pair reacted as quickly as if they had been sober, turning back to back, dropping their packs and drawing their *gladii* in one motion, and within no more than two normal heartbeats of time, the men who led the attack on either side, the men with cudgels and who both executed the same kind of overhead, downward swing left themselves open to a thrust to their bodies, and neither of them were wearing any kind of armor. Atilius' man let out a low moan, but Didius' victim issued a piercing scream because, unlike his comrade, Didius, using the strength that was second only to Pullus in their section, and perhaps the entire Century, ripped his blade across the man's midsection, opening his abdomen and causing his intestines to come bulging out through the rent in his tunic. Not surprisingly, Didius' victim collapsed immediately, his blood spattering all over Didius' legs, while Atilius' man went staggering backward, clutching his stomach just beneath his breastbone, but in doing so, he unwittingly aided Atilius because he collided with the second man, this one armed with a *gladius*, who was rushing to the attack.

Didius' next opponent, also armed with a *gladius*, barely broke his stride, able to hop over the prone body of the first man, but while he didn't make the same mistake of trying to bring his blade down onto Didius' head and instead executed a thrust, it was so poorly done that Didius actually laughed aloud, which served its own purpose, startling his foe and instantly followed by the ringing sound of iron meeting iron as Didius contemptuously knocked the man's blade aside so that it stabbed nothing but air to Didius' left. And, just as he had been trained, and had practiced more times than he had once thought necessary but had learned to appreciate, Didius' blade, now across his body with blade pointing downward, came back up in a backhand slash, one of the only slashing maneuvers the men of the Legions were trained to perform. Even in the dark, there was no way for him to miss, and his aim was perfect, catching this man in the throat, but with the hood being pinned to the tunic of his victim, to Didius' disappointment, he wasn't able to decapitate the man and send his head tumbling in the same manner he had seen the night that Pullus had whatever it was that happened to him that every other man of both First and Second Centuries still insisted saved their lives. Even in this moment of extremis, there was a dark corner of Didius' brain that was occupied with that bastard Titus Pullus, although it had the hidden benefit of fueling his rage in this moment so that, even as his blade sliced through the neck of his second assailant, he was already moving towards his third and final attacker, who turned to run but was too slow, taking a thrust to the back and only making it two steps before collapsing. With the third man out of action, Didius spun about, just in time to see that Atilius had dispatched the second man, while the third had dropped his *gladius* and fallen to his knees.

"No! Wait! Please don't! I didn't want to..."

Despite the voice being muffled by the hood, Didius recognized it, and he shouted to Atilius, whose arm was already drawn back, his blade glistening from his two victims, "No, Marcus! Don't kill him!"

"Why not?" Atilius demanded, though he never took his eyes off the kneeling man, but more importantly, his arm hadn't plunged downward.

"Because," Didius replied grimly, "I know him."

As time passed, Aulus Didius became increasingly nervous, although he hid it from the small crowd that, now that the sun was down, were crammed into Proserpina's Grotto. The only vacant tables were the two his men normally sat at, while Septimus was sitting at one of them with his passion of the moment, a new arrival from Gaul named Abruna, a buxom girl of perhaps sixteen but with hair the color of burnished copper who, in imitation of his father, he had perched on his knee. Otherwise, it was the normally busy night, with men occupied in playing dice at several tables, while there was traffic going to the back of the *taverna* to where the staircase was located leading upstairs, and even over the buzzing of conversation and laughter, the sounds of counterfeit passion were still audible over the background noise, which as it always did, elicited raucous jibes from the companions of one of the men who had gone upstairs. Aulus was usually amused by this almost as much as the customers, but on this night, he barely noticed, and while he tried, he couldn't seem to stop his eyes from going to the door, waiting for Prixus and the other men to return. The door was opened at regular intervals, but it was always either one or perhaps two men and an occasional woman arriving to join their friends. It was, he thought absently, a good night, even a bit more lively than usual, but this didn't lighten his mood at all. Only when he snapped at Septimus, who asked him a question that was in no way irritating about the plans for the next day did Aulus realize that his foul humor was being noticed, so he tried to smile, even recalling his favorite whore, Diana, to come back to sit with him so that he could at least pretend that all was normal.

It was perhaps a third of a watch before midnight, the traditional closing time, or the time when most of the patrons of the Grotto chose to go home to get some sleep, that the door opened, and Aulus saw that it was Prixus, and he felt the tension drain from his body. His relief was destined to last no more than a handful of heartbeats; his first indication that all wasn't what it seemed was by the way Prixus entered the *taverna,* suddenly lurching forward violently enough that he stumbled, though he kept his feet and quickly regained his balance, but it was long enough for Aulus to see that the figure behind him wasn't one of the other men. Even in the dim light of the dozen lamps hung from the ceiling at various points around the *taverna*, Aulus recognized his son; more importantly, he also saw the *gladius* in Didius' hand, and that it was glistening in the lamplight from the blood coating it. Naturally, those patrons nearest the door noticed Prixus' awkward entrance, but it was the sudden silence that was most telling. For a second time, Aulus suddenly shoved Diana off of his knee to stand up, but this time, he hurried to position himself so that he wouldn't be trapped in the corner. Septimus, who had been told that his half-brother would be returning to visit, had also come to his feet, but with a smile on his face that suddenly froze as his mind caught up with what his eyes were seeing.

Without looking away from where Prixus, who they could

now see had his hands bound behind him with leather thongs, Septimus called to Aulus, "What's this about, Father?"

"I have no idea, my son," Aulus said louder than necessary as his mind raced, but he tried to portray that he was both concerned and puzzled as he addressed Didius. "*Ave*, my other son. What seems to be the problem? And," he indicated Prixus, "why do you have Prixus trussed up like a hog?"

"You know why," Didius snarled, and nobody had to know him to see that he was truly angry.

Meanwhile, although Atilius had followed his comrade, he stopped just inside the doorway, and like Didius, his *gladius* was unsheathed...and as bloody, though his expression was unreadable.

Aulus licked his lips, but this was the only sign of his nerves as he asked, "Why would I know? I have no idea..."

"Shut. Your. Mouth."

It wasn't the words as much as it was Didius lifting his *gladius* and pointing it directly at his father, now just a half-dozen paces away, although Prixus was partially blocking Didius' path to Aulus, who did the wise thing, though he still held his hands out in a supplicating gesture, trying to maintain his expression of puzzled innocence, but Didius didn't address his father, turning instead to Prixus to prod him with the point of his blade, commanding harshly, "Tell Septimus why you're tied up." Prixus shook his head, though he bowed his head so that he didn't have to look at either Aulus or Septimus. Infuriated, Didius jabbed him in the back with the point, causing Prixus to yelp with pain, and he roared, "*Tell him!*"

Prixus opened his mouth, but it took him two tries to rasp, "I...I...I was ordered by your father to kill Spurius and his friend."

There was a chorus of gasps from the onlookers, while Septimus spun to face his father, who was glaring at Prixus, demanding, "Is that true, Father?"

Recognizing the futility of it, Aulus didn't try to deny it, saying simply, "Yes, it's true." Now, there was a small uproar as the patrons of the *taverna* began muttering excitedly to each other, either expressing their shock that a man would have his own son killed, or their complete lack of surprise given that it was Aulus Didius who was the father, and it required Aulus to raise his voice, and while he was frightened, he was also angry, and he pointed an accusing finger at Didius as he said, "He came here after I told him as the *paterfamilias* that he was to never set foot in Gades again! I'm within my rights under Roman law to punish him however I see fit!"

The problem for Didius, and to a lesser degree for his half-brother, was that Aulus was speaking the truth; Roman law and custom was very clear on this point. The *paterfamilias* of a family, no matter what class they belonged to, exercised total and absolute authority over every member of his family, up to and including the right to kill them if he deemed it necessary. However, while this wasn't unheard of, it was almost always over a serious matter, such as a son committing a serious crime like murder that brought dishonor to the family, or more commonly, a daughter who was wantonly unchaste, and not just because a father forbade his son to return to his birthplace.

Didius didn't bother to address Aulus, choosing instead to turn to Septimus and ask him bluntly, "How long do you think you have before Aulus decides to do away with you, eh, Septimus? If he'd kill me, his oldest son, what makes you think that you're safe?"

Septimus' face clouded, communicating his confusion, and a concern that he clearly had never thought about, and he replied hesitantly, "But if he had you killed, I'd be the only son he has left!" Suddenly recognizing how his words could be interpreted, he added hurriedly, "But I didn't know anything about this, Spurius, I swear it on Jupiter's Stone!"

"I know you didn't," Didius assured him, but while he smiled, it was a grim one. "Because if you did, you'd end up like everyone but Prixus here." Now, he matched his father's volume to announce, "You're going to need to hire more bully boys, Septimus. Five of them, I think." He cocked his head as if he was thinking, then prodded Prixus with his *gladius*. "Or maybe six; I haven't decided."

"But that's Father's decision," Septimus answered automatically and without thinking.

Returning to the original subject, Didius countered, "And what happens when he sends those new men after you? Yes, you would have been the only son left if his plan had worked tonight, but how long do you think that's going to last, eh?" He pointed to Diana, who was still standing at the counter, and Didius asked Septimus, "Do you know what I see when I look at her, Septimus?"

"No," Septimus replied cautiously, but he suspected he knew, which was confirmed when Didius replied flatly, "I see Livinia. Your mother. That's what I see."

"Don't talk about my mother, Spurius," Septimus showed his anger for the first time; this subject had been a point of contention between the pair for some time, but as Didius had matured, he had realized that his anger at his half-brother was misplaced, although he could never truly control the bitterness he felt.

To Septimus' surprise, Didius said, "I don't really blame your mother either. Not," he allowed, "anymore, because I know the only way she would have...done what she did," even now, he couldn't bring himself to use the word "murder," if only because, while he was almost certain this was the case, he didn't really know, "was because Aulus wanted her to do it." Now, he did turn to face Aulus. "Isn't that right...Father?"

"I told you," Aulus answered tightly, his lips set in a thin line, "your mother became ill, that's all. Neither Livinia nor I had anything to do with it."

"But you had everything to do with what this *cunnus* and the other men tried to do tonight," Didius retorted. Making sure that his eyes were locked with his father's, Didius' tone was lacerating with the scorn he felt. "And you should have known better than to send someone like this," he prodded Prixus again, "after two men of the Legions, and if you had really been under the standard and not a *mentula* liar, you would have." The blood drained from Aulus' face, yet he still just stood there, prompting Didius to turn his head, not much, but enough so that he could be heard by all of the spellbound onlookers. "How many of you in here have been told by Aulus that he marched for Lucullus against Mithridates?" Almost every person either raised their hand or mumbled in a manner that affirmed that they had, in fact, been told this. "Well, he lied," Didius said flatly. "It was his brother, Gaius Didius, who actually served, but after Aulus tricked his brother into leaving Gades so that he could take over our family's business, he told all of you that it was him."

As Didius intended, Aulus was growing angrier, and he shifted slightly so that his hand was closer to the hilt of the *gladius* that was in the sheath attached to the underside of his table, while he tried to recall if he had ever shown Spurius this trick. He was also aware of the manner in which Septimus was staring at him, but it was the eyes of all of the other people sitting there that were of most immediate concern. He had ruled by fear for years, and the basis for it had been his supposed status as one of the hard men of the Legions, although he had certainly committed a number of acts in the intervening years that reinforced that belief, and now here was his son Spurius telling everyone it was a lie. Aulus was under no illusion that this would stay within the walls of the Grotto, and he could easily imagine the eagerness of some of the onlookers to rush out into the city to spread the tale, especially to the leaders of the rival *collegiae* in the city. Then, he thought grimly, the wolves will come, and it was all because Prixus and the others had botched the job of ridding him of what he viewed as the most potent threat to his hold on his family and his *collegia*. Suddenly, Aulus was almost blinded by a flash of white-hot rage, fueled by the frustration at Prixus' failure and his son's taunting, so he was as surprised as anyone to find his hand snatching for the *gladius*, drawing it from under the table, and before he could stop himself, rushing at his son. The only person in the room who didn't seem to be caught off guard was Didius himself, his only response being to take a single step to his right so that Prixus, still bound and struck motionless by all that was transpiring, wasn't between himself and Aulus. Aulus came hurtling at Didius, but when he was just out of reach of a thrust, he stopped, clearly hoping that his son would do that very thing.

All this earned him was a sneer from Didius, who was standing in a slight crouch, right arm pulled back, his blade at waist level and parallel to the ground, and he taunted his father, "You're going to have to do better than that, old man. We learned that trick our first week of sparring! Not," he finished with a sneer, "that you would know anything about that, since you never served a fucking day under the standard."

As he intended, this further enraged Aulus, who roared a challenge. This time, his attack was in earnest, and like his son, his blade was held low but out farther from his body, the only difference being that his blade was held vertically. Whether it was because Aulus had never faced a man wearing mail before and didn't compensate for it by adding more power to his thrust, or, in what would be the last few heartbeats of life, he couldn't bring himself to plunge his blade into his son's body, nobody would ever know. From Didius' perspective, he was surprised by Aulus' speed, and in that instant, he realized how he had come to rely on training with a shield, because his left hand automatically raised to a position that, had he been holding it, meant that he would have easily blocked the thrust. Instead, the blade shot underneath his forearm, the point punching him in the stomach, but not only did it not penetrate his mail, it only partially drove the wind from him. His right arm was already moving, while his father only had a tunic protecting him, and Didius put his strength behind the attack. Because he had oriented his blade in the way they had been trained, rather than cutting through Aulus' ribs, the blade slid in between them, about midway up Aulus' thorax, with sufficient force behind the blow that Didius felt the impact of the handguard striking his father's body to the point that, if it had been a punch, that alone would have knocked the wind out of Aulus. The more unsettling aspect for Didius was that it brought his face less than two feet from his father's, and even in the dim lighting, he couldn't miss Aulus' eyes going so wide that the whites made the colored part look ridiculously small, but it was the blast of his father's dying breath, the odor of wine, garlic, and the rot of teeth that was common to men of Aulus' age that Didius would remember for the rest of his days.

To his credit, Aulus didn't scream, although it was probably because he had no breath, nor did he try to speak, yet his eyes never left Didius' as he sank slowly to his knees, looking up at his son, not with hatred or anger, but with what, later, Didius would conclude was resignation, as if this was what Aulus had always expected would be his fate. Without being aware of doing so, Didius almost gently laid his father's body down onto the wooden floor, withdrawing his blade as he did so, leaving his father lying face up, his eyes still open but now with the black part almost obscuring the brown of his father's eyes, the sign that he had crossed the river in Charon's Boat. Only then did he become aware of the utter silence, but he also realized that his back was turned to Septimus, and he spun about quickly, his blade back up and in position. This was when he saw that Atilius had moved from his spot at the door, putting himself in a position so that even if Septimus had any thought to avenge their father's death, he would have been cut down immediately by Didius' close comrade, yet another thing that Didius would remember for the rest of his days.

Septimus was standing as well, but his weapon hand was empty as he stared down at Aulus' corpse, his mouth open, and it took some effort for him to finally say, "I never thought anyone could kill him."

"Well," Didius said roughly, "I have." He paused for a fraction of a moment, then asked quietly, "And what do you intend to do about it, Septimus?"

This jerked Septimus' attention away from their father's body, and he stared, hard, at Didius, giving his older half-brother the impression that he was trying to divine what was happening in his soul. Didius also noticed that the shock was wearing off, and he deduced that this could be a moment where matters became more explosive. The crowd in the *taverna* were also coming out of their stupor, and it quickly grew noisy again as men began talking to and over each other, despite their eyes remaining on the pair.

Understanding that he needed to wait for Septimus to commit himself, Didius returned his brother's gaze, and to his eyes, it was as if Septimus was growing up even as he watched, his expression becoming harder, his jaw setting in a line that Didius had learned signaled that Septimus had come to some sort of decision, one from which he would not be dissuaded.

In a signal that he understood that this involved more than just the pair of brothers, Septimus said loudly enough for all to hear, "While you did violate our Father's order never to return to Gades, you didn't deserve the treatment you received." He turned and addressed Prixus, who, like Atilius, was standing there mutely, although his hands were still bound, and Septimus demanded, "Is what Spurius said true? Did you and Percennius and the rest try to kill him and his friend here?"

Prixus licked his lips, and it was plain to see that he was trying to calculate the best approach to take, but while loyal and willing to do as ordered by Aulus no matter what it was, Prixus wasn't known for being clever; in fact, he was quite the opposite, which meant that it took him several heartbeats to conclude that honesty was in order.

"Yes, Septimus," he answered at last.

Septimus didn't look surprised, which he confirmed by saying, "I believe you, Prixus. And," his voice hardened, not much but enough to be noticeable, "you'll refer to me as *Dominus* from this point forward, is that understood?"

Didius could see that Prixus didn't like it, and for a bare instant, it appeared as if he would make an issue of the matter, but Didius guessed the fact that he was still bound convinced him that the proper course of action was to answer, "Yes...*Dominus*."

Addressing both Didius and Atilius, he asked, "Where are the other men?"

"Where we left them," Didius answered indifferently.

"They're all dead?"

"All but Prixus," Didius agreed.

Septimus considered this for a moment, then he announced, "I have no quarrel with my brother Spurius, nor his friend here..."

"Marcus Atilius," Atilius supplied, and Septimus continued, "...Marcus Atilius, and I swear by Jupiter Optimus Maximus that they're safe from any kind of retribution while they're here in Gades." In a quieter tone, he said, "Enough blood has been shed tonight as it is." With one hand, his left, Didius noticed, Septimus indicated his table, asking, "Would you two care to sit while I attend to our father?"

Didius was about to say no, still not fully trusting Septimus was being sincere, but Atilius caught his eye, whereupon he whispered to Didius, "You *did* promise that we'd get drunk and have our pick of the whores."

That was true, Didius thought, and it was a sign of not only their times, but of the nature of men under the standard that the pair of Legionaries came, sat down, and after a quiet few moments, the crowd resumed doing what they had been doing before their appearance. Before they sat down, they asked Pacula's daughter to bring them a couple of cloths, and while people were talking now, they were all still watching the pair as they used the cloths to wipe down their blades. Only when they both sheathed their weapons did the people turn away and resume their conversation normally, although there wasn't much laughter, and there was a muted, urgent tone as every person present discussed what this meant to their own futures. Neither Didius nor Atilius noticed how the people were constantly glancing down at Aulus' body, which was soon removed once Septimus had cut Prixus' bonds, and the pair picked Aulus up and carried him into the back of the *taverna*, moving through a passageway that led to the storage room and small office, while Pacula's wife and daughter were pressed into service by scrubbing the bloodstain from the floor, which anyone observant would have seen they did as if it was a routine matter. Neither man said anything to the other, both content to resume their drinking, although Atilius was slightly miffed that he had sobered up considerably.

He broke the silence by grumbling, "Now I have to start getting drunk all over again," although he said it as much to lighten the mood, and while Didius didn't laugh, he did smile.

He was staring down into his cup, and Atilius wondered what his comrade was thinking, but wasn't about to ask, and he tried to think about how he would feel if he had been the one to kill his father instead of his mother doing the deed. Honestly, he didn't know, nor did he dwell on it that long, giving only an imperceptible shrug as he drained his cup. When Septimus returned, he took his seat, his demeanor once again impossible for Didius to interpret, despite essentially growing up together, but in that moment, Didius realized that he hadn't paid much attention to Septimus, never seriously considering him a rival for what, less than a year ago, he had been sure would be his *collegia*; although, he thought with grim humor, I would have probably been content to wait for Aulus to die. Or, he thought, maybe not; it was impossible to say.

Septimus, whether by accident or design Didius would never know, broached the subject by asking Didius bluntly, "Now that Aulus is dead, what are your plans, Spurius?"

This startled Didius, and he glanced over at Atilius, but his friend was too busy pouring himself another cup to react.

"What do you mean?" he asked, but Septimus wasn't put off.

"You know what I mean," his half-brother countered. "Are you going to stay here?"

Now, this *did* get Atilius' attention, because it had never occurred to him that his close comrade might consider this an option, and by this point in time, he and all the other new men of the 10th had heard the tales of the fate of men whose close comrade deserted and their Centurion was convinced they were somehow involved, so he looked at Didius with something close to alarm.

Thankfully, Didius only hesitated for a bare fraction of a moment before he said, "*Gerrae!* What kind of *cac* are you talking? Do you know what happens to deserters, Septimus?" Judging by the expression of surprise on Septimus' face, he didn't, which he confirmed with a shake of his head, and Didius went on, "Deserters who get caught while on campaign are either crucified or forced to run the gauntlet, while deserters who do it when we're not are flogged with the scourge, a minimum of fifty lashes." Leaning towards Septimus, Didius asked, "Have you ever seen what scourge does to a man's back?" Again, Septimus shook his head, and Didius assured him, "Well, I have. And the poor bastard could barely lift his *gladius*, let alone his shield. He was basically crippled for life!"

The truth was that Didius had never seen anyone who had been scourged, although a few of the veterans salted into the 10th had been flogged, or as the rankers called it, "striped," and they were all ashamed of the scars crisscrossing their backs, but he felt his untruth was in a good cause. He *was* being honest about the punishment, but it was more than that; it surprised Didius almost as much as Septimus as he realized that, while running the family *collegia* had once been his dream, that was no longer the case. Even before his confrontation with Aulus, something had been nagging at Didius, and that was the fact that, as he and Atilius walked the streets of his home city, he didn't feel as if he belonged there any longer.

Aloud, he assured Septimus, "I've got no desire to stay here, Septimus. The business is yours to run now. I," then he hastily amended, indicating Atilius, "I mean, *we* are going back to Corduba." He could have been content to leave it at that, but there was enough residual anger and bitterness in Didius' soul that he couldn't resist adding, with an elaborate shrug, "Now, whether you'll be running it a month from now, let alone a year, only the gods know. Although," he offered Septimus a smile that might have been considered cruel, "if I was you, I'd be running to the temple of Hercules Gaditanus and make an offering to give you the strength you're going to need."

Didius was both slightly disappointed and ashamed that, rather than angering Septimus, he was clearly worried, and he leaned over the table closer to Didius to ask, "What advice do you have for me, Spurius? What would you do in my place?"

Despite himself, Didius experienced a twinge of what, while he hadn't experienced it in many years, was what he dimly understood was a familial connection, and a feeling of concern for his brother that surprised him, so he pretended to consider the question as he struggled to control his emotions.

After a pause, he said, "The first thing I'd do is figure out where Prixus stands. He was Aulus' longest serving man, and you either need his loyalty or..." He didn't finish, but there was no need because Septimus gave a grim nod of understanding.

"What else?" Septimus asked, and again, despite himself, Didius found himself warming to the task of helping his brother by returning his mind to the world of the back alleys, docks, and dark corners of Gades.

"You need to arrange a meeting with Pulcher," Didius went on, naming the head of one of their father's rival *collegiae*, but at this, Septimus didn't immediately agree.

"Why Pulcher first?" he asked. "Shouldn't I meet with Vulso? His gang is bigger than ours, and we can't afford to have problems with them because we share the docks."

"Because," Didius explained, "Vulso is a man of honor. He and Aulus have had that agreement about the docks for, what, ten years?"

"About that." Septimus nodded thoughtfully, and Didius continued, "But we had the trouble with Pulcher just last year, when he got greedy and thought that he should expand beyond the forum."

"That's true," Septimus acknowledged, but pointed out, "but it was just that one block along the edge. I didn't think it was worth going to war over."

"I know you didn't," Didius agreed, but while he wasn't excessively harsh, he did say firmly, "but you were wrong. That wasn't the first time Pulcher has tried poaching what's ours to run. Which is why you need to either meet with him. Or," he hesitated, because the idea had just come to him, "use that as your loyalty test for Prixus. Send Prixus to take care of Pulcher so that he's not a problem anymore."

Although Atilius was unfamiliar with the names, it wasn't hard for him to follow the conversation, and he happened to have a mouthful of wine when Didius said this, and rather than spit it out, he swallowed it down, along with air, causing him to choke and cough.

Septimus' reaction, however, wasn't much different, as he gasped, "Kill Pulcher? Are you mad?"

Rather than anger Didius, this made him smile, although he was pounding Atilius on the back as he did so, and he replied, "I've been told I'm mad more than once." Turning serious, he went on, "You're going to have to prove to all these jackals that you're not a young, green weakling, and Pulcher has been a problem for some time. How many times did we hear Aulus say that he needed to do something about the bastard?"

"More than I can count," Septimus admitted, and while he didn't look happy, he was once more nodding thoughtfully. After a span of perhaps a half-dozen heartbeats, Septimus nodded. "All right, I see what you're saying, and I see that I do need to make a...demonstration. And," he concluded, "your advice about using Prixus is good. I'll tell him that I'm not certain of his loyalty, and that I..."

"No," Didius interrupted sharply. "Don't say that, say the opposite. Tell him that because you *do* trust him so much, he's the only man you considered for the job. But," he finished grimly, "have him watched in case he decides to betray you."

Fortunately, Septimus immediately saw the sense in this, and he nodded acceptance.

Then, trying to disguise his anxiety, he asked Didius, "Will you stay here in Gades for a few days? Until I take care of this and get my feet under me?"

Didius opened his mouth with the intention of assuring Septimus that he would, but what came out of his mouth was, "No. We need to get back to the Legion, and if there *is* trouble with the *duumviri*, I can't be involved."

Septimus, while disappointed, didn't look surprised, and he asked, "When are you leaving?"

"Tomorrow," Didius answered immediately, but then he gave his brother a grin as he indicated Atilius, "but I promised Marcus here a night to remember before we leave."

"You mean you haven't had one already?"

This made both Didius and Atilius roar with laughter, and in the former man's case, this was an exceedingly rare event in itself, and Septimus made sure that it was. As they made their way back to Corduba, Didius would think more than once about how the night that he killed his father was one of the only happy memories he would have of his life under Aulus' roof; what he never did was think about what that meant.

Quintus Ausonius, who never thought of himself by his nickname Cyclops, was seated at the table in the small but tidy house, and as he always did at this time of day, sat watching as his wife Lydia busied herself preparing the evening meal, a small smile on his face. Not for the hundredth time, he found himself marveling that, somehow, he had found true happiness with Livia Pullus, and it was a running joke between them that his trading one of the mules he raised for his wife had been the best trade he ever made. Despite the transactional nature of their marriage, and despite Livia's initial fears that she was being essentially sold to a man who might prove to be as cruel and depraved as her father, she quickly learned that Quintus was nothing like Lucius, and almost as quickly, she fell in love with him. Now, she was stirring the pot that contained the stew she was making with the rabbit that Quintus had found in one of the traps set on their property, which Quintus had bought from another old Legionary who, like so many men under the standard, discovered that life on the farm was not to his taste. While they grew some olives, and Livia had a small vegetable garden, Quintus made his living as a mule breeder, using the skills he had picked up as an *immune* in the Legions, originally enlisting with Lucullus, but then serving under the renegade Roman patrician Sertorius. He never spoke to Lydia about his time under the standard and the things he had seen, and had done, although Lydia had been present when her brother Titus and his best friend Vibius, just before their departure to Scallabis, had prevailed on her husband to speak more openly about what they could expect. Perhaps it was because her huge brother was on her mind that, when they both heard a shout from outside their house, while Quintus didn't recognize the voice, Lydia did.

"That's Titus!" she said excitedly, although Quintus was already on his feet and moving to the door, and while he drew the *gladius* hanging from the hook next to the door, it was more out of habit.

Opening the door, even with one eye, Quintus could see just by the bulk of the dark figure striding across the small yard that his wife had been right, then the light spilling through the unshuttered window caught the glittering of what Quintus quickly discovered was a set of gleaming *phalarae*.

"*Salve,* brother!" Titus called out, but even before Quintus could reply, he was shoved aside with surprising force by Livia, who dashed outside and, with a squeal of delight, threw herself at her brother, who in turn was forced to drop his pack to catch her.

They were both talking and laughing at the same time, and as he had been doing for a couple years now, Titus lifted Livia up off the ground, extending his arms as she protested at being treated like a doll, both of them knowing she didn't mean it. By the time Pullus had lowered her back to the ground, Quintus had stridden up to him, although he was content with thrusting out his arm, which Pullus took, squeezing as he always did, while Quintus refused to wince, as he always did.

"It looks like you didn't take my advice to stay out of trouble," Quintus joked, indicating the *phalarae*, but Livia's eyes went elsewhere.

"What happened to you?" she cried, pointing down to the livid scar running down Pullus' forearm.

"Pluto's cock," Pullus groaned, though he was still smiling, "not you too! I had to listen to Gaia scold me for being clumsy enough to get stuck by some barbarian."

"Well," Livia replied tartly, "she's right!" She smiled then, turning to lead her brother in as she told him, "You're in time to eat. Quintus trapped a rabbit, so we're having a stew."

"I just ate," Pullus complained, though he was following her inside, and he was grinning like his sister.

"So? When has that ever mattered?" Livia countered, and he couldn't deny that, in fact, it never did matter, because he was always hungry.

Before they sat down, Pullus opened his pack, rummaged around in it, and withdrew a couple of items. One of them was a necklace made of gold filigree, the links very tiny, an example of the kind of work that the tribes of Gaul, to whom the tribes of Lusitania were connected in some way, though none of them knew how, were famous for, with a polished piece of jet hanging in a pendant, which he presented to Livia.

"I'd ask where you got this, but Quintus told me that it's not a good idea to because you probably took it off a body," she commented.

Pullus had originally intended to do that very thing, but he couldn't resist the opportunity of teasing the sister who was closest in age to him, and he seemingly assured her, "Oh, this didn't come from a body." Winking at Cyclops, he went on, "We found this *under* a body in one of the huts we cleared."

All he got for his troubles was a roll of the eyes, but Pullus was already presenting Cyclops with a ring, this one made of silver, but with a flat surface, upon which a rearing horse was etched.

"I know a mule would have been more appropriate, but I couldn't find one," he joked, but while Cyclops laughed, Pullus could also see that he was genuinely touched.

They sat then, and as Livia dished out the stew, Pullus related some of his experiences, although he took pains to avoid being too graphic, but Livia would still gasp, or put her hand to her mouth.

Finally, Pullus said in mock exasperation, "How is it that you women can go through all the mess of childbirth, but talking about killing barbarians has you going pale?"

"Because that's different!" Livia said indignantly, but when Pullus pressed her on why this was the case, she finally gave up, saying only, "Oh, I knew you wouldn't understand. Men never do!"

All Cyclops did was offer his brother-in-law a slight shrug, signaling that it was as much a mystery to him as it was to Pullus.

"Have you gone to see Phocas and Gaia?" she asked him, forgetting that he had mentioned her and slightly offending her brother for thinking he would not do so.

"Of course!" he said, but when Livia asked him about Lucius, he suddenly shifted uncomfortably, looking down at the table as he replied with a shrug, "Yes, I saw him."

Sensing that this was a potentially sensitive subject, she asked quietly, "Do I want to know about it?"

"Probably not," Pullus answered shortly, and she wisely took the hint, moving on to other subjects.

Once the meal was over and everything was cleared away, Livia kissed her brother, then retired to the other room, and while Pullus had been happy to see Livia, he was also relieved, because now he could talk freely.

Waiting for Cyclops to pour a cup of unwatered wine, Pullus began by saying, "You were right. Nothing you could have told us would have prepared us for what we saw."

Cyclops didn't gloat; it wasn't in his nature for one thing, and for another, he had been in Pullus' *caligae* himself, so he only replied, "I don't think anyone can warn a man what it's like, not really."

Taking this as a tacit signal, Pullus began to talk, and this was unlike the things he had said while Livia was present. He held nothing back; talking about the horror of seeing Vinicius essentially roasted alive, and all that had taken place, and what Pullus had done himself during the taking of the first town. He described the men of his section, even Didius, although for him Pullus had nothing good to say and felt nothing but scorn, viewing him as a cheat and a likely coward, although he grudgingly acknowledged that his performance at the last Gallaeci stronghold had been better. The time passed, the night creeping towards day, but Cyclops didn't stop Pullus and insist they get some sleep, just sat there listening, but it was past midnight before Pullus brought up the ambush.

"I won these," he indicated the *phalarae,* which, while they were still attached to his harness, he had taken off and laid on the end of the table, "for that ambush. But," he turned to look at Cyclops with a troubled gaze, "I don't remember any of it, Cyclops. I just remember the Pilus Prior telling me that he was going stripe me for leaving my post, and how it was so loud, and in the darkness, it was almost impossible to tell who was one of ours and who was one of theirs. But all that mattered to me was Crastinus being angry at me just for coming to help when those bastards breached our wall. And," he took a breath as he tried to think of how to describe it, only able to say, "I got angry too. The next thing I remember is how I was standing there and I couldn't move because I was surrounded by all these bodies."

"How many?"

"They told me they counted twenty-two around me," Pullus replied, but then he said honestly, "but I don't remember killing one man then, let alone twenty-two."

"Was it like what happened with Vibius?" Cyclops asked, not needing to elaborate, and in confirmation, Pullus flushed, though he didn't hesitate to admit, "No, that time, I meant to do what I did. I was angry about Juno, true, but I remember doing it."

Knowing that chastising Pullus further about what had happened about a year before, when in a fit of teenage jealousy, Pullus had punished his best friend because Juno had clearly chosen Vibius, wasn't necessary; instead, Cyclops thought about what Pullus had just told him.

"Maybe," he spoke slowly, as the thought began forming in his mind, "it's some sort of gift from Mars, Titus. Maybe he gave it to you so that you could use it in moments like that where you could save your life and the lives of your comrades."

"Scribonius said that," Pullus admitted. Then, more to

change the subject, he said, "Pilus Prior Crastinus speaks highly of you."

"Crastinus is a good man," Cyclops replied. "You can learn a lot from him."

"I already have," Pullus laughed, "but sometimes I have trouble deciding whether I hate him or love him."

This made Cyclops smile, answering, "That means he's a great leader, because you respect him out of equal parts love and fear. And in a place like the Legions, you have to have both."

This was the last they spoke that night, both of them retiring, with Pullus feeling better than he had in some time, as if a weight had been lifted. The next morning, when he was packed and ready to make the trip to Valeria's farm, Pullus took Cyclops aside.

"When you go into Astigi, you're going to hear some...things," he informed his brother-in-law.

"What sort of things?"

"You remember Marcus and Aulus?"

At first, Cyclops didn't, but then after a moment, his expression lightened and he said with a laugh, "Wait, are those the two *mentulae* who were dunking Vibius' head into a bucket of *cac* when you came along?" When Pullus nodded, he asked, "How old were you then?"

"Ten," Pullus answered, but he went on quickly, seeing Livia stirring inside the house through the open door, preparing to come say goodbye. "Well, we ran into them when we came into Astigi, and there was some...trouble."

"Trouble?" Cyclops' eye narrowed, certain there was more, but even he wasn't prepared for what was coming. "What kind of trouble?"

"We had some words," Pullus' tone turned flat, Cyclops recognizing it as a man under the standard giving a report, "and Aulus took offense to something Vibius said. He pulled his *pugio*. And," he finished without any discernible emotion, "I killed him."

"*Gerrae!*" Cyclops muttered, though not because he doubted Pullus, but because, even for their time, a man of the Legions killing a citizen wasn't an everyday occurrence.

Thinking of something, he asked, "Does Cornuficius know?"

"Yes," Pullus confirmed, Cornuficius being the commander of the town watch and a former Legionary himself. "And he ruled that it was a case of self-defense. I just wanted to tell you so that," he lowered his voice and nodded his head back behind him, having heard Lydia's footsteps, "in case she hears about it, she'll know I'm not in any trouble."

"Trouble about what?" Livia, who only heard the last part, asked suspiciously.

"Oh," Pullus grinned at Cyclops before he turned to face his sister, "trouble for thrashing busybodies who listen in on other people's conversations."

Livia laughed and retorted, "If you men didn't think you were clever enough to hide things from us, we wouldn't have to!"

In answer, Pullus swept his sister up again, spinning her about as he kissed her. When he turned to face Cyclops, he extended his arm, but he was caught completely off guard, and was absurdly pleased when, instead, the normally taciturn former Legionary enveloped Pullus in a hug, then kissed him on both cheeks as if he was a family member.

Softly, so that only Pullus could hear, he whispered, "I'm proud of you, Titus. I think you have a great destiny in the Legions."

Not knowing what to say, Pullus mumbled his thanks, but he had little memory of the walk to Valeria's farm, so absorbed in reliving what, to that moment, was the greatest praise he had ever received from a man he admired and respected almost more than anyone else alive. No *phalarae*, no crown, perhaps with the exception of the Civic Crown, could compare with the praise from this one-eyed former Legionary, and Pullus hoped that he would be able to return again, unaware that his destiny and that of Cyclops would be intertwined for years to come, just not in the way he imagined.

For some of the others in the Tenth Section, what would turn out to be their last weeks in Corduba passed uneventfully; neither Scribonius nor Calienus returned to their homes, although it was for decidedly different reasons. For Calienus, his home was now the Legions, and besides, returning home was something that men did after their first campaign; for men who had participated in several, their return home was generally because of a death or some sort of emergency in their family, and that was only if it happened during the winter months. Otherwise, as the new veterans would discover on their own, usually after their first visit, home would become a foreign place, one where they didn't feel comfortable, either because they realized they no longer had anything in common with the people they had left behind, or because they grew tired of being considered a curiosity, or in some cases, as a potential menace. For Scribonius, he never gave his reason for staying in Corduba, aside from making a vague statement to Pullus and Domitius about how he didn't feel the need to return home, and neither of his friends pressed him on the matter. Romulus and Remus returned home with one singular goal in mind; they were going to force the young Livia Plautus they both claimed as theirs to make her choice, then and there. What they found on their arrival, however, was that she had in fact done so...and neither of the brothers had been her choice, the proof being that she was not only married to the son of another farmer, but she was already pregnant. On their return to Corduba, despite some initial acrimony and recriminations between the brothers about whose behavior had been most responsible for essentially driving her into the arms of a third man, they had reached the conclusion that they were both better off without her.

Vellusius' visit had only served to reinforce the conviction that had compelled him to join in the first place, that the life of a farmer held absolutely no appeal for him. Surprising no one, it was Pullus and Domitius' return to their home in Astigi that was the most dramatic, although in something of a rarity, it wasn't Pullus who announced to their comrades that he had killed another man on their arrival. Not surprisingly, this elicited many questions, but while Calienus noticed that Didius and Atilius weren't among the interrogators, he noticed them exchanging a grin that, to the Sergeant, seemed conspiratorial. However, try as he might, even cornering Atilius one night at the *taverna* frequented by the Second Cohort, Calienus never learned the nature of the secret the pair was keeping, although he was silently relieved to see that there was at least one man who could tolerate Didius' company. As far as their time in Astigi, Domitius was clearly more eager to talk about what had happened than Pullus, who, if anything, seemed more embarrassed by the incident. It was left to Scribonius to recall how Domitius and Pullus had met one night as they were seated at the table in their section hut waiting for the evening meal.

"Wait," he spoke up as Domitius began telling the story, "weren't those the two that ducked your head into a bucket of night *cac*?"

Not surprisingly, this elicited a ripple of snickers, but while he flushed, Domitius affirmed, "Yes, that was them. Now," he asked pointedly, "can I keep going?" Without waiting for Scribonius to reply, Domitius continued, "We had just gotten to Astigi and we were in the forum talking to the woman who sold us meat pies, when who do we see?" His face creased into a smile. "Marcus and Aulus! So, naturally, we went to renew our acquaintance and catch up..."

"Of course," Calienus interjected dryly, "that's all you had in mind, eh?"

"Exactly!" Domitius lied cheerfully. "That's all we had in mind, truly. But then," the grin faded, and despite it being in the past and all that had happened, he was still clearly angry about it. "Marcus had to go and say something about Juno." He paused in his story to remind the others, "You know, she's my..."

He was immediately drowned out by a chorus of groans, as Romulus, still smarting from the rejection of him and his brother snapped, "Yes, yes. We know! You and she have been chosen by The Fates to be together forever. Get on with the story!"

"You bastards are just jealous!" Domitius countered indignantly, but he relented, and continued, "Anyway, Marcus...said what he said about Juno, and I," he shrugged, "took exception to it."

"What he means," Pullus broke in, speaking for the first time, and to Scribonius at least, the giant Roman didn't seem to particularly relish this tale, "is that he had his *pugio* out so quickly, I didn't even see it happen, and had it at Marcus' throat.

He even drew a little blood," he added, then became silent again.

Domitius, tacitly understanding, resumed the story. "As I was explaining to Marcus why this was a really, really bad idea," this elicited some chuckling, "it was Aulus who decided to *really* be foolish, because he drew *his pugio*. At least, he started to, but," he turned to indicate Pullus, "Titus saw it, had his *gladius* out quicker than Pan, and pinned Aulus to the wall of the building we were standing next to. He got him," Domitius made no attempt to hide his satisfaction, "right through the mouth, and pinned the *cunnus* to the wall."

Unsurprisingly, all eyes went to Pullus, who only offered a vague shrug, muttering, "He shouldn't have done that. Not with us anyway."

"So what happened?"

It was a natural question to ask, but to Calienus, Atilius, who was the man who asked the question, seemed intensely interested in the outcome.

If the others were waiting for some sort of dramatic result, they were to be disappointed as Domitius shook his head and replied simply, "Nothing."

When he said nothing more, it was Pullus who spoke up.

"The commander of the town watch was under the standard, and Marcus and Aulus had been causing trouble for years. He said they were suspected in robbing travelers who were passing through Astigi, but he could never catch them. So," he concluded, "their reputation and all that they'd done meant that Cornuficius didn't think it was worth pursuing."

"I've said it before," Romulus said with mock disgust, "the gods really do love you, Pullus." He laughed then, adding, "Only you can kill a bastard while you're on leave from the Legion and get away with it."

The others joined in, but while Calienus was one of them, he noticed something in the manner in which Atilius and Didius shared another look that, to his eyes, seemed both amused and, once again, conspiratorial. I wonder what that's about, he mused, but he quickly set it aside; there was a lot to do to prepare for the march from Corduba to Narbo Martius now that all of the men were back.

Chapter Nine

The march from Corduba to Narbo Martius, or as it was commonly called by almost everyone, just Narbo, took the 10th Legion almost a month to complete. It could have been done more quickly, but none of the men complained, much, at what was a leisurely pace now that Caesar was back in Rome. It wasn't the entire Legion, however; left behind were those men who had been wounded in the last fight on the island who were still recovering, along with a skeleton staff of rankers and a handful of *medici* to attend to the convalescents. Otherwise, it was a routine march where the men weren't required to wear their *hamatae*, their shields were covered and lashed to their backs, and their helmets were attached to their harnesses. While they all carried a javelin, it was used as a walking staff, while the second missile was carried as part of the baggage train that accompanied a Legion of Rome on the march.

As they progressed eastward, not only did the landscape gradually change, so did the reception they received as they marched through one settlement to another. There had been speculation that their route would take them south to the coast and through Nova Carthago, a prospect that appealed to almost all of the men save one, with the speculation that it would fall conveniently on the fifth day of the march, which was traditionally a day of rest on a march like this, according to the more experienced men. Fortunately, at least as far as Atilius was concerned, the hope for a southern route was extinguished by the middle of the second day when, arriving in Castulo, instead of taking the road south, and up over the line of low mountains that protected the interior from the more fertile coastal area, they turned north, heading instead for the settlement of Mariana, so named for the great Gaius Marius, much to the consternation of the majority of the Legion, save for one. As far as Marcus Atilius was concerned, if he never set foot inside the walls of Nova Carthago again, it would be fine with him. He did miss his sisters, but the prospect of being anywhere near his mother and her madness was more than enough to quell any homesickness, the subject of which he only divulged to Didius, feeling as if he was the only man in the section whose family compared to his now that he had seen Didius' situation with his own eyes. On the subject of what had taken place in Gades, neither Atilius nor Didius ever spoke of it, not only to the others, but to each other, thanks to an agreement they reached on their first day's journey back to Corduba.

"What's done is done," was how Didius put it, "and I don't see that talking about it anymore will make any difference."

For reasons of his own, which Atilius never divulged to his close comrade, he was happy to agree, and it was a promise he kept to the end of his life, another thing that Didius would come to appreciate as time passed. Now that they were on the march, most of the talking done in the ranks was either about the campaign, or about their time in Corduba, but not for the first or the last time would Atilius notice that, when speaking of the campaign itself, most of the men who engaged in this banter didn't speak of the fighting in a serious manner, choosing instead to relate some humorous moment, even if it happened during battle, and they certainly didn't talk about some of the darker deeds they had participated in, like the sacking of the first town they had taken. It wasn't that the officers forbade it, but Atilius sensed there was some sort of unwritten rule that men didn't introduce topics that might take some men down a darker path as they relived their own actions in those moments. As Atilius would learn, this wasn't destined to last; within a couple of years, the men of the 10th would be a hardened bunch of veterans, inured to the misery and terror they inflicted on their foes, and these topics that were currently forbidden would be no longer. At this moment, however, he and the others were happily ignorant of this development and what would cause it, and once they had accepted their fate in not getting to Nova Carthago, they began talking about the next largest town they would be passing through.

Another pleasant reminder that they were no longer on

campaign was that their marching camps were different, without ditches and walls, although there was always a Century on guard, which rotated so that everyone gripped the dirty end of the sponge. They were commanded, at least in name, by one of the Tribunes who had been left behind, but Gaius Trebonius was one of the few fine young men on the *cursus honorum* who, if not respected on his own merits, was tolerated by Primus Pilus Favonius, if only because Trebonius was wise enough to ask Favonius beforehand whether the orders he issued were appropriate for the moment at hand, and most of the time, they were. It was now December, but while the weather was cold, as long as they were in Hispania it wasn't anything more than a minor inconvenience. Those men of the 10ᵗʰ who had come from places other than the Roman provinces of Hispania warned their comrades that, as they moved further north, things would change, and they were quickly proven right.

About two weeks into the march, just after they left Tarraco, the last settlement of a respectable size, it began to rain, a cold, miserable rain that, to men like Pullus and Domitius, who had spent their lives in warm, sunny Astigi, was a new and quite unpleasant experience. Compounding matters, once they were on the coastal road, they were unprotected for the most part from the winds roaring across Our Sea, which at this time of the year, meant the wind was usually in their face once they followed the curve of the coast east. It became commonplace for the men to not only start the day wearing their *sagum*, but to keep them on for the entire day, then using them to curl up under in their tents at night. It was the only unpleasant aspect of the march, which men like Calienus were quick to remind their tentmates.

"Imagine if we were having to dig a ditch and build a wall in this *cac*," he counseled the others, although he had to raise his voice to be heard over the drumming of the rain on the leather surface of the tent. "And we had to worry about some fucking Gallaeci *cunnus* trying to sneak into camp to cut our throats."

While it helped, it wasn't by much, but the grumbling and curses were to be expected, since it was an article of faith among the ranks that Mars and Bellona had given soldiers the right to complain about their treatment. Nobody knew from where this belief came, nor when it had started in the Legions, just that it was as hard and fast a rule as if it had been inscribed on a bronze tablet and stored in the Tabularium. And, as the more experienced men reminded their comrades, when Fortuna gave with one hand, she took away with the other, which the men were about to learn.

The 10th arrived in Narbo Martius two days after the Kalends of Januarius, where they immediately learned that, while they had been spared laboring at the end of every day's march to fortify their camp, they were now faced with the prospect of several weeks of toil. An advance party sent out ahead of the Legion had surveyed and staked out what was destined to become a permanent encampment just outside the walls of Narbo, with the men of the 10th supplying the labor to construct what would become their winter quarters, and unbeknownst to any of them, their home for the next two years. Instead of digging a ditch, some men were put to work constructing a wooden wall, while others were charged with first building the *Praetorium*, which was initially a single-story wooden structure.

One by one, the tents under which the men were living during their work were replaced by huts, although the organization was the same, with a section occupying a hut. These were made a bit longer than the tent so that it could accommodate the brick oven that served both as their kitchen and to provide heat when it was cold, and they were whitewashed, with the cracks between the boards filled with pitch. Best of all, at least as far as most men were concerned, they were made with wooden floors, while their bunks were constructed in tiers, which meant there was room for a long table that could seat the entire section. It was, in most respects, a good-sized town, although its citizens were all male, and it was organized in a manner to which the men had become accustomed to one degree or another. By the Ides of Februarius, most of the Legion was sleeping under a solid roof, save for the Ninth and Tenth Cohorts, but they were similarly quartered by the first week in March. Even before the camp was fully complete, Tribune Trebonius gave the order to conduct the annual lustration ceremony, the sacred consecration of the Legion and its standard to the gods, the second of the 10th's existence. Then, with this flurry of work done, the Legion settled into its first peacetime routine, which would provide another learning experience for the new veterans who were in their first full season. And, as they would all learn, some of those lessons would be bitter.

For Marcus Atilius, once the Legion settled into its peacetime routine, there was really nothing to keep him busy. Whereas some of his tentmates were also *immunes*, giving them extra duties; Domitius, for example, because of his experience with tanning, was a leatherworking *immunes*, making the *caligae* and *balteae* to replace those pieces that men had either damaged or worn out, Calienus was an armorer, Romulus worked with the animals, and Pullus was the weapons instructor for not just the Century but the entire Second Cohort, but for a *Gregarius Ordinarius* like him, there wasn't much to do. And, at first, he viewed this as a boon, because it also meant that he was free to go into Narbo Martius more often; that he had to do it by "going over the wall" as the men put it, wasn't an issue, in his mind anyway. The problem, at least as Atilius saw it, didn't lie with him, but with the civilians of Narbo, especially those of the Head Count and for whom he quickly developed a loathing as he realized that, aside from the name and location, Narbo was essentially as much of a *cac* pit as Nova Carthago. It was left to Didius to point out what, at least to the Sergeant, was obvious.

"Narbo is a port town," he reminded Atilius. "Just like Gades, and just like Nova Carthago, and you know that port towns attract all manner of scum."

Only after Didius said this did Atilius realize, with a fair amount of chagrin, this should have been obvious from the beginning, but when he thought about it, he had supposed that the presence of the Legion would somehow counterbalance that. In fact, if anything, it made Narbo even worse, at least for men like Atilius, because it attracted all manner of opportunists who, from experience and long practice, had learned how to milk the Roman army, particularly its Legionaries. The number of *tavernae* almost doubled, seemingly overnight, with names like The Happy Legionary, and The Broken *Vitus*, names specifically designed to attract men wearing the soldier's tunic. Despite himself, Atilius found himself drawn to these places, and while he didn't give it much thought, it was because it was familiar to him, since as Didius had pointed out, once you scraped away the veneer of the Legions, at its heart, Narbo was still a port town, whose inhabitants had long practice in dealing with sailors putting in and hailing from all points across Our Sea, meaning it really wasn't much different than Nova Carthago. Very quickly, he learned which spots to avoid, not because he feared those who frequented such places, but because he did *not*, in fact, fear them, and he knew himself well enough to know that he posed as much of a danger to them as they did to him. Somewhat to his surprise, Didius wasn't willing to go into Narbo illicitly; this didn't mean that he wasn't engaging in anything that would earn him some form of punishment, even if it wouldn't be official.

"I haven't worked the boys in the third line Cohorts yet," he had explained to Atilius when, finally in some exasperation, Atilius had demanded to know why his comrade wasn't willing to participate in his own favorite pastime of getting drunk. "There's some big fat birds in that bunch, just waiting to be plucked!"

It was the manner in which Didius smacked his lips, as if savoring the prospect of a good meal that made Atilius laugh, although he did warn his friend, "Just don't get caught again."

"That only happened once," Didius protested, but when Atilius only gave him a level look, he grumbled, "All right, it happened twice. Still," he insisted, "I'm being careful."

Consequently, Atilius' illegal forays into Narbo were usually solitary affairs, although fairly quickly, he learned there were other men like him who couldn't seem to resist the allure in the form of the filthy streets and back alleys of Narbo, even if what drove them was different. For some, it was the prospect of carnal delights, their appetites simply not satisfied by the twice a week forays that were allowed by Primus Pilus Favonius. For others, it was the sound of dice rattling in cups, these men having grown tired of seeing the same old faces gathered around the table. This, at least, was their claim, but Atilius wasn't fooled, knowing that these were men like Didius, the sharp operators who needed fresh meat because their comrades had grown suspicious of them, which was one reason it was hard for Atilius to understand Didius' reluctance to flout the regulations. Finally, there was the group of which Atilius was a part, though he never viewed himself in this way, men who loved Bacchus to the point that it was worth risking punishment to seek the god out. Unfortunately for Atilius and these men, on their illicit forays, they had to avoid the newer *tavernae* opened to cater to the men of the Legions, because officers weren't restricted to camp like the rankers were, which meant that, despite his best efforts, it was inevitable that Atilius would find himself down by the docks. It wasn't just the Centurions and Optios that Atilius and the other men like him had to avoid; Tribune Trebonius commanded a staff of men who weren't attached to the Legion, but attached to the *Praetorium*, provosts whose job it was to prowl the streets, looking for men like him. Rather than put him off, it added another element of risk that excited Atilius. This was a new development in his character; when he had been working the streets of Nova Carthago, more than once, his father had thrashed him for being too cautious and unwilling to take chances to cut a purse, or to snatch a loaf. Despite his lack of introspection, Atilius at least knew that this newfound taste for danger was a direct result of the campaign, when, despite the fear, he had never felt as alive as he did when he was standing in his file, waiting for his turn to fight the barbarians who were just a matter of a couple paces away, screaming their hatred and trying their best to kill *him*, or shuffling in a *testudo*, the racket of missiles clattering on the shields making it so loud it was impossible not only to talk, but even to think. It was almost as intoxicating as wine...almost, and it was this reality that would find him crouched in an alley on a night waiting for a pair of provosts to pass, when his comrades were in their section huts, or perhaps visiting friends in other Centuries, enjoying activities that weren't all that different than the scene in an average *taverna*.

For Atilius, the difference was that, while the men were

allowed wine in permanent camp, it was rationed, and it was always watered...and there were no women, at least for the rankers. Fairly quickly, the men of the ranks would learn that there were Centurions who flaunted the rule that women weren't allowed in a Legion camp, but any man who asked one of their more experienced comrades how this could happen, the older veteran would either wink and touch the side of his nose, indicating that it was a secret, or rub their fingers together in the gesture that every man knew represented money changing hands. As they became more accustomed to a life when not actively campaigning, Atilius and his comrades would learn that not even the Legions were immune to corruption; fairly quickly, they would discover that many, if not most Centurions, were amenable to being paid cash in exchange for missing certain duties, like a guard shift on a night when the Century was scheduled for guard duty but the rest of the Legion had the freedom of the town, provided you got to your Centurion first, and were willing to pay enough. There were also limits that were strictly enforced, at least in the Second Cohort; punishment duties, for example, weren't negotiable with Pilus Prior Crastinus, although not all Pili Priori were of the same mind. Labor details were another category where Crastinus forbade his Centurions to take payment, although this was for more practical reasons, knowing that it would foment resentment on the part of those men who either didn't have the cash on hand or it was committed for other purposes, just to avoid repairing a road or erecting a new structure in the camp.

No more than a month into their time in Narbo once the camp was completed, and on perhaps his sixth or seventh foray over the wall, Atilius' dice came up Dogs, when he was snatched up by a provost who just happened to be turning the corner at an intersection at the same time as Atilius, but in the opposite direction. Dragged back to camp, he was deposited at the *Praetorium*, where he was collected by a very angry Pilus Prior Crastinus and his *vitus*, which he used on Atilius all the way back to the Second's area, leaving the ranker with a black eye that he couldn't see out of for a week and which turned a variety of colors. Aside from the physical beating, he was confined to camp for a month, even on those days when his comrades had the liberty of the town, had his pay deducted, and was put on the latrine detail for the same length of time. Regardless of this punishment, and despite the urging of Didius and the rest of his comrades to curtail his activities, while Atilius was willing to abide by the official length of punishment, no more than a week after it ended, he once more slipped out of camp. This time, however, he wasn't caught by the provosts, but by one of the pair of rankers manning the walking posts who made a circuit of their section of the camp wall when he had just slipped over it and back into camp. Even then, Atilius wasn't terribly concerned; this had happened before, and a couple of coins always convinced them to look the other way, but in a similar manner to his encounter with the provost, their *Tesserarius* had just emerged from the *Via Decumanus* on his way to check with these two men. This time, the punishment was harsher; not only was it more painful, it was also more humiliating, which was by design, because the entire Second Cohort remained behind after dismissal from morning formation two days later to witness *Gregarius* Atilius receive ten lashes. Punishments were carried out every day of the week, but it was done by Cohort, so that every man of a particular Cohort who had been sentenced to a punishment that warranted being lashed to a frame in the forum, or worse, had to wait for their Cohort's day in close confinement in the cage that was built behind the *quaestorium*.

In that sense, Atilius was fortunate; some men had to wait nine days on nothing but barley bread and water in a cage that was barely large enough for them to lie down in, and while there was a roof, it was otherwise open to the elements. On the Second's day, Atilius was one of three men, although while they were for the same offense, it was another ranker's misfortune that this was his third infraction, meaning that he would be receiving ten lashes, but then another five with the scourge. Consequently, this man, a member of the Fifth Section of the Sixth Century, would go last, while the other man, of the First Section of the Third Century, another new veteran who, like Atilius, had an irresistible appetite for the grape, went first. For Atilius, this was a mixed blessing; while he had witnessed punishments often enough to know what to expect in one sense, it also meant that his mind had time to imagine just how painful it would be. As he stood there, he refused to look over to where his comrades of the First were standing, though he was somewhat thankful that being in the Tenth Section meant that he couldn't see any of them clearly, save one man, and it was Pullus' gaze he wanted to avoid, even more than Crastinus', who, being responsible for reading out the charge, and the punishment, was standing in front of the frame, facing his six Centuries.

"*Gregarius* Atilius," Crastinus' voice was flat and emotionless as he read from the wax tablet, which in some ways made it worse, "four days after the Ides of April, you were apprehended when you attempted to return to camp when you did not have the liberty of the town. Since this is your second offense, Tribune Trebonius has passed sentence. You are to receive ten lashes, without the scourge." He paused, then barked, "*Gregarius* Atilius, step forward to receive your punishment!"

Although this was his first time as one of the men being punished, since Atilius had stood in formation for other men, he didn't hesitate, knowing that his reluctance would make things worse; more importantly, it would shame his comrades. He passed by the first ranker returning to the spot he had occupied at the beginning of the punishment formation, the man's face streaked with tears and his tunic tied around his waist, but despite an almost overwhelming urge to do so, Atilius didn't glance over his shoulder to see the other man's back, certain that seeing the aftermath of a flogging this closely would make his nerve fail. Standing at the punishment frame was one of the provosts, though not one of those who patrolled the town. This man, the rumor went, was one of four such who were used by the commander of the army for special matters; in simpler terms, he was a member of the torture detachment, and when they weren't torturing people, usually slaves who had been accused of theft from the section or Century they served, one of them was expected to carry out the punishment because of their experience with the whip and the scourge. The man, squat, burly, and quite hirsute, wearing a plain brown tunic with a broad leather *baltea* and not the soldier's version, barely glanced at Atilius as he began his instructions.

"If you can get your arms out of your tunic without taking it off, do that. Your *baltea* will hold it up. If you can't, then you're going to have to strip down." Whereas it would have been impossible for Pullus, or even Didius, Atilius was able to pull one arm inside his tunic and bring it up through the wide neck opening, then the other, and he shrugged out of it, pulling it down so it was bunched at his waist. "Put your right hand here," the man's voice sounded like a bucket of gravel being shaken, and he pointed to one of the loops of rope, tied with a slip knot which was fastened to the horizontal support at shoulder height.

When he did so, the man pulled the knot tight as, without being told, Atilius extended his left arm, wondering if his comrades could see his legs shaking from where they were standing. Once both of his wrists were secure, the man withdrew the leather-wrapped wooden dowel from where he had tucked into his own *baltea*, and Atilius could see that it was still wet and gleaming from the saliva of the first man, making his stomach churn even more.

"You don't have to use it," the man said, making it clear that he didn't care one way or another, "but I'd suggest it."

Swallowing hard, Atilius' mouth was too dry to speak, so he nodded and opened it to accept the gag, clamping down on it with his teeth as he wondered what was worse; the saliva of another man that still soaked the leather, or the feeling of the indentations in both leather and wood from men clenching their teeth with all of their might. Even as he was considering this, the man disappeared from view, moving behind Atilius.

As with all things associated with the Legions of Rome, everything was done according to the letter of the regulations, which, for the most part, were unwritten at this point in time, but every man, especially of officer rank, had been forced to memorize when they attained their post.

What this moment required was for Pilus Prior Crastinus to order the sentence to be carried out, but while he wasn't really expecting a reprieve, Atilius still felt a stab of despair when Crastinus called out, "Carry out the punishment!"

Perhaps a heartbeat later, Atilius had a bare fraction of warning from the whistling sound before the half-dozen leather straps, each one cut on a bias because it did more damage that way, slapped across his back, the pain literally taking Atilius' breath away. It was easily the most agony he had ever experienced, yet at some point between the moment his name had been called and this one, Atilius had decided that he wouldn't cry out, no matter how much it hurt. By the third lash, it was all Atilius could do to only give a muffled groan; by the sixth, he was panting rapidly and heavily through his mouth past the gag, fighting the urge to spit it out, knowing that if he did, he might inadvertently bite his tongue off. Somehow, he never really knew how, Atilius managed to refrain from doing anything more than groan, although he now understood why his predecessor's face was streaked with tears. Once his arms were released, he used his hand to take the gag out of his mouth, though it was difficult to do so sticking to his teeth as it did, but he somehow pried it from his jaws, handing it to the man who barely gave him a glance as he took it and thrust it back into his *baltea.*

"Have one of your mates use vinegar on those cuts," he grunted. "Don't want them to corrupt."

Atilius simply nodded, and copying the first man, he walked on wobbly legs past Crastinus, who was standing there holding his *vitus* with both hands, his face registering the same amount of emotion as the man who had flogged Atilius, but he did look Atilius in the eye as he attempted to march past.

"Don't fuck up again, Atilius," Crastinus said quietly, "or you're going to end up like Terentius here."

Terentius was the ranker who was about to be scourged, except that he was being dragged physically to the punishment frame by the provost, not because the man was struggling but because his legs kept collapsing.

"Yes, Pilus Prior," Atilius responded. "I understand, and I will obey."

It was the ritual response every man under the standard used when acknowledging an order from a superior in a formal setting, but while Atilius had every intention of doing so, even he wasn't sure he'd be able to resist the allure of Narbo in a couple months. That, however, was a problem for later. Of more immediate concern for him was the response of his comrades now that he was the first of them to be flogged, and after witnessing Terentius' punishment, which, as it was meant to be, was gruesome to watch and meant to be a deterrent, he was dismissed to await them in the section hut, the only concession a flogged man receiving was being exempt from duties for the rest of the day. He heard them coming before they opened the door, but while they weren't in their normal boisterous mood, none of them refused to look him in the eye, and Scribonius offered him an awkward pat on the shoulder.

Calienus actually stopped and sat down next to Atilius on his bunk, and his tone contained no censure, only sympathy as he said, "I'm going to use vinegar on those cuts, Atilius. It's going to sting."

"I know, Sergeant," Atilius assured him. "The bast...the man who flogged me told me that's what I needed to do."

"You need to thank Fortuna," Calienus told him, causing Atilius to turn and stare incredulously, prompting Calienus to explain, "If it had been Carbo and not Vistilia, you'd be in worse shape, believe me. Now," he smiled, "Vistilia *is* a bastard, and a few other names I can think of, but he's still better than Carbo."

Remus, overhearing their Sergeant, asked curiously, "Why do you say that, Calienus?"

"Let's just say that Carbo truly enjoys his work," Calienus answered grimly, and there was something in the manner in which he said it that prompted Scribonius to ask, "How do you know them, Calienus?"

"They came with us from Pompeius' Legions," Calienus explained. "So I got to see Carbo's work up close, you could say." When nobody said anything, and instead looked at him expectantly, Calienus sighed, understanding. "One of my section, my first section, got caught a third time." At this, he looked back directly at Atilius, and while he continued in the same tone, Atilius received the message. "And it was Carbo who had the duty, but more than that, Carbo has his own special whip that he likes to use. It has three more lashes and it's longer, so he can attach more gouges to them." Gouges, as the men called them, were the tiny pieces of iron, and just as their name described, they were designed to gouge out hunks of flesh from a man's back. Recalling the event, Calienus shook his head, his expression a combination of disgust and sadness. "And, in Pompeius' Legion, third offenses called for eight lashes, then another eight with the scourge."

"That's not right!" Domitius exclaimed. Then, with a hint of doubt, he asked, "A Legate can't just change the regulations, can he?"

"He can if his name is Pompeius Magnus," Calienus countered. Feeling obligated to defend his former general, Calienus went on, "After our campaign against the pirates, many of the men just..." he searched for the right word, "...ran wild, I suppose. And the usual punishments didn't work, so Pompeius added the extra numbers to get us back under control."

Nobody argued this, and Scribonius asked, "What happened to him? Your comrade, I mean?"

"I know who you mean," Calienus assured him. "Carbo turned his back into nothing but bloody raw meat. You could see the bones of his spine sticking out, along with some of his ribs. Even if the cuts hadn't turned bad, he would have been crippled for months."

"You mean he *died*?" Romulus gasped, to which Calienus gave a curt nod.

"He lasted a week, but he was out of his head the last two days. We took him to the hospital two days after his flogging. And," he finished simply, "he never left."

"And you think it was because of this Carbo?" Scribonius asked.

"No," Calienus retorted. "I *know* it was because of Carbo. Some men don't survive a scourging, everyone knows that. But," his mouth twisted into a bitter grimace, "only the men who were scourged by Carbo during that time died. Everyone else punished by one of the others like Vistilia, they all survived." The laugh he gave offered only bitterness. "So, either the gods *really* don't like Carbo and want to haunt him with the men he killed, or he likes his work a bit too much." He scanned the faces, seeing that they were all listening, and finished, "I know which way I'd wager."

Not all of Atilius' forays into town were done illicitly, however, and on one sultry summer night during that first year at Narbo, after a period of what for him was exemplary behavior, to his delight, he finally talked none other than Pullus into accompanying him for a night of debauchery. He didn't even bother to ask Didius this time, knowing that once he learned his nemesis would be present, he would want nothing to do with it, but Romulus, Remus, and Vellusius were happy to participate. To Atilius' surprise, Domitius, who could usually be counted on to go wherever Pullus went, demurred, but he quickly learned why.

"Sextus is writing a letter to Juno for me," Domitius explained, something that he did religiously at least once a week, and Atilius accepted this.

What only Pullus knew was that Scribonius was not just writing a letter, he was teaching Domitius his letters, Pullus' best friend determined that by the end of the year, he would be able to write a letter to Juno in his own hand. Which, of course, Juno would still have to take into Astigi to have read for her, but Domitius had given her money of her own to pay for that service from one of the clerks of the *duumvir*, a normal enough occurrence in towns and cities across the Republic.

Consequently, it was the five comrades of the Tenth Section who walked through the *Porta Praetoria*, following a line of men attired in their red tunics and their *balteae*, but with only their *pugiones* allowed inside the walls of Narbo, another army regulation. For Romulus, Remus, and to a lesser extent, Vellusius, this was a common occurrence, but for Pullus, this was his first time taking advantage of the opportunity to spend a night out without having another reason to go into town. It wasn't because Pullus was a prude; indeed, one reason he said yes was because the needs of the flesh had become overpowering to him. His hesitance to participate in the kind of debauchery that, for most men under the standard, was one of the few pleasant aspects of their lives, was based in his ambition, and in his recognition that, as fraught with obstacles as his path already was, running afoul of the Legion regulations about causing trouble in town was one of the most common over which men stumbled. Not even his best friend knew of Pullus' real ambition, mainly because he was acutely aware of how it could be viewed, as extreme hubris, particularly for a man of their class, but it didn't make his aspiration any less real. In its simplest terms, Titus Pullus was determined to achieve a level of fame in the Legions that would enable him to accrue the necessary funds to be elevated into the Equestrian Order, the first step up the ladder to respectability in their world. In some ways, it was good that Pullus was still so young; he had turned seventeen in April, five days after the Ides, making him only now legally eligible to enlist in the Legions, a carefully guarded secret that only his best friend knew, but he was also naïve, because if he had truly understood the monumental undertaking he was attempting, and how many men of the upper classes would not only disapprove but would actively work to thwart his ambitions, he might have given up then and there. The gods, however, had other plans for Titus Pullus, and he had convinced himself that a night out in Narbo wouldn't prove fatal to his ambitions. It would be a decision that he would be questioning in the immediate future.

"We'll start at The Happy Legionary," Atilius announced, having appointed himself as the unofficial guide for his comrades. "It's mostly First and Second Cohort men who go there. And," he turned to walk backward so he could leer at his friends, "Penelope's Den is right across the street. It's one of the best brothels in Narbo."

"Best as in expensive?" Pullus asked doubtfully.

"Best as in the women there will take you to places you've never dreamed of," Atilius boasted.

"That sounds good to me!" Romulus laughed. "I love visiting new places like that!"

The others laughed at this, including Pullus, but he nevertheless said, "So yes, it's expensive. I'll save that for a really special occasion."

It was a long-running argument with Domitius at this point, that Pullus' parsimony was excessive, but Pullus would always retort that he wasn't the man always asking for a few *sesterces* to go into town. Still, he made the decision that, tonight, he would treat himself to one of the cheaper options when it came to whores and match them drink for drink and, in doing so, prove to the others that he was as ready and willing to debauch as any man under the standard. Even in this, there was a burning competitiveness imbued in Pullus that would never be fully quenched; if he was going to debauch, he would be the best at it!

The streets of Narbo were crowded, but most of the party earned barely a glance from passersby, all of the citizens in what was almost a small city now having become accustomed to seeing men in soldiers' tunics walking about. There was one exception, but it was a reaction to which Pullus was long accustomed; when a Roman was a foot taller than most of the people around him, and so broad across the shoulders that he effectively took up the space of two men, it was natural for people to gawk. It was simply a part of his life, and while he certainly couldn't say he always enjoyed it, he was at least resigned to it, and he rarely registered the muttered comments and being referred to as "Ajax" and "Hercules" as something worth responding to; that it was also flattering didn't hurt. While Pullus had been in Narbo several times, he had restricted himself to the area around the forum for the most part, and had occasionally gone with Domitius just to have a look around, but Atilius led them away from the forum until he was in the northwestern quarter of the city. They heard the sounds of revelry before they turned the corner, where they saw a sign, still brightly painted and portraying a man in a red tunic, seated on a chair with a woman on his knee, one hand cupped around a bare breast, with a cup in the other hand and a leering grin on his face, above which was its name, The Happy Legionary.

"Do any of the women here have tits that big?" Pullus demanded of Atilius, pointing up to the buxom woman depicted on the sign. "Because that's what I want! Big tits!"

"I don't remember," Atilius answered absently, getting impatient because there was a small crowd around the door. "But I haven't seen all the serving girls yet. And," he assured them, "they're available for more than serving drinks."

This was typical of such establishments, even at places like

Proserpina's Grotto in Gades where the women were the wife and daughter of the proprietor, although some owners, like Pacula, refused to pimp their women out. Once inside, they paused, looking for a table, and Atilius pointed to one in the middle of the main room that was being vacated by some men they recognized as belonging to the First Cohort, and they quickly replaced the previous occupants, while Atilius grabbed a woman walking by around the waist.

"Bring us a jug, *meum mel*," Atilius said, laughing when the woman, who appeared to be in her twenties, but with a hard quality in her eyes that to Pullus spoke of a difficult life, slapped his hand away, although she was smiling as she did so. Atilius added, "And don't serve us that horse piss either! We're Second Cohort men, and we know what's what!"

"Why, of course, *Dominus*!" The woman's Latin betrayed an accent that spoke of Gaul, which explained her wider hips, more voluptuous figure, and light brown hair, saying mockingly, "I'll bring our finest Falerian immediately! Or," she suddenly looked directly at Pullus, "would you prefer something else, soldier?"

The others all roared with laughter, while Romulus, who was sitting next to Pullus elbowed him in the ribs, hooting, "I don't think she's talking about wine, Pullus!"

Pullus flushed, but he was grinning as broadly as his companions, and he called out, "I very well may. What are you offering?"

Rather than reply directly to Pullus, the woman instead glanced over her shoulder, where a burly man in his forties was standing behind the counter, and even without seeing the missing three fingers on his right hand, Pullus and his companions would have been certain he had been under the standard. Leaning over slightly to examine Pullus, he straightened, and with his left hand, held up three fingers.

Turning back, the woman smiled down at Pullus, and he was happy to see that she still had all of her teeth, and in the dim light of the *taverna*, could even be called attractive, and she told him, "For you, soldier, I'll give you a ride you won't forget for three *asses*."

"Three!" Pullus squawked, and proving that he wasn't

completely unfamiliar with transactions of this nature, he protested, "We were told that it was only two *asses* for...that!"

The woman shrugged, not really caring whether Pullus paid her or not, because not only did she know that there would be other takers that night, but because the owner of the *taverna* was going to take half of it anyway, but she was also experienced dealing with soldiers, so she put on a smile as she flattered, "Look at you, soldier. You're *huge*. That means that your prick is the same size, doesn't it? So," she added, "I probably won't be able to walk, let alone give anyone else a ride tonight, and Dento," she jerked her thumb over her shoulder at the man, "sets the prices, not me." Putting a hand on her hip, she finished in a challenging tone, "But if you don't think you can handle me, soldier..."

And, as she had known it would, this proved to be too much for Pullus' pride, especially in front of his friends. The whore was fortunate that their paths crossed now and not just a couple years later, when Pullus wouldn't be so easily baited, yet despite his size and all that he had experienced in the previous months, in many ways, he was still a teenage boy.

Standing up, he raised his voice as he shot back, "There's nothing I can't handle, woman. And," he gave his friends a grin, "I'll prove it."

Knowing better than to behave smugly, the woman reached her hand out and took Pullus', leading him not to the back of the *taverna*, where there was normally at least one small room for such transactions, but towards the door.

"Where are we going?" Pullus asked, though he continued to allow the woman to lead him.

"Outside in the alley," she replied, smiling over her shoulder.

"I'm not lying down in a filthy alley." Pullus stopped then, but the woman wasn't put off, and in fact seemed amused.

"Who said anything about lying down, soldier? Once Plautia is done with you, *then* you might want to lie down!"

"Don't worry, girl," Remus called out, "this won't take long! You'll be ready to serve the rest of us quicker than Pan!"

This earned a roar of laughter, and not just from Pullus' comrades sitting at their table, but most of the other men in the room, while Pullus glared at Remus, who offered him a wave and a grin that was completely unrepentant. The huge Roman didn't turn around and return to the table, as they knew he wouldn't now that his pride was involved, and the couple left the *taverna*. This was the normal course of business, with a couple leaving every few moments, and while the men were usually different, it was always with one of the women of The Happy Legionary who served the men of the Legions in more than just one way.

"Did you see him?" Romulus laughed. "His face was as red as his tunic!"

"How long do you think he'll be gone?" Vellusius asked the others.

"I doubt he lasts to a count of a hundred," Remus said confidently, and Vellusius didn't hesitate.

"I've got a *sestertius* that he lasts longer than that," he challenged.

"A *sestertius*?" Remus mocked. "Are you sure you can afford it, Vellusius?"

"All right, two, then," Vellusius answered stubbornly. "I say he stays out there longer than a count to a hundred."

"When did the counting start?" Romulus asked, but it was Atilius who answered, "I started when the door closed."

At first, Vellusius thought he had gotten away with it, but then Remus frowned, and giving Vellusius a suspicious look, said, "Wait. We're talking about how long he lasts fucking Plautia, not whether he waits outside so he doesn't have to take a ration of *cac* from us." Vellusius tried to avoid betraying that he had been counting on Remus missing that distinction, but he clearly failed because Remus hooted triumphantly, "Ha! I knew it! You were trying to pull one over on me. Well, my lad, the sun hasn't risen on a day where you can get one past me! So," he pointed to the door, "it's when *Plautia* comes inside that counts, not when Pullus does."

As it turned out, Vellusius won his wager without any trickery; once Atilius reached one hundred, he stopped counting, and when Remus offered to double the wager for a count of two hundred, Vellusius demurred.

"No," he patted his coin purse, smiling broadly, "I think I'll take my two *sesterces* and leave it at that. And I should thank you now for paying for my own ride with Plautia. Although," Vellusius turned and pointed to another woman, one of the other five who were working the tables, "I might fancy her. Anyone know her name?"

"Daphne," Atilius supplied, already on his third cup of wine, which prompted him to belch. "Her name is Daphne. Or," he cocked his head, "maybe that's Niobe. I get them mixed up."

Although the door opened and closed several times, as either new men entered, other men left, or similar transactions to that of Pullus and Plautia took place, finally, Plautia entered, with Pullus following behind her, grinning broadly. And, just as he had given Plautia an extra *as* to do, that she didn't tell Dento about, Plautia clutched her belly and made a show of having trouble walking.

The final piece was, as she passed their table, she groaned, "I'm going to have to tell Dento that I'm only going to be serving wine the rest of the night."

Pullus, right behind her, dropped onto the bench, still grinning broadly, and he snatched up the jug, poured himself a cup, then took a long draught.

Setting the cup down, he wiped his lips before he said, "So, what were you girls talking about while I was away?"

As he suspected, his comrades swore that what they certainly weren't discussing was their wagering on his performance with Plautia, and he laughingly called them liars. Very quickly, the wine was flowing, and the conversation raucous as they swapped stories about each other and some misdeed or mistake they had made, argued about what type of gladiator was the hardest to defeat, and the chariot races that, while the most famous were held in Rome, every Roman town and city held with varying frequency. Since they were new to Narbo, none of them had developed a strong loyalty to any of the four local teams, each named for a color, but as time passed, men would form a passionate love for one of them. The hippodrome at Narbo was small, comparatively speaking, holding only five thousand people, but with the arrival of the 10th, it had quickly become apparent that the structure would have to be expanded. By the end of the first night watch, which began at sunset, The Happy Legionary was packed, and there was a dull roar of noise that, while nothing like a battle, still made it hard to be heard, so Atilius suggested a change was in order.

"There's another spot I know," he told the others. "It's the newest *taverna* that caters to us. It's called The Rudis, and it won't be this crowded. And," he added as an incentive, "the man who runs it only uses women from Gaul."

By common consent, they agreed that relocating was a fine idea, and as they filed out, Pullus threw Plautia a wink, while her only response was to reach into a pocket sewn onto her shift and withdraw a coin; whether it was the actual extra coin Pullus had given her to help perpetrate his fiction he didn't know, but it still made him laugh. While it was only a half-formed thought in his mind at this point, this was the first but would not be the only time Pullus sought out Plautia, becoming one of her regulars for the entire time the 10th was in Narbo. Once outside, as Atilius led them unerringly across to the opposite side of the town, they passed within a block of the area surrounding the docks, and down one street, they could clearly hear the sounds of revelry, on a scale that was much like the scene they had left but, if anything, louder.

Temporarily forgetting this was why they had vacated The Happy Legionary, Romulus called out to Atilius, "What about that place down the street? It sounds like a festival!"

Atilius shook his head, replying immediately, "You don't want to go to that one. It's called Charybdis' Lair." When this had no impact on his comrades, Atilius patiently explained, "Anything with that kind of name is a place where sailors go. And," he shrugged, "most of us aren't welcome there. Besides," he warned, aiming this mostly at Pullus, "it's also one of the first places the provosts come looking when there's word of trouble in Narbo, and we don't need that kind of worry, do we?"

For a moment, the brothers appeared as if they were disposed to argue the point, both of them drawn to the place because of its illicit nature, something that many soldiers shared; Atilius was one of them, and under other circumstances, the fact that he would have been leading the way was what made this sudden example of sober restraint unusual, although his comrades put it down to the now-healed scars on his back. However, the truth was that his hesitance was because of the presence of one of their section, and for Atilius, it was a simple enough calculation; he was equally frightened of arousing Pullus' enmity and ire as he was about any potential punishment at the hands of the army, still recalling that night on the hill. Fortunately, the brothers quickly acquiesced, and they resumed their progress, and as Atilius had predicted, while the establishment was doing a brisk business, it wasn't as packed as The Happy Legionary. Even better, as Atilius had promised, the women working the tables were, if not unanimously Gallic, were definitely not the common variety of whore. There was a blonde, and two women had hair that, while not the flaming red that was such an enticement for some men, had a darker reddish tint to it, and the Mallius brothers immediately forgot their recent heartbreak at the hands of Livia Plautus. And, surprising none of the others, the pair immediately selected the same woman as their choice for a quick tumble.

It was Vellusius who noticed, and he was a bit nervous as he said quietly, "None of the others here are from the First or Second."

Pullus glanced around, and while he agreed, he wasn't worried, assuring Vellusius, "I recognize a couple men from the Fifth Cohort and some from the Ninth. We'll be fine. Besides," he grinned down at his friend, "do you think anyone is going to start trouble with me here?"

This made sense, not just to Vellusius but to the others, and at first, it seemed as if the time would pass without incident. Romulus and Remus, unable to agree, decided to share the girl, for that was what she was, no more than fifteen but plump, with auburn hair and a rounded figure, the pair flipping a coin over who went first. Remus won, a fact that he crowed about, leaving Romulus to grumble as the girl obediently followed his brother, not outside into the alley but into the back, where rooms of sorts had been fashioned by stacking wooden crates to close off one part of the storeroom, creating three cubicles that were just wide enough for a couple to lie prone provided neither of them rolled over much.

"You know there are others here. That one looks like she

might be the sister of the one you two wanted," Pullus pointed out to Romulus, but he wasn't surprised when the other Mallius brother demurred, while Pullus, on closer examination of the woman he had suggested, amended his initial assessment of sisterhood, thinking it more likely they were mother and daughter.

The wine was almost identical in quality as that served at The Happy Legionary, or The Broken Vitus, or Charybdis' Lair, the only requirement of the beverage being the effect and not the taste, and they resumed their drinking, and their conversation, where they had left off. Perhaps the one difference was that, because of the smaller crowd, cups didn't remain empty nearly as long, which meant that Pullus, and to a lesser extent, Vellusius, were consuming wine at a higher rate than normal. For the first time since the end of the campaign, Pullus felt himself completely relax, which was why he didn't pay attention to something that he normally would have noticed. Not the extra attention he was receiving from some of the other men, but in the nature of the glares and muttering that came with the scrutiny.

Remus finally returned, a broad grin on his face that was as much from his satisfaction that he had beaten his brother as it was from sexual gratification, but while he was still grumbling about it, Romulus got up and followed the girl back to the rear of the *taverna*, pretending that the smile she was offering him was not only genuine, but broader than it had been for his brother. Atilius and Vellusius had resumed their argument about the Greens, calling on Pullus to adjudicate the dispute, but he was finding it hard to follow the course of the debate; at that moment, all he could say was that Atilius was certain that the Greens were cheating bastards, while Vellusius' argument was that it was just because the Whites, Blues, and Reds were so pathetically inept it made it appear as if the Greens were winning by underhanded methods.

So absorbed was he trying to follow this convoluted argument that, when he heard a deep, hard voice demand, "Are you Pullus?" it took him an extra heartbeat for it to register, and because of his state, he was even slower to react, turning his head to look up at the man.

"Yes," he replied, although, despite his intoxication, there was a voice in the back of his mind that warned him something was amiss. "Why?" Leaning back slightly to get a better look, he vaguely recognized the man, and exclaimed, "I know you! You're in the..." it took him a moment, "...the Third of the Ninth?"

"That's right," the other ranker said, but while Pullus was still slow to grasp the situation, Atilius, even as intoxicated as he already was, recognized what was happening, and he reached over and tapped Vellusius on the shoulder. Meanwhile, the man's eyes never left Pullus as he announced flatly, "I'm Publius Bassus."

While he was sitting down, by this moment, Pullus saw that, while not as tall as he was, Bassus was about as tall as Scribonius, and was nearly as muscular as Pullus, but it was his features that bespoke of the man's nature, and, Pullus was beginning to realize, the likely reason why Bassus was standing there. His nose might have been aquiline at some point, but it was now a misshapen mass, while his brow ridge was even thicker than normal because of the scar tissue, and part of his right ear was missing. He was, Pullus now understood, a brawler, and more crucially, he was looking for one now which, despite his condition, Pullus was more than happy to oblige, the wine making him forget why he was reluctant to come into Narbo in the first place.

This was why Pullus answered indifferently, "I've never heard of a Publius Bassus." Then, in an exaggerated show, he turned and asked his three companions at the table, "Have you ever heard of a Publius Bassus?"

"I have," Vellusius spoke up, nervous now.

"And?" Pullus demanded. "Is he famous or something?"

Before Vellusius could reply, Bassus said menacingly, "I'm the fucking champion of Pompeius' 2nd Legion, that's who I am!"

Pullus appeared to keep his gaze away from Bassus, who was standing at the end of their table, but he was watching for movement out of the corner of his vision as he seemingly addressed Vellusius, feigning puzzlement. "Aren't we in the 10th?" Vellusius could only nod, while Atilius sat there, cup to his lips, but his eyes weren't on Bassus; they were on the men at the table that he had gotten up from, though he listened to Pullus as he continued, "Then why the *fuck* would we care about the *mentulae* in the 2nd Legion?"

"Who do you think you are, pup?" Bassus challenged, then taunted, "What is it? Because you won a trinket from Caesar, you think that means anything? That you're a *hero* of the Legion?" Bassus offered a mocking laugh. "This was your first campaign, boy! When I was with Pompeius, we..."

"You're in the 10th now," Pullus cut him off, and in contrast to Bassus' glowering bluster, his voice was oddly, and jarringly, quiet. "And we march for Caesar. He's our general, not Pompeius." Before Bassus could respond, for the first time, Pullus showed that he was paying wider attention than just on this ranker trying to start a fight by leaning back to look past Bassus at the table where he had been sitting. Pointing up at Bassus, he demanded of the men sitting there, "What about you boys? Who do *you* march for, eh? Are you like Batius here, thinking he's still under Pompeius' standard? Or do you march for Caesar?"

As he knew it would, Pullus' deliberate mangling of his name enraged Bassus.

"Stand up, boy, and I'll make sure you never forget my name!"

Pullus was still looking past Bassus, and he saw that his words had at least caused a couple of the rankers at Bassus' table to break eye contact and look down into their cups, while one of them muttered something. By this time, Pullus knew there was going to be a brawl, but his hope was that it would be confined to just him and Bassus, and for a brief instant, it appeared as if he might be successful.

Then Bassus, not getting the reaction he wanted, or expected, from Pullus, who he viewed as just another large boy from the farm who had never faced someone who knew how to fight without a *gladius* in their hand, shattered Pullus' hope by saying, "Caesar's nothing compared to Pompeius Magnus! Besides," for the first time, Bassus smiled, revealing the jagged stumps of his front teeth, "everyone knows that Caesar's Nicomedes' wife in all but name."

The sudden uproar that this slur that had haunted their general for years created, as several men from the surrounding tables who had been listening leapt to their feet, would likely have precipitated what was coming, but it was the speed and ferocity of Pullus' response that the participants and witnesses would have cause to remember.

"I'm never going into town with you again. You're fucking made for trouble," Pullus whispered.

He, along with his four comrades, were crouched in a ditch that, as they immediately discovered when they dived into it to avoid the group of men who were hot in pursuit, served as the drain from the public latrine.

His words were aimed at Atilius, who had, wisely in Vellusius' view, placed himself with the Mallius brothers and Vellusius himself in between him and Pullus. Atilius didn't answer, only because the pounding footsteps of several men had drawn closer, and they all pressed themselves against the side of the ditch closest to their pursuers.

"Where did those *cunni* go?" A harsh voice, with an accent that indicated a Greek heritage, sounded frustrated. "They can't have gone far."

"What about there?"

Since they couldn't see, the five rankers were forced to guess where the unseen man was pointing, but they got their answer quickly enough.

"In the sewage ditch?" the first man scoffed. "And then they'd smell like *cac* for the next week? No," he dismissed his companion, "they're somewhere between here and their camp." There was a brief pause, then he ordered, "Let's get to the western gate and cut them off. They still have to watch out for their provosts."

The sound of running men resumed, leaving the five men relieved, although even in the darkness, Vellusius could see that Pullus was glaring past him at Atilius, who, still behaving sensibly in Vellusius' opinion, was staring intently up at the top of the ditch, oblivious to Pullus' gaze, or at least pretending to not notice. And, Vellusius thought, Pullus isn't wrong to be angry. Yes, his brawl with Bassus had undoubtedly drawn the attention of the provosts, Vellusius recalling seeing one of the girls darting out the door and into the street in the heartbeats before the first punch was thrown, and at this moment, he felt reasonably certain that she had been sent to fetch the provosts, at least one of whom always stayed in the forum, waiting for just such a call. But then, in Vellusius' view, Atilius had lost his mind, because rather than getting stuck in, like he and Remus had, throwing punches at the occupants of Bassus' table who had come rushing across the *taverna* an eyeblink after Pullus had rendered Bassus unconscious with his first punch, then managing a left and another right before Bassus had hit the floor, Atilius had headed straight for the owner of the *taverna*, a greasy sort who, somewhat unusually, hadn't been under the standard, nor had he even been an auxiliary. From Vellusius' perspective in the moment, while Pullus and two of his comrades moved to face the men of the Ninth, out of the corner of his eye, he saw Atilius move, with similar speed, except in almost the opposite direction, heading for the rear of the main room of the *taverna* and the long wooden counter, behind which the owner was standing, mouth open and shouting something. In the ensuing mayhem, where at least three stools were broken because they were used as a weapon of convenience and two tables were overturned, sending the cups and jugs flying, with shards of pottery flying and liquid spraying everywhere, Vellusius had been too busy to notice what his comrade had done. It was only when the door burst open, but instead of provosts arriving to break up the fight, it turned out to be a half-dozen men armed with cudgels, at least three of them wearing the leather armor that former gladiators wore almost as a badge of honor, which indicated to Vellusius that it was Atilius' attack that was the reason for their arrival.

While it wasn't their intent necessarily, it did serve to break off the hostilities between the Ninth's men and the outnumbered Second men, and for a brief instant, Vellusius thought that for reasons he didn't understand, they were allies of himself and his other comrades, because the first man through the door immediately lashed out with the cudgel, striking one of the Ninth's men on the side of the head, dropping the ranker like a stone. Vellusius was disabused of his belief in the span of the next heartbeat, when the second man, who to Vellusius bore a striking resemblance to Bassus in terms of build and misshapen nose, also swung his cudgel, except that he aimed it for Vellusius. He didn't know how he did it, yet somehow the second-smallest man of the Tenth Section managed to evade the blow, though he felt the disturbed air as the end of the cudgel swung past his face. Despite the miss, the man's attack had an unexpected benefit, because while he missed Vellusius, he didn't miss a ranker from the Ninth who actually had a fistful of Vellusius' tunic in one hand, with his other drawn back about to deliver a punch when he was smacked full in the face. Releasing his grasp of Vellusius, the Ninth ranker went staggering backward, clutching his nose, the blood already streaming through his fingers, while their attacker drew the cudgel back again, his eyes blazing with the same kind of fury that Vellusius had witnessed as he looked over his shield at a Lusitani. Vellusius was already moving, however, leaping over the table that, just a matter of heartbeats earlier, he had been sitting at, enjoying the change that came from swapping stories in a different setting, so the man's second swing missed him again. He heard the bellow of frustration, but he was now focused on where Pullus, standing over Bassus, who was clearly unconscious, was being attacked by two of Bassus' Ninth comrades, which turned out to be a blessing in disguise for the huge Roman since the pair were actually between Pullus and this newly arrived threat.

The Ninth men also had their backs turned to the door, meaning that neither of them saw the first man bring the cudgel down a second time, and despite the circumstances, Vellusius winced when it struck one of Pullus' attackers in the back of the head, who, completely unsurprisingly, crumpled to the floor like his two comrades. Remus had moved behind Pullus to his left, but with his back to their giant tentmate, swinging wildly at a trio of Ninth men who had clearly thought to attack Pullus from the rear. Thankfully, since these men were facing the doorway, their attention suddenly shifted to the threat posed by the new arrivals, and they had actually begun to skirt around Remus, undoubtedly spurred by the sight of their comrades being struck down. Bassus, it seemed, was completely forgotten, and in the less than a full heartbeat of time that the leading attacker, who was also one of the men wearing the leather armor, had to decide who to make his third victim, he clearly chose Pullus, despite the fact that the second Ninth ranker was still not facing him, although he was now clearly aware to the threat and looking over his shoulder just as he began to pivot. Once he had time to think about it, Vellusius recognized that it was understandable that the largest man standing would be the gladiator's next target, but it was a mistake, one for which he paid dearly. Probably because Pullus was facing in his direction and had undoubtedly seen this man using a downward overhand blow to knock both Ninth men senseless, the gladiator decided a different attack was in order, which he initiated with a thrust aimed for Pullus' midsection, clearly intending to knock the wind from his foe first. Probably with any other man Pullus' size, it would have worked, since it was rare for someone that large to be agile, but as Vellusius, his comrades, and the barbarian tribes of Hispania had learned, rare didn't mean there wasn't such a man. It wasn't that the gladiator missed, but Pullus not only twisted at the waist, he bent his upper body backward at the same time, thereby lessening the force of the blow to his midsection and redirecting it more to his left side than squarely underneath his breastbone, although Vellusius, and everyone else, heard Pullus bellow with pain, but what Vellusius and Remus also heard there was the rage, the same roar they had heard on an anonymous hill in Hispania.

In another moment that would last with the men who witnessed it, Pullus demonstrated his strength by clamping his left hand around the shaft of the cudgel before his foe could recover it, but instead of pushing it away from his body to shove his attacker backward, Pullus moved his hand outward from his torso, while adding to the power of his momentum by swinging his left arm the opposite way, behind him, with enough force to jerk the gladiator towards Pullus, clearly surprising the man. Perhaps if he had let go of his cudgel, the gladiator could have saved himself from the humiliation, and the pain, from the punch that Pullus threw with perfect accuracy at the exact instant he was pulling on the cudgel, meaning that the former gladiator essentially walked into the blow. In another ignominy, he fell directly on top of the prone body of the first Ninth man he had just clubbed, and in the same state of unconsciousness. The prudent thing for Pullus to do at that moment was to retreat, but Vellusius was completely unsurprised that, instead, Pullus began to move towards the man who had swung at Vellusius, who, having just seen what happened to his ostensible leader, was understandably cautious. Despite himself, Vellusius took a step in the same direction, intending to cover Pullus' back when, from out in the street, a shrill blast sounded, one that men under the standard knew all too well.

"*Provosts!*"

If things had been chaotic before, what occurred next made the moment before look almost sedate as, without exception, every man wearing the soldier's tunic instantly stopped pummeling each other and began rushing in seemingly every direction at once, including Pullus, who whirled about, his eyes searching the room for another exit.

"Second boys! This way!"

Vellusius spun about at the sound of Atilius' voice to see that he was standing behind the counter and in the entrance to the passageway leading to the quasi-brothel area. Before he headed in that direction, he started to turn to call to Pullus, but there was no need, and he saw that Remus was already moving as well.

"I'm right behind you! Go!"

As much to avoid being run over by his huge comrade as to escape the provosts, Vellusius broke into a sprint, crossing the few paces by hurdling one of the tables lying on its side, just beating another man to reach the spot where Atilius had already spun about, with Remus just ahead of him.

"Romulus! Come on! Provosts!" Remus shouted, but his brother was already stepping out into the narrow passageway, his tunic on but his *baltea* in his hand.

Vellusius didn't see it, but he heard the collision between Pullus and the man Vellusius had beaten to the doorway, but he didn't even turn his head to look back, certain he knew who won. Besides, his eye had been drawn to a sight that, once back in camp, would be the topic of much debate.

Even so, in the moment, he shouted at Atilius' back, "Did

you just throw him through that wall?"

Atilius didn't answer, having already rushed past the cubicles, while Remus slowed just long enough for his brother to step into the passageway and fall in behind Atilius, who, with unerring precision, led them to the back entrance of the *taverna*, somehow knowing to take a right at the intersecting corridor that ran in both directions and not left. As Vellusius ducked around the corner, he glanced to his left and saw a staircase that undoubtedly led upstairs to where the owner and presumably the man's family lived, the same man now draped over the ragged hole in the wall behind the counter, his lower half in the main room and his upper body in the first of the cubicles, the sight that had caught Vellusius' attention.

"Hurry, those bastards are right behind us!"

Vellusius didn't recognize the voice, but he assumed it was the man of the Fifth who both he and Pullus had preceded down the passageway, but then he was suddenly outside in the alley, where Atilius, Romulus, and Remus were waiting, quickly joined there by Pullus.

"What did you do?" Pullus gasped at Atilius, but before his comrade could reply, a pair of men, one of them with a torch, materialized at the entrance of the alley.

"You men! Stop!" Before any of them could react, the shrill whistle blast sounded again, blown by the second provost, who shouted, "We've got some trapped here!"

Vellusius hadn't had the time to look in both directions, but when he spun about, he saw what appeared to be a solid wall blocking the other end of the alley, and he just caught a glimpse of the Fifth man ducking back inside, evidently willing to take his chances by going back into the *taverna*.

"We're fucked," Romulus muttered, but once again, it was Atilius who saved them.

"No, we're not," he promised them. "Follow me."

For an instant, Vellusius was certain that Atilius had in fact lost his wits, because he went dashing directly for that wall as if he intended to run right through it, but when he reached it, he suddenly darted to their left, promptly vanishing. The Mallius brothers rushed to follow, and when Vellusius got there, he saw that there was a gap between two buildings, not wide enough to be an alley but just wide enough that a man could walk between them, although the sleeves of his tunic would brush the sides of the two structures. At least, every man but Pullus, who was forced to turn sideways, and he cursed Atilius roundly, though he didn't hesitate to sidestep as quickly as he could, all of them hearing the pounding feet of their pursuers who were rushing down the alley behind them. Emerging out onto a street, they now had more choice in escape routes, but when Atilius led them to the nearer intersection, then began to turn to his right, which meant they were essentially doubling back, the others balked.

"That takes us back towards the fucking *taverna*," Romulus hissed. "Besides," he jerked his thumb down to the opposite end of the block, "the camp is that way."

"Which is where the provosts are going to look," Atilius answered calmly. They were now gathered in a small knot, but they could hear the shouting of what sounded like protests by more than one man back behind them, which Vellusius assumed meant that some of the Ninth and Fifth men had been caught, but Atilius was still talking. "We need to get behind them, then we can get out through the northern gate and just walk around. Then," he shrugged, "we'll just be rankers coming back to camp."

It made sense, besides which they all knew how experienced Atilius was in evading the provosts, but Pullus did think to ask, "What about those *collegia* boys? Won't they be looking for us? Since you," Pullus was close enough to poke Atilius with a finger, "are the reason they showed up."

"Yes," Remus actually shoved their comrade, "why did you do that?"

"Do we really need to talk about this now?" Vellusius asked.

Aiding his cause, there was another blast of a whistle, but this one was louder, although Atilius did answer Pullus, "They came to rescue Dukanos." When he saw the others' expression, he explained, "The owner of The Rudis." With a shrug, he said, "Now that they're there, there's no reason for them to get involved with the provosts in an army matter."

Again, it made sense, and when Atilius began to move, not

at a run but a brisk walk in the direction he'd indicated, they all followed. They actually made it two blocks, and were within sight of the northern wall when they learned Atilius had been wrong about being no longer of interest to the *collegia* men, precipitating another dash that ultimately led them to the sewage canal, where they were now, listening to their pursuers debate their likely whereabouts.

It seemed as if they were there for a third of a watch, but after perhaps a hundred heartbeats, the unseen leader of the group gave his command to head for the western gate. Waiting long enough that their footsteps couldn't be heard, and only after peeking up over the edge of the ditch did Atilius clamber out.

"Wait here," he told the others. "Let me make sure it's clear."

"I'm not spending another heartbeat in this," Romulus declared, and ignoring Atilius' protests, hopped up, followed by the others.

They moved slowly, but they reached the northern gate, requiring them to take the longer route back to the camp, which also meant that Atilius had to undergo an interrogation from his understandably agitated comrades as they took it.

"Pluto's cock, Atilius, why did you go after that Dukanos bastard?" Remus asked again.

"Yes, why?" Romulus echoed, then added the real cause for his ire. "I hadn't finished with Aphrodite yet. We were having a perfectly wonderful time, then all of a sudden, it's like Dis unleashed Cerberus in the fucking place!"

"Aphrodite?" Remus laughed. "Is that what she called herself?"

"That's her name!" Romulus shot back.

In response, Remus shoved his brother as he chided, "Idiot. She told me her name was Niobe."

"I don't fucking care what her name was," Pullus growled, and he reached out to yank Atilius by the tunic, earning him a squawk of surprise. "I want to know what the fuck you thought you were doing. He wasn't part of any of that with Bassus!"

"I know," Atilius admitted, but he wouldn't look up at his comrade, although he realized that he had to say something.

What he came up with was a slight shrug as he said weakly, "I just don't like pimps."

Pullus wasn't sure what he had been expecting, but this wasn't it, and when he glanced at the others, he saw they were as mystified as he was.

Thinking for a heartbeat, Pullus said, "But Dento is a pimp! Why didn't you go after him?"

"He," Atilius said as if it was obvious, "was under the standard. That *mentula* Dukanos is a civilian. And," he spat to emphasize the point, "he's a fucking Greek."

Pullus had no idea how to respond to this, and when he glanced over at the Mallius brothers, all he got back was a pair of shrugs.

It was left to Vellusius, who, as his comrades had learned, didn't think with any real swiftness, but if you gave him time, he would chew on a problem and get to the bottom of it, which was why he asked, "So...you hate pimps who are civilians, but not pimps who were under the standard?"

"No," Atilius replied, "I hate pimps in general." For the first time, he grinned as he said cheerfully, "I just hate civilian pimps more."

This made the others, including Pullus, laugh, but while he was still smiling when he said it, the huge Roman was serious when he said, "One of these days, Atilius, Fortuna is going to be busy doing something else, and when that happens, you'll be fucked."

"I know," Atilius answered simply, but he didn't seem all that upset about the prospect.

What he didn't say was that he had known that his string would run out sooner rather than later for most of his life; he was, after all, an Atilius.

It would be, Marcus Atilius decided quickly, a secret he took across the river with him. And, as usual, he reflected bitterly, it was entirely his fault that he and his four comrades found themselves huddled in a sewage ditch. While he had been telling the truth about hating pimps, that wasn't why he had seemingly rushed at Dukanos and, as Vellusius had seen, grabbed the *taverna* owner by his tunic, and with savage force, rammed his head into the wall behind the counter. The whole truth, the real truth, was far more complicated, because, while Atilius had been telling the truth about The Rudis, and that it was new, it wasn't until he led his comrades into the place where, for the first time here in Narbo he had laid eyes on Dukanos, that he learned that he actually knew the Greek from his days at Nova Carthago. Even worse was the reason he knew Dukanos, but while his first instinct was to turn around and lead his friends out, he had seen Dukanos, from his spot at the rear of the *taverna*, look in their direction. Not surprisingly, he had been extremely nervous, but he had actually locked eyes with Dukanos, and the Greek hadn't given a flicker of recognition, and when nothing out of the ordinary occurred, Atilius had begun to relax. It *had* been a few years, he reflected, and I've changed since I was thirteen...or was it fourteen? However long ago it had been, it had been his father's idea to target the customers of the *taverna* nearest to the docks of the city, where his father would indulge the fondness for wine that he had passed down to his son, becoming a regular customer to the point that the owner, Dukanos, would view him as part of the furniture. Every *taverna* had at least one such man, who somehow had enough money to keep themselves in a perpetual state of drunkenness, and like most proprietors, Dukanos didn't ask, nor did he care from where the money came. That, at least, had been what Atilius' father insisted, but as Marcus knew, the money came exclusively from other customers of Dukanos' *taverna*.

As Gaius' schemes went, this one wasn't a bad idea necessarily; the problem became that, true to his nature, Atilius' father didn't know when it was time to quit and move on to some other endeavor. Among his more dubious characteristics, nobody who knew Gaius Atilius would deny that he was an engaging, affable man, one who was a seemingly good listener and was happy to provide an outwardly sympathetic ear to the tales of woe of other people, even if his purpose in doing so was for his own gain. Not surprisingly, a *taverna* was considered a good place for a man, or woman, with troubles to come unburden themselves, and there would be Gaius, willing to listen and, even better, buy a cup or two for the troubled. The fact that he was doing this with an eye towards plucking them like a chicken was something that, at first, nobody suspected at Dukanos' *taverna*. While Gaius was inside, Marcus would be outside, down the street and tucked away in an alley, watching for his father's signal that he had found a target. After plying them with drink as he listened to their woes, Gaius would insist on walking out with the man, still commiserating with him, and then bid the man farewell with a friendly pat on the shoulder. This was the signal for Atilius that the man was sufficiently inebriated to be an easy target for a sneak thief to come and slice his purse strings, a skill that Atilius had become quite adept at by this time. Following his father's orders, Atilius would stalk the marked man, waiting to strike until the man was at least three streets away from the *taverna* in order to avoid suspicion about some sort of connection. And, Atilius acknowledged, it had worked, but like with all things involving his father, despite repeated warnings from Atilius' mother and Atilius himself, Gaius refused to stop, or even move on to another *taverna*. The reason for Gaius' obstinance was revealed when, one night back at their *insula,* while Gaius was still in the grips of Bacchus, he had blurted out the real reason.

"That Greek *cunnus* looks down on me!" He had shouted this, seemingly out of nowhere, as he sat at their table, punctuating his declaration by slamming his hand down on the table hard enough to rattle the cups and bowls sitting on it. "He thinks I don't understand Greek, but I do, and I heard him tell his bitch of a wife that I was nothing but a drunk!"

As he said this, he glared across the table at his son, but Atilius wasn't mature or confident enough to challenge his father; his mother held no such compunctions.

"That's because you *are* a drunk," Domitilla had retorted, even as she was preparing their meal.

"Shut your mouth, woman," Gaius had snarled. "The only reason I drink as much as I do is because I'm married to a shrew who doesn't respect her husband the way she should!"

As it always did, this devolved into a screaming match between them, while Atilius and his two sisters silently ate their watery porridge, all three of them accustomed to the scene. In fact, the only reason Atilius remembered this exchange was because of what happened the next night, when Dukanos proved that he was aware of what was happening to some of his customers, and had made the connection to Gaius. Things had progressed normally; Gaius had disappeared into the *taverna*, leaving Atilius to watch from his spot in the alley, knowing that it would be a while before his father got what he called the "pigeon" drunk enough, and he settled down to wait. And, he would acknowledge, what was about to happen was just as much his fault as Gaius', because he stopped paying attention to his surroundings. Specifically, he stopped glancing over his shoulder to the opposite end of the alley, where it opened out onto the next street over. The result was that, when the door opened, and a man emerged, followed by Gaius, Atilius was caught completely by surprise by the rough hand that clamped around his mouth from behind, but it was the feeling of the cold iron of the dagger pressed against his throat that he would remember.

"Keep your mouth shut, boy," a voice growled in his ear, "and don't do anything stupid, or I'll cut your throat quicker than Pan. Understand?"

Even if his assailant had released his grip of Atilius' mouth, he couldn't have spoken, so frightened was he, but thankfully, his nod was sufficient. Only then did another figure materialize, stepping past him to slowly peer around the edge of the building, and instinctively, Atilius refused to look at the man, keeping his eyes on the ground, not wanting to give these men the excuse to kill him. Nevertheless, out of the edge of his vision, Atilius could see enough of the man's features to recognize him as someone who he saw entering Dukanos' *taverna*, usually shortly before dark, every night he had been there with his father. Although he understood that these men had something planned for his father, he wasn't certain how they intended to trap Gaius, since once he gave the signal to Atilius, he went back inside so that he wouldn't draw suspicion. He found out only after the intended victim walked past the alley, weaving slightly and muttering to themselves, and once the drunken citizen turned the corner at the end of the block, the man with his hand over Atilius' mouth lifted Atilius by the back of the tunic and stepped out into the street, with the other man leading the way. Half-carrying and half-dragging Atilius, they headed for the *taverna*, and once he understood that they intended to take him inside, Atilius began twisting wildly in an attempt to break the man's grip so that he could at least have a chance to escape. This earned him a cuff on the head that made his ears ring and left him half-stunned, so he didn't really have much memory of the last few paces to the *taverna*, only regaining his senses when they were already inside in the dimly lit room. People coming and going at this time of the evening was a common enough event that the customers already there barely glanced up, but Atilius heard the sudden drop in the volume of noise as it became clear that something unusual was happening. It wasn't his age, he knew; it was the fact that just after they entered, the man holding him removed his hand from his mouth to draw his dagger, which was now pressed against Atilius' neck.

"*Eyo* there, Gaius Atilius," the second man, a heavyset man with a Greek accent called out. "We've got something of yours here!"

For the span of several heartbeats, to Atilius, it appeared as if his father had no intention of acknowledging his son as Gaius sat there, blinking in what appeared to be bleary surprise and, to Atilius' dismay, seemingly not recognizing his son. Dukanos had been behind the counter when they entered, and he moved now to stand just behind Gaius, who was apparently unaware of this, but even if Atilius hadn't been scared out of his wits, feeling the blade pressed to his throat, as he grew older, he recognized that he probably wouldn't have warned his father about what was coming. It was, after all, he would think, what Gaius deserved, and in fact, he got off lightly considering what could have happened, with just a severe beating, started when Dukanos, whose normally affable manner was nowhere in evidence when he slapped Atilius' father with an open hand, striking the side of Gaius' head with enough force that, even with an open hand, it knocked Gaius out of the chair and onto the floor. The second man moved quickly to stand on the other side of Gaius, who was shaking his head, trying to clear it, whereupon he unleashed a kick that struck Atilius' father in the stomach. Atilius was forced to watch with the dagger to his throat as Dukanos and the second man administered a savage beating, while the crowd watched in almost total silence, although Atilius did notice that nobody seemed that distressed...or surprised, which indicated to Atilius that his father hadn't fooled the other regular customers as much as he thought. By the time they were through, Gaius was semiconscious, bleeding from mouth, nose, and from a scalp laceration from a kick, and had curled up in a ball. Only then did the man holding Atilius relent, dropping the dagger away from him to give him a hard shove, as Dukanos seemed to examine the youth for the first time.

Pointing down, Dukanos asked in heavily accented Latin, "Is this your father, boy?"

For an instant, Atilius thought of denying it, but as if on its own, he felt his head bobbing up and down.

"Your father is a thief," Dukanos said flatly, then pointed a thick finger at Atilius, "and you're his whelp. You helped him rob my customers. No!" he snapped when Atilius opened his mouth. "Do not try and deny it, boy. It will only make it worse for you." To Atilius, this sounded ominous, and he braced himself for a similar beating, but instead, Dukanos stepped over Gaius' body to stand in front of Atilius, staring down at the youth with hard eyes. In a slightly softer tone, Dukanos said, "But he's your *paterfamilias*, neh? That's what you Romans call it?" Atilius nodded, still not sure whether it was wise to speak, and Dukanos continued, "And your law says that your father must be obeyed, and if you disobey him, he can kill you, yes?" Another nod by Atilius, then, without warning, Dukanos slapped Atilius across the face, and there was enough power behind the blow that his tunic was jerked from the grasp of the man still holding on to it, and he staggered to his right, colliding with another man, seated at the nearest table who, thankfully, didn't bash Atilius for sloshing his wine, and in fact helped steady him, while Dukanos continued, "So that's your punishment...this time. But," Dukanos' tone returned to its harsh quality, and he raised his voice, telling Atilius that he was making something of an announcement, "know this, boy. If I *ever* see you again, I do not care where it is...I will kill you. Because," at this, he turned, and leaning over Gaius, spat on him, "once a thief, always a thief, and you are probably going to follow in your Tata's footsteps. So," he turned back to look at Atilius, "if I see you again in one of my businesses, I will assume you are there to steal from me. Now," he pointed down at Gaius, who was just beginning to stir, "take your father and get out of here. I do not want your kind of trash in my *taverna*."

Somehow, Atilius had managed to drag Gaius to his feet, and with one of his father's arms draped across his thin shoulders, he had helped Gaius out of the *taverna*. And, for one of the only times Atilius could remember, Gaius Atilius steered clear of Dukanos' *taverna* from that moment onward. Oh, he talked about getting revenge, but that was all it amounted to, and in time, Gaius had other people angry at him, and while Atilius always remembered that incident, he also assumed that Dukanos had forgotten about him. As he learned that night, the Greek had not, and this was something that Marcus Atilius never told anyone, not even Didius, but only because he was worried that Pullus would find out at some point.

Fortunately for the five of them, the regulations on reentering camp only required that they know the watchword answer to the challenge that was issued every given day, not that they not be covered in *cac* and smell badly enough to cause the Optio at the gate and both guards to begin gagging. And, as time passed, the humor of that night would be what they remembered, although before that moment came, they were forced to endure spending that night outside, and they were actually excused from morning formation by Crastinus to go to the camp bath that was now functional. Their tunics had to be washed not once but twice before the odor was gone. True to his word, Pullus never went into town with Atilius again, and in fact only rarely ventured out, and when he did, it was always with Domitius, or almost as often, Scribonius joined them, along with Vellusius because he was Scribonius' close comrade. They also steered clear of The Rudis, sticking to The Happy Legionary, but as always happened, word of what had taken place at the other *taverna* was common knowledge. And, again as always happened, the description of what took place became more lurid, with the beating Pullus administered to

Bassus becoming even more brutal with every telling. The fact that Pullus had felled Bassus with a single punch wasn't as compelling a story as the tale that developed, that Pullus had administered one of the worst beatings in anyone's memory to a man who, before this, had been one of the most feared brawlers in the Legion. Initially, Pullus felt compelled to set the record straight, but it was his Sergeant, taking him aside a few days later, who persuaded him to do no such thing.

"If you keep telling everyone that you knocked him out with one punch, men will become convinced that it was just a matter of Fortuna favoring you, and they'll tell themselves it's not likely to happen twice. Then," Calienus assured him, "every time you're out in town, there will be some stupid bastard who challenges you. This way, men are more likely to steer clear of you, and the fact that Bassus has made it clear he wants no part of you to get revenge, that works in your favor."

And, Pullus reflected later, it was true that Bassus had seemed reticent to pursue any kind of settling of accounts; in fact, they had crossed paths, both in camp and in town, and every time, the former 2nd brawler had seemed to make it a point to either be looking the other way or walking in a direction where their paths wouldn't cross. Over the course of the next several weeks, word began to spread that Bassus seemed like a different man, as if he had been shaken to the point that he wanted no part of what many of his comrades in the Ninth had been urging, for their own purposes. It was just another anecdote that was added to what would become the legend of this young Gregarius, and while he was perfectly happy for Bassus to come for a rematch, he began to appreciate the value of how matters actually transpired, although there would be more conflict between men of the Tenth Section and the men of the Ninth, just not with Pullus.

Otherwise, the army settled into the routine of what peacetime under the standard looked like, but while many men were content with this life, others chafed at it, though not always for the same reason. For Didius, he had been serious about his intentions of making extra money using his skills learned before he enlisted, and with the men of what were called the third line Cohorts. While it was true that, during their time in Scallabis, he and his comrades hadn't worked with the Fifth, Sixth, or Seventh much, the men of the third line had even less to do with their comrades in the front line, for a number of reasons, all of them predating the creation of the 10th Legion. When not on campaign, the men of each Cohort heartily detested their counterparts, at least when there weren't men of another Legion on whom they could focus their hostility. As long as it was individuals or groups of two or at most three men interacting with each other between different Cohorts, such actions were tolerated, if not encouraged, but when all or most of the men from one section crossed the forum into a different Cohort's area, that was when matters could become contentious because it signaled intentions.

Despite their growing friendship and the bond Didius felt for Atilius after Gades, their interests lay in different directions, which meant that Didius was on his own when he began to seemingly wander into the Eighth, or Ninth, or Tenth's Cohort streets. He worked slowly, and carefully, using the time-tested method of losing just a bit more than he won on his first few trips as he rotated his visits from one Century to the next, knowing that if he didn't win at all, it would alert his potential victims. This was one of the few areas where Didius demonstrated patience, though this had been a hard-won skill, typified in the form of a few beatings and near-beatings he'd managed to avoid by fleeing, and it chafed him to do it. Gradually, as the summer months came, Didius worked, never returning to the same section he'd fleeced, and always taking care to lose the next night with another section, although it was never more than he had won from their comrades, stopping when he had won roughly the same amount as the night before. And, just as gradually, he began accruing a tidy sum, but while some men had grumbled about the possibility that Didius had cheated them, that was all it had been, grumbling. What surprised Didius was how he had begun missing spending time, not just with Atilius but most of the others in his section, although he would never admit as much. His period of banishment had been extremely trying, yet even after it ended, his comrades had treated him with varying degrees of coolness, with Atilius the one man who didn't exhibit any kind of judgmental behavior towards Didius, while on the other end of the spectrum, Pullus, and to only a slightly lesser degree Domitius, who would at least deign to speak to him occasionally on topics not strictly related to their duties, such as they were, never tried to hide their feelings towards him. There were two formations a day, one in the morning, where the orders for that day were given, and then in the late afternoon, when they would be released from duty, prompting a stampede for the *Porta Praetoria* to get into Narbo for those men who had the freedom of the town. Twice a month, Tribune Trebonius took the Legion on a forced march out into the area around Narbo, usually about twenty miles long, although they didn't have to construct a marching camp. In between their marches, men were sent out on working parties, while the *Immunes* were kept busy to one degree or another, and as Didius learned through Domitius, the only *Immunes* busier than the leatherworkers were the men responsible for the care and maintenance of the pool of Legion mules, oxen, and the handful of horses for the officers.

"These bastards run through a hundred pair of *caligae* a week!" Domitius had complained, more than once. "It's better with their harnesses and *balteae*, but not by much, and that's only marching twice a month."

It did explain why, when a Legion began a campaign in earnest, there was a stock of *caligae* in one of the Legion wagons, enough to refit every man once, and there were enough flat sheets of tanned leather to provide another two pair, while there was a spare *baltea* for every man, and enough sheets for one more, along with a barrel of hobnails, and another barrel of the metal disks, called *bullae*, that were attached to the hanging strands of the *baltea*. Since Didius was one of the men who hadn't been assigned as an *Immune*, it meant that, like his close comrade, when it was the First of the Second's time for a working party, he was guaranteed to be on it, provided that he didn't conjure a way onto the sick list, which he did more frequently than anyone in his section. The best that could be said of this time, their first full year in Narbo, was that the men of the Tenth Section tolerated Didius, and he had learned to curb his natural tendency towards surliness and combative behavior, even with Pullus, the pair loathing each other and making no attempt to hide it. Didius knew that the others viewed him as being the problem; what would have astounded Didius was their belief that, perhaps if he wasn't so unceasingly hostile towards Pullus, the giant Roman wouldn't treat him in kind, and that the rest of the section viewed Pullus in a much different light than he did, but this never occurred to him. It was also the one thing that Atilius never brought up, sensing that Didius would be incapable of seeing what appeared obvious to the others. As Didius had learned in training, there was a limit to Pullus' tolerance when it came to his comrade's taunts and jibes, and the way Pullus communicated his displeasure was when they sparred. While Pullus had never thrashed him to the same degree as their first bout, which was now the cause for Didius' nose taking a decidedly sharp bend about halfway down the bridge, he would limp out of the ring, badly bruised and aching for days. Despite all of this, Didius began curtailing his nightly forays to the other side of the camp, and increased his time in the section hut, but while he went into town almost every time it was their turn, he didn't gamble when he went, for the simple reason that in a port town like Narbo, there would be men who were as skilled at cheating as he was, and that invited trouble of a kind he didn't want. He was secretly proud of himself for displaying this kind of discipline, and he correctly attributed it to his time under the standard, and while he didn't think of Aulus that often, nor did he feel any residual guilt about killing him, he would find himself wondering occasionally how things might have been different between them if his father had been the one to serve under the standard and not his uncle. One night, and on a whim, Didius decided to go out in town, but in what could be considered a minor shock, when he approached Atilius lounging on his bunk, his close comrade waved him off.

"Not tonight," Atilius said, then gave Didius a wan smile. "Bacchus and I need to take a break from each other."

"*Gerrae!*" Didius exclaimed, not believing his ears. "You? Since when have you ever turned down a chance to debauch?" Suddenly, Didius realized something, and he lowered his voice. "If you're cleaned out, I have enough to pay for both of us."

"No," Atilius shook his head, "but thanks for offering." He laughed as he said, "I just want to see what it's like waking up without a sore head and a sour stomach. We haven't been on campaign in almost a year, and that's about the last time I can remember. Besides, we're sparring tomorrow."

Didius was disappointed, but he said that he understood. Romulus and Remus had already left, while Pullus and Domitius were playing tables, which Scribonius had taught them, and Vellusius and Scribonius were both stretched out on their bunk, although Scribonius was reading from a small scroll. He knew better than to ask the pair from Astigi, and while he actually respected Scribonius, he also thought the lean ranker was a bit of a bore who was unlikely to be interested in the kinds of things Didius intended to do. That left Vellusius, but he appeared to be asleep, although he suspected that Vellusius had overheard his invitation and was feigning his slumber, so he didn't bother. Without saying a word to them, and only giving a nod to Atilius, Didius headed out into town, where he was about to finally make a mistake.

Despite Didius' feelings towards Pullus, he had taken Atilius' warning about The Rudis to heart, and he had no intention of going there. However, what neither Didius nor any of the other men of the section knew was that men from the Ninth Cohort hadn't accepted Dukanos' apologies for what had taken place, even as the Greek was still recovering from his own injuries, when he had sent a slave to the camp, explaining that it was a case of mistaken identity and that it had been the five men from the Second Cohort who were supposed to be the targets for ejection. The fact that the half-dozen men of the *collegia* to whom Dukanos paid for protection arrived within a matter of heartbeats after the brawl erupted didn't help reduce the collective outrage by the men of the Ninth. And, as Fortuna would have it, there was already a new *taverna*, and not only was this one owned by a man who had been under the standard, he had been in one of the Legions raised by Pompeius Magnus. While, like every man of the 10th, Didius had heard about the new *taverna*, named Bellona's Den, he had no idea that the men of the Ninth had transferred their business there, and he only learned shortly after he walked through the door.

Part of the problem for Didius was that, whenever a new establishment opened, there was a period where the customer base of a place catering to men under the standard fluctuated in terms of which Cohort claimed it as their own. None of this was official, of course, but over the decades, it was a proven, time-tested formula that worked for everyone, keeping the number of men on the punishment lists for brawling outside camp lower, while for the citizens of the nearest town, it saved their businesses and their owners and employees from being damaged in the process. Narbo inevitably grew because of the business opportunities created by the presence of the army, and while *tavernae* and brothels began popping up like weeds in a garden, it also attracted merchants, most of them in the Equestrian order, all of whom competed fiercely for contracts to supply the raw materials that sustained a Legion of Rome, meaning that what was taking place in Narbo with its explosive growth was typical. Naturally, none of this was in Didius' mind when he found Bellona's Den and entered; it was located on the same street as The Happy Legionary, but one block removed from the place, the minimum distance for competing soldiers' *tavernae*, as decreed by the *duumviri*, who knew from either first or secondhand experience that putting two such businesses next door, or even worse, directly across the same street, was an invitation to disaster.

Didius stood inside for a moment, allowing his eyes to adjust from the light of long summer days, and it just so happened that he saw men he recognized from the Fifth of the Second first, although he didn't approach them, instead crossing to the opposite side of the room. There was a table of men where there was an empty spot at the end of one bench, and since none of the faces of the men sitting on the opposite side looked familiar, he approached with a sense of caution. The man who he would be sitting next to glanced over his shoulder, and this man Didius did recognize, and he froze in his tracks, his mind racing as he tried to remember. He was in the Ninth, but in a different Century than the men who had been with Bassus, and he felt fairly certain that he was in the Sixth of the Ninth.

The seated ranker clearly recognized Didius, but there was no hostility in his voice when he called out, "*Oy!* I know you. It's..." his eyes narrowed as he thought about it, then came up with, "Didus, isn't it?"

"Didius," he corrected, and that was when the name came to him, "and you're Torquatus, isn't it?"

"That's right," Torquatus confirmed, then waved to the empty spot with a grin. "Come, sit down with us. I'll give you a chance to win back what I took from you when we were in camp."

It couldn't have been a better situation for Didius, because Torquatus' section had been one of the first he had visited, when he had lost more than he had won, and he hurried to sit down.

"Boys, you remember Didius, eh?" Torquatus called to the others, which was barely acknowledged by three men at the opposite end, although he could see they were clearly engaged in some sort of debate, but another man, across the table and seated in the middle, gave Didius a grin.

"Oh, I do!" he said, then happily lifted his cup. "You paid for several cups of wine, eh, Didius?"

This earned laughter, and while Didius joined in, not only was he pretending to share the humor, he was thinking savagely, You're about to be a plucked chicken, you *cunnus*. Later, he would reflect that perhaps this hadn't been a wise decision on his part, but he was aroused now, and while he was still laughing, he reached into his purse and extracted a pair of dice.

"I did, Herennius," Didius seemingly agreed, happy to have remembered the ranker's name, "but since I'm here, what do you say? Are you up for giving me a chance to win it back?"

And, not surprisingly, Herennius thought this was a perfectly splendid idea, whereupon Didius went to work.

On the opposite side of the room, the men Didius had recognized from the Fifth of the Second were holding a quiet conversation as they hunched over the four-man table.

"Should we tell them? I know they're from the Ninth, but..."

The man who asked the question addressed it to the other three, but it was the oldest, Gaius Ventidius, who also happened to be the Sergeant of the Third Section, who spoke first.

"And what do we tell them?" he asked challengingly. "That we're *almost* sure that that bastard Didius is cheating them, but since we never caught him ourselves, we can't be completely sure that he did?"

One of the other men who had yet to speak did so then, pointing out, "No, we didn't catch him, but the boys in the Eighth Section did."

"And," the ranker who had posed the original question added, "so did the boys in the Second Section of the First of the First. I know Quintus Balbus, and he wouldn't lie about something like that. They caught him with a second pair of dice, but their Optio showed up and stopped them from thrashing him, and they wouldn't inform on another ranker, even if he is a cheating bastard."

"That's true," Ventidius allowed, then he sighed. "So, what do we do?"

"I think we just sit here," the first man, Gnaeus Poplicola, suggested, "and keep an eye on him as we enjoy a cup. Or two." He grinned. "We'll be able to tell if Didius is winning by the way the other men at the table are acting."

The others agreed, while Ventidius signaled the girl to bring another jug of wine, and they resumed their discussion of which gladiator style was superior.

He hadn't intended it, but Didius got carried away. After three throws where he lost, which was the moment most men passed the cup to another man, once it came back to him, he was ready, so when he switched the dice while calling Venus in a practiced move with his right hand, just as he expected, the edges of the pair of dice that had been shaved so finely that you needed to be in strong sunshine, and have keen vision, to see it, did what they were supposed to, and he won the pot.

He won five throws in a row then, before losing the sixth as he intended, except he immediately passed the cup to Torquatus, and it was early on in the evening when the ranker asked Didius with a casualness that didn't fool Didius at all, "I forget; you're in the First of the Second?"

"That's right," Didius replied, though his eyes never left the man at the opposite end of the table who was rattling the dice in the cup.

"So you must know that big bastard, what's his name? The one who Caesar decorated?"

"Pullus," Didius spat the word, relieved that he didn't have to pretend about his feelings. "The bastard's name is Titus Pullus."

"I suppose," Torquatus said carefully, "you heard what happened between him and Publius Bassus?"

"I heard," Didius replied shortly, then lied, "but not any details." The truth was far different, because between Romulus, Remus, and Vellusius, it was all they talked about for the next few days after that, and while Didius took a great deal of pleasure at the idea of Titus Pullus cowering in a ditch and covered with *cac*, that part of the tale was only mentioned once. Only Atilius had, wisely, refrained from bringing the subject up with his close comrade. "Besides," he added, and offered Torquatus a grin, "you know how it is. The truth may be that the *cunnus* was blessed by Fortuna and landed a lucky punch, but by the time it's told a few times, it becomes something else."

Torquatus surprised and angered Didius then, shaking his head.

"No, I saw it happen. We were at another table, but what that beast did wasn't because Fortuna loves him. I've seen Bassus whip men Pullus' size," he stopped, then amended, "well, *almost* Pullus' size, but I've never seen a man that big move that fast."

Partially hating himself for it, Didius allowed, "*That* is true. He's fucking quicker than Pan." Without planning on it, he pointed to his nose, confessing, "He gave me this when we were *Tiros*."

"*Gerrae!*" Torquatus exclaimed. "How?" Didius tersely explained the circumstances, and his pride was rubbed even rawer when Torquatus' reaction was to laugh and say, "I'm guessing you're not an admirer of his, then, like some of his comrades seem to be."

"I," Didius' tone turned savage as he said with completely honesty, "*hate* that bastard."

Torquatus looked over at Didius, eyeing him for a moment

before he said, "Then you and Bassus should become good friends, because so does he. And," Torquatus sighed, "he hasn't been the same man since then. Maybe knowing there's another man under the standard who feels the same way about the bastard will cheer him up."

Later, Didius would decide that this was what had spurred him to become overconfident, because the next time the cup came to him, he again won on six straight throws, and was tempted to try for seven but decided he could wait, and he threw Dogs, but did it twice this time before passing the cup. The night was progressing well; it was noisy but not raucous, and there were easily four other games going on around the *taverna*, and while Didius occasionally glanced over to where Ventidius and the other Second men were seated, they were always engaged in conversation and not paying attention. This contributed to what was coming, as Torquatus took the opportunity to relay to the other Ninth men at the table that they had found in Didius a kindred spirit who had no love for Titus Pullus. If Torquatus told them why, pointing to Didius' nose, with a bit too much relish, and if the others laughed a little too hard for his taste, Didius reminded himself that this was actually helping his cause by allaying suspicion because of his status as a man of the Second, and the First of the Second at that. The one thing that Didius did *not* relay to Torquatus was that he was in the same section as Pullus and the other combatants of that night, and thankfully, none of the others thought to ask. It was on his fourth pass that Didius made his mistake, making ten straight throws, the pile of *sesterces* in front of him growing bigger and bigger. While this wasn't unheard of, it *was* unusual, and as often happened, word that a man was riding a streak made its way from one table to the next so that, before he realized what was happening, Didius became aware that there was a crowd around the table. This, he knew from experience, was dangerous; winning was one thing, but you didn't want to do it so much that you drew more eyes, because more eyes meant a higher risk of getting caught.

In fact, he decided that he was done for the night, and was about to scoop up his winnings, when Herennius, seeing what he was about to do, protested, "You can't quit now! We need a chance to win our money back!" Turning to the others, he asked, "Don't we, boys?"

His query was answered with a chorus of agreement, but not just from the men at the table.

From behind him, a voice he recognized said, "That's right, Didius! You can't quit now, not with the honor of the Second on the line!"

Ventidius' challenge was immediately seconded by a voice Didius knew belonged to Poplicola. "You can't quit now, Didius! We need to show these boys from the Ninth what the Second is all about!"

Didius, completely unaware of his comrades' true intentions, was torn; a part of him was screaming that things had gotten out of control, that it was time to call it a night and make off with what he estimated was at least a hundred *sesterces'* worth of winnings, almost ten percent of his yearly pay. But, despite his hatred of Pullus, and his resentment for Crastinus and Rufio, who he felt picked on him unfairly, Spurius Didius was also proud that he was a man of the First Century of the Second Cohort, which made his decision for him.

Shrugging, he said loudly enough for the small crowd to hear, "Well, if you boys insist, I suppose I can ask Fortuna to keep smiling on me for a bit longer!"

As he expected, this was answered by jeers and taunts that Fortuna had grown tired of him, and she was about to smile on one or more of them the next time it was Didius' turn with the cup. This happened a short while later, after Torquatus threw Dogs on his second throw, and he thrust the cup disgustedly to Didius.

"That bitch has been pissing on me all night," Torquatus groused. "Let's see what you can do this time."

Even as he took the cup, there was a part of Didius that recognized that the prudent, and in many ways, the only thing to do was to throw Dogs when he switched the dice; the difference in throwing Venus and throwing Dogs entailed a subtle but distinctly different use of the wrist, a skill that had taken him months to learn, and years to perfect.

And, he was planning on doing this when, from behind him,

Ventidius leaned down and whispered, "Take these Ninth *cunni*, Didius. For the Second."

Consequently, he threw Venus, to a mixed chorus of groans and shouts of happiness from those men ringing the table who were making side bets on the action.

Scooping the dice up, Didius continued the patter he had been using from the beginning, "All right, blessed Fortuna! Keep showing us that you love Spurius Didius!"

He threw Venus once again, eliciting the same reaction, and he scooped up the dice when, from just behind him, he heard Ventidius snarl, "What the fuck did you just say to me, Poplicola?"

"I *said*," Poplicola shouted back, "that your fucking head is so big, it's blocking my view!"

This was when several things happened, almost simultaneously, beginning with Poplicola shoving Ventidius, hard, sending him staggering backward and into Didius' back, with enough force that it threw Didius forward, his upper stomach slamming into the table, and in the process, jarring Didius' right hand holding the cup. What Didius would remember as much as the sight was the sound of not two, but four dice bouncing across the table, the bones making a clicking sound on the wood as they tumbled across the table before, in almost slow motion, they stopped, the final one toppling over to land so that the two pairs of three dots faced up to join the other three, which were also sixes. Even in that instant, the thought that flashed across Didius' mind was: What are the odds of four dice showing Venus at the same time? All the noise around the table had stopped, as every pair of eyes stared down at what was, when all was said and done, incontrovertible proof that Spurius Didius was cheating. And, to his credit, he was the man who reacted the first, leaping up from his stool, turning as he did so, and when he turned to face eye to eye with Ventidius, he saw the look of triumph in the Sergeant's eyes, and he knew this had all been by design. His fist lashed out, striking Ventidius flush in the face, and while he was certainly enraged about being discovered, his striking the Sergeant was based in practicality, because as he intended, the punch sent Ventidius reeling backward into Poplicola, giving Didius just enough space in the press of bodies, creating a gap where, tantalizingly close, he could see the door to the *taverna.* Shoving the man next to Ventidius, also sending this one staggering, Didius, without even a glance at the glittering pile of coins on the table, made his dash for the door. And, because he hadn't hesitated, he almost made his escape.

Down the street at The Happy Legionary, the Mallius brothers had decided to call it a night, enduring the mostly good-natured taunting from their fellow Second Cohort comrades for leaving while there was still drinking to be done.

"It's not your turn to spar with Pullus tomorrow," Remus retorted. "It's bad enough to face him without having a banging headache and wanting to puke. And," he wagged a finger at the other men, "you bastards would be doing the same thing, and you know it!"

He was walking backwards, following Romulus as he said this, then when he got to the door, he grabbed his crotch while giving their friends an obscene gesture, grinning broadly as the brothers emerged onto the street, followed by jeers and taunts. In every way, it was a perfectly normal night, and the pair walked down the street in the direction of the western gate, which would take them past the new place, Bellona's Den. As was the custom, there were only torches in sconces at intersections in Narbo, while those businesses that remained open after dark, exclusively the *tavernae* and brothels, advertised their presence with an oil lamp placed in such a way to illuminate the sign designed to lure customers to their door. It meant that, while they could see a group of men down the street the next block over illuminated by an oil lamp, it wasn't until they got to the intersection that it didn't appear to be a routine matter.

It was Romulus, grabbing his brother's tunic, who noticed, "It looks like someone's getting a beating."

This wasn't unusual, and Remus correctly guessed the cause, saying indifferently, "They probably caught some bastard cheating, so he deserves it."

They were standing in the intersection then, and Romulus suggested, "Let's go down a street. We don't want to be in the wrong place when the provosts show up."

Remus agreed, and they had turned and were about to resume their progress on their altered route when Remus idly glanced over to catch a last glimpse of what they could now also hear was a savage beating, with men snarling and hurling curses as they kicked at the prone man who had curled up into a ball, pulling his arms up around his head to protect it, and muffling his cries of pain from every strike. It was when a man, whose back was turned to the brothers, lifted his leg, bringing his foot up to above knee level in preparation to stomp down on the man that Remus saw the face of the victim, peeking out from between his arms.

"Pluto's *cock*!" he gasped, reaching out and yanking hard on Romulus' sleeve. Before his brother could snap at him, Remus pointed, "That's Didius! He's the one they're beating!"

He was moving as he said this, directly for the knot of men, and it was Romulus' turn to grab at Remus' sleeve, momentarily stopping his brother.

"If it's Didius, he probably deserves it, Marcus," he said quietly. "We should just leave it be."

At such moments, Remus tended to defer to his brother, but then he turned his attention back, and in the lamplight, he saw the features of one of the men standing over Didius, just as he delivered another kick.

"I recognize him! Those bastards are from the Ninth!" he exclaimed to Romulus. "This might have nothing to do with his cheating!"

Then, without waiting for Romulus' reply, Remus unleashed a bellow of rage as he broke into a run, heading for the now-identified men of the Ninth. Romulus' hesitation was barely a full heartbeat, so he was close behind his brother when Remus, without slowing down, threw himself bodily at the Ninth ranker who had just finished his stomping of Didius. The man was in the process of turning when Remus slammed into him, and when the ranker reeled backward, he tripped over Didius' prone body, giving Remus the opportunity to unleash a wild swing at the man who had been standing next to his first victim. It was poorly aimed, but it landed solidly enough, smashing into the cheek of his opponent with sufficient force to snap his head back, and then Romulus arrived, also shouting at the top of his lungs. He, however, wasn't as fortunate; despite it only being a heartbeat later, it was enough to allow a third Ninth ranker to pivot about and raise his fists, launching one of them just as Romulus arrived. If it had landed cleanly, it would have been devastating because of Romulus' momentum, but instead, it was a grazing blow to his jaw, while like his brother, Romulus' aim was better, though not perfect, missing the point of his opponent's chin to strike the man at the base of his throat. It could have killed the man, but most of the force of Romulus' punch landed on the bony region of the man's upper chest. Nevertheless, it was enough to stagger this man as well, but now that the initial surprise was over, the Mallius brothers were still outnumbered three to one, and while Remus was first to arrive, Romulus was fated to take the first punch from Herennius, although neither brother knew his identity, who struck Romulus on the side of the head. While it was painful for Romulus, it was almost as damaging to Herennius' hand, and his yelp of pain was louder than Romulus', but it did force the older Mallius to shake his head in an attempt to clear it. For the next span of heartbeats, the predominant sounds were the harsh breathing, muttered curses, and the meatier sound of fists striking flesh as Remus and his brother exchanged blows with the other men. While they were doing damage, the brothers were waging a losing battle, but they were saved when Ventidius, who felt a bit guilty by this time, and the rest of the Second men, decided to come outside in the event that the Ninth men had gotten carried away. Recognizing the Mallius brothers, the Sergeant and his comrades immediately pitched in, and the Ninth men were driven off, with Herennius carried away, unconscious from Romulus' second punch, which this time landed where he had aimed.

"That's right, you bastards!" Remus bellowed, shaking his fist, blood streaming from his nose and with the neck of his tunic torn. "Run from the Second, you gutless *cunni!*"

"You haven't seen the last of us!" one of the Ninth men promised, but he was walking backward and away from Bellona's Den. "We'll be seeing you boy-fuckers again!"

What mattered was that the men of the Ninth were moving

away from the battlefield, the need for which was accentuated when, from what sounded like no more than a couple of streets away, the Second men heard the shrill blast of the bone whistle used by the provosts, the same used by Centurions.

"Didius, can you walk?" Romulus asked his prone comrade, who was only then beginning to stir from his defensive ball.

"I...I think so," Didius mumbled, but while he did get to his feet, it was only with help from Remus.

It was next to impossible to make out Didius' features, his face a mask of blood, some from his nose, some from his mouth, but the most from a gash just above the hairline of his forehead, caused by the hobnail sole of the stomp by the man who Didius had seen while peeking out from between his arms was Herennius.

Once on his feet, the brothers wasted no time, Remus snapping, "Come on, we've got to get out of here. The provosts are on their way."

Now that he was on his feet, while he was still unsteady and dizzy, Didius was nevertheless aware enough to see Ventidius and his other tentmates, and it was a good thing that his expression was disguised by the blood that covered his face almost as thoroughly as the red paint worn by a triumphing general.

Still, his glare was enough to alert Romulus that something was amiss, but he assured Didius, "Ventidius and his boys saved our bacon, Didius. If they hadn't come outside, Remus and I would have been on the street with you."

For a number of reasons, it was fortunate that when Didius opened his mouth to accuse Ventidius and Poplicola, both of whom were staring at him without expression, the stab of pain to his jaw was enough to stifle him, and he thought it might be broken. Instead, he gave a curt nod that he understood, and allowed his tentmates to help him on their way, while Ventidius and the others watched dispassionately, and without any sympathy.

Once the three men were out of earshot, Ventidius said, "I think he got the message, don't you, boys?" There was a muttered chorus of agreement, and the Sergeant said, "Let's get back inside. When the provosts come, we need to be back at our table and as solemn as Vestals."

Didius knew that he should show some gratitude to his rescuers, but the truth was that he was still seething from what he saw as a betrayal by Ventidius and Poplicola. The fact that he was, indeed, cheating at dice was, in his mind, secondary to the fact that he was a man of the Second Cohort, and it was considered an almost sacred duty to defend a man of your Cohort no matter what their offense might have been. It was only the next day when, after a fitful night of sleep, Didius recalled that, early on, he had fleeced Ventidius and the rest of his section, but by that time, the damage had been done with his own tentmates, and he had avoided Ventidius and his section when seeking shelter during his banishment. It began when they were still in the town, where the three had stopped at a fountain next to the western gate, where Didius did what he could to wash the blood from his face, but when Romulus tried to probe what was the most serious wound, the gash on his scalp, Didius slapped his comrade's hand away.

"I don't need your help," he snarled, and while Romulus desisted, it was with a muttered curse.

This was bad enough, but once they resumed their progress back to camp, it was Remus who said, "You know, a thank you would be in order here, Didius."

Before he could stop himself, Didius snapped, "For what? I didn't need your help!"

This brought both brothers to a standstill, their expressions mirroring each other, reinforcing the mistaken idea that they were twins.

"*Gerrae!*" Romulus exclaimed. "What kind of *cac* are you talking, Didius? You," he pointed downward, "were on the ground! You were getting the *cac* kicked out of you! If we hadn't come along, there's no telling what those bastards would have done." Turning to his brother, Romulus demanded, "Did they look like they were planning on stopping?"

"No," Remus answered without hesitation, his tone as adamant as his brother's. "They would have stomped this ungrateful bastard to death if we hadn't shown up."

In his heart, Didius knew they were right, yet he couldn't

bring himself to say the words.

Instead, he stubbornly insisted, "I had it under control!"

They resumed walking, but neither brother said anything more, which suited Didius; with every step, he was becoming sorer, and was feeling the effects of what was, while not the worst beating of his life, close to it, the pain occurring seemingly in a new place with every step. The bleeding had stopped, at least, and while he had prevented Romulus from doing so, Didius began probing his scalp, groaning with pain despite his barely touching what felt like a gash of at least three or four inches, running parallel to his hairline but perhaps a finger's width into his hair. His jaw hurt, but he didn't think it was broken, although he wasn't sure about his ribs, since every breath sent a jagged stab of pain through his chest. When they got to the *Porta Praetoria*, while the duty Optio gave Didius a long, hard look, they were allowed to enter without being questioned about why one of their party looked like he had just undergone a beating. That this was a nightly occurrence certainly helped Didius' cause, but he was more concerned about what was coming, and he seriously thought about not entering the section hut, standing instead outside the door. However, since Remus assumed he was coming, he had left the door open, and some of his comrades were still up and seated at the table, but it was the sight of Pullus sitting there that seemed to make the pain even worse. Naturally, once the brothers entered, their comrades glanced at them, but before Didius could make up his mind what to do, Remus took it out of his hands.

"We just saved someone's bacon," he jerked a thumb over his shoulder outside, "but you wouldn't know it."

Once the attention was turned on him, Didius realized there was no point in escaping, so he entered, pulling the door closed, though he refused to meet anyone's eyes, ignoring the sudden gasps from his comrades.

"Pluto's *cock*," Domitius exclaimed, his eyes wide at the sight of Didius' battered face. "Who did that?"

"Bastards from the Ninth," Remus answered for Didius, who braced himself, waiting for his comrade to divulge what, to him anyway, was obvious. Instead, Remus went on, "They're obviously still angry about what happened at The Rudis."

It was understandable that, now that everyone was roused, with Atilius sitting up, blinking sleepily, as was Scribonius, all eyes were on Didius.

"That's who did this, Didius?" Pullus asked quietly, but while Didius didn't reply, he nodded in answer.

"The only strange thing," Romulus had dropped down onto the bench and was grabbing at the jug of water on the table, "was that this was at the new place Bellona's Den, and there were Second men there too."

"Oh?" Domitius' eyes narrowed in what Didius felt certain was suspicion that this was more than a feud between the two Cohorts. "Who was it?"

"Sergeant Ventidius, Poplicola, and three others from their section," Romulus answered.

More to forestall further exploration about this, Didius, ignoring the pain, spoke up, "They came outside. But," he insisted again, even as he knew it was stupid, "I told you, I had it under control."

"By the gods," Remus groaned. "Not again!"

"What does he mean?"

"Our dear Didius here," Romulus answered Scribonius' question, "insists that, despite the fact that he was on the ground, curled up like a baby, and getting the *cac* stomped out of him by a half-dozen of those *cunni,* he didn't need our help."

It was the laughter at this that lacerated Didius almost as badly as the real cuts on his body, but now that he had committed himself, he was far too stubborn to relent, and with as much force as he could muster, he bellowed, or tried to, "I had a plan! I was just waiting for the right moment! Not one of those Ninth bastards could take me, and I was about to show them!"

"I thought," Calienus' voice was calm and measured, in stark contrast to Didius' impassioned tone, "Romulus said there were six of them, Didius. What," he asked with a small smile, "was your plan? To challenge them to face you one at a time?"

It was, Didius knew, absolutely ridiculous, yet he still couldn't bring himself to admit as much, so instead, he muttered, "Something like that."

"Well," Romulus interjected, "the next time we see you on the ground, getting beaten to a pulp, we'll know that it's all part of your plan, and we won't lift a fucking finger to help."

Pointedly, Romulus turned his back to Didius, his brother following suit, and they began talking to Pullus and Domitius about a new whore that had just started at The Happy Legionary, leaving Didius standing there, feeling foolish as well as being in pain. Limping to his bunk, he dropped down on it, where he sat, head down, staring at the floor, then he felt the bunk sag from another man's weight. He wasn't surprised to see that it was Atilius, but what did catch him off guard was the sudden surge of gratitude that at least one of his section didn't think he was a miserable piece of *cac*.

"You know," Atilius spoke quietly so that he couldn't be overheard by the others, although they were all pointedly ignoring the pair, "that gash is going to need stitches."

Atilius didn't need to say anything more to identify which cut he was talking about, and Didius sighed, "I know."

"And," Atilius went on, "you know that you can't present yourself to the sick and injured list tomorrow morning at formation." This, too, Didius knew very well, although he just nodded. "Well," Atilius said lightly, "you should thank Fortuna that I know someone who can stitch that up without having to go to the *quaestorium* to do it."

Didius looked up in surprise now, and he knew he sounded a bit hurt when he said, "You never mentioned you knew anyone like that before!"

"You didn't need him before." Atilius shrugged. Then, he grinned at Didius. "But I did, a couple months back." Seeing he had startled his close comrade, he explained, "Remember when I said Pullus hurt my ribs after one of our sparring sessions?" Didius nodded. "Well, I lied. It was the night before, and I got into a scrap with some civilian, and the *mentula* pulled a dagger and slashed me on the side. I was already wrapped up when we sparred that day. Now," he slapped Didius on the knee as he stood up, "we need to get moving. I doubt we'll be back before the call to retire, but when has that ever stopped us, eh?"

When the tears started pushing against his eyes, Didius told himself that it was from the pain, but he followed Atilius out the door, aware that their exit was noticed but ignored.

Because of Didius' predicament, it meant that he had no choice but to put on the padded tunic under his *hamata*, slide on the padded sleeves, attach the faceguard made of wicker to his helmet, which he put on gingerly, despite the felt cap they wore, and when the time for him to step into the square formed by the men of the First Century to face Pullus, he did so, if not with any enthusiasm, at least with no hesitation.

"You've seen what we're working on today," Pullus said in a neutral tone. "So, let's see how your shield work is."

Even as he hefted the heavier training shield, Didius' groan was not just because of the pain, but what he took as a sign that Fortuna wasn't through pissing on him that this would not only be the day for sparring with his nemesis, Pullus had decided that his comrades would be forced to defend themselves from the onslaught from their weapons instructor's *rudis*. In fact, Didius suspected that this had been a deliberate choice by Pullus based on Didius' condition from his beating the night before; while he never learned the truth, he was right. When Pullus had seen Didius' condition that night, he had originally planned to work on their javelin throwing since it had been some time since they had last practiced this skill, but this was too good an opportunity to pass up. Not surprisingly, he didn't tell Domitius, but he knew by his best friend's expression that he wasn't fooled, and judging from the level look Scribonius had given him when he announced this, neither was the man who had become his second closest friend. If Pullus had bothered to ask, there were several more men in the First Century who saw through Pullus' ploy, but none of them were willing to voice their suspicions, for a simple reason; they, after all, had to face Pullus as well.

Didius hefted his shield, squaring himself up, but somewhat unusually, Pullus called out, "Are you ready, Didius?"

"Yes," Didius snapped, already sweating, which made the cuts sting even more.

"Are you sure you're ready?"

"*Yes*, damn you! I'm..."

And, not for the first time, Pullus was moving and doing it so quickly that Didius didn't have time to think, relying on his reflexes and the watches of practice to move his shield just enough to block Pullus' first position thrust that was aimed at Didius' right thigh, which, to Didius' consternation and pain, turned out to be a feint. Before he could bring the shield back across his body and into a normal defensive position, Pullus launched a third position thrust that shot into the opening behind his shield created by Didius falling for the feint, the blunted point striking Didius right in the ribs. It would have been a painful blow under any circumstances, but this was his injured side, and the agony was so unbearable that he dropped his shield altogether, crying out in agony. Which, of course, meant that Pullus struck again, except this time with his own shield, his arm shooting out in the same manner as if he was punching with his fist, the iron boss of the wicker shield striking Didius squarely in the chest, knocking the wind out of him as he took a staggering step backward before his legs gave way. Before he could react, Pullus was straddling him, the point of the *rudis* a matter of inches above his face, and Didius knew that, even with the wicker faceguard, Pullus could have easily broken his nose again as he had the first time...if not worse. Instead, the point just hovered there, and when it became clear that Pullus didn't intend to strike him, Didius focused on the other man's face instead of the point, but Pullus' expression was unreadable.

"I know you're hurt," Pullus said so quietly that none of the other men could hear, especially because they were still shouting and talking excitedly as if they were watching a gladiatorial game. "And I know that you can't go on the sick and injured list. But the next time we're out there, and there are barbarians spraying their spit in our faces as they try to spill our guts on the ground, do you think they're going to care if you're hurt?"

At first, Didius thought the question was rhetorical, but he saw in Pullus' expression that he was expecting an answer. He was still trying to catch his breath, but he managed to gasp, "N...no."

"No," Pullus agreed, then with an abrupt motion, he thrust the *rudis* into the ground to offer Didius his hand. "Now, get up, and let's try it again." Didius hesitated, and he felt certain that Pullus had some sort of trick in mind, but he took Pullus' hand and tried not to groan as Pullus pulled him to his feet. Once he was vertical, Pullus spoke into his ear, "Now, let's try it again, and no matter how much it hurts, you're going to handle it, right, Didius? Because that's how you'll stay alive when it's real, ignoring the pain. Our section hasn't lost a man fallen yet, and we need to keep it that way for as long as the gods allow, eh?" Now, Didius was more confused than anything else; this was the only time in their association where Pullus spoke to him with anything resembling warmth or respect, and all he could manage was a nod, which was enough for Pullus, who slapped him on the shoulder, though not hard, saying briskly, "Good. Get back into position. And this time," he turned and walked a few paces away, finishing over his shoulder, "be ready."

And, to Didius' pride, he was; it was torture, and by the end of his bout with his large nemesis, he was in more pain than when they had started, but he kept his shield up, and for the first time, he blocked the rest of Pullus' thrusts. Deep down, Didius suspected that Pullus had gone easier on him after the first clash, but for the rest of the time they were destined to serve under the same standard, and beyond, Titus Pullus never admitted it...and Didius never asked.

It was shortly before the Ides of September that the men of the 10th were confronted with another enemy, this one almost as deadly as any screaming barbarians. As one of the only intact tent sections, not just in the First Century, but in the entire Second Cohort, it was probably inevitable that the men of the Tenth never thought much about the fact that a man of the Legions wasn't always felled by an enemy blade, despite the older veterans like Calienus trying to warn them.

Indeed, shortly after they settled in at Narbo, one evening, Calienus called a meeting of the section, forbidding any of them to go into town until he talked to them, whereupon he warned, "If we're truly going to be here for a year or longer, you need to prepare yourselves for an outbreak of some sort of plague or deadly fever."

They had heard this before when they were in Corduba, and Crastinus and the other officers had stressed the importance of proper hygiene, particularly in the form of attending the baths regularly, along with keeping the latrine pits below a certain level. Now, Calienus was reminding them of this, but he could see that it didn't make much of an impression, and for the first few months when there were no outbreaks, the men teased Calienus about worrying over nothing.

"We'll see," he would say with a shrug. "Maybe you're right. Maybe the 10th is blessed as no other Legion has been before us."

They had become somewhat accustomed to the boredom that came from a period of peace, although it chafed on some more than others, but as they quickly learned, there was no real way to prepare for this new enemy, even as inevitable as it turned out to be. Compounding the tension, this sickness, that in later times would be called dysentery, seemed to have no cause for it. Everyone knew that, if you spent enough time in an area with swampy ground, it was inevitable that men would be stricken with a fever, especially the dreaded quartan variety, where men would go from a raging fever to suddenly be shaking from cold, even if it was temperate. This sickness, however, known as the flux, or sometimes the bloody flux in extreme cases, originated in the Tenth Cohort; that this Cohort was closest to the latrines wasn't considered particularly noteworthy, since in the past when it struck, it could seemingly originate with any Cohort or Century. One of the reasons for the siting of the camp was because of the Atax (Aude) River a short distance from the camp walls, and as was common practice, a channel had been dug that provided the flow of water through the latrines, where the waste of thousands of men were carried the half-mile out into the protected bay that recommended Narbo as the capital of Transalpine Gaul in the first place more than a half-century earlier.

The Roman system of sanitation was the most advanced in the known world for its time, which was why the arrival of the flux wasn't considered a result of poor sanitation, but because one of the gods had been angered. This was what found men scrambling out of camp and rushing into Narbo, besieging the various practitioners and healers, willing to pay almost anything for what the seller would declare was a certain protection from the flux sweeping through camp. Some of these counterfeit healers swore by a potion that they had concocted, and declared to every prospective buyer that they would cross the river themselves before they divulged the ingredients and the process required to manufacture what usually came in a small stoppered bottle, only insisting that it would ward off the flux. Others offered amulets that were, according to the seller, well known to protect the wearer, either because the object, such as amber, was sacred to the gods, or because a powerful magic had been worked over the object that provided a protective spell.

As the illness swept through the camp, and the first men began to die, the search for some form of protection became more frantic, and it wasn't uncommon to see, in every section hut, that a corner of the room had been turned into a small altar, upon which men put either the figurines or symbols representing the deity they thought would be the most receptive to their offerings, which usually consisted of a portion of their daily meals. That, at least, was how it started, but about a week after the first men began to die, men were buying small live animals, usually doves, although sometimes chickens were used, and sacrificed on the altar, the lifeblood of the sacrifice staining the floorboards. The Tenth Section was no different than any of the other sections in the Legion; each of them had their own personal beliefs that guided them to the type of protection they purchased. For Scribonius, who privately doubted the existence of any of the vast pantheon of gods Romans worshipped, he preferred purchasing an elixir, knowing the power of certain herbs and plants for curative powers; for example, if the scrapings of willow bark helped reduce fever, he reasoned, then it was likely that there were ingredients in the potions offered that would ward off the flux. Where he was agnostic was in not relying on just one healer, and over the course of the plague, which raged for more than a month, he had purchased several different concoctions and downed each one.

Calienus didn't do anything other than participate in the daily prayers and sacrifices at their makeshift altar, while Pullus, Domitius, and Vellusius eschewed potions for a magic talisman. In Pullus' case, it was the withered claw of a hawk, its talons curled up into a fist, that he wore outside his tunic on a leather thong, having been assured that it was very important that he display this symbol so the gods could see it. Scribonius considered, very briefly, pointing out to his giant friend that if the gods truly existed, and were as all-powerful and all-knowing as commonly believed, they would have no need to actually see the hawk's claw outside his tunic, but correctly decided that the risk of a beating wasn't worth it. Didius and Atilius favored a combination of sacrifice, potions, and talismans, although in Atilius' case, he had to rely on Didius' hoard of coins from his winnings that hadn't been lost at Bellona's Den. Of all of them, only Romulus and Remus scorned such measures, although if the truth were known, Romulus would have preferred to do *something* to appease the gods, but Remus scoffed at all of it.

For the rest of their time together, each man would carry the memory of Remus, during their evening meal early in that time, declaring, "If the gods want me, they're going to take me no matter how many magic potions I drink, or how many of those things," he pointed to Pullus' hawk claw, "I wear around my neck! Besides," he had shrugged just before he shoved a spoonful of chickpeas into his mouth, "if those barbarians couldn't kill me, I'm not worried about whatever *numen* is behind this."

His words created a ripple of movement, as the more superstitious men, like Vellusius, dropped one hand beneath the table to make the symbol that was known to repel these invisible, and usually malevolent spirits that, depending on one's viewpoint, were either the instruments of the gods, or operated independently of the gods, making their mischief capriciously and driven by a whim known only to them. Remus' words weren't challenged, but he could tell by the murmurs that he was essentially alone in his view, and one cause for his comrades to remember this moment was because, the next morning, Remus was stricken with a fever.

Quintus Mallius, forever known as Remus to the men who knew him best, save his brother, who would always think of him as Quintus, died five days later, with his brother clutching his hand, as the other men who, while not brothers by blood, considered themselves bound by an even stronger bond, crowded around his bunk. None of them were surprised; once the camp physicians and *medici* had determined that a man was beyond saving, his comrades were summoned to carry him back to their respective huts, where he could at least die among men who cared for him. This was the stated reason, but many men, Scribonius among them, deduced that there was a practical aspect to it, because having more than a half-dozen men clustered around one of the cots in the part of the *quaestorium* that served as the hospital made it difficult for the staff to do their jobs. And, of course, it didn't do the morale of the others afflicted with the flux any good to see men dying all around them.

While conscious, Remus had stopped making sense in what would be his final night, suddenly crying out to his mother that he had performed his chores, and he wanted a slice of bread slathered with honey like she had promised. One blessing, the others were certain, was that whenever Remus called out for Marcus, Romulus immediately answered him, and they were equally sure that over the last three or four watches of Remus' life, Romulus never let go of his brother's hand. Aside from Remus' ramblings, there was a low murmur from his comrades, as each of them, even Didius, offered up prayers, some of them choosing the goddess Febris, despite the fact that Remus wasn't technically dying from a quartan fever, but because his body had expelled every drop of moisture from his body, and it was that lack that was burning him alive. Another small mercy was that he was no longer fouling himself, and shortly after, they were all reminded that the business of the Legions never ended by the *bucina* call that was the official signal to rise, Remus died, and now, while they hadn't had a man fall in battle, their section was down to the more traditional size of eight men. None of them thought of their tenth member, Artorius; in fact, only Vellusius remembered his name because of their short stint as close comrades, but they all felt the loss of Remus keenly, while Romulus was inconsolable, only ceasing his sobs when, at last, he slumped over his brother's body in exhaustion. What sobered all of them was knowing that their section wasn't unique, as similar scenes had been playing out in every Cohort in the camp. Then, as always, this affliction that had stricken a full tenth of the numbers of the Legion and killed more than half of those, vanished as mysteriously as it had come. And, as always, the *bucina* sounded the call to rise every morning, sounded the change of watch, the call to both formations, and ended with the call to retire, just as always. By the end of that first year, life in the 10th was back to normal, and the first wave of births had begun, as what would become known as the "tail" of the Legion grew, and some men, not all but some, began to think that this was what their lives would be like for the rest of their enlistment. All of the surviving men were thankful when another full year passed without a reappearance of the plague, while the first wave of infants were now toddling about, making for the strange sight of a hard-bitten, browned man in a red tunic tossing a child in the air, both of them shrieking with laughter. Then, in March of the Year of the Consulships of Lucius Calpurnius Piso Caesoninus and Aulus Gabinius (58 BCE), their third year in Narbo, everything changed in ways that no man under the standard of the 10th could imagine, although almost more than any man, it would be the fortunes of a Gregarius in the Tenth Section, First Century of the Second Cohort that would change dramatically.

That man was using his free time on this day, just before the Kalends of April, to work at the stakes, with a *rudis* and a training shield, his tunic soaked with sweat already as he performed the same motions, over and over. Every time his massive arm lashed out, there would be the sharp crack of wood on wood, as Pullus' *rudis* struck the wooden stake, and while he wasn't alone, there was only a handful of other men who demonstrated this level of dedication to what was, when all was said and done about the Legions, the most vital skill any Legionary could possess. Although the men scattered around the other stakes were essentially performing the same exercises, creating a clattering sound since they were all working at their own pace, the sound made when Pullus' *rudis* struck was distinctly different, not only louder, but with a sharper quality that made it distinctive.

So intent on what he was doing, he didn't see Calienus approaching, making him jump slightly when his Sergeant said with a laugh, "I could find you blindfolded just by that sound."

Since this wasn't the first time Pullus had heard this, his response was just to shrug, then he asked, "Did you come out here to get some work in? Or," he gave Calienus a challenging grin, "do you want to spar again? Who knows?" He shrugged, though the smile didn't leave his face. "Maybe this time, you'll beat me."

"I gave up on that idea months ago," Calienus replied honestly. "But that's not why I'm here. I wanted to let you know that Primus Pilus Favonius is going to be calling a formation."

"But why?" Pullus asked, his tone reminding Calienus of a child being told he had to put his toys away and could no longer play. "It's just past noon!"

"How should I know?" Calienus replied, already turning away, but he wanted to walk a few paces away before he called over his shoulder, "But I do happen to know."

Cursing under his breath, Pullus had to trot to catch up to the Sergeant, knowing that was why Calienus had done it, enjoying the idea of the large Roman running after him like a tot chasing his Tata.

When he was still a couple paces away from catching up, he demanded, "Well? What's it about?"

"Apparently," Calienus answered casually, "Caesar has sent for us."

This brought Pullus to an abrupt halt, his mouth open, then he had to resume his trot to catch back up to challenge, "*Gerrae!* You're making this up!"

"Am I?" Calienus lifted an eyebrow. "Maybe. But why else would Favonius be calling a..."

Even before he finished, they heard the sound of the *bucina*, playing the order to assemble but at a time that wasn't normal, giving Pullus the answer, and he broke into a run with Calienus following behind him, both men heading for the *Porta Sinistra Dextra*. Caesar had called for the 10th! And, considering his promise that he would only call on the 10th in the event they were needed, it meant that they'd once again be marching with Caesar; where and for what purpose didn't matter to Titus

Pullus, nor to most of the men. That Caesar had called was enough, and Titus Pullus and his comrades of the Tenth Section, First Century of the Second Cohort, would be ready for whatever came, but not in any of their wildest dreams, even Pullus', could they imagine that they would be marching into history as part of one of the greatest feats of arms ever accomplished, in any age.

Printed in Great Britain
by Amazon

82795639R00222